The Lion

REDEMPTION DUET BOOK 2

SHERITTA BITIKOFER

Moonstruck Writing

MOONSTRUCK WRITING

Cover art by Angela Quincoces Rivera at http://www.dream-designz.com

EBook ISBN: 978-1-946821-40-9

Print ISBN: 978-1-946821-41-6

Contents

To those fighting a battle that no one understands or knows about. Stay strong and keep going. You are never alone.

Chapter 1

B elle blinked hard as she continued to scroll through the online ads, as if she hadn't spent enough time researching on the internet the day before. She had expended all her morning perusing through more advertisements for stallions for sale in Arkansas.

Since the week before, life had never been the same. With her new stable and barn completed, she was finally free to make a solid plan for growing her farm just outside her hometown of Levi. Her family would have been proud if they could see her stumbling along in their footsteps to make her ancestral home the great sheep farm it had once been. Of course, Belle wanted to make one addendum to that dream and use half of her pastures for breeding and boarding horses.

The only thing she was missing was a stud of her own.

She rubbed at her tired eyes and leaned in the rickety dining chair before stretching out her arms high above her head to work out her stiff back. For the thousandth time, her gaze roamed to the window that overlooked her farm and the rolling stretches of acreage that would one day soon be covered in ewes and rams.

But she wasn't staring in hopes to see a vision of the future. Belle's attention was torn between finding the right stallion for her three mares and to the man who made all of it possible.

Leo, the man who had mysteriously shown up in her barn that stormy night – which seemed like ages ago – had been slowly teaching her the value of choices. The handsome, charming Scotsman with a past that could only be described as stranger than fiction, gave her something she hadn't had in a long time. Peace. When all the rest of the world made her stomach knot and roll, he had become a solid foundation. He was the rock she clung to when the waves of anxiety tried to drown her in self-doubt.

Before Leo, Belle had to wear a mask to hide her true fear that people would think less of her if they saw who she really was. But each day, in his own special and blunt way, he showed her that their opinions didn't matter and that she had the freedom to be herself. To say and do things without panicking. The only thing stopping Belle was her own mental strongholds.

She still wore her mask, but she allowed herself the choice to take it off in front of certain people, like her coworker Ivy and select ladies at church. It was a slow process, a slow deconstruction of the imposter she had created, because she thought that other self was necessary to be accepted. And Leo was the one taking down the bricks, one by one, and building a pedestal he believed she belonged atop.

If only he knew that he was the one who belonged on a pedestal. Rugged, strong, and incredibly attractive, Belle constantly wondered what it was about her that made him say yes when she asked him to live with her and help on the farm. Maybe it was that first moment they met, when she threatened him with a crowbar for breaking into her barn. Or maybe it was all the little moments since then, when she let herself be real and candid with him.

Either way Belle felt blessed to have Leo in her life, and she sincerely hoped that whatever they had together would grow into something more. If only he would stop holding back. She wasn't the only one with strongholds.

She straightened in her chair again and resumed her search, scrolling through site after site looking for a reasonably priced stud that would be a good fit.

A few moments later, the backdoor opened and Leo entered, smelling of soiled hay and mud. Ranger, the Australian shepherd puppy Leo had bought for her, came bounding in behind him, tracking in bits of wet grass and dirt. The pup went straight for the water and full food bowl on the other side of the kitchen, his little tail wagging vigorously.

"Are you still looking?" he asked as he kicked the dirt from the bottoms of his boots on the threshold.

"Yeah," she sighed.

"Any luck?"

Belle sat back and shook her head. "Not really. There's one, but he's way too expensive."

After shutting the door, Leo made his way to her. "Which one?"

"He's in Fayetteville," she said as she opened the saved webpage. "Not too old, broken, he's sired before, and it looks like he could double as a good trail horse too."

Leo leaned one hand on the back of her chair and the other propped next to the laptop as he read the listing. Of course, she wasn't looking at the screen and let her eyes rove over him. His striking, ice blue eyes never failed to steal the air from her lungs, even when they glared below dark furrowed brows. He looked every bit the man that he was. Fighter, laborer, blue-collar worker, mechanic, farmhand, and a million other things he hadn't told her.

She took a muted, deep whiff of his masculine scent, mingled with the tang of his sweat that never really bothered her. That was surprising, given that she'd always run away from her father after he had spent hours working outside, because he stank to high heaven. Leo never stank.

"Looks like a brill match," he said, his Scottish brogue flavoring every word from his perfectly formed lips.

Belle pointed to the price tag on the ad. "Yeah, but you see that?"

One of his brows shrugged. "Forty-five hundred."

She snorted. "You say that like it's the weather report. I don't exactly have that kind of money."

"What about those funds your da gave you?"

"That was for emergencies," she replied as she folded her arms. "And I used up a big chunk of it to help rebuild the barn after it burned."

As soon as she said that, Belle regretted it. She knew how sensitive Leo was about what happened to the barn, though he wouldn't tell her why. His face would wrinkle in that odd, pained way as if the very memory left a bad taste in his mouth. It left a bad taste in her own, but as she accepted weeks ago, it was all in God's plan and timing. If the barn hadn't burned, she wouldn't be looking for more horses, because she wouldn't have had the room. With the rebuilt stables, she did.

"Can't take out a loan?" Leo asked before making his way to the counter for his second cup of coffee. After it was decided that he would be a – hopefully – permanent resident of the farm, Belle broke down and bought a true coffee maker and shelved the French press. That man could drink three or four cups a day, and she was sure he got up in the middle of the night to make another pot. The smell of percolating coffee would be infused in the wallpaper if he kept it up.

Luckily, the smell proved to be just as soothing as Belle's lavender candles. Maybe the smell of coffee calmed her nerves, because it was connected with Leo somehow. Or maybe she should give the caffeinated brew another shot. It used to turn her stomach, but so much had changed in so short a time.

"I'd rather not. I'm sure my credit is fine, but I don't like the idea of being in debt." Belle closed the tab and resumed her search. "I'm trying to find one for just a few hundred, a thousand at the most. But anything that cheap is listed as a stud fee and they're way too far away and I'd have to buy a horse trailer, and there's no way my truck will pull that kind of rig."

"You're in a tight fix, m'eudail," he said as he poured his second cup.

The Gaelic word rolled off his tongue so beautifully. If only she knew what it meant. He had used it several times before, but she never asked, unsure if she really wanted to know.

Ever since last week, and then the night before the barn burned, when they'd shared their first kiss, Belle had spent hours trying to come up with an answer to a haunting question. What were they?

Not lovers, because they hadn't slept together, nor had they given any obvious declaration of their feelings. They were closer than friends, but there was still so much she didn't know about him and his past. The only real date they had ever been on was the one time at the diner when Leo beat up Drake Henson for getting too fresh with Belle. But they knew one another's routine, their triggers, and sometimes finished one another's sentences. Belle had spent so much time around Leo that she could almost replicate his accent on demand. That had to count as something.

But when it came to defining what they were or if she could even claim him as a boyfriend, she was clueless. Belle had never been in a serious relationship due to her social anxiety, and demurely turned down any man who tried to ask her out. Leo had been the only one to penetrate her defenses, but now that he was inside her walls, she didn't know how to act.

They hadn't even kissed since that day on her porch when she asked him to stay in Levi, after he had already decided to leave them for good. Whatever she had said to convince him to live with her, Belle wasn't about to question it, lest the spell should break, and Leo change his mind again.

For now, she'd enjoy it, and hope that they could both slow down and figure it out together.

Between researching how to properly raise up a bigger flock of sheep and what it took to start her own horse boarding services, Belle's mind was full. And what gaps did exist were filled in with thoughts of Leo. That made for one absent-minded shepherd, who was late for her other job at the only bookstore in Levi.

Belle glanced to the clock and let out a startled noise before bolting to her feet and running for the living room. "I needed to leave fifteen minutes ago!"

Leo laughed at her hurriedly roaming around looking for her purse. "I try to time it just right, so that when I come inside, you should be headed out the door."

She snatched up the sofa pillows to check underneath, but still no purse. "Well, you went over a little on the time."

"And you were occupied."

He cleared his voice to get her attention just as she was ready to kneel onto the floor to check under the coffee table. Leo stood in the cased opening between the kitchen and living room, her purse dangling from one finger as it swung back and forth. The smile that curved his mouth was mocking, but in a sweet way. When she ran up to snatch it away, his hand curled around the strap and held it tight.

Their eyes met, and all humor had left him. "I might not be here when you come home."

Panic streaked through her and Belle's eyes went wide. "What're you talking about?"

Leo lowered his chin. "Nothing like that," he assured. "I'll be back in the morning. I just wanted to tell you that you'll need to take care of the evening chores, because I won't be here. I'll put Ranger inside before I leave."

With that announcement, he released her purse and her shaking hands nearly dropped it. "But, where are you going?"

Leo turned away and acted as if he hadn't just tugged the rug out from beneath her. "There's just something I have to do."

She closed her eyes. More secrets. It wasn't uncommon, but she had hoped they were past all that. Whatever it was, Belle tried not to be unreasonable. They had no openly spoken claim on each other, and he wasn't asking her permission. So she couldn't demand that he stayed.

"Promise to be safe?" she requested, shouldering her purse, though she was far from interested in going to work now.

Leo gave her one of those dazzling smiles and nodded. "I promise I'll be safe. Go on, you're going to be late."

Belle quickly petted Ranger, who had finished his breakfast and now staggered into the living room with a full belly. Then, she stole one more glance into the kitchen before stepping out the door. The last sight of him until the next day would be of Leo sipping his second cup of coffee and walking toward her laptop, still open on the table. She had nothing incriminating on there, and they not only shared a bathroom, but everything else in the house – including the computer. She didn't mind, as long as the virus protection program stayed active.

But what she did mind was never knowing exactly what he did during the day while she was gone. He had admitted that he wasn't an avid reader like her, so the bookcases packed with novels and reference books would be of no interest to him. Mr. Tale had called him a few times in the past week to help work on a few construction sites or remodeling projects in town, but to her knowledge, he didn't have any new work.

Leo remained a puzzle since day one, and though she had filled in a few of the corners and part of the center, many pieces were still missing. She could only pray that someday, the final masterpiece could be completed, and she wouldn't have to feel like she lived with a stranger.

The heaviness continued to drop onto his chest as Leo drove further and further away from Levi. Further away from Belle. It always happened every time he distanced himself from her or the farm. The only way he could reason it was that it must have had something to do with all that praying she did.

Ever since that night when she first dispelled the darkness with one small, impromptu prayer, Leo began to see the pattern. On those days she prayed, the darkness stayed away. His nights weren't tormented by dreams of fire and death. His soul didn't feel as weighted and burdened. So, each morning, he asked if she prayed and if she said she hadn't yet, he would slyly drop a hint that she should. Of course, she didn't complain. Why should she? It was nothing to her. Just a string of words sent up to God to protect them and the farm from evil.

But to Leo, it was everything.

It meant the difference between walking around with an easy smile, because he had finally settled where he wanted to stay, or looking over his shoulder and starting at every loud noise, thinking it might be the demon coming to collect his payment.

It took a great deal of courage to mount his motorcycle and head south toward Little Rock, far away from Belle's protection and deeper into the world he had tried to leave behind. It was all for her, though. If he didn't do this, it'd take that much longer for Belle to achieve her dreams.

One call to an old acquaintance – the only one he had left that would still speak to him – sealed his plans for the evening and with a little money in his pocket and a change of clothes in his duffle bag, he left in the late afternoon.

The two-and-a-half-hour drive did little to settle his nerves or clear his head. He used to love riding on the highway. Of all the vehicles he had ever driven, the maneuverability of a motorcycle appealed to him the most. He could weave in and out of traffic, zoom on and off exits and effectively lose whoever might happen to be chasing him. On those drives when he could relax, let the wind pound his face and feel the grind of the wheels on the blacktop, Leo could zone out and not think so much. He didn't have to think about his past or his future. Just this moment with only him, the road, and the deafening rumble of the engine beneath him.

He could do anything but relax now, because he knew exactly where he was going and what he'd be doing that night. Something he thought he'd never have to do again after he arrived in Levi.

It didn't take long to find the place. Mack gave detailed directions that a toddler could follow. Even over the roar of his bike, he could hear the multitude of voices and music booming out of the warehouse just outside of town. The parking lot was packed, but he managed to find a cramped spot on the side closest to the river.

Leo didn't make eye contact with the people he passed as he made his way toward the entrance. Smokers, groups of men with beer bottles in hand, couples displaying their affection in obscene ways, bookies, dealers, and thugs. It wasn't so long ago that he knew this scene by heart. Being in Levi had cleansed him somehow and as he approached the bouncers at the door, he began to question himself again. The darkness practically lived here, and in places like it where sin went unchecked. He could feel its pull, like a black hole that Leo had once dangerously skirted the edges of not so long ago. And here he was again.

Did he really want to do this? He was capable of it. He was completely capable of winning the money for Belle's stallion. But there was no turning back now. He had already called the man in Fayetteville and made the deal. He was expecting the money first thing in the morning.

"Mack called me in," he told the two bouncers who were just a hair bigger than him.

The bald one flipped through his clipboard while the other sized Leo up, taking in his jeans and leather jacket. Leo could admit that he didn't look like he was ready for a fight, but he never needed a fancy rig to pound another man into the dirt. He learned bareknuckle boxing when he was just a teen in Brooklyn. Most who did this for a living couldn't say that.

The bouncer made it to the final page and tapped at the bottom of the sheet. "He penned you in."

"Realized he couldn't leave out his best guy." Leo gave them both a cocky smile and they reluctantly let him through. In a place like this, arrogance was the common language.

The stench of cigarette smoke and beer hit him, making his eyes water a bit before he could adjust. The bass from the speakers beat against his ears and made the fabric of his clothes vibrate, once more dazing him before he could get a handle on his senses. He squinted against the flashing strobe lights as he pushed his way past the throngs.

The tip of his boot hit something on the floor and sent it rolling. He didn't have to look to know it was a syringe. His arms reflexively jerked away from the seductive touches of the women who tried to grab his attention as he looked for Mack in the crowd. The fight was still a quarter of an hour away. If he guessed right, the man would be near the bar, taking more bets and organizing the tournament tree one last time.

Leo felt something brush at his pockets and he turned just in time to seize the hand that tried to make off with his keys. What he didn't expect was for his fingers to connect around a small wrist. The boy looked up at him, the colorful lights like a kaleidoscope across his youthful face. He couldn't have been more than ten years old.

He snatched away what was his and set the boy free, knowing he would just steal again from someone else. As much as he hated it, the boy wasn't his responsibility and it wasn't his place to correct him. With a sigh, he skimmed the crowd again and found the Red Socks ball cap bobbing lively across the sea of strangers.

Leo pushed through a cluster of drunken college students and edged past a tight grouping of ladies in leather skirts dancing with martini glasses before he could put his hand on Mack's shoulder.

The manager jumped and spun around, wide eyes looking through a pair of tinted glasses. When he saw who had grabbed him, he let out an exaggerated breath.

"Scared me, man!" he shouted over the trap music. "Lookin' good!" Mack reached out and squeezed Leo's bicep in the kind of way that reminded him of a man who looked to buy a piece of livestock and wanted to test its sturdiness.

Leo smacked his hand away, effectively startling the manager. "I need a place to put my stuff," he said, jerking his chin toward the duffle bag slung across his chest. Mack recovered and offered out his hand to take it there for himself. "Someplace no one will get to it," he clarified, unafraid to sneer at him. It didn't pay to be friendly in a place like this.

Mack's throat worked when Leo dropped into that serious tone and then nodded. "All right. All right. I've got a locker in the backroom. You can put it there." He handed Leo the tiny padlock key and gave him his usual thorough directions.

"When's my fight?" Leo asked, making the key disappear in his fist, so no one would try to pinch it.

"You're my first matchup!" Mack announced proudly, his one gold tooth blinking in the club lights. As if to prove that he wasn't lying, he took the dry erase board he had been working on at the bar and showed him. The column of names on one side of the tree didn't matter to him. The one blank spot where the winner's name would be written did.

"Rules?"

Mack began to list out the scant regulations set down for the tournament. The only restriction appeared to be the usual. No eye gouging and no groin shots. Everything else was permitted until his opponent tapped out or passed out.

"Kicks and grappling?" Leo asked.

The manager grinned. "All fair game."

"Payout?"

"Six Gs."

More than enough. Leo nodded in approval and pulled out his wallet to count out the bills.

"Buy-in's five hundred."

He froze in the middle of his count and shot Mack a glare that could peel paint. "You told me it was four."

The wanker only shrugged. "Must have misspoke."

Leo feigned a smile. "Must have." He stacked what bills were needed to get him into the fight and held them out for Mack between his two fingers. Before the manager could take them, Leo grabbed for his shirt collar and pulled him in close. "You better not cross me on this," he growled in warning. "If I find out you skimmed my winnings again, I will find you."

And Mack knew Leo could. He didn't have connections, but he had his demon who loved a good fight. The bookie's hairy brows shot up and he nodded quickly, hands raised as if he had already been caught in the act.

"We're clear," he assured. "But I didn't cross you that time, you know. It was – "

Leo shoved him against the bar counter, knocking over a few beer bottles in the process as Mack's feet were nearly lifted off the floor. He could have easily snapped this weasel's spine if he wanted to. Good thing for him, Leo still needed the money.

"I know it was you," he snarled, getting close enough, so only Mack could hear him. "Be grateful I'm in a forgiving mood tonight. Otherwise, you'd be in the river by now."

Before Mack had a chance to open his mouth and dig himself a deeper grave, Leo tucked the wad of bills in his front shirt pocket. Under the watch of several patrons to the bar, he let Mack nearly crumble in a heap and strode away to find the locker room.

He regretted nothing. Mack was a snake, no different than any of the other managers and bookies he had met across the country. They would sooner double-cross someone they thought wouldn't notice and take a bigger portion of the payout. Leo wouldn't be fooled. Not tonight. Not ever again.

Once more, he had to maneuver his way through the crowd, upsetting plenty and spilling drinks along the way. The long hallway to the locker room might have been the only empty place in the club. Can lights lit the path that stretched in a straight line toward the back of the complex, but shadows lined the walls and spaces between.

Leo gave himself permission to breathe again, but the darkness was close. He could tell in the subtle drop in temperature and the way the lights flickered and dimmed. It didn't surprise him that the demon would show up here. Away from Levi, away from his lighthouse of calm, Leo was vulnerable again. But this was what the darkness wanted. Pain, fear, blood.

"I almost thought we'd never be here again."

The voice scratched at the corners of his mind, slinking with him along the corridor. He knew, if he cared to look, what he would see. Either a floating immaterial orb of black mist, or a form that appeared much less sinister, like a swindling gambler or underhanded dealer ready to make bargains on souls. By the more substantial presence in his peripheral vision, he knew it was the latter.

"Don't get excited," Leo said. "I'm not staying."

The demon edged closer in the form of a man wearing a neatly pressed suit and jacket, jet black hair and coals for eyes gleaming in the fluorescent light. "Oh, come on. You know you miss this."

Leo scoffed. "Yeah, I totally miss the smell of piss, alcohol, and weed. Such a pleasant smell."

A disturbing laugh bubbled up from the demon's throat. "There's that humor I missed. See, we're so much better off here than in that little town in the middle of nowhere."

He slid a scathing glare to the darkness, but wouldn't slow or protest. "Here to collect payment?"

"You've had a week off, Leo. Thanks to that little – "

"If you call her anything but a lady, I'll – "

"What?" he snapped. "Punch me? Strangle me? You forget that you can't do anything, Leo. You're powerless and always will be."

He didn't need to be reminded. Whatever the darkness wanted to do, he could do it. Except when Belle prayed. That was his only saving grace, but there was no way her prayers could reach this far. Could they?

"Just pay attention during the fight and you'll get all the payment you need," Leo directed, slamming the door in the demon's face as he walked into the locker room.

It did little good. The darkness rematerialized beside him as he worked the padlock with the key he had been given.

"I know why you're doing this," the demon said, grinning to show his perfectly straight white teeth. "You're trying to make your girl happy. It won't work."

"Watch me," he dared.

"I'll make you throw the fight. Take you out of the first round before you can get anywhere close to the semi-finals."

"You won't do shi-" Leo stopped himself and bit back the word he wanted to use. "You won't do anything. Think of all the lads I'll beat into the floor tonight. You need that payment. Remember our deal?"

Leo stripped off his shirt and wadded it up before zipping open his bag to shove it inside. He then set to taking off his shoes and socks to join his shirt.

"And you remember what I told you? I need more than the typical payment, especially since your brother is getting closer."

One thing about demons, he had learned, was that they didn't have an ounce of loyalty in them, not even for the man who had tethered them to a victim. Twelve years he had lived with this curse, the darkness serving as the constant thorn in his side. But he did have one useful thing going for him. He told Leo when Matthew was catching up.

Leo shot a look to the demon to see if he was lying just to get a bigger blood payment. That was the agreement they had made months ago. If he did his part and gave the darkness what he wanted, Leo and Belle would be left alone. Of course, the game changed when Leo decided to pursue her. Now that they were living together in a hotspot that the darkness didn't care to be in, the cost of their protection went up.

"How close?" he asked, hoping for an honest answer.

"Very. And I would rather not be around when he does come. Think of how mad he'll be when he finds out I've been masking your trail for the sake of an extra fix."

That was laughable. "You poor wee thing," he mocked. He crammed his duffle bag in the locker, thoughtless to how the luggage would damage Mack's package of cigarettes or the tiny bundle of cocaine tucked away in the back. Leo hoped he busted the plastic bag.

"Why don't we stay in Little Rock? It's such a fun town," the darkness suggested as Leo began the methodical process of wrapping his hands in the gauze and athletic tape to protect his knuckles. By the end of the night, they would be stained red with blood.

"After this is over, I'm going to Fayetteville."

The demon came around to face Leo. "There's nothing in Fayetteville worth seeing."

"And then I'm going back to Levi," Leo stated impatiently, as if he had been saying it all night in one way or another. He wouldn't leave Belle, no matter how much the darkness wanted him to. Like she said that day when he almost skipped town without telling her, he needed to take control of his life, one choice at a time. This choice, though made for odd purposes, was what he wanted, and the darkness would not pressure him into returning to this way of living – if it could even be called that.

"Why not stay a few days?" he said, almost whining like a child who was denied candy and was one refusal away from throwing a tantrum. "We could use some of the winnings to get a hotel, order room service, order some girls and – "

Leo shot daggers with his eyes that instantly made the vile mouth shut tight. He would have threatened to leave Little Rock right then if he thought it would do him any good. The darkness was smart enough to know that Leo needed this money just as badly as he needed the blood payment.

He finished wrapping his hands and left the locker room just as he heard the music dim for a minute to allow the presenter to publicize the first match. He didn't care if the darkness followed or not. He'd be in the crowd, watching, absorbing the pain and misery of Leo's opponents. It'd be just like old times.

Unceremoniously, Leo entered the main hall where the fighting would take place. His bare feet slapped against the cold concrete floor, wetted by the spilled beer and liquor from earlier that night. Mack was by his side as if he were a personal sponsor and hyped up the crowd when his name blared over the intercom. Men roared and cheered while women let out whistles and offers that were lost in the din.

He was led to the center of the room where one bright light hovered over the space sectioned off for the tournament.

Spectators leaned on the rope partitions to get a look at Leo as he swaggered forward to meet his first opponent. As always, his stomach tangled, but then he reminded himself that as long as his brother's curse tarnished his soul, there was little man could do to him. He was kept alive to suffer and cause suffering for others. He'd get hurt, but death wasn't in his near future. Not yet.

The ropes were closed behind him and he raised his fists, keeping his stance easy and light. The other man, leaner and an obvious novice, blew air past his protective mouthpiece and hopped about like an eager boxer.

Don't waste your energy, he told himself. *You've got a long night to go.*

When the bell sounded, and the crowd shouted for their favorites, the thinner man came charging forward with a wild hook. Leo dodged and sent an uppercut into his ribs. The guy recoiled and put a hand to his side, eyes wide like he had never expected to be hit.

Leo shook out his hands and flexed his unpracticed knuckles. His fight with Drake was the last time he'd ever hit bone that hard. He readied himself again for the next assault, but was disappointed when the man came at him again with a similar greenhorn move.

He left himself open and Leo took the opportunity. He ducked and wrapped him in a chokehold from behind. One kick to the back of his leg buckled him to the ground. For a minute or two, they grappled with one another. Leo saw stars each time a punch connected with his head, but he willed himself to stay conscious during every reversal. Limbs twisted as they rolled across the concrete, scraping the skin of their arms and backs along the way.

Each time he thought the guy would tap out, he kept coming at him with more desperate jabs and kicks. Leo felt a bit of blood trickle from his nose after an elbow slammed into his face. He could taste its metallic essence on his lips.

He was kicked off and stumbled backward, giving his opponent time to jump to his unsteady feet. Leo wouldn't give him the chance. He landed one solid punch to the jaw. He heard the crack, but didn't care. The man finally crumbled to the floor and he waited for a hand to smack the pavement.

When it did, Leo spat a bit of the blood from his mouth and looked up. His eyes instantly met the devilish stare of the darkness in the crowd. The black pits that bore through him told enough. This tournament wouldn't be a walk in the park for him like it used to be. The demon would drag this out and make the poor boys he fought think they had a chance against him.

The darkness wasn't just in the business of making Leo's life a living hell. He'd also drag along any other susceptible soul with him. That was why he needed to protect Belle, the only thing he cared about anymore.

Chapter 2

Belle had never passed a more restless night in her life. The only one that could come close was the night her father told her about his cancer. Even then, she could sleep a little knowing that it was all in God's hands. But with Leo, she wasn't so sure.

No matter how fervently she prayed that he would come back safely, her stomach never stopped turning. It only got worse when she woke up to find his bike was still missing from the driveway and there were no new messages on her phone. She tried calling him, but he didn't pick up. The fact that it rang and didn't skip straight to voicemail both relieved and terrified her. It meant that, wherever he was, he had cell service and kept his phone charged. But was he ignoring her calls? Or did he lose his phone?

No word, no sign, and she couldn't recall if he said when exactly he'd return from this mysterious errand.

It had been so long since she suffered like this that Belle had almost forgotten how to hide it from her coworkers.

Thankfully, the bookstore wasn't so busy that Saturday and she had plenty of alone time that was spent struggling to get her thoughts together. She tried to tell herself that Leo was a man of his word, but was he? If he said he'd come back, would he really? Had she done anything to make him want to go away? Or did this have nothing to do with her?

As she stood on the windy sidewalk with Ivy, locking the doors to the shop for the afternoon, her hands betrayed her. She couldn't get the key to slide effortlessly into the lock. Ivy must have noticed.

"Want me to do that?" she asked, her long blonde hair tangling in the breeze.

Fall was quickly approaching, along with a million other things to consider. Holidays, her lambing ewes, and church events. She despised this time of year. Too much going on, too much to think about, too much to dread, because it all involved being part of a community. And though she loved Levi and the people in it, Belle would have rather stayed home than help with the pumpkin patch at New Hope Church or man the store's booth at the annual festival on Main Street.

Just the reminder of the cold snap that could potentially endanger her animals heightened her current frazzled state. She simply handed the keys to Ivy and backed away from the door to let her lock it.

"You've been kind of a mess today," she said gently. "Are you all right?"

Belle hated that her mask kept slipping off all day. Once, a customer accidentally dropped a book and the loud boom of the hardcover hitting the floor made her visibly jump. Another time, she froze after a truly disturbing thought crossed her mind. What if Leo hadn't come back that morning, because he had been hurt and had no way of contacting her? For a solid two minutes, she willed her tight chest to release her lungs, so she could breathe again.

Ivy, however, didn't lord it over her. She didn't mock her or tell her to get a grip. Besides Leo, she might have been her only other friend who began to see more and more of her true self. The scared, anxious, sometimes blunt and unpleasant person that she hid behind that mask. And because of that, Belle was willing to show a little more every day until a line was crossed.

"It's Leo," she confessed, wrapping her army green canvas jacket around her middle. "He left yesterday and I haven't seen him since."

Ivy's big brown eyes widened. "Left? What do you mean he left?"

She had to choose her words carefully. No one knew that they were living together, but it was common knowledge that he worked on her farm. "Yesterday morning before he left after doing the chores, he said he wouldn't be back that evening. He said he had something to do, but he wouldn't tell me what."

Ivy propped a slender hand on her hip. "Just like that? He left? And you haven't heard from him?"

Belle shook her head. "I thought he'd be back this morning, but he never came."

"Do you think he came by after you left for work?"

She shrugged and let her finger obsessively rub the zipper handle on her purse. The leather had been worn down in that spot over the years. She fiddled with it when she became too nervous. "I'm not sure. I've been trying to call him, but I'm also trying to not be too crazy about it... I'm sure he's fine."

They walked a few paces to the space of brick wall next to the bookstore display window, the spot where they always stood during Ivy's smoking breaks.

"The least he could do is send you a text or something," she said. "Are you afraid he's left, like, for good?"

Belle felt her insides chill. "I've been trying not to think about that, after the last time he almost skipped town without telling me. I've gone over it again and again in my head, but I can't remember any hint that he would leave."

Ivy angled her body toward her and placed a hand on her trembling shoulder. "Maybe it's not all that extreme. He might be on the farm right now doing the evening chores... But the man better have an excuse or I might come and beat it out of him myself."

She let herself smile at the comment, but shook her head. "Even if he didn't, I wouldn't want you to... It's not like he owes me anything."

"If he's a decent man, he'd tell you why he ghosted."

Belle pursed her lips for just a moment, hating that she was about to divulge more of her innermost fears to Ivy, who probably already thought she was over reacting. "That's just it. I don't know if he is a decent man. I mean, I know he's kind and thoughtful when he wants to be, but... there's something else that he's not telling me. It's like every time I think I'm really getting to know him, he shuts the door. He's an iceberg and there's so little above the surface. It's frustrating and I just... I just wish he'd trust me, you know?"

When she looked up to her friend, she found a pair of empathetic eyes gazing back at her. She nodded. "I know exactly what you mean."

Belle's overactive mind whirled at that statement. What did Ivy know about all of this? Did she once have a guy who did the same? Or a friend? A pang of conviction struck her out of nowhere, and she let out a defeated sigh. Ivy had been in her shoes, all right. But instead of a love interest playing the guessing game with her, it was a coworker.

"Are you two... Are you dating? I mean, I know you said you weren't before, but that was a while ago and so much has happened between you two since then." Ivy smiled. "Do you really like him?"

Oh, Ivy didn't know the half of it. Belle didn't either, but that didn't stop her from embracing every confused, thrilling, and terrifying aspect of these feelings she had for Leo. But this much she did know. "I do like him... A lot. And I know I shouldn't. After this stunt, you'd think I'd learn my lesson that he doesn't care about me in the same way, but..."

"There's the mystery of it all," Ivy finished with an understanding nod. "I know exactly what you mean."

To Belle, it wasn't just the mystery, that fuzzy image of Leo behind sheer curtains that taunted her to come closer, to see more. When she'd try to pull back the veil, another dropped in its place and she would get nowhere. After every talk, after every kiss, every naked look of those blue eyes that enraptured her soul so completely, she thought she had caught a glimpse of the real him. Only to find out that he was so much deeper than all of that, so much more broken.

"Tell you what," she continued eagerly, "I'm going to a party tonight. It's in your neck of the woods. If Leo still doesn't turn up, why don't you come with me? It should be fun and I was told there'd be food. A lot of people we know are coming too."

Belle didn't know what was more terrifying. The prospect of going to a crowded party packed with people she knew or coming home to find that Leo was still missing. The last thing she wanted after the long, emotionally exhausting day was to go to an equally exhausting party, food or no food.

She found her excuse at that thought, however.

"I actually have to go grocery shopping and..." She paused and bit her lip. "I'm really not in the mood for a party. I know it'll be fun and all, but I'm just not up for it."

She expected to see Ivy discouraged, but instead she gave another sympathetic nod and patted her arm. "That's all right. I do hope Leo is there though, for your sake. I don't like seeing you so stressed out."

She returned the smile as best she could. "Believe me, I don't either."

"Keep me posted if he turns up," Ivy requested as she made her way to the silver Honda parked near the corner.

After agreeing, Belle moved to the driver side of her truck, only to remember that there was a crucial flaw to her plan. Though she had her purse, she had forgotten her checkbook on the counter in the kitchen. The habit of leaving her money at home started weeks ago when she realized that paying Leo for his work would put a dent in her cash flow. Now that his payment was room and board, she could be a little less frugal, but the habit hadn't died. And with her anxiety frying her brain, it was no surprise that she would leave the house without it.

But if Ivy saw her drive out of town, she might think that Belle had been lying. Just another lovely part of her anxiety that made her overthink something so simple. So, she sat in her truck and waited for the little Honda to turn down one of the few branching residential streets off of the main road. Then, she checked her phone one more time for a message that wasn't there, and left for home.

As she neared the farm, Belle could already feel it building in her core, that tense anticipation for something potentially good or devastating. If Leo was there, what would she say to him? What would she do if he wasn't? How many cups of tea would she need to drink until she passed out or started to feel normal again? What about a bubble bath? Would she even bring herself to leave the house again for grocery shopping? The way she felt in that moment, she wasn't even sure she could eat anything. It'd all come right back up.

The climax came when she pulled down the drive and saw Leo's black Harley propped on its kickstand by the porch steps. The tiny gasp was involuntary, as was the stab of pain through her abdomen. She couldn't get out of the car fast enough and even left her purse in the passenger seat.

The door was unlocked when she bounded in, half expecting to see him in the kitchen with a cup of coffee. Instead, she was met by

Ranger who yipped and slid across the smooth floor, his big awkward paws slipping beneath him.

Belle stooped down and ruffled his ears as she always did when she came home, but her energy couldn't be poured into an effusive welcome just yet.

"Leo?" she called out as she made her way toward the stairs. Over the pounding of her heart in her ears and her shoes against the treads, she heard a door open on the second floor.

When she reached the top, Belle froze, her feet cemented in place. Steam rolled out of the bathroom and pooled into the hallway. Standing in the middle of this puddle of mist was Leo, wearing nothing but a towel tucked securely around his waist and water rolling down the tan, scarred skin of his chest and arms.

Belle's insides quivered at the sight of him, his dark hair glistening in the hall light, locks sticking out in all directions like he had tried to dry it off just before she came in. Those blue eyes never looked so inviting and if she wasn't so terrified, she might have run to him – naked or not.

Her lips parted and she could feel her mouth go suddenly dry, unable to blink or look away, even for modesty sake. It appeared that he suffered in the same way, motionless with one hand gripping the point where the towel ends connected and the other on the doorframe to the bathroom. The posture showcased his form so beautifully, so erotically. Muscles, rippling and toned, were so unlike anything she had ever seen in real life. Only magazine models and action movie stars were this ripped.

She had seen him like this once before, the night they met. Only then, he had been wearing a pair of mud-splattered jeans that hung low around his hips. He didn't have as many scars then either. Since they had known one another, a few more were added to his left arm and some speckled across his shoulders where he had been burned in the barn fire.

And there was a new one, fresh and still red, right across his cheekbone. The white butterfly-closure bandage was a plain give-away and stood out just above the dark stubble on his jaw.

That small detail reminded her why she had rushed inside and why she had been going out of her mind for the last twenty-four hours.

"Where were you?" she nearly screamed, startling them both. Belle never screamed, and it seemed she couldn't stop. "I tried calling you and you didn't answer."

Leo's mouth closed and he blinked a few times as if to get himself out of the same daze she had been in. "I was busy. I didn't have my phone on me."

"I thought you would be back this morning." Belle reached out and held onto the baluster for support.

"Well, it didn't work out that way," he said with a sigh and shrug of his brows. Leo took one step, then another.

Belle flinched back just a tad before she realized that he intended to walk into his room and not toward her.

"You could have..." Her voice trailed off as he turned to look at her, standing in the doorway.

No, he didn't have to let her know where he was or what he was doing or why he would be so late. Like she had told Ivy, he owed her nothing. They didn't belong to each other.

"Say it," he demanded in an encouraging way. "Say whatever it is you're thinking."

He asked for it. And even if it ruined everything, she'd give him what he wanted.

Belle squared her shoulders and tried to keep her stare fixed on his face, though the scar and everything else was incredibly distracting. "You could have told me that you didn't think you'd be coming back until later. From the start, you could have told me what you were doing. And I'm guessing it's got something to do with that cut on your face. Did you clean that?"

One corner of Leo's mouth quirked up at her question. "Aye, I cleaned it." Then, he closed the door and Belle was alone in the hall, now even more dazed if that were possible.

She stormed to his room and stamped her foot. "You're not off the hook! Why didn't you return my calls?"

She heard the towel drop to the floor and a flash of heat creeped up her neck.

"I didn't even know you called until I got back," he replied over the scrape of the wooden dresser drawer opening.

"And where did you go? How did you get that cut?"

There was more movement on the other side of the door and her mind betrayed her by creating the image of Leo sliding each masterfully shaped leg into a pair of jeans. She crossed her arms, willing her heart to settle down in her chest.

When he didn't answer, she knocked again. "Leo, please answer me? I was... I was worried sick."

The admittance came out soft and tenderly, so different from her previous biting tone that Belle wondered if she had used up every ounce of anger she had in that one outburst. She had only ever been that openly mad once in the last few months, and again it was directed at Leo because of something he had done to make her come unraveled.

A few seconds later, he reemerged, the door swinging open so suddenly that her recoil was delayed. Leo towered over her just barely five-foot frame, still shirtless but a little drier, with a black shirt in one fist and a sheet of paper in the other.

Before she could get lost in the delectable smell of his body wash and deodorant, he presented the paper to her. "I was taking care of this for you."

Belle glanced down to the paper and read the tiny print. Before she could even finish, her hand was on her mouth to keep herself from screaming.

"The deal was made early this morning and I hoped to be back before you left for work, but – "

She cut him off with a squeal and lunged toward him, arms reaching for his neck. Leo caught her up against him and held her there, her feet kicking excitedly just inches from the ground. The dampness of his hair chilled her face and some of the residual water on his shoulders and chest transferred to her blouse, but she didn't care.

"You got the stallion!" she cried, completely forgetting that he was half naked in her arms.

Her shirt rode up a bit in the excited embrace, and the skin of her stomach touched the skin on his abs. His warmth seeped into her and sent a skittering thrill down her spine. To have him so close, and so near to a bed...

Thankfully, he was the only sensible one between them and took two long strides away from the darkened bedroom and into the hall. She clung to his neck like a child who refused to let go.

"I did. I even negotiated the asking price down to four grand."

Belle buried her nose against his neck and smiled as she breathed in that scent she had missed so much. She closed her eyes, and just for a moment, she could pretend that they were together as more than friends. That this hug was normal, and not something impulsive or purposeful as their first kisses. She could pretend that this was how she hugged him every day. It felt so right to hold him and be held.

Harsh reality, however, came crashing through and when her body began to feel heavy and weighted, her hold loosened, and she dropped to the floor. Leo was the only one to hesitate and his arm gradually slid away from her, but the warmth of it remained like a painful reminder of what could be the norm.

"Thank you," she said, unrequited passion and gratitude stealing some of her voice as she took the bill of sale from him.

"He'll be dropped off on Monday and I'll be here to get him settled, so you don't need to worry about any of that."

She nodded and instead of looking up into those eyes that would sever her grasp of reality, she read the paper over and over again. Leo tugged on the clean shirt, the smell of detergent now mingled with his already tempting scent.

Downstairs, Ranger whimpered and she could hear him struggling to get up the steps that his stubby legs couldn't climb.

"But, how did you even get four grand?" she questioned as Leo moved around her toward the stairs. Belle marveled at how they could have shared such an intimate embrace and then act as if it didn't happen. Maybe that was for the best, but her heart couldn't pretend.

"That was what I did last night," he called back to her.

Hurriedly, she followed after him and watched him scoop up the puppy with one hand, carrying him into the kitchen. She giggled at the way Ranger squirmed and tried to mouth at Leo's forearm.

"I went to Little Rock," he continued. "Got a hold of one of my old fight managers from about six months ago and he got me into a tournament."

Belle reached the bottom of the steps, but her legs couldn't take her any further. The blood drained from her face. "A tournament? Like, a fighting tournament?"

Ranger was set on the ground as Leo picked up his empty water bowl and filled it at the sink. "A fighting tournament. Seven rounds."

"And I'm assuming you won?" she asked.

"I did. Won the four grand and a few extra thousand on top of that." He sounded so smug and she didn't need to see his face to know he was smiling.

Quickly, Belle tried to reason through it.

Seven rounds. That meant he had fought seven men for the prize. Leo had gone out of his way, drove all the way to Little Rock just for the chance to win that money. He risked his health and maybe even his life to get her this stallion, so she could continue building the foundation for her dreams. He had done all of that for her, and she had been angry that he didn't return a phone call.

How ungrateful could one person be and still breathe?

"Hey."

His voice drew her out of the thoughts that were speedily veering into a dark place. Belle looked up and realized he had been staring at her, brows furrowed in concern.

She opened her mouth, but the words were slow to come out. "You... You didn't tell me, because you thought I'd try to stop you."

Leo let out a long breath. "Either that, or you'd be mad. So I thought it best not to tell you."

Was that his reasoning for everything? He did something to make her happy, but left out details, so she wouldn't become upset? What did that mean?

She couldn't let herself hope. Not when so many mixed signals were being thrown around on both sides.

"You're right. I probably would have... I'm glad you didn't get hurt worse than you did."

Leo smiled and she wondered if it hurt for his cheek to pull at the little cut.

They stared at one another and Belle's mind drifted back to just moments before, replaying the way their bodies had been pressed together, how the water rolled down his skin. It was clear his thoughts weren't in the same place, because he cleared his throat and thumbed to the refrigerator. "I noticed there wasn't any food."

Belle smacked her forehead and motioned to her abandoned checkbook on the counter. "Yeah, that's why I came home. I need to go shopping."

He swiped the checkbook and flipped it in his hand a few times. "Want some company?"

If he was doing that just to charm her, it was working. With a steadying breath to expel all the pent-up energy that had tormented her all day, she nodded. "I'd love your company."

She didn't quite mean for it to come out the way it did, but she wouldn't correct herself or take it back. His smile was enough to tell her that he didn't notice that sly hint. Leo was the only person on the planet who was welcome by her side anytime, anywhere. It didn't matter if he was fighting or if they were strolling down aisle seven looking for canned green beans. She'd want to be with him all the time. No matter what.

Chapter 3

The fatigue and ache in his ribs were well worth that hug. He didn't care that Belle had slammed right into his chest, furthering the lingering pain from the tournament. He would have held her there until the world turned to dust.

He was glad to be back in Levi. The darkness nearly dropped from him as soon as he crossed the city limits. After spending the night in the club, smoking cigarettes just to stay awake and sipping on beers to keep himself from thinking too much about the blood caked on his knuckles, Leo was happy to be back. He could finally breathe, knowing that Belle had her horse and the darkness would be kept away for a little while. The blood payment he made had been substantial.

For now, he'd settle for watching her amble down the grocery store aisles while he leaned on the cart, easing some of the pressure off his throbbing hip. Toward the end of the night, it had been twisted unnaturally, and he was sure a muscle had been strained. But he wouldn't tell Belle that. She would only know of the cut, because that was the only visible wound so far. Bruises would appear soon, if they haven't already, especially across his back and legs, so he'd have to be more careful about when and where he took his shirt off around her.

He smiled when he thought on those few moments they shared in the hall. Her fury, her presence, the way she looked at him with such unguarded eyes, all of it drove him mad. If the darkness had been there, he was sure there wouldn't be much to hold him back from acting on an instinct he had been resisting for a while now. It was a good thing that he respected her more than that.

Leo listened to Belle's soft voice rambling about what they would need for certain recipes or talking about her favorite products as they passed them. The story about how she came to love a certain brand of cereal as a child proved especially entertaining. Much of it went over his head, like when she talked about how much ground beef she would need in proportion to how much meatloaf she intended to make that night. But in those sparkling moments when she talked about her childhood or personal preferences, he hung onto every word. It all seemed so simple, so innocent and genuine.

This is what life was supposed to be. All he had ever known was the rough, wild sort of living that created one crisis after another. But this, with Belle, was easy and comfortable. It was safe. He wanted more of that.

They reached the cold and dairy section when she turned, her face transformed by some startling thought.

"What?" he asked, then glanced to the bag of shredded cheese she held.

"All this time, I never even asked you what you wanted to eat."

Leo couldn't stifle the laugh and it bothered his sore ribs. "It's fine, really. I'm not picky."

Belle lowered the bag of cheese into the steadily filling grocery cart, but he could see the way she looked at the contents, wondering what she could put back or trade.

"Belle, really. It's fine."

"But, don't you have a favorite food or something? Or maybe some other embarrassing story about breakfast cereal so I won't feel so silly?" Now she was laughing, but Leo knew she was at least partially serious.

What she didn't know was that he had been trying to fight the flashbacks since they arrived to the store. When he was a kid, he used to live for trips to the supermarket with his mother and sister. Such memories were tainted, forever touched by sorrow and grief, because he was the last.

However, Belle was right. It wasn't fair for her to be the only one to share her childhood, and it was about time for Leo to face the deepest of his wounds that had never properly healed.

"When we'd go to for messages – that is, going to the store," he began as they continued toward the shelves of milk and orange juice jugs, "my little sister, Kaitlyn, would ride in the cart. She was four years younger than me. My mum would split the list and give me one half, so I'd run all over the store to get things and bring them back."

One look to Belle walking beside him told Leo that he had successfully captured her attention.

"The manager of the store knew when we came in, because he'd see me darting down the aisles. Sometimes, I'd grab things I wanted that weren't on the list like Irn-Bru bars, Soor Plooms..."

"What's all that?"

Leo swooned at the question, remembering when he snuck all those things into the cart. His mother would find out what he did, only give him a look, and then finish out the purchase. "It's the best candy, but I doubt you'll find any here."

"I'll have to try it someday... You never mentioned you had a sister."

With a heart full of regret, he nodded. "Yeah. I had a younger sister and an older brother."

"Had? Did they…"

She already knew that his parents were gone, but he had never mentioned his siblings. He never wanted to. One was an angel and the other a devil. Leo, caught between, wanted to put them all out of his mind forever. Easier said than done.

"They did," he replied flatly, hardening so she wouldn't see the truth in his eyes. It was better she didn't know about Matthew. If she stayed ignorant, maybe that would be enough to keep her safe.

But what about him? Belle reached out and put a hand on his arm. "I'm sorry. I didn't mean to make you relive things."

He passed her an easy smile, willing to move on after some salt had been rubbed into that old wound. "I know… If you really want my input, I haven't had mince and tatties in ages."

"Mince and what?" she giggled.

"It's a mincemeat dish with some mashed potatoes. It's not hard to make. We just need some carrots. That's the only ingredient you're missing."

So now, it was Belle's turn to listen to him go on and on about comfort foods from his childhood. Black pudding, haggis, and Scotch pie being just a few. He told Belle about the food fights during breakfast with porridge instead of cereal. He could see them all now, flinging spoonfuls of the mush across the table. Even his father laughed and teased with them. That was before everything went to hell in a handbasket. Quite literally.

It had been so long since he thought of the good times. But Belle made the reminiscing less painful. He didn't feel that blade cutting into his stomach when he envisioned Kaitlyn giggling or when all the men of the house teamed up to throw scones at the girls. Belle laughed along, imparting a piece of his childhood that he could never get back.

They were halfway to the produce section when they were nearly T-boned by another cart zooming out from the end of an aisle.

Leo stopped just before they could collide. Belle gasped and his thoughts went instantly to her. His hands tightened on the handle of the cart and he was mildly frustrated by the woman who wasn't paying attention to where she was going, chatting away on her phone. But for Belle, it could be a trigger. She fixed her gaze straight ahead, eyes a little wide and staring dumbly as if she had just been slapped.

They had talked about them once and she hadn't mentioned sudden collisions with grocery carts, but that didn't mean this wouldn't affect her. So instead of shooting a glare at the careless woman, he turned to Belle and reached out.

Leo wasn't sure what he was thinking. Maybe he wasn't. His hand found the small of her back and stayed there, pressing against the fabric until he could feel the tense muscles around her spine. He meant the gesture to be supportive, to help ground her instead of slipping into a panic attack – if it should come to that.

Instead, it became something more intimate, at least for him. The shiver spread like a domino from the nape of her neck down to meet his hand. A bit of her warmth seeped into his fingertips. He could envision them kissing again, right there in the grocery store. All he'd have to do is apply a little pressure and she'd be in his arms.

"Belle!"

He looked up to see the woman they had almost hit. The phone was angled away from her cheery face. Belle stiffened under his touch and now he knew how she'd react. The mask would come first and what would follow would be nothing more than a show. And Leo would be a spectator.

The look of shock tightened into a grin brimming with identical joy portrayed in the stranger.

"Mrs. Levinson!" she said, taking a few steps away from Leo and the cart, abandoning his hand to the cold air. "How are you?"

The woman, Mrs. Levinson, quickly hung up with whoever she had been talking with on the phone and gave Belle a brisk hug.

They exchanged pleasantries, the kind that Leo detested. Shallow and unauthentic. The play was performed by all the people of the town when they saw someone in public they knew. Leo, though the pretense had almost been forced on him plenty of times, refused to be anything more than polite. But not this effusive, mawkish exchange.

He couldn't wait for the day when Belle would drop that mask in front of people, just for a second, so they could realize she wasn't just sweet and fluff. There was so much more to her than they could have ever guessed.

"It's been so long since we visited," Mrs. Levinson said, looking genuinely regretful of that fact.

Leo was sure that she was, but could Belle say the same?

"I know," she replied, imitating her friend's tone perfectly. Faked. "It's been a crazy time."

"Mrs. Johnson told me about what happened to the barn. Is the new one built?"

Belle perked up. "Yes, ma'am. All built and..." Finally, Leo was remembered. She glanced over her shoulder and took a small sidestep so Leo and Mrs. Levinson could get a good look at one another. "I've had Leo help me on the farm, too."

Her smile took on a bit of disdain, but stayed firmly in place on her lips. "He's working on the farm?"

Belle nodded and went into explaining all that Leo did to help her through this trying time. No one else knew he was the one to create it for her. The exclusion of that fact instantly made him more agreeable in Mrs. Levinson's eyes.

"Well, it's a pleasure to meet you, Leo. I'm so glad Belle has a man like you looking after her."

He smiled, but the effect of it didn't reach his eyes. "Just glad I can help in what way I can."

Mrs. Levinson brightened. "Oh, you're from Scotland?"

And just like that, Leo thought better of her in return. "Most people around here think I'm Irish. Thank you for recognizing the difference."

She waved her hand and he could see a bit of color rise to her slightly wrinkled cheeks. "Oh, it's easy to get the two mixed up, but my husband and I went to England one year and took a tour through Edinburgh before we left."

"I lived in a small town outside Edinburgh." Even Leo was a little surprised that he had offered up that bit of information. Belle had opened the flood gates and apparently, he had a hard time closing them again.

"Very interesting," Mrs. Levinson said, and then suddenly became somewhat distracted. The buzzing phone in her hand must have been the reason. "Listen, I would love to stay and talk, but I've got to get these home. I'll see you at the party tonight, won't I?"

Belle straightened. "Party?"

Mrs. Levinson dropped her chin. "Don't tell me my husband forgot to invite you!"

"I'm sorry," she replied with a shake of her head. "I didn't get anything."

Leo's teeth clenched tight to keep himself from saying anything.

"He said he would since he came over to help with the barn a week or so ago."

Belle seemed just as confused as Mrs. Levinson, but Leo wouldn't clear the air for either of them. It wasn't his place to say that Mr. Levinson did mention about the party and extended the invitation to both him and Belle. At the time, he didn't know the man. Leo had been trusted to relay the message, but that was just days before he had planned to leave Levi and he had no intention of talking to Belle about a party she wouldn't want to attend anyway.

"Well, if you don't have any plans," Mrs. Levinson continued, "it's tonight on the farm. Very informal. This is all groceries for the cookout."

Leo looked to the overflowing shopping cart and saw packages of hamburger patties, hotdogs, buns, and dozens of bags of crisps. Tucked beneath all of that must have been the condiments and fixings.

"What time?" Belle asked.

The very question itself made him look up, brows snapped together. Even if she was being polite, Leo didn't expect her to be interested in this party. She said she hated crowds and the chance to embarrass herself.

"Seven o'clock. Do you two think you can come?"

Before she had a chance to regret it, Leo replied with, "No."

At the same time, however, Belle had said, "Yes."

Their eyes met, and he hoped that something in his expression would tell her enough. Her mask faltered for a split second and she almost looked angry with him. Leo was only trying to save her. Couldn't she see that?

"Well, the invitation is open to you both. I do hope you can come." Mrs. Levinson gave Belle's arm an affectionate squeeze and then answered her phone. By the tail end of the conversation, Leo could guess it was her husband and she was not happy that he didn't tell Belle about the party.

He looked to Belle and could tell that she wanted to discuss it further. Thankfully, she would never make a scene in such a public place. So, Leo turned the cart down the nearest empty aisle and he faced her.

"You want to go to this party, or were you saying yes, because you thought it's what Mrs. Levinson expected you to do?"

With the mask dropped, the true Belle emerged, and she stuttered for a bit before she could articulate her answer. "It's... It's not that I think it's what's expected of me. I guess... I don't know... If... If you're with me, then I'd like to go. If you don't go, I won't. I don't want to go alone. If I'm guessing right, Ivy will be there, and so will a lot of other people I know."

He blinked and leaned a little more on the cart to take some of the weight off his hip again. "If Ivy's there, you won't be alone."

Belle's eyes dropped away, and he watched her lips tighten and pull as if she were in some discomfort. "It's... It's not the same."

Then, he understood. Belle wanted someone there who would keep her steady, who would keep her from tripping into an anxiety attack. She wanted him, because he was her safety blanket. As much as he didn't like to be used, not by the darkness or anyone else for that matter, he didn't mind being used by Belle. He just wished he could have been more than just a bodyguard or comforter. He wanted to be her everything, just like she was everything to him.

"If you want to go, then I'll go with you. It's not like I have anything better to do."

She lifted her head and gave him a half-way convincing smile. "I think I'd like to. If I know the Levinson's, it'll be a decent party with dancing, and it's been a while since I danced."

Wonders never ceased. "You dance?"

She stood up to her full height, beaming with confidence. "My dad was the best line dancer in the county and he taught me everything he knew."

Out of respect for her and her father, Leo didn't laugh. But he almost did. "Then you'll get to dance tonight. We'll leave whenever you want to, whether that's five minutes after we get there or five in the morning."

Belle snorted. "I hardly think I could last until five."

Twinkling Christmas lights flashed across the dashboard of her truck. The cheerful laughter and voices coming from the pole barn behind the Levinson farmhouse made Belle want to both draw closer and run away screaming.

It had been ages since she attended a party of any kind, small or large, formal or not. When she told Leo and Mrs. Levinson that she would come, at the time, she thought she could handle it. But the longer she sat there, staring at the silhouette of the barn-like roof against the dusky sky, she could feel that assurance begin to crack and splinter like a mirror under too much pressure.

In the growing darkness, she couldn't recognize the other cars and trucks parked in the field near the house, so there was no telling who was there. What if there were people from church? What would they think when they saw her with Leo? Belle couldn't forget the way Mrs. Levinson looked when she introduced him, and her mind filled in the blanks of what she was unwilling to say for the sake of politeness.

What if she wanted to dance, but no one else did? What if she did dance and made a fool of herself? What if her nervous stomach made her toss up anything she ate? Would Mrs. Levinson read that as an insult?

"You're hyperventilating."

Leo's voice in the passenger seat brought her back to the present after spending a hot minute in the potential future.

"I can't breathe," she gasped as her mind continued to spiral with a thousand thoughts and fears. Church, she could handle, because it was routine. Work was a little less predictable, but she managed. Trips to the grocery store were chaotic, but she was under no obligation to socialize.

This was a battlefield and if she didn't navigate it perfectly, she'd be blown away.

"What can I do?" he asked.

Belle finally looked to him and how the residual light from the pole barn left half of his face in shadows, one blue eye glistening with empathy.

"Just give me a minute."

Instead of seeming impatient, Leo turned his head and gazed out the windshield. They were too far away to distinguish faces. Just a mass of moving bodies around a buffet table. A band, comprised of four musicians, stood near a narrow stage toward the opposite end with an open space of dirt and hay for the dance floor. Children ran and squealed with delight as they chased each other in and through the shadows around the pavilion.

It all looked like so much fun and part of Belle knew that it could be. These were just the initial jitters, the minor panic attack before plunging off the diving board into the cool, refreshing pool.

They're just people. You'll be fine. You will survive this. You're safe.

All the little things she told herself helped most of the time. But right now, all she wanted to do was tell Leo that she had changed her mind.

"We don't have to go," he said, as if reading her mind. "If it's too much, we can go back home. There's no reason for you to stay."

Belle gripped the steering wheel until she heard the old, cracked leather crinkle. "I shouldn't run."

"You don't have anything to prove."

She closed her eyes and took one deep breath, summoning it from her core rather than her chest. "Yes, I do. I have to prove it to myself."

Suddenly, she felt a hand on her wrist. That one touch was like the turning of a release valve. Every tense muscle slowly loosened, the raging tide of anxiety calmed with a simple command. Her hands went limp and Leo slipped in. His rough fingers laced between her own and the elephant on her chest finally stepped off.

"You remember what I said?"

Belle nodded and let her fingers close over his knuckles, feeling his steady, calm heartbeat in his palm. "We'll leave when I want to."

"Five minutes or five in the morning."

She cracked a smile and looked to Leo, the only person on this earth who might have really understood her. "Thank you."

With Leo's hand in hers, Belle was able to climb out of the vehicle within a matter of minutes, instead of being stuck in her typical quarter of an hour preparatory ritual. Her panic attack subsided, and her confidence rose with each step she took toward the pavilion.

Somewhere between the cars and the edge of the light coming from the party, Leo dropped her hand. The cool early autumn air hit her clammy palm and she wondered if she had been holding on for too long. One look to Leo told her enough. He did it for her, not because he was uncomfortable. If it were up to her, she would have held on through the whole night. But if she had been that concerned about what everyone thought, it would have been better not to seem too attached.

A good variety of townspeople were present. Churchgoers, farmers, ranchers, and all their families were present. Belle knew most of them or at least knew of them. A few heads swiveled in their directions, waves and hellos were exchanged, and before she had much of a chance to get used to the noise and the crowd, a shriek of joy rose up from somewhere near the buffet line.

Lena Kirkland came skipping between the other partygoers. An old high school friend and fellow farmer's daughter, Lena dropped off the map when she went to community college half an hour away. Belle had heard through secondhand whispers in the church pews that she had come back to Levi for a brief stay with her parents before going on to becoming a nurse in Little Rock. That always seemed to be the story in Levi. People moved away and lived their dreams. Few stayed.

"Oh my gosh!" she cried, wrapping her skinny arms around Belle's shoulders. "It's so good to see you!"

Belle returned the hug and greeting, and before she knew it, she was being led under the pavilion.

"Mrs. Levinson said you may come, and I was so hoping that you would!" Lena said excitedly, holding onto Belle's arm as if she'd run away at any moment.

She was right.

"I almost didn't, but you know I couldn't pass up the dancing."

Lena grinned, her dark curls bouncing with each step of her loud heels. "Oh my gosh! I remember you loved our school dances."

She went on to reminisce about all the times when she, Belle, and several other girls would stand around at the dances in the gym. They would watch the boys or talk about teachers, shows, the unfairness of life as teenagers, and a multitude of other topics. Belle had pretty much forgotten about all of that up until now.

It wasn't until she was in the thick of the crowd, spreading acknowledgments to those she passed by, that Belle turned to find Leo. He stood near the edge of the pavilion, watching her intently from a distance. While Lena was busy talking about how they would tease their P.E teacher for his receding hairline, Belle gave him an apologetic look. She had fully intended to stay by him all evening, but the mob had other plans.

They soon joined a group of girls, all of which she knew from church or her school days. Soon, the mask was in place and she was able to smile and add her own input into the conversations. All the while, she thought of her words to a nearly obsessive degree, playing them back in her own head to assess if they were innocuous. Would she offend? Was she talking enough? Too much? Did they even want her in their circle or was she only there because of Lena?

Their smiles seemed genuine, their questions and comments easy and unforced. Their mannerisms, too, gave off the feeling that her presence was unoffending, and Belle was truly welcome with them. That made her relax and she could feel the muscles around her spine begin to relax.

Every given chance, she looked to the spot where she had left Leo. He had gone from watching her to watching the crowd, band, and buffet line. Belle had already given up on the idea of eating right then. She had been far too nervous, and it was better not to risk it.

She looked over one more time and saw that Leo had moved. A spike of panic wedged herself from the conversation, disconnecting her for only a moment while her eyes darted over the many heads to find him.

"Are you all right?" Lena asked, a thin hand touching her shoulder.

Had her mask dropped a little? Her brows arched, and she nodded hastily, composing herself. "Yeah, I'm good. I was just looking for my friend."

As if realizing the error she had made, Lena gasped and began to look as well. "That hot guy? I'm so sorry! I didn't realize you two were together."

Belle didn't want to read into that too much. Had Lena assumed that just because Belle never had a boyfriend in high school, she would never have one as an adult either? Or did she assume that just because Leo was hot, he would never want a girl like her?

"Well, we're not together," Belle began nervously, feeling heat creep up her neck. "I mean, he works on the farm. My ewes are about to lamb, and I need all the help I can get, so I hired him. He helps with other stuff too. On the farm, I mean. I don't know him all that well, but I'd say we're friends. Just good friends."

When she caught the eye of Mrs. Levinson's married daughter, Jessica Greene, Belle shut herself up. That knowing, almost entertained look like she saw through the rambling and didn't believe a word of it, even though it was the honest truth.

"There he is!" Lena cried, probably a little too loudly for Belle's comfort.

She looked and saw Leo had gravitated toward a group of men. Seeing they were a few of the other workers from the crew that helped build her barn, she let out the breath she didn't know she had been holding. But she sucked it in again when she noticed the brown beer bottle in his hand.

It shouldn't have startled her. If he smoked, it was logical that he would drink too. She just never thought that she would kiss lips that had touched alcohol. Not that she thought it would ever contaminate her, as some of the traditionalists within her church would believe. Somehow, she had just always pictured herself with a purist in the end. A man who never smoked, never drank, and a virgin. Leo broke that perfect image in every way, she was sure.

That thought alone further cracked a bit of her heart and whatever delusions she had about her and Leo. He had probably been with women. After traveling as much as he did, how could he not? If they ever married, their wedding night would be an awkward affair to say the least. Belle knew nothing, but Leo must have been so experienced.

All at once, she felt inadequate. Every condemning thought about herself and this strange, undefinable thing between her and Leo threatened to drown her.

The impulse to run for a safe spot flared up, but she squelched it quickly. This was not the time or the place to have a meltdown, not even over Leo.

So, she turned back to Lena and the rest of the girls before she could meet the blue eyes that were about to look her way. If Belle did, she might not have had the strength to stand. She'd think about it at another time, in another place. Not here, not when she had to stay in character. None of them knew that Leo mattered to her as more than a farmhand, and she had to keep up that appearance.

"He's pretty cute," Jessica said, the only taken girl of the lot.

"He's totally smiling this way!" Whitney squealed, another bachelorette from her school years.

"Do you know if he's dating anyone?" Lena asked hastily.

Belle opened her mouth and tried not to stammer. "He... I don't know."

Whitney's eyes sparkled with some wicked scheme and Belle suspected that she knew exactly what would happen later that night. She only hoped that she wouldn't be around to see it. If she thought that alcohol could ever cure her anxiety, she would have downed a whole six pack just to keep her stomach from doing backflips against her lungs.

One thought continued to echo, even as the conversation diverted from Leo. They never should have come. If they hadn't, Belle could have stayed happily ignorant about whatever it was they shared and she wouldn't feel the green monster of jealousy and black cloud of doubt suffocate her.

Chapter 4

Letting Belle be dragged off into the middle of the party might have been a true test of Leo's willpower. He stayed on the edge of the pavilion and watched her leave. It was clear she knew the girl well enough, so she was in no danger, but Leo's pounding heart didn't believe it right away. He had wanted to stay by her all night, available for support if she should need it. But something told him to stay back, give her space and let her swim on her own. If Belle needed him, he would be there.

What might have been even harder was to see her slip into the shoes of someone he didn't know. The mask was up, the curtain was raised, and Belle starred in her own show with everyone here as a spectator to her performance. The girl who talked and laughed with the other ladies in that tight-knit circle wasn't Belle. He knew that, because he saw her true character in the way her eyes darted at each sudden noise, at the way she raked her hands through her long brown hair to release that nervous energy. She didn't want to be with these people, not really.

So what was the point of it all? Why did they come here? Dancing wasn't a good enough reason. Not to him, anyway. There was no obligation, no purpose. Why would she put herself through this? Did she like diving headlong into a panic attack? Did she enjoy the feeling somehow? He might have never understood whatever tiny voice in her head told her that she had to prove to herself, and the world, that she was capable of facing a crowd of friends and strangers.

One thing he did know, though, was that she was stunning. He never thought that someone could pull off a long skirt and simple white blouse the way she did. The drawstring collar came off her shoulders, sleeves so loose that they filtered the light when she lifted her arm just the right way. The skirt, too, with its tiered seams accentuated her curves while also hiding them from some angles. With her hair undone, cascading in subtle, thick waves down her back, Belle looked the part of a free spirit, a wild horse ready to break free. If she did, Leo wouldn't hesitate to run beside her.

It was some improvement on her usual jeans and button-down shirt that made her look plain. But nothing could compare to her pajama pants and long, baggy t-shirts. That look, with her messy hair and face clean of all makeup, was his favorite. Raw and real. He needed more real.

Much like Belle, he had been spotted by someone who knew him and pulled into a group, much against his wishes. But with a cold beer in his hand and four other men he knew and trusted to some level, Leo wouldn't argue. Mr. Tale and the other men on his crew could be crude at times, but they showed themselves to be good people in one way or another. Besides, from his new vantage point, he could better watch Belle and the majority of the party. Even with the darkness paid off for a substantial amount of time, Leo wouldn't let his guard down.

But it soon occurred to him that the darkness was not what he should have been wary of.

"Who's that girl you came with?" Hunter asked, casually gesturing the neck of his beer bottle toward Belle and the other ladies.

"That's Belle Clearwater, ya loon," Winston replied before tipping back his own beer.

Hunter, the youngest on the crew and fresh out of high school, stamped his boot into the soft dirt of the pavilion floor and let out an oath. "When did she get hot?"

Leo had to consciously keep a light grip on the bottle, so he didn't crack the glass.

"She does look different with her hair down," Tucker commented. Tucker was engaged to be married next spring, but he still eyed Belle like a man who was unattached.

Mr. Tale, the boss and eldest of the bunch with his salt and pepper beard, was the one to end the string of insinuating comments that made Leo's blood boil. "Watch it, fellas. Just remember whose daughter that is."

Leo looked to Mr. Tale and narrowed his eyes in question. Belle said her father had died. What difference did her relations make?

Tucker cleared his throat and seemed to suddenly remember the vows he was destined to give. Winston, the only one who was even remotely close to Belle's age, turned his attention toward the band tuning up on the stage. Hunter, however, wasn't all that deterred.

"Who's that? Is he here?"

Tucker swung his free hand and popped the boy on the back of the head. "No, he ain't here."

"What does Belle's da have to do with anything?" Leo asked, the first time he had spoken since they started talking about her.

"Her father's Chad Clearwater," Winston answered.

"I knew that. He passed a few years ago, didn't he?"

Mr. Tale gave him a reproving look, as if speaking of the dead was some taboo thing in this community. "He did, but you didn't know him."

For a moment, Leo felt as if he were in one of the Twilight Zone episodes his great-uncle used to watch late at night. What was Belle not telling about her family? From what he understood, her father was a decent man. Better than her mother, anyway. And she didn't cringe at his memory or the mention of him like she did with her mother. Did she have more skeletons in her closet that he didn't know about?

"My dad and Mr. Clearwater were close," Winston added.

"Every man over thirty was close to Mr. Clearwater," Tucker said before taking a swig of his beer.

Leo still didn't understand the connection. "Was he an important man?"

"A well-liked man," Mr. Tale clarified. He would have been old enough to know Belle's father personally. "He had his hands in every church function, every community event, and helped out on all the farms and ranches in and around Levi... I think he had just about every family over to his house at least twice before he went on to be with the Lord."

Leo blinked at that euphemism, but didn't question it.

"When he did pass on," Winston said, "the whole town showed up for his funeral. I've never seen that church so packed, not even during Christmas and Easter."

Mr. Tale nodded in agreement. "Any man who messes with Chad Clearwater's daughter is digging a ten-foot deep grave for himself."

"Graves are only six foot," Hunter corrected.

Tucker laughed. "You best believe that man will get pounded down an extra four feet for good measure."

The others laughed, but Leo could only think back to that day at the diner when Drake had almost assaulted Belle. Where had all the men of the town been then? Were there other social politics at work that protected Drake? Or did Leo do such a good job of warding off the jerk that no one bothered to come behind and finish the job like Mr. Tale implied?

It also made him think deeper. Not about Mr. Clearwater himself, but how his choices had affected Belle. Everyone knew her and loved her through her family. When her mother left, what other mothers came to her aid? There was a saying that it took a village to raise a child. Could that have happened here in Levi? Maybe that was why Belle felt some obligation to attend these parties, even though her nerves could barely handle the social interactions.

If all of that wasn't enough, what about her father's actions? His absence from the farm, the constant revolution of guests through their home, their involvement in the community. What if it all added to her anxiety? What if that only built upon the foundation that her mother had laid for this emotional handicap and mental illness?

Leo felt as if he understood her a little better, but it all seemed superficial and too much like guesswork. If her father had truly made her anxiety worse, then she might not have adored him as much as she did.

And what did this bit of information mean for Leo? Nothing good. He was bound to hurt her eventually. If not directly, then the darkness would work through him like he promised. Belle would be his downfall and the town would run him out with torches and pitchforks in true village style.

He took a long draft of his beer until it was nearly empty, wishing it could make him forget about a bleak and unhappy future ahead. He had to live in the moment or he'd lose a hold on everything.

"Speaking of men who need to be ten feet under the sod..." Tucker tipped his beer toward the other end of the pavilion.

Materializing out of the growing darkness were two new guests. One tall and obviously feminine, her long ponytail swaying with each stride. Her partner cut a masculine shape, steps powerful and slowing more and more as they neared the pole barn. It took a moment for Leo to recognize them, but when he did, he never felt a stronger urge to growl.

"Who invited him?" he grumbled.

Mr. Tale let out a heavy sigh. "I think Jessica invited Ivy, and she decided to bring Drake along."

"They're dating now?" Winston questioned, his voice dripping with the staunch disbelief. Leo was a little surprised too, given what Ivy must have known about the man she had brought to the wrong party.

"Have been for weeks now," Hunter replied. He didn't sound too happy about the arrangement either. "The dude won't stop talking about it."

Mr. Tale's hand was already holding Leo back the moment he moved to intercept them. He must have known the kind of hate rolling in his chest at the very sight of Drake. He must have also known the kind of scene Leo would cause if he were allowed to confront him on an impulse.

"He's not doing any harm," his boss warned. "It's too early to cause any trouble anyway."

That was easy for him to say. He didn't know the meaning behind the lurid look Drake gave Belle in that moment. She noticed it and quickly looked away, her face now suddenly pale. Leo ground his teeth and could feel himself shake with rage. But he wouldn't move. This was just another opportunity for him to screw up.

At least if Drake did make a move, Leo wouldn't be alone. There were plenty of other men here who would come to Belle's rescue. Despite her anxiety, he hoped she understood how safe she really was.

"Belle? You okay?"

She heard Jessica's question and even felt the hand on her shoulder, but she couldn't begin to form a response. The words kept buzzing in her head, all jumbled together and getting lost in the panic she felt when she saw Drake.

He was with Ivy? This was the party she had invited Belle to earlier that day? Was she falling back on Drake as a date or were they going to come together anyway?

And most importantly, she feared what Drake would do. Not to mention what Leo would do. She slid a checking glance his way. Yep, he saw Drake. But did Drake see Leo? One more look confirmed it. The two men stared one another down and neither appeared as if he was willing to give an inch to his rival.

Belle caught herself at the thought. Rivals? There was no competition. Not to her. Her choice would always be with Leo, but did he know that? Was Drake aware?

"You look like you're going to be sick," Whitney remarked.

She turned back and saw all eyes were on her, watching and concerned. Her face felt chilled and bloodless and if any of them bothered to look at her hands, they'd see how badly she was shaking.

Get it together. Play the part. Don't make them worry.

Belle somehow managed to smile, though she was sure it wasn't a convincing one. Luckily, she didn't have to tell any of them what had made her blanch.

Lena propped a hand on her hip. "Who invited that piece of trash?"

The ladies turned in unison toward Ivy and Drake.

"I don't know," Faye, a distant cousin of Whitney, said with a screwed up face. "But someone needs to take it out."

Whitney snorted at her humor, though Belle couldn't help but wonder who exactly they were talking about. Drake was universally disliked by most of Levi, but Ivy had her share of enemies as well, especially among the other women of the town. One rumor about a scandalous affair was enough to make her name like mud, especially to the girls within the family that were said to involve the scandal. That happened to be at least one-fifth of the guests present.

Belle never gave into such gossip, but she reasoned that if Ivy was willing to show up to a Levinson party, then the rumor must not have been true at all.

Only Lena's next question cleared the air.

"Is he still as conceited as I remember from school?"

Before the word could be stopped, Belle practically blurted out an overly confident, "Yep."

Gaping smiles turned her way, eyes brightened in awe as if they were pleasantly surprised by Belle's rather rude, but poignant answer. Too aghast by her own brutal honesty, her hand clapped over her disobedient mouth. A few beats of silence passed before they all erupted in laughter that caught the attention of almost everyone around them.

Belle's pallor brightened into a mortified blush. She had never openly tried to defame anyone before, not even Drake. She was everyone's defender, whether they deserved it or not.

Lena gave her a comforting side-hug. "Girl, that was awesome. Didn't know you had it in you."

Although her heart could never justify criticizing someone so openly in that way – whether it was true or not - Belle tried to breathe easy that she was amongst people who shared her thoughts on Drake. Her temperature cooled, her face became less flushed, and her pulse didn't feel as if it were pounding out of her neck.

This might have very well been the tipping point of her evening, the last time she spoke until she told Leo she was ready to leave. But the band was just beginning to play and she knew the song. A new flavor of anxiety swelled up in her as couples began to pair off and make their way to the open dance floor.

Jessica left the group to find her husband, Faye grabbed for her boyfriend, leaving only Belle, Lena and Whitney. That wouldn't be the case for long. Whitney gave the two girls one last flirty look and turned to saunter toward the other end of the pavilion, toward Leo.

What beer was left in Leo's bottle became warm, but he didn't have the stomach to down the last of it. He kept his eyes riveted upon Belle and Drake. He should have been comforted by the slightly intimidated look he received from the latter before he went off to get food at the buffet with Ivy. That calm was shattered by the episode in Belle's circle.

He didn't know what they were laughing about, but whatever it was had embarrassed Belle so much that her mask slipped again, this time quite possibly for good. The temptation to go over and whisk her away from the rest of the party was strong, but nothing in her gaze begged for a rescue, so he didn't move.

The other men continued to talk, but none of them seemed to notice that he wasn't even in the conversation anymore. Mr. Tale, however, must have noticed where his focus had been for the last few minutes.

"Why don't you go ask her to dance?" The older man pointed toward the stage. "I know she can dance pretty well."

Leo glanced to him, then to the band as it struck up the first few tunes. Couples everywhere scrambled for one another and moved to the dance floor, but he stayed contently rooted in his spot. Even half of the men in their circle left to find partners, abandoning their half empty beers.

The invitation to ask Belle to dance seemed more like a blessing coming from an influential member of Levi. If Leo wanted to think whimsically, it was as if Mr. Tale spoke for all of the town and gave him permission to approach the eligible bachelorette. What had he done to deserve that kind of approval? It could have been from a variety of things. The fight with Drake, helping with the barn, or serving as her platonic escort. Maybe it was in the way he was ready to come to her rescue a few times already that evening. Mr. Tale knew about it all, but there was still much more he didn't know.

"I don't think she wants to dance," Leo replied, raising his voice over the band.

Mr. Tale cocked a graying brow his way. "Every girl wants to dance. You just have to find the right song."

Leo turned to the dance floor and watched the ever-revolving carousel of two-steppers. It was an easy dance, one he could figure out if given a few minutes to observe. But he also saw the way the partners held one another so close. How could Belle like dancing with him in that way? He knew he would enjoy it, but would it be too much to think about how near they were, along with the steps of the dance and trying not to bump into another couple?

While he tried to make sense of the unchoreographed, but seemingly fluid swirl of dancers, he was aware of someone coming up close to him. He looked to meet the matte brown eyes of one of Belle's friends. She smiled sweetly and flipped her blonde hair over one shoulder, as if that would impress him.

"Wanna dance?" she asked, her shrill and oddly unpleasant girlish voice cutting through the sawing of the fiddle coming from the stage.

He looked her up and down. Slender, dressed in clothes both appropriate to the weather and event, while still showing off her feminine assets, Leo might have found her attractive. And if she had asked him months ago in another time and place, he might have agreed. He had danced with women before in bars, so he wasn't unfamiliar with the concept.

Without consciously thinking about it, Leo looked to Belle. She was watching too, but quickly turned away when their gazes met. It was just long enough for him to see the brokenness behind those green eyes. She didn't want him to dance with the girl any more than he did.

How to tell her though? In any other place – like a bar or club – Leo could have turned her down in some rude, condescending way. He could send her off with a, "I don't have the time for you" or "I'm not paying". But with Mr. Tale watching his every move, Leo knew he couldn't be so callous.

He took a minute to fight through the many inappropriate responses and said, "I'm not interested in dancing right now. Hunter might." He gestured toward the youth who was without a partner.

Hunter's eyes went a little wide with pleasant surprise, and the girl didn't seem to mind the alternative. Their gazes raked over one another and Leo was all but forgotten. As the two joined arms and went to take their place among the other couples, Mr. Tale gave an appreciative nod.

"Nicely done," he said. "Now, will you go dance with Belle before any other girl tries to move in?"

Leo made a disgruntled face that elicited a laugh from the older man. How did he know the refusal had nothing to do with whether he wanted to dance or not? If Belle had been the one to ask him, he would have agreed in a heartbeat.

With the separation of Hunter from their group, that left Leo and Mr. Tale alone. He hoped that they would either be given to comfortable silence or he would talk about work. No such luck.

"So, what's your story?" Mr. Tale said as he nursed on his Solo cup of sweet tea.

Leo shrugged. "No story."

The disbelieving look on the old man's face wouldn't make him talk. "Everyone's got a story. You're a Scotsman in America. That's a story in itself."

"And that's as much as I'm willing to tell."

He turned his attention back to Belle who seemed to have recovered from whatever anxiety she had felt a few moments before when the girl came to ask him to dance. What did she feel when she saw that? Fear? Anger? Sadness? What he wouldn't have given to know just how she felt at that very moment or what she and the other girls were talking about. All smiles and the occasional giggle, but about what?

"It'll come out eventually," Mr. Tale said coolly. "And most of the time it'll come out in gossip. Best to clear the air with your own words than let people run their mouths. Like you riding into Levi early this morning. You drove straight through, looking like sin. All tired and like you'd had one rough night."

He had, but that wasn't for Mr. Tale to know. It wasn't for anyone to know. If he thought the town would gossip all by themselves, nothing they concocted could be any stranger or more condemning than the truth.

"I don't think it's anyone's business what I do." That smart remark might have ruined whatever esteem Mr. Tale had for Leo, but it was what needed to be said.

The older man huffed. "That's what I thought when I first moved here thirty years ago, but I'll tell you something. It'll become their business. You stay here long enough, everyone will eventually learn your shoe size. They'll know everything about you and there really isn't anything you can do to keep it from happening. Not too many secrets in this town unless you get really good at hiding things."

Luckily, Leo was good at keeping secrets. That neat skill had kept him alive and out of trouble so far, and Levi would be no different.

It also made him wonder, however, if that was another reason Belle kept her true self locked up from the rest of the world. If she didn't want the whole town knowing about her social anxiety, that mask came in handy.

"I don't know what you did to her," Mr. Tale began, "but I like it. She seems happier."

Leo's brows pinched together at the sudden comment. Happier? Belle never looked more like a scared rabbit in the whole time he had known her, save for the one instance at the diner when she was ready to dart out the front door. Maybe Mr. Tale wasn't as observant as he thought.

"No, I mean it. That smile isn't faked like it usually is."

Or, maybe he was. He was the second person in Levi to confess that they noticed Belle's charade. First, Ivy had commended him for luring the true self out of her friend, and now Mr. Tale voiced his own appreciation. Who else knew? And who else saw the change?

"She... She doesn't like big crowds," Leo said, breaking whatever trust Belle had in him.

"I know," Mr. Tale replied. "Even when she came to cookouts or church socials with her father, she never seemed quite at home. Always very prim and overly sweet. Never disagreed, never offending. Always smiling and hugging everyone like she meant it, but I knew she didn't. My wife was the same way for a while, but she coped differently. She just didn't show up and everyone labeled her as rude and unsociable. She's better now, but no one invites her to things and when she goes out, they just kind of brush her off."

There was more evidence for Belle's case. Leo shook his head at the shamefulness of it all. If people would just be more understanding, maybe people like Belle and Mrs. Tale wouldn't have to suffer the way they do.

"Well, whatever your story is, wherever you came from or what you're running from, do right by Belle and you're good in my book."

Mr. Tale clapped Leo on the back and walked toward the buffet, leaving him alone to lean against one of the rough poles holding up the pavilion roof. He could have let his mind wander over the man's words, turning them over until he went crazy thinking how all of these things were so interwoven with Belle. He could drive himself mad trying to make sense of this town and how everything was connected, how secrets couldn't stay hidden in the dark for very long.

It made him wonder, more than anything, if his days here were numbered. They would find out about him eventually. Covering his tracks was something he had become rather good at, but gossip would still drive him out. And if he was right, this thing with Belle would be the catalyst for it all. The moment their relationship became public knowledge, all eyes would be on them. Belle wouldn't be able to handle that kind of attention, and neither could Leo. Not when so much was at stake.

Two options lay before him, the only two he ever had. Stay or run.

As long as Belle still wanted him here, as long as the darkness was held back by blood payments or by that terrible, unspeakable, unseen force, then Leo would stay. He would just walk on eggshells until the last possible moment.

The music changed from that steady, plodding two-step rhythm, to something he vaguely recognized. It was bouncier, more lively. A few whoops and hollers rippled through the party as singles and couples scurried to form the rows for a line dance.

Leo immediately looked to Belle and saw her face light up with the same giddy excitement shared by the other girls around her. They screamed and fled for the dancefloor. He grinned and wanted to laugh at this burst of enthusiasm. There wasn't a doubt in his mind that she knew this song and the dance that was paired with it.

Belle stood toward the far end of the second row from the stage. It seemed rather close in his opinion, but he saw his opportunity in the empty spot next to her. She only glanced back to him once, her eyes glinting with an unspoken invitation to join him. He didn't know the song, the dance, or how much of a fool he would make of himself. But he didn't care. How could he refuse her when the mask was gone and she looked like she was about to have a craic? He wanted to share in it, to jump up from the sidelines and be with her while she enjoyed herself. Hell, maybe Leo would enjoy himself too.

So he tossed his beer bottle in the trash and made his way to stand beside her.

Chapter 5

The steps to *Boot Scootin' Boogie* were so ingrained in Belle that it was like breathing. The first dance her father ever taught her, she was sure she could do it in her sleep. But the familiarity of it couldn't dampen the joy she felt when she lined up with a dozen or so other people to do the dance. It might have been the only social function she could do without thinking too much, without overanalyzing who was watching. Because she'd know that everyone was watching, but she was just another dancer in the crowd. There was no pressure to be the best, no pressure to show off. Just them, the music, and the dance.

There was something about stepping in time with the song with other people that made it feel comfortable and downright enjoyable. So many smiling faces, flirty exchanges between neighbors, whoops and yee-haws that for a few minutes, Belle could forget about everything. Even when Leo came to join her.

She looked to him and saw that, without much prompting, he was ready to learn. So Belle pointed directions and called out the moves. She even picked up her skirt a little higher so he could watch her boots. Stepping to the right, then the left, forward and back.

The crisscross jumping and heel kicks took a little longer for him to master, but by the middle of the song, he was adding his own flourishes that made her giggle. Leo, too, smiled and laughed as they moved synchronically until the very end of the song.

When it was all over, her tired legs finally got the best of her. Claps and hollers rose up as the dancers finished strong with spins, heel-clicks, exaggerated bows, or a salute to the band. Belle, however, lost whatever touch of grace she had mustered and tripped over the tapered toe of her boot. She went sailing to the side, arms out to catch herself.

Leo received her instead. She let out a great laugh, still high from the fun of it all and mindless to her little fall. He laughed with her, both breathless and holding onto one another.

Her hands wrapped as far as they could around his massive biceps for support, his arms the only things keeping her upright. Her blouse, as thin as it was, allowed her to feel every curve of his torso, the ridges of his sculpted abs and chest pressing into her soft flesh.

She looked up and met those icy blue eyes that had the power to melt away every bit of tension in her muscles. For a second, her legs didn't want to right themselves. She wanted to lean into him for the rest of the night. He smelled so good, clean and yet tinged with the piney scent of the outdoors and slightly tangy bit of the sweat he had worked up while dancing.

Everything about Leo sent her world off kilter, like falling upwards or diving into the clouds. He was her safe ground and her oxygen supply. And it took this dance to make her realize that she could never lose him, or she would lose herself.

That sobering thought of dependency gave her the strength she needed to find her footing, but he didn't let go right away.

The band, seeing that the guests needed something slow to counter the workout, slipped into a slow, easy ballad that she recognized all too well. And it was that recognition that made her want to shy away.

Her smile faltered and she came crashing back down to earth. No longer on Cloud Nine, she realized where she was. This was Levi, and she was in a place packed with people that would be watching her every move. Belle resisted the urge to meet their stares. That would only make it worse.

His hold had loosened out of respect when she pulled away. Her hands slid from his biceps to his forearms, and she could feel how they tensed and bunched beneath his jacket sleeve. The only reason she kept holding on was because she feared a total collapse if she didn't have some connection with him. If she let go completely, would she be able to stand on her own under the weight of this sudden freefall?

"Dance with me?"

Leo's voice was so soft, so calm that it was almost lost in the rest of the noise. His question served as her parachute for just a moment and she felt as if her descent had been at least slowed for a bit.

One thing blew a few holes in that parachute. The image came to mind of Whitney walking to Leo after proclaiming that she'd ask him to dance. She wasn't alone. Even Lena wanted to take a shot at him before the night was over. Belle should have taken comfort in the fact that Leo turned her down. They didn't dance, and he had been watching her from a distance all evening.

Doubts of her adequacy combatted with the heart that was ready to fling itself off that ledge again and ride whatever wave Leo was sending her way. To go wherever this weird twisted thing was leading her, or to pull back to safety and guard what sanity she had before he stole it all again.

Belle didn't want to hurt, didn't want the kisses they shared to be meaningless, didn't want to think that he had been playing, or that she really meant nothing to him in the end. Leo had done so much already. Why shouldn't she believe that he had the best of intentions with her?

The screams for intimacy grew louder in her head and she finally nodded.

They joined hands, and one arm swooped around her waist. On cue, they stepped and swayed to the song that held so much meaning for her. Though Belle could feel his stare, she wouldn't look up. She kept her eyes on the ground beside them or on her hand resting on his broad shoulders.

When the chorus came, she found her voice again.

"This was my dad's favorite song," she said. "They're not singing the lyrics, but it's *Red on a Rose*... He loved Alan Jackson's music. He played it all the time when he was in the hospital."

She could almost feel his smile and his fingers tightened over hers. "Sing it to me."

Belle grinned and shook her head, the waves of her hair tickling her cheeks. "No way," she laughed.

"Why not?" he purred, his breath stirring the flyaway hairs on the crown of her head.

Heat rose up her neck and she knew wearing something that came off the shoulders was a mistake. Everyone could see her blush creep down her collarbone if they cared to look.

"I can't sing."

"Sure you can," he replied. "I've heard you sing plenty of times." Belle's eyes snapped up. "When?"

The gentle smile he blessed her with revealed one important thing. This wasn't one sided. It couldn't be. Not when he spoke to her so soft and tenderly. "In the morning when you're getting ready, or when you're cooking supper. Right before I walk in, I've stopped and listened. You can sing just fine."

Her cheeks tingled with the inching blush and Belle thought she'd lose it right there on the dancefloor. Only, they weren't on the dancefloor anymore. Somehow, he had steered them into the shadows outside the pavilion. The glow of the string lights wasn't as bright against his face, but she could still see that luster in his eyes.

"What else do you do when I'm not looking?" she asked, tucking her chin to hide the glossy film of happy tears.

He never answered her. Instead, he did what he had asked her to do and sang.

"*And I love you like all little children love pennies. And I love you like good times, of which I've known many. And I love you 'cause I know you give me a heart of my own... You're where I belong... You make my blood flow... Like red on a rose.*"

That was it. That was all Belle needed to know that she was falling for Leo. Hard and fast and recklessly.

"I've watched you read on the couch after supper," he said. "I've watched you smile when you're happy and when you're on the verge of breaking down. I've watched you so much I know when you're holding your breath and the exact moment when you release it. Like now. Right now, you're holding your breath, but you've been so good at hiding that I'm sure no one else notices it."

Belle hadn't even realized and forced out the air, sending it shuddering through her nose. Did he mean all those things? Did he mean to hold her so tight that she could practically feel his ribcage expand against hers?

"I don't want you to hide anymore." Leo leaned down until his lips were nearly grazing her ear. "Not from the world... and not from me."

Her whole body shivered at his whisper, but his solid embrace made it impossible for him not to know how he affected her.

"You should know by now that I can't hide anything from you, even if I tried."

Leo's head rested against her own and she found it hard not to be intoxicated by everything about him. And then, a rather important thought resurfaced. One that she would have preferred to beat back with a baseball bat if she could. But it was there, rearing its ugly head again and she eased away.

"You know so much about me. You know about my parents, about my mask, and all the little things in between... but I don't know you." Belle felt the need to emphasize this again. They had agreed long ago that he would start divulging more, but she had yet to see the fruits of that. He confessed a little in the grocery store, but it wasn't enough. He saw her scars and those wounds that refused to heal, but she still hadn't seen all of his.

If anyone should have been coming out of hiding, it was him.

Leo looked at her, a good portion of affection gone from those eyes that seemed so dim now that they were retreating further from the pavilion.

"You're right," he replied. "You don't know me."

"And I want to," Belle pleaded. "But every time I get close, you deflect. I know a bit about psychology and you're definitely deflecting. I've let you get deep with me, but it's like I need a jackhammer to get anywhere with you."

He smirked at the analogy, but nothing about this should have been amusing. "Yet, you still know more than anyone else on this planet. Every time I come to a new place, I come up with some story to tell people. I never tell them the truth."

Belle blinked in confusion. "So, is this just another story? Have I been pounding away at the wrong wall?"

"No, you're hitting the right wall," he replied with a soft chuckle. "What I'm saying is that you may think you don't know a lot about me, but you know more than anyone."

She shook her head. "But I don't feel like I do. I... I don't even know how your parents died, or why you decided to leave Brooklyn or... or why you cut your arm before."

He stiffened at the mention of that one dark secret that taunted her every time she caught a glimpse of them. Whatever had troubled him enough to cause such pain, she could handle it. But she couldn't handle being shut out like this, not when she bared her soul. This mess was so one-sided, but Leo didn't seem to care.

"Am I ever going to know all those things?"

The tenseness alleviated for just a moment and then he nodded. "You will. Just keep chipping away at that wall. It may take a while, but you'll break through. I promise."

Before she could realize it, Leo's face descended upon hers. It would have been their third kiss if a voice hadn't called to Leo from the pavilion. Afraid that anyone had seen them, Belle jerked away.

"Hey, Leo!" Looking to the party, she saw Mr. Johnson waving. "Come here for a minute. Marshall's tractor won't start and he wants you to take a look."

This sudden intrusion from the outside world made Belle realize that the song had stopped playing quite some time ago. Now, the band was in the middle of another fast-paced dance. It seemed as if the rest of the world had forgotten about them just for a little while. Too bad it couldn't last.

Leo's hands immediately dropped away from her and Belle couldn't help but feel dazed when he stepped back to give her space. The cold night air rushed in to take his place. He didn't run off right away as she expected, but continued to stand near. Only then did she realize he must have been waiting for some sort of dismissal.

She tried to smile through the disappointment. "Go on. Mr. Levinson's been complaining about that tractor for a while. If you could get that old Bug to work, you can probably give them a few pointers."

Little did Leo know that he wouldn't be over there for just a minute. Her father would get called away for similar reasons and be away for hours. Only a small percentage of that time was dedicated to actually looking at the broken-down farm equipment or vehicle. The rest was spent visiting and yacking.

Belle, unlike most wives and girlfriends to the farmers and laborers in Levi, understood what happened when men of like interests came together. They were as bad as old women at a church social. Nothing but talk and gossip for hours.

Leo gave her hand a quick squeeze. "You can keep bashing down those walls later," he said before taking a few steps toward the pavilion.

"I'm counting on it."

"Get yourself something to eat, if you feel you can."

As if he could read the invisible cues, Leo must have predicted her growing hunger. He had a weird way of taming her anxiety, and the thought of eating no longer made her uneasy. Her stomach rumbled, but there was no trace of the nausea she had felt earlier when they arrived. A more important factor was whether there was any food left at all.

So as Leo walked in one direction to join the other men who made their way toward the barn, Belle steered to the buffet. Many couples were too occupied by the dance, leaving only the older folks who had grown out of their dancing days and the little kids who had no interest in the music. So Belle was without anyone her age to talk to.

When she was about halfway through the buffet line, she realized she had been wrong.

The all too familiar Axe body spray hit her before Drake came within three feet. She refused to look up, but felt her hands begin to shake.

"Nice spread, isn't it?" he said close enough that she could smell the beer on his breath.

She wrinkled her nose and took an extra step to the side as she reached for the spoon to the potato salad. "What do you want?"

"Nothing. I'm just getting some food. It isn't all about you, Belle."

She glanced to his plate and saw it loaded with baked beans, rolls, pasta salad, and a double-stacked burger with every condiment the Levinson's offered. "That's got to be your third plate," she commented.

"Oh? Were you watching me?"

Belle slid him a nasty look that she wasn't afraid to hide anymore. He didn't deserve the mask, the demure smiles or anything polite. "It isn't all about you either."

Drake chuckled and continued to follow her. "There's that fire I like."

They were the only ones at the buffet table. But the closer he came, the more she lost her appetite. Now she was just taking small spoonfuls of everything, so she couldn't say that she didn't try something. She even took a small portion of Mrs. Levinson's broccoli salad. The nuts were always too rancid for her taste.

"Didn't you come with Ivy?" she suddenly asked, hoping to throw Drake off her trail. "Shouldn't you be dancing with her or something?"

"She went up to the house for a bit."

Belle couldn't help but wonder if it was to go to the bathroom or just to get away from her date for a little while. She still couldn't believe that she would agree to go anywhere with the guy who practically assaulted her friend. Then again, remembering Ivy's track record in the boyfriend department, it shouldn't have been surprising. She always picked the damaged ones, the ones that needed saving. It never ended well for Ivy, but she never lost hope that one day she'd find the right guy.

That guy was not Drake.

"I was actually hoping to talk to you for a bit."

They reached the end of the table where the two-liters of soft drinks and lemonade were set up along with the red Solo cups. "Well, you know what the Bible says. Hope deferred makes the heart sick. And your heart's about to get real sick. Leave me alone."

Drake didn't take the hint. Even after she poured herself a cup of Dr. Pepper and moved away from the table, he followed her like a lost puppy.

Belle found an empty seat near an outer support pole and sat in it. Drake sat beside her. If they weren't so near to an older couple, she would have demanded that he leave again. They were well within earshot.

"Just give me a few minutes?" he asked, sounding more than a little desperate.

After stealing a glance to make sure no one was paying any real mind to them, she sighed. "You have five minutes." Though she wasn't sure how well she could hold down any food anymore, she slipped a tiny forkful of baked beans into her mouth and savored the barbeque flavor while he talked. All the while, her eyes were fixed on the light pouring out of the barn. If Drake did try anything, Leo was too far away to beat him to a pulp. Considering the death threat he had given so convincingly the last time they met, maybe that was a good thing.

"I wanted to apologize for what I did at the diner. It was inappropriate and I'm sorry. I know you're a good Christian girl, so you'll forgive me."

Belle blew air from her nose, but wouldn't say what she truly felt. She might have been a Christian, but she wasn't a saint. Drake had given her more grief than anyone else in this town. The abuse he dished out on her nerves came in close second to her mother, and that was saying something. She never knew if she'd run into him and he'd start making passes at her like it was mating season and she was the only eligible doe in town.

"I promise I'll make a real effort to respect you from now on."

She passed him a look that should have told him enough. This was nothing new. She'd heard this before out of him. The first time was when Ray had to ban him from the bookstore, because he wouldn't stop coming around to pester her. The second time was when one of her neighbors had to intervene on her behalf inside the hardware store when Drake almost made a scene in the plumbing aisle. That was the last time she ever stepped foot in the place.

And now, he had been scared by Leo and called out for his rudeness again. This time, the whole town knew about it and that might have been enough to keep him accountable from now on. One could only hope.

But Belle was far too jaded to believe him now. "I hope that you do."

Drake leaned in. "I won't make your heart sick, Belle. Really, I promise."

Now she wished she hadn't even tried to be clever earlier. Coming out of his mouth, it sounded like a stab at romance. If only it weren't him trying to woo her. Now, if Leo had said that...

"Let me prove it to you," he continued. "Why don't we go out tomorrow? Just us. We can get away from this old stuffy town. I know a great Thai place in – "

"Not interested," she said quickly, feeling her anger rise.

"Don't like Thai food?"

She set her plate in her lap and turned to face him more directly. "I like it just fine. What I don't like is a guy who's dating one of my best friends to come around and ask me on a date."

Drake's face quirked with mock disgust. "You mean Ivy? We're not dating."

Belle's brow arched.

"Okay, we went out a couple of times," he admitted. "But it's not exclusive."

"Where do you get off being this way? You can't be serious."

Drake put his plate on the ground in front of him and he took her hands in his. There was no buzz, no spark at all. Not like when Leo touched her.

"Belle, I've liked you ever since we were in school."

She huffed. "You didn't even notice me in school. The only stuff you cared about were football and cheerleaders."

His expression brightened with earnestness. "But I remember you. You sat on the front row of the bleachers at the home games."

"I only ever went to one home game and I sat at the very top."

He made it clear that he didn't appreciate being shot down at every turn and his grip tightened over her hands until it hurt. "Whatever. You were there. And I remember looking up and wondering about you. Why you always looked so sad and I wanted to make you smile. I still want to make you smile."

"Right now, you're just making me mad." Belle tugged to free herself, but it was no use. "I don't care if you think we're soul mates. I'm not going out with you."

"Why not?" he asked, his voice deepening into a frustrated growl.

"You don't know me and you don't care about me. You just want me, because you can't have me. You've always been that way. You chase after the ones who give you a challenge and when it's not fun anymore, you ditch them."

One of her knuckles popped and she winced, but he wouldn't let go.

"I'm not that way anymore," he pleaded, his hot rancid breath spilling over her face, their knees almost touching now. "I want to be better for you. Don't you get it?"

From a young age, Belle had been taught to give people second chances, especially when they asked for them. That was the only reason she let her mother back into her life when she became an adult. But Drake hadn't just been given a second chance. He had been given a third, fourth, and fifth. Each time, he proved that he didn't respect her and probably never could.

"I understand plenty, Drake," she affirmed, dropping her voice so no one else would hear. Though, she wished she could have been screaming. Maybe then he would listen.

"Is this about that other guy?"

So observant. Belle glanced back to the barn, wishing Leo would poke his head out and see what Drake was doing. Violence might not have been the answer, but she wanted to see Drake flat on his back again, cowering for his life while Leo stood over him with rock-hard fists.

"This has to do with you and your attitude." Drake let go of her hands just long enough to move up to her arms. Panic rose and like a caged animal, she finally began to fight back. "Let me go," she demanded, still trying against everything to keep her voice down.

"Not until you agree to go out with me."

If he had tried to pull something like this months ago, she might have given in just to avoid making a scene. This wasn't her party or her farm. But this was her life. Drake, like Belle's mother, was trying to steal her freedom of choice. Either agree to a date just so he would let her go and give her space, or he'd keep holding on until she agreed.

There was a third option. One he wouldn't have considered in a million years.

Belle might not have been a fighter like Leo, but she wasn't about to take this sitting down.

Braving embarrassment, failure, and the fact that everyone would be looking at her in that moment, Belle stood up from her seat. The plate fell from her lap and spilled over Drake's boots and pant leg. A bit of potato salad and barbeque sauce leaked onto her dress, but the stains would be worth this.

Maintaining her balance, she used his temporary shock against him and wrenched her hands free. Before Drake could raise some defense, she coiled back a fist and threw a punch as hard as she could. Her knuckles connected with his nose. Bones in both her hand and his face popped. The force of the jab was enough to throw him clean out of his chair and into his own food laying right in his landing zone.

She scrambled away, expecting him to grab for her leg or clothes to keep her there. The music came to a clumsy pause as the band, and the rest of the guests, were drawn to the commotion. Gasps and tiny exclamations snaked through the crowd as they all realize what she had just done.

At the same time, she realized too.

She had just punched a man in the nose for grabbing her. Though he deserved it, how many would see it that way? What would they think of her now? In the span of just a couple of seconds, she felt as if every eye under the pavilion was on her, pinning her with looks of complete amazement and disapproval, especially from the older women.

What could she tell them? How could she talk her way out of this? She had been the victim, but she fought back, which was so unlike her that it was possible no one would believe it. But there was no one she could shove the blame on. No one was close enough.

Such a violent and angry act was unforgiveable to them, even if Drake deserved it. Thoughts began to whirl and spin in her mind, too many to sort or reason through. Feelings she couldn't name or give a voice to swelled in her chest and tears were already pushing at the corners of her eyes. She felt like she'd explode if she didn't move, didn't do something.

She turned and ran straight for the barn, her skirt getting caught in her legs as they pumped harder to carry her to safety. To Leo.

After they heard the band had stopped playing, a few men poked their heads out from the open doors of the barn. It was improbable that they could see her sprinting through the darkness, but one set of eyes must have.

Leo left the barn and came straight for her. In a rush of incoherent sobbing and heaving for air, she tried to explain what had happened. Her heart was pounding too hard and her mind too frantic to properly form the words.

His wild gaze, however, wandered back to the pavilion where she had left Drake to the other guests. No doubt Drake would spin some story about how she had attacked him for no reason. He had done the same when he and Leo fought at the diner, but no one believed him. Hopefully no one would believe him now.

Scared that there would be some real retribution for her actions, scared that she'd never be welcome to the Levinson's again, all she wanted to do was crawl into Leo's arms and cry. She had stood up for herself, which was progress, but she wished she had done it in some place more private. In the moment, however, she hadn't been thinking about privacy. She just wanted Drake to leave her alone. Had that been too much to ask for?

In her hysteria, one word came out clear and strong. "Home."

Leo nodded and wrapped his arms around her convulsing shoulders as her whole body became wracked by the terrified sobs of a girl who had just committed one of the bravest acts of her life. "Alright, alright. I'll take you home."

They were well on their way to the truck when Mr. Levinson came out, asking for explanations that neither of them could give. They ignored their host and everyone else who might have come up to inquire about the incident. Leo shielded her as they hurried the entire way to her truck and sped off the property.

Chapter 6

Leo poured the hot water into the mug that was already prepped with a bag of Belle's soothing chamomile tea. In the living room, he could hear her take deep breath after deep breath, drawing the air into her diaphragm and letting it all out in a controlled release. Ranger, who must have sensed the trouble when they came home, had curled up in her lap the moment she sat down on the sofa.

Once he put the pieces of hysterical speech together and realized what had happened, it took all of Leo's self-control not to make a U-turn in the truck and speed back to the Levinson farm, so he could bash in Drake's skull. Though the man deserved it, his first priority was taking care of Belle. Besides, he had gotten what was coming to him. Leo was just sorry that he hadn't been the one to deal out the punishment. And Belle would have rather he had been there with her than beating up Drake.

Careful not to spill either his hot chocolate or her tea, Leo made his way back into the living room with both. The fire he had kindled in the fireplace grew, giving off a homey and comfortable warmth that he hoped would further ease Belle out of this panic attack. He still wondered what exactly she had freaked out about. Did Drake touch her before she punched him, or did this have to do with the way everyone under the pavilion flew into their own bit of hysterics? They hadn't stayed long enough to find out anything, and Leo wished he had been there for her. He might have prevented it or saved her the trouble.

Stepping lightly across the hardwood floor, he approached and set the mug down on the table in front of her. Belle's bloodshot eyes stared ahead at the mantle, the only movement coming from her therapeutic breathing. Not wanting to spook her or rile her in any way, he sat on the farthest end of the couch and blew on his drink to cool it. His only regret was that it wasn't spiked with anything a little stronger to get him through this ordeal. Then again, he didn't need a mind doused in alcohol at this moment.

When he took a sip and let his gaze drop from her panic-stricken features, he finally noticed the red marks on her pale knuckles. He might not have noticed it if the rash didn't pop out against Ranger's scruff where her hand was resting. Her first battle scars. Her first physical ones, anyway. She had been fighting for most of her life. And right now, she was fighting another war inside her own head.

Leo waited patiently for her to come out the victor. When she did, he'd be there. Every time.

Belle was so much stronger than she gave herself credit for. When anxiety crippled others, she managed to get herself out of bed every day and face the reality of her condition. She both accepted her feelings, but she didn't let them control her. Life wouldn't keep her down, and Leo wondered if he was the only one to recognize that. Belle was so much braver and stronger than him in so many ways.

As if she had finally noticed the tea, she blinked a few times and looked down to the coffee table. With deliberate slowness, she reached out. Her hands were less than steady. In fact, it might have been the last of her symptoms, but the most severe.

She gripped the handle and lifted the mug, but he could already see how unstable she was.

Leo quickly set down his own mug and scooted closer. He cupped the bottom of her mug in his palm and supported it as she brought it closer to herself. The ceramic burned his skin, but Leo didn't care. He'd hold it forever if he thought it would help.

She took a sip and lowered it back to her lap next to Ranger's head. Leo didn't let go. His hand wrapped around hers, keeping the mug steady as it rested atop her thigh. She was still wearing her skirt from the party, the smear of barbecue sauce evident on the fabric. That stain would need to be treated before throwing it in the wash. But Leo was sure that was the farthest thing from her mind.

In an effort to distract her, he said, "Looks like you gave him a run for his money."

Belle didn't see the jerk of his head toward her roughed up knuckles. Her eyes closed as she took one more shuddering breath and held it. Maybe that's not what she wanted to hear.

"What did he do?" Leo asked slowly.

She shook her head. "He didn't do anything."

"Don't defend him," he replied, mastering himself enough to not raise his voice. "You wouldn't have hit him unless you had a good reason."

Belle looked to him and he could see the way her facial muscles twitched as if she'd burst into tears again. "He really didn't do anything. He didn't hit me, he didn't yell at me. He was trying to apologize for that day at the diner. But when he asked me on a date and I turned him down, he wouldn't let me."

Leo's eyes narrowed into angry slits. "What else did he do?" He sounded like a broken record.

"He just grabbed my arms. That's all." He waited for more, the more that he knew was sitting on her tongue, waiting to be spoken. "He... he wouldn't let me go when I asked him."

If the date and the grabbing wasn't enough, Drake trapped her.

A single tear rolled down her cheeks and the moisture captured the dancing firelight. "I shouldn't have done it."

Leo was angry enough to kill Drake for this. It was bad enough that Belle had to fight her own thoughts. She didn't need someone coming along and making her feel like she was in the wrong when all she had done was defend herself. Fear drove her to do what she did, and no one could blame her for that.

"No, you should have," he corrected. "You should have done a lot more to him."

Belle crimped her eyes shut until her lashes brushed her cheeks. "I'm not like you, Leo. I don't go out and beat up people. It's not right."

He cradled her face with his free hand and hated to feel the wetness of her tears. "Drake should have never laid a hand on you. Quit telling yourself that you did something bad. It's all lies. You can't believe that the better way to handle that would have been to do nothing."

Belle leaned into his hand. "I don't, but I didn't have to break his nose."

He cracked a smile. "I don't know if you broke his nose, but I hope you did."

"We should never wish evil on someone like that."

"I wish a thousand plagues on him for all the trouble he's caused you. And I'll wish the same for anyone else who makes you feel like being yourself is wrong."

Her green eyes opened, and he thought he saw a spark of humor in them. "You do realize that includes me too, right?"

"You only think that, because you've never been taught to think differently."

Belle turned away from his touch. "You make me sound like a victim in this whole thing. Drake's against me, the town is against me, even I'm against my own self."

Forgetful of all he had resolved before, to stay somewhat distant, so Leo wouldn't be added to her already growing list of enemies, he hung his arm around her shoulders. "Start with yourself. Once you start learning to love yourself just the way you are, everyone else's opinion doesn't matter anymore."

After a moment of deliberating, Belle let herself melt into him. Her head rested against his shoulder, her side leaning into his, right where she belonged. Ranger, who had been asleep for the most part, let out a cute puppy snort and rolled off Belle's lap to lay fully on the couch.

For several long, blissful minutes, neither of them spoke. Only the crackling of the fire in the fireplace disturbed their silence. The one good thing that might have come out of this whole episode was this show of absolute trust in him. What he wouldn't have given to have her stay just like this. As long as Leo held Belle, she didn't seem so lost or broken.

"Where did you learn all of this stuff?" she asked, her word soft and tired.

He smiled, though the memories were anything but happy or funny. "Years of experience."

Leo didn't have to look down to know that she was brimming with questions. Maybe now was a good time to let her chip away at that wall she had been talking about. But could he be as brave as her and talk about a life spent on the run, constantly believing himself to be bad luck incarnate. To be alone and driven to near madness by grief. He had fought battles of his own that no one knew anything about.

Maybe that's why he could understand her mind so well. They were on similar ends of a battlefield, working their way into No Man's Land, so they could finally take a breath.

"It hasn't been easy for me," he began with a little hesitance. Finding the right words while not saying too much would be a challenge. "Growing up, I never thought I'd be on my own like this. I remember the day I told my mum I wanted to go to the University of Edinburgh when I graduated from high school. I thought I'd pick a major, go on to have a career and a normal life."

"And then your parents died."

Leo closed his eyes. It was so much more than that. It started long before that day, before everything finally fell to pieces in front of him. But for her sake, he only nodded. "Aye. I left Scotland and you know the rest. I was bullied in Brooklyn for my accent and my great-uncle was no better. He had broken away from the family over some petty disagreement before I was born and he didn't want to take care of me. I spent years believing life had just cast me into the trash bin and left me to rot... I have to remind myself that it isn't true. One day, things will get better. I'll stop being followed by the... by this storm cloud and finally find a place I can belong."

Unexpected, but most certainly welcomed, Belle twisted her hand around to hold his as they had done when they sat in her truck before the party. Earlier that evening, he had reached out to comfort her. Now, she was repaying the favor.

"You can belong here," she whispered.

Leo swallowed and found his mouth was dry. "I want to... but it may be too soon to tell."

Belle's head moved in just the slightest way that signaled she wanted to look up at him, but something stopped her. He wasn't the only reticent one on the sofa. "If it has to do with me –"

"No, no." He brought her in tighter. "It's not you. If I ever leave, it won't be because of you." Planting a kiss on the crown of her head, he hoped that she wouldn't see through his lie. If he ever left, it would be because he couldn't hold the darkness back anymore, because she was put in too much danger, because if he stayed a moment longer, she'd be killed. That was his only reason for ever abandoning her.

"I can't imagine what it must have been like for you," Belle said. "You lost everything, and your life has never been the same. My problems are nothing compared to yours."

"That doesn't invalidate you or what you've been through. I'm just saying that I'm not talking out of my arse."

She gave a slight start at the word, but otherwise didn't reprimand him for it. Instead, he heard a tiny, struggling laugh.

"What?"

"I was just thinking how often I had prayed for something to happen that would take away all this anxiety. I prayed that God would somehow help me to be free from all of it... And he sent me you."

Leo stared into the fireplace, letting the heat and light burn his eyes. He had never thought about God. Never wanted to give the concept much consideration at all. If there was some all-powerful creator in the sky that really cared about everyone here on earth, then why did he continue to suffer under the manipulation of the darkness? Why wouldn't God save his family? Why wouldn't God take away all the evil in the world, so its population could live happy all the time?

They were questions for theologians and philosophers. Not for him, and not for Belle. If she wanted to believe that some man with a long white beard in the stars directed him to her barn that stormy night, then so be it. He wouldn't ruin her delusion. He was there now, and he'd continue to help her in whatever way he could.

"You said you had never been in a relationship," Belle said after a long stretch of silence. "Was that part of the story you were trying to tell, or was that true too?"

Leo sighed. "That's true." She wouldn't know quite how true it was.

"But you've been all over the place. You never found anyone to be serious with?"

Telling her the truth that he had found her and that was more than enough, was out of the question. The darkness might have been held at bay for now, but as he said before, leaving Levi was still on the table.

"Not really," was all he'd say.

Belle wasn't content with that. "So, this isn't going anywhere?"

Leo frowned. "It could."

Another small laugh bubbled up. "Did I ever mention that part of my anxiety is that I hate not knowing where I stand with people?"

"I figured it was," he replied, closing his eyes to give them some relief from the flames. He could still see the bright amber glow burn through his lids.

"So where do we stand?"

Leo shifted to get as comfortable as he could as the building fatigue began to catch up with him. The amount of sleep he had gotten over the last several days was barely enough to keep him functioning as it was. And if he wasn't going to drink coffee this late in the evening, he'd crash soon.

"We are on solid ground for now, m'eudail," he replied tiredly. "If the sands ever shift, you'll be the first to know."

"Are we... I mean, what do I... What do you..."

She must have been more tired and confused than he was if she couldn't form one simple question.

"What are we, you mean?"

Belle nodded against his shoulder.

He could hardly blame her for being as befuddled as she was. His mind turned over word after word, searching for the right thing. They weren't dating, because she didn't like dates at all. This wasn't some casual fling, but they were both well aware of just how temporary this could be. The hugs, the kisses, and the words they exchanged, the way they felt all pointed to one bright neon sign that should have been obvious from the start.

But Leo couldn't bring himself to call Belle his girlfriend. It seemed so immature, so shallow compared to what they shared. It wasn't a crush or an infatuation as he thought it had been from the start. It had become so much deeper than that. She wasn't his lover, and probably never would be, but he couldn't deny the way his heart, as cold and stony as it was, longed to be in her hands.

"Just know that no matter what happens, I'm here for you. Only you."

Belle nuzzled deeper into her feather pillow and watched how the morning sun filtered through her window. Beyond the panes of glass, she could hear songbirds. How could such a beautiful morning come after the kind of night she'd had? It was as if nature were trying to make up for the tears and the hours spent tossing and turning. Her mind had been inundated with confusing thoughts that left her tired and with no answer.

Leo had been more than helpful in getting her home and comforting her on the couch. But he was useless when it came to deciphering this relationship - if she could even call it that. It turned out that not even he knew for certain what they were.

In the end, she had to do what she could never do no matter how hard she tried. Let it go. Let it all go and just accept what they had. Let go of the questions, the wondering, the uncertainty of everything and just believe what he said last night. He was here for her and no matter what, she wouldn't scare him away. She'd never be the reason he left Levi, and Belle tried to convince herself that was good enough for now.

Yet, she couldn't bring herself to crawl out of bed. It was Sunday and church would start in just a few hours. There was so much that needed to be done before she left, starting with letting Ranger out of her bedroom. The pup had mastered the stairs for the first time the night before and followed Belle onto the second floor. He needed a little help to climb into bed with her, but he was perfectly capable of letting her know that he needed to relieve himself.

Belle never thought that a dog could keep her so accountable, but Ranger was proving himself to not only have the makings of a great sheepdog, but also a fantastic support animal. He cuddled with her all night and she wished that had been enough to calm her anxiety. One day, maybe Ranger would be enough, and she wouldn't need tea or Leo to make her feel normal again.

She climbed out of bed and let Ranger romp his way down the hall toward the stairs. When she passed by Leo's room, Belle paused for a few seconds to listen. She wasn't sure what for. Maybe she hoped to catch him while he was getting dressed or hear him gently snore as he sometimes did. But she heard nothing. Absolute silence.

She thought to knock and ask if he wanted coffee, but she knew well enough that he did and Ranger had confidently tried to work his way down the steps, but ended up flopping over himself a few times. His little whimpers spurred her forward and she carried him down to the living room, leaving Leo to snooze.

She left the back door open, so Ranger could come bounding back inside when he finished his business, but it was as if the puppy had forgotten all about his bladder and continued to follow her around the kitchen. He nipped at the end of her robe belt as she spooned out the coffee grounds for Leo's brew, all the while doing her best to enjoy this little morning ritual.

She wondered how it would feel to do this all the time. Make his coffee, make their breakfast, watch him come down the stairs and rub the sleep from his eyes while she smiled up at him. How long would they do that? Forever wasn't conceivable, but a few months? Maybe a year?

Belle shook her head, letting the tangled strands whip across her face. No need to think about the future. It did no good. Live in the moment. There was a saying she once read that depression was constantly looking back and anxiety was constantly looking forward, but true peace stayed in the present. That'd be the only way she could enjoy whatever time she had with Leo, or anyone else for that matter.

Taking the basket of eggs that had been collected the day before, she washed them in the sink and readied the frying pan. But when she turned the knob on the stove, the ignitor glitched again. Belle rolled her eyes and impatiently began twisting the knob back and forth as she usually had to do. The gas turned on and off, but there was no click from the electric starter.

Thinking the cold air from outside was doing something to the stove, Belle left the burner to shut the back door.

The moment she did, Ranger pealed into a furious string of barks and growls. All of which were directed at the stove. They had used it several times over the last week. The dog shouldn't have been startled by the smell of gas at all.

Fearing that the dog would wake Leo unnecessarily, she tried to shush him. But Ranger only barked louder, ears folded back and his tiny tail sticking straight up in aggression. Belle went to pick him up, but the dog turned and nipped at her finger, drawing blood. She popped him on the nose, which seemed to snap the pup out of his hostility. He whimpered and that erect tail tucked between his hind legs.

Belle couldn't be angry at him. Something had spooked him enough to make him that upset, and she'd pushed too hard. He didn't know any better and she had been in similar positions before. All she could do was run her hand under the sink to clean the tiny cut and wrap it in a paper towel until she had the time to properly bandage it.

She came back to the stove, turned the knob, and heard the ignition click.

A balloon of fire exploded over the stove. Belle shrieked and fell backward as the heat blasted her in the face. Ranger resumed his crazed barking, but this time at the destructive tower of flames roaring up from all the burners.

She gaped in shock as the tendrils of fire curved around her vent and licked at her upper cabinets. Over Ranger's incessant and useless barking came the pounding of bare feet down the stairs. Leo stood in the entryway to the kitchen and stared at the spreading inferno.

All Belle could think about was that she had to move, had to do something. But her legs and arms wouldn't obey. Frozen in fear, she couldn't even rationalize what she could do. The fire extinguisher was old, and she didn't know exactly how to work it. Not only that, but she couldn't remember where it was. Did she store it over the stove or was it somewhere in the living room?

Leo only spent a second or two assessing the situation before jumping in. He moved so quickly to the cabinet under the sink, as if he knew the extinguisher was there all along. He managed to duck below the inferno and switched off all the burners, cutting off the gas supply, and then went to spraying the stovetop and the upper cabinets.

In less than a minute, her pristine kitchen had turned into a train wreck. White powder caked the stove, countertops, and all the cabinets that had been affected by the fire. Belle was on her back on the floor, her supporting arms becoming weaker as the adrenaline ebbed away. Ranger had stopped barking and scuttled out of the mess he had made on the tile. Leo, the only clear-headed and sensible one in the house, set the extinguisher on a dining chair and knelt beside her.

He asked something, but Belle's ears only heard rumbles as if the stove fire had deafened her for a minute. Or maybe it was the shock of it all.

"Are you okay?" he asked again, this time a little impatiently.

She looked to him and realized that she hadn't blinked. Her eyes burned from the heat and the strain, so when she nodded in response, it felt as if she had broken the terrified fixation.

In the relative quiet, the coffeemaker beeped. She looked, but couldn't even find the machine under the mounds of extinguisher foam that suffocated the counter space. Somehow, Belle found that hilarious enough to laugh at. She laughed until she couldn't breathe and let herself fall onto her back, arms raised to cover her face.

None of this was funny. The kitchen was a disaster, her stove was probably broken, and who knew what was left of her cabinets. It didn't take long for the flames to spread, but there was some serious reconstruction work ahead for them.

Her giggles and gasps for air became infectious and Leo began to laugh with her. Ranger trotted up and licked at her hands, his little puppy heart wanting nothing more than to be useful. She grabbed for him and rubbed her nose into his shoulder until he squirmed.

When she finally caught her breath, her head rolled to look at Leo. He sat cross-legged beside her, wearing nothing but a pair of pajama pants. Sweat glistened on his face and broad shoulders and there was some white matter on his forearms, presumably from the extinguisher. His expression, so full of relief and something like admiration, made her almost forget about the stove and the kitchen.

"Well, I guess I'm not going to have any breakfast this morning," she said, giving a helpless shrug, a smile still plastered across her lips.

Leo's abs tightened when he let out a fresh burst of laughter and he rubbed at his face. "No coffee either," he added.

Belle looked to the wreckage and didn't even know where to begin. Her first thought was to take that stove and throw it out. It took catastrophic failure for her to finally seriously consider getting a new one, and that was pitiful in itself. She should have taken her mother's advice. That was something she never thought she'd admit to.

Funny enough, however, Belle didn't feel like she needed it. Yes, her stove was officially retired, her cabinets were trashed, and it'd take hours to clean up the mess, but she didn't feel anxious enough for self-medication just yet. Her house didn't catch on fire and everyone was safe. That was all that mattered. There was the question of where she'd get the funds to buy new cabinets and a stove, but something of her resolve from earlier that morning began to kick in. Live in the moment.

"Did you at least make any tea for yourself?" Leo asked, glancing toward the barren dining table.

She shook her head. "Nope. I think they should have tea at church though."

Well, if the accident didn't kick start her anxiety, the thought of going to church did. She'd have to tell this story dozens of times. She'd have to walk into the church kitchen and make her own tea.

Would the older parishioners get mad at her for sipping on her tea during service? There would be people at church who were also at the party last night. They would know what she had done to Drake and though that trauma was behind her, the thought of revisiting the embarrassment was less than ideal. She wanted to forget she had done it at all. Or better yet, somehow make a time machine and stop herself from breaking his nose.

"Do they have coffee at church?" Leo asked.

Belle blinked and regarded him questionably. "Oh, they always have coffee."

"Breakfast?"

Still unsure of where he was going with this. "Yeah, I think one of the deacons always brings in donuts."

Leo turned thoughtful for a minute and then nodded, more to himself than to her. "What time do you need to leave?"

Glancing to the clock, she gave him a wry smile. "Service starts at nine."

He checked and mimicked her look. "I guess you better go get ready then. I'll clean up and take care of the animals before we leave."

We. Did he just say that they would be leaving? Together?

Belle's lips parted like she'd speak, but her mind went totally blank. Leo had never given her any indication that he wanted to have anything to do with church or God.

"You don't have to go," she told him as he moved toward the supply closet. "I've been to church a thousand times without any emotional support. I mean, I went to church the week after my dad passed, even when I didn't feel like it."

A flash of something like disapproval streaked across Leo's face, but his next words didn't reflect that. "I'm not going, because I think you need emotional support. I'm going, because of the coffee and donuts."

Even though Belle didn't want to talk him out of coming, she didn't want to make him feel forced in any way. "You can easily get that from Josie's Diner."

Leo pulled out the broom and dustpan and began to quite literally sweep off the residue from the counters. "Ivy works there on Sundays, remember?"

That thought had slipped her mind and after the episode with Drake, Belle didn't even want to think about going to work on Monday. "Good point... Do you have something nice to wear?"

"Would jeans be too casual?"

After a moment of thought, Belle shook her head. "No. Plenty of the other farmers go in jeans and a tie."

At the mention of the tie, Leo passed her a skeptical look over his shoulder. "I've never had to worry about a tie."

She smiled and pushed herself off the floor, testing her limbs to see if they could hold her after enduring both the fall and the rush of adrenaline. "I'll tie it for you. I have a lot of experience with that. I had to help my dad with a tie every week."

Belle lingered in the kitchen a little longer to let Ranger outside and watched the way Leo's muscles moved beneath his tanned and less than flawless skin. So many scars. So much history. She wanted to touch each and every one of them and know their secrets. How long would it take for him to tell her? Or should she be the one to ask first?

The memory came to mind of Ranger when she tried to handle him in that agitated state. The puppy, as docile and cute as he was, didn't want to be touched and she crossed a line. A line that, with Leo, should never be crossed. Her curiosity and need to understand would have to wait and he would have to come to her, no matter how long it took.

Chapter 7

L eo wasn't sure what he was thinking. Maybe it was the need for coffee or to be close to Belle and make sure that she really was okay after the accident. There was no doubt it was the darkness that caused the stove to explode. They were all vulnerable, especially after what happened at the party. The house was open to attack and the stove was the best tool the darkness could use to wreak havoc. When he heard Ranger barking his little head off, he should have known and run down before it could get worse.

He was just thankful that Belle wasn't hurt and seemed to be taking it surprisingly well. That laugh, the genuine belly laugh that echoed through the house, told him that in that moment, she was fine. How long that would last could prove uncertain.

But more than anything, he felt like going to church with Belle and putting on one of her father's old button-down dress shirts was nothing but scratching an itch. He had been curious about her church and the people she faced every day. He wanted to know if they were adding to her condition or somehow helpful. Religion was supposed to be soothing to the soul of the believer. He never understood why, but that didn't mean he couldn't try to understand Belle's need for it.

So instead of letting her go alone week after week or asking about the sermons when she came home, Leo decided to go himself. It'd be like ripping open the stitches with no anesthesia, but he'd have to do it. He hadn't stepped foot in a church since he lived in Scotland and back then, he only saw it as something he had to do with his family. His mother shoved him into the car wearing a tiny suit and then he endured two hours of sitting in a pew, twiddling his thumbs until it was time to go. The words, the prayers, it meant nothing to him. It still didn't.

But for Belle, he'd park it in a pew one more time and listen. He wondered what he'd do with all the new information he'd glean from the experience. Would it give him the fuel he needed to convince her to stay home on Sundays, or would he have an excuse to send her off to more church functions if it helped her anxiety in any way.

The longer he stared at the mass of people flooding in and out through the front entrance, the more he was convinced of the truth. This place wasn't Belle's idea of paradise. And the five extra minutes of sitting in the truck was proof of that. Just like the night before, she had to prepare herself for any and all social contact that was inevitable now.

Approaching the humble white-washed church, Leo could feel a certain energy about the place. The peace and good vibes were so palatable. He likened it to the way the house felt after Belle prayed. He didn't even have to be in the same room with her to know the exact moment she bowed her head and closed her eyes. The radiating power stretched throughout the farm, and that same force resided here. Leo wondered how much of a connection existed between the two.

They didn't go straight to the main church building. They followed the sidewalk around to one of the auxiliary buildings behind the church. Children and parents swarmed through the halls and Belle led the way past classroom after classroom where toddlers and grade-schoolers screamed and laughed over the adult voices just inside the doors.

Belle gave out greetings to everyone they passed as they edged their way toward the church's kitchen. Leo, thankfully, was not spoken to and he ignored the confused and intrigued looks he received from the other churchgoers. He recognized a few faces from the party, but many others were unfamiliar to him. Undoubtedly, they all wondered what he meant by trailing after Belle.

He could smell the rich dark roast before the kitchen came into view. One turn around a corner and they found themselves on the edge of a herd of men and women all talking and gabbing away. Some held a cup of coffee in one hand and others held donuts, but all wore smiles. As soon as they realized who was coming to join them, however, those smiles faded and faces were transformed by their concern for Belle and themselves. Leo felt like a lion who had approached a crowded watering hole.

Belle, on the other hand, played her usual role and grinned to them all. That alone seemed to put them at ease and the roar of conversation picked back up.

"Popular one, aren't you?" he muttered in her ear as they wedged their way toward the counter where an attendant was passing out the steaming Styrofoam cups.

"My dad was a deacon here, so yeah, everyone kind of knows me."

Leo would not be ashamed of his ignorance today. There would be no hiding how little he knew about church or religion in general. "What's a deacon?"

Belle turned to him, slightly off guard by the question. "Uh... A deacon is kind of like a church elder, but they don't have to be old. It's more of a title. They serve in a specific ministry with the church and help make decisions about funding, events, and that sort of thing."

"So, he was a pretty important man?" Leo asked, pulling out the fresh memories of what Mr. Tale and the other men had talked about.

With a smile, she replied wistfully, "Yeah, he was pretty important I guess. Everyone loved him, even if he did go through with the divorce and all."

Leo wasn't quite sure what the divorce had to do with anything, but he let it slide. The fact that her father was a church deacon solidified what he had already presumed. Belle had an image to keep up as her father's survivor, which must have placed a heavy obligation on her shoulders. Maybe that was why she went to church every week, even when she didn't want to.

The older woman at the counter grinned, her red lips spreading between deep laugh-lines on her cheeks. "Good morning, Annabelle!"

"Good morning, Miss Georgina."

Something in Belle's tone told him that she wasn't all too pleased to see Miss Georgina, and he guessed the reason as soon as the old lady's eyes fell on him. A twinge of disgust made her mouth falter, but she recovered quickly. He seemed to have that effect on everyone Belle knew. None of them expected her to be in the company of a man like him. Big, intimidating, dangerous.

"Who's your friend?"

"This is Leo." Belle's hand came up as if she were going to touch his arm or shoulder, but her fingers didn't so much as graze the ironed fabric of his shirt. Her fingers curled away and then dropped as if remembering some reason why she shouldn't show such affection toward him in public. He wouldn't hold it against her.

He offered out his hand to Miss Georgina and out of politeness, she shook it. "A pleasure to meet you, Leo. I'm Georgina Harrison. I'm normally in the sanctuary with the music directors, but they needed some help here this morning."

"I noticed it was a little crowded," Belle remarked, thumbing toward the others who had already gotten their coffee.

"Yes, it's strange. We normally don't see these numbers unless it's getting close to Christmas or Easter. Can I get you two coffee?"

"And a couple of donuts, please."

Leo reached for his billfold in his back pocket and both women jumped to correct him.

"Oh no, honey," Miss Georgina laughed. "This one's on God. No need to pay."

On God? Leo tried not to look as confused as he was and slipped his hands back into his front pockets where they had been lodged for most of the morning.

"Can I actually get a tea?" Belle said quickly before Miss Georgina poured the second cup.

The older woman raddled off the list of different kinds of tea they had, rambling on how some were donations and others were left in the kitchen after certain church events. Finally, Belle said she preferred plain black English tea and they moved aside to wait.

Leo watched Belle's expression as she scanned the crowd behind him, studying the way her mask never slipped. Not once, even when he made that minor social blunder. His father had said something once about churches being nothing but a hole in the ground where people threw their hard-earned money, so he assumed he'd have to pay double for the coffee and donuts. Maybe churches in Scotland were different than churches in Arkansas.

"How are you doing?" he asked, wanting to make sure that Belle wasn't falling to pieces behind that mask.

She looked to him, eyes a little wide. "I'm fine."

Leo bent his head a little lower. "Really fine?"

There was a second of hesitation before he saw a fracture in her defenses. "Well, not completely fine... But I'm here and I'm breathing. I am breathing, right?"

"Aye, you're breathing," he replied with a playful turn of his voice. "Maybe not when we were passing by that screaming passel of brats at the front door, but you are now."

Belle shushed him, and her gaze darted to the people again. "That's someone's children you're talking about," she murmured.

Leo's shoulder shrugged, and he felt the seams of his shirt stretch a bit against his movements. Her father wasn't nearly as built as he was, and it made for an uncomfortable, tight fit, but he could tolerate it for a little while.

"I'm sure you were thinking it. I just thought I'd say it out loud." He jerked his head toward the counter. "Did you see the way she looked at me? Like I was some thug here to take all of her coffee and tea bags." Leo screwed up his lips and imitated the old crone. "I'd take all of her black tea, white tea, green tea, herbal tea, jasmine tea, lemongrass tea, blueberry tea, mint tea, peach tea – "

Belle was laughing so hard that all she could do was put her hand against his lips to make him stop. Leo smiled against her fingers, knowing he had succeeded.

"What's so funny?" Miss Georgina asked as she came back with their two cups with donuts balancing on napkins on top. Her disapproving look shifted from Belle to Leo, to the hand that had made contact with his mouth.

Belle cleared her throat. "Nothing. I'll see you at the service?"

Leo was ready to turn away the moment he took the cups and donuts, but Miss Georgina spoke before he had a chance to make his speedy escape.

"By the way," she said to Belle, "if I don't get to talk to you after the service, I've got a favor to ask of you. I know it's last minute, but a booth became available for the Farmer's Fall Festival next Saturday. As you know, I'm head of the committee and I just can't have a booth go empty. It'll be an eye sore. While I was talking about it with Miss Marlene yesterday, she mentioned that you sometimes brought eggs and wool to the farmer's market when your papa was still running the place. Do you think you could take that booth and sell some things? It'd be great advertisement for that farm of yours and you said yourself that you wanted to build it up a little bit. Having a booth would be a great way to get the word out about your sheep and horses."

He watched the flicker of doubt and panic in Belle's eyes, though he was sure the older woman wouldn't have noticed it at all, even if she were paying the slightest bit of attention. Did Miss Georgina understand what she just asked? She was giving Belle one week to get some kind of display together. It was too last minute. Something like this needed to be planned out well in advance.

Leo would have answered for her if he didn't think that Miss Georgina would misconstrue the intent. He'd be turning down the offer in order to save Belle's already fragile sanity, but she might not see it that way.

With his arms full, he couldn't reach out to help ground her. Instead, he cleared his throat. When she lifted her eyes to him, he tried to convey his thoughts and concerns without words. He asked, wordlessly, for her to make her own decision and not let Miss Georgina's silver-tongued request blind her. Whatever she chose, he would support her in what way he could, even if it meant dumping this scalding hot coffee over Miss Georgina's apron if she tried to push Belle any harder.

But Belle straightened to her full height and gave her answer. "You're right. It would be a good opportunity for the farm. I don't have a lot to make the booth pretty, though so – "

"Oh, honey, don't worry about making it pretty," Miss Georgina said with a wave of her bony hand. "If you need anything, don't hesitate to ask."

They then went into some of the details of the event. Location, time, what the committee could provide, and what to expect. Belle listened, but didn't seem overwhelmed as he expected. He thought there might have been a bit of truth in how she answered Miss Georgina. Having a booth at the festival might be a good advertising point for the farm as it began its first growing stages. Because it was for the farm, Belle would brave the anxiety storm that would be waiting for her on Saturday.

One thing was a given, though. Leo would be with her the whole time, as long as she'd let him.

When they said their final goodbyes and an older man came to order his own coffee, Leo turned to lead the way through the crowd. Belle had stopped on a corner, still in the thick of the cluster, but he wouldn't let her stay in this suffocating place. He retraced his steps back toward the door, ignoring the way Belle called after him. Only when he tasted the fresh, crisp morning air, did he finally stop and offer up her meager breakfast.

"We need to go back inside," she said breathlessly. She always had trouble keeping up with his stride.

"Why?" he questioned, taking the first sip of his incredibly strong coffee. For once, he wished he had asked for a little sugar to go with it.

Belle opened her mouth to answer, but she had nothing. "Well... I mean, we just should. No one else is out here."

Leo gave her a clever half-smile. "That's the point."

Admitting defeat, they moved off the sidewalk and leaned against the brick wall, their feet sinking into freshly mowed grass.

"My dad used to get donuts every Sunday, whether we ate breakfast or not," Belle began, a bit of partially glazed dough stuck in one of her cheeks. "He would stand in the hall like those other men and talk and socialize. I'd usually be with him or I'd go into one of the Sunday school rooms."

Driving Belle out of the building had been a simple act of preservation. She didn't want to be jostled or crowded any more than he did, but it never occurred to him that she would have wanted to stay there for sentimental sake.

"Do you really want to go back in?"

She shook her head, her perfectly curled hair swaying against her shoulders. "Nope. I did see the way they were looking at you."

"Embarrassed?" Leo took a bite of his donut.

"No, I'm not embarrassed. Not for myself anyway... I don't like it when people look at you in that way. They probably don't think you're a thug, but they'll be a little hesitant of you and I don't... I don't want you to feel like you're not welcome, because you are. They just forget their Christian hospitality when fear gets in the way."

At first, he thought she was just rambling. Then he realized that Belle was only being honest. One thing he did remember about church. Those times when his mom took him and his sister to the services, especially in those last few years they shared as a family, everyone seemed so supportive. They saw through her lies when she said she was fine, and they didn't ask about the bruises, but Leo could tell they cared.

Those people in there cared too, but not about him. They were worried for Belle alone. If he made a better impression, if he weren't so naturally threatening, then maybe they would approve of him. But then, he'd be in the same boat as Belle. He'd be faking it, putting on a show for people whose opinions didn't matter.

"I wouldn't have been embarrassed to stay in there," he said. "I'm used to people not liking me right away. If you want to go back in and talk to them, I won't stop you."

Belle smiled up to him, but it was flavored with something akin to pity. "I don't want to. But I do want people to like you."

Leo turned the warm cup of coffee in his hand as if he were examining every side of it. "I don't care what they think, and neither should you. We've been over this."

"I know, I know," she said, waving her donut. "It's just a hard habit to kick, that's all."

"But it does need to be kicked. Straight to the curb. And those hags can spraff all they want about you and me."

"Spraff?" she laughed.

"One other thing you can do is just roll with my highland slang," he said, turning up his nose in exaggerated haughtiness. Once more, he succeeded in making her laugh. "It means gossiping. And I'll take it that Miss Georgina does a lot of it."

Belle bit her lips together as if they were having some scandalous conversation and only nodded in reply before taking a swig of her tea.

"If I wasn't here, what would you be doing right now?" Leo asked as he watched a family of five make their way down the sidewalk. The mother frantically plucked at her children's hair and clothes while the father looked to be half asleep on his feet. It looked like he needed coffee more than anything else that morning. And with three kids, Leo wouldn't doubt it.

"I'd probably be in the sanctuary talking with people, sitting in my usual spot."

Leo waited until the family was out of earshot before replying, "So, do we go in when we're done or...?"

"You really are new to this, aren't you?"

Her expression bordered on utterly mystified.

"Is it that obvious?" he grumbled with the coffee cup tipped against his mouth.

"Yeah. It's pretty clear you've never been to church if you try to pay for the coffee."

Leo shrugged again and wondered how long it would take him to completely tear the shirt open if he did that too many times. "How was I supposed to know?"

"Have you ever been to church?"

"Only when I was a kid and that was in Scotland."

Realization dawned in her eyes and Belle fell speechless for a few beats. "So... Anytime you went to church, it was with your family."

The memories didn't quite sting like they used to. "It was, but I couldn't get into it. All that kneeling, praying, big words in the Bible. I didn't care to go, but my mum told me it was important, so we went."

"I was kind of that way," Belle said. "But my dad put me in the Sunday school classes and they made the Bible sound a lot more interesting. It's not all praying and kneeling, though. There's the fellowship, the music, the... the feeling when the pastor says something and it just all kind of clicks for you in one minute. It's going to the fundraiser events and knowing you're doing something good for someone somewhere. It's not just the routine and the religiosity of it all. There're some spiritual aspects too, as a kid, I didn't really understand. But I do now and maybe that's why I keep coming."

Leo watched her, enraptured by the wealth of feeling and conviction in her explanation. Maybe he had been wrong. Maybe there was something hidden behind the stained-glass windows, piano music, terrible coffee, flowery dresses, and ties that Leo couldn't see. Maybe it wasn't all about the people and the building. Belle genuinely liked going to church. Whether he could share in that kind of enjoyment, he wasn't sure. But he'd make an effort to stay open.

"Well, hurry up and eat your donut so we can go in."

Belle hadn't anticipated it to be so crowded, and she was sure that if Leo wasn't there, she would have suffered a lot more for it. Instead, she felt strangely calm, especially after finishing off her donut and tea outside the Sunday school building.

Inside the sanctuary was almost no different than near the kitchen. Voices rose and reverberated off the high rafters, unable to drown out Miss Cynthia's piano in the far corner near the choir platform.

Here was the real test. Running the gauntlet between the front doors and her usual pew seat would be that much harder with Leo in tow. People would ask about him, introductions would need to be made, and she'd have to endure that look. That almost sneering look like they didn't think he belonged there with her. If only she could have been like Leo and not care about their opinions.

She remembered that day on the front porch when the pastor's wife, Mrs. Kendall, warned her about any further association with Leo. Of course, she went against her warnings and even welcomed Leo into her home to stay. What would she think now when they came in together?

Another thing she hadn't expected, which seemed so different compared to the reception they had received at the kitchen, was how many of the old farmers called out to Leo and at least waved, if not shook his hand. Leo looked just as puzzled by the gestures as she was, and then the explanation soon came out.

It happened when Belle was approached by Jessica Greene and her husband.

"Are you all right, Belle?" Jessica asked after giving her a warm and sincere hug.

"Yeah, I'm fine. Why?"

Jessica looked warily between the two. "You both left so quickly last night after what happened and we didn't know if Drake did something. He said you had just hauled off and hit him for no reason, but no one believes him anymore. It took Mr. Tale threatening to bash his head into a pole to get him to talk. Mrs. Robinson had been there too and heard little bits of the argument. It was a big thing."

Belle grimaced. "I hope I didn't ruin anyone's fun."

"Only Drake's," Jason Greene answered. "Me and some of the other guys dragged him out to the barn and gave him one hell of a talk."

Jessica lightly backhanded her husband's beer gut. "Don't talk like that in here," she hissed.

He only gave her a crooked smile and kept going. "Anyway, Drake won't be a problem anymore. Mr. Levinson called up his mama and told her about all the stuff he's been doing. He'll be leaving town soon."

Aghast that she had caused all of that, Belle's jaw dropped. "All because I punched him?"

Jessica reached out and grabbed her hand. "Girl, it's not just you. He's been pestering everyone in town. Even me. But you're the first one he's ever gotten physical with."

"We should have ran him out after Leo beat him up outside Josie's."

Could that be why all the other men seemed to know and esteem him all of the sudden? Because he and Belle had done what no one else dared?

Mr. Levinson, Jessica's father, came forward and wedged his way into the conversation much as his daughter did. He asked if Belle was all right and told her about what they did to Drake after she left.

"I'm so sorry if I spoiled the party at all, and I completely understand if Mrs. Levinson doesn't invite me over anymore. I'm sure she doesn't want to risk anyone else getting a broken nose because of me."

The old farmer's face screwed up with confusion. "Not invite you? Spoiled? My wife throws fine parties, but this one was the most exciting of them all because of what you did. This beats the one time that boy got so drunk he climbed on top of the barn and puked over the side. Who was that? Do you remember?"

Jessica pressed her fingers between her brows like she was developing a headache while the two older men listed off the possible names of the boy. All the while, Belle wondered if Mr. Levinson was only saying that to make her feel better. She didn't know the man to sugarcoat anything, but when it came to Belle, she wondered if everyone in town coddled her a bit because of who her father had been.

When he turned to Leo, Belle wasn't ready for what Mr. Levinson would say.

"What are you doing on Tuesday morning?" he asked. "Does Tale have you doing some job?"

Belle had almost forgotten that Leo was technically still employed by Mr. Tale's construction company, if not temporarily.

"Nope," he replied casually. "He hasn't told me about anything."

"Great. Why don't you come out to have breakfast with some of the men here? We go to the coffee shop by Blanche's sewing store at eight every Tuesday morning to chat. You should join us."

Jessica slid Belle a look that told her enough. Even they were a little surprised at the invitation. She bit her lips shut to keep herself from answering for Leo. Chances were that he wouldn't find out what the meeting was really about until he got there.

Her father had started the tradition of coffee on Tuesday mornings with the men and elders of the church. It was a way for them all to get together once a week and talk about God, the Bible, and be open with each other about things that only men really understood. Belle always thought they just got together to complain about women or politics, but she had spied on them once and found out she was totally wrong.

Being invited to Tuesday morning coffee was like being welcomed into an exclusive club. When her father had started the tradition, it had only been him and three other men. The number of attendees typically fluctuated, but it never grew to more than eight. If Mr. Levinson was inviting Leo to sit with them, it was a big deal.

It took a moment, but Leo finally agreed. "Sure. I can come over after I finish with the chores at the farm."

It was settled, and they exchanged phone numbers.

"I'm sure you know where it is. You practically live right down the road from it."

Again, Belle said nothing. No one knew that they were living under the same roof. If Mrs. Kendall or Miss Georgina found out about that, there was no telling what kind of reprimand she'd be in for.

They moved on and talked with more folks, made more introductions, but she still couldn't get over what she had been told about Drake. He would be gone soon. Very soon. While she could feel a little guilty for leaving a man without a job or home, she couldn't regret that he wouldn't be bothering anyone else in Levi anymore. She could glean some relief from the fact that no one was mad about what she had done. As usual, her anxiety had beaten her up for no reason.

Her usual reserved seat in the middle pew was within sight when they were cut off just one more time by Mr. George Calloway.

Though he wasn't someone she normally talked to, she recognized him instantly by his shock of pure white hair pulled back in a thin ponytail, and dark wrinkled face. One of the biggest rice farmers in town, he didn't attend services often. He came even less frequently since his wife passed away last November. But no one could ever doubt his supreme level of faith. Belle often wondered if the man didn't come as often, because he didn't feel like he needed to. His commitment and open communication with God sometimes surpassed that of Pastor Kendall's, which almost seemed like heresy to even think.

Mr. Calloway and her father often differed on some theological points of view, but their discussions were always civil, and both kept an open mind to the other's argument. Belle remembered her father would often come out of one of their long talks, quiet and pensive as if he were stewing over everything that had been said. They weren't close, but her father never turned down a conversation.

He gave her a light side-hug and shook Leo's hand with a firm grip.

"So, the Lord told me that you need something."

Beyond her own control, her eyebrows arched high. "He what?"

Mr. Calloway smiled and smoothed down his clip-on tie. "The Lord said you needed something, so I want to see what it is."

Nonplussed was an understatement. Belle tried to wrap her mind around it. She hadn't prayed that morning or asked God for any intervention, but she did need a new stove and new cabinets.

"Belle told me about her broken stove this morning," Leo answered for her. "The burners were on the blink and it's not safe for her to use anymore."

Mr. Calloway's face lit up like fireworks on the fourth of July. "Isn't God good? I just bought a new stove and was looking to get rid of my old one. Want to take it off my hands? It's only about two years old. I just remodeled my kitchen and there's nothing wrong with it."

Moved by his generosity and the timeliness of it all, Belle couldn't speak. Leo did answer for her and arranged that they would pick it up from his farm later that afternoon. The only thing that could break her stupor was Pastor Kendall announcing that they would begin service in a few moments. That was everyone's cue to find their seats and fast.

She gave a heartfelt thanks to Mr. Calloway before he turned to leave, and she mindlessly walked toward her pew, still trying to process it all. This might have been the best Sunday service she had ever attended. Leo had been invited to Tuesday coffee, her stove problem was resolved, and her fears about being ostracized for her behavior the night before had finally been put to rest.

By the time she sat down, Belle almost felt like she didn't need the mask to smile for her. When she looked up to the elaborate stained-glass window behind the pulpit and rows of choir singers, she didn't feel drained or fatigued after talking to so many people. In fact, she was happy.

And when Leo sat down beside her, in the place where her father used to sit, a kind of surreal emotion washed over her. It was like in that one simple move, in the span of just an hour, the end to an era had finally come. Her dreams of being anxiety-free didn't seem so far-fetched anymore. The answer to her prayers for relief and revelation had come in a single, rather attractive package.

Leo had shown her so much already, but today he proved just how magical and special he really was. Maybe he didn't understand her faith or why she needed to come to church, but he was here with her. He was supporting her and, in that moment, she was complete again. She hadn't felt that in a long time.

As the voices hushed and the piano tunes rang out across the sanctuary, Belle slipped her hand into Leo's and gave his fingers a squeeze. He replied back with his own squeeze and smiled down to her. There wasn't a single person on this planet that could make her feel so comfortable. She had sat in this same church, surrounded by people that loved and cared about her, but she had never felt at home. But with Leo, she was at home.

Chapter 8

Leo had to shake his head and smile one more time while he waited at the next traffic stop. The lunch that Belle had forgotten that morning was safely secured under his zipped-up jacket, the bulge was minimal, but still noticeable.

Ever since the day before, after they left church, Belle's head was full of plans. They picked up the new stove from Mr. Calloway's in the afternoon, but Leo was on his own to install it. Belle's afternoon and evening was occupied with searching for marketing plans and taking notes of all the things she'd have to do to get ready for the Farmer's Fall Festival in the coming weekend. He let her ramble on as she talked about signs, business cards, everything that would have to be done with the sheep in preparation for the event, how she should present the products, and everything in between. The idea of taking one of the more docile ewes with them to pen up near the booth had been tossed around.

He listened and gave whatever advice he could, but he still questioned the wisdom in Belle putting herself out there like that. If she was wound up after only talking to people she'd known for most of her life, how would she do with strangers? She had said multiple times that he didn't have to go with her, but Leo wouldn't think of doing anything else. Someone had to keep a level head between the two of them.

Hence, why he was driving to the bookstore with a chilled lunch-box under his coat. The sandwich and bag of carrots had been prepared the night before, but Belle became distracted with an early morning internet search and she left it sitting in the fridge for Leo to find.

Even though Belle had told him the ewes would start lambing soon, so he couldn't afford to leave them alone for long, he didn't want Belle to feel obligated to go out to get her lunch, nor did he want her to starve. She had enough to worry about and Leo had a few hours before the new stallion would arrive from Fayetteville.

He parked his bike next to the bookstore's sign – whether it was legal or not – because all the other stalls were occupied. From his limited experience, the store had never seemed so busy. Inside was no different. There was actually a line to the front counter and every customer held the same book. One look in the display window confirmed it. There was a new release today.

Belle hadn't mentioned it before and he wondered if she had forgotten. If new release days were this hectic, there was no telling how she would be handling it.

Leo recognized that he had become almost hyper-aware of every little possible trigger. From the beginning, he didn't want to be that protective, overbearing friend who tried to shelter Belle. The only way to grow was to expose herself to these uncomfortable situations, but after all he had seen and learned, he understood that spreading herself too thin was the last thing she needed. Especially now, with everything the darkness continued to throw at them, she needed a little peace and rest. If Leo had the chance to intervene and save her from that, he would.

With the lunch box in hand, he maneuvered his way through the bookstore, passing by customers as they browsed down the aisles. All the while, he kept his eyes peeled for Belle's deep brown ponytail.

He spotted her struggling with a box near a table piled with discounted books and moved to intercept. She wasn't paying attention and they nearly ran into each other. Almost predictably, Belle let out a tiny squeak of surprise and closed her eyes in embarrassment when she realized who she had just squeaked at.

He chuckled as he took the box from her. To him, it wasn't heavy at all, but to her it seemed like quite a load. He was able to balance it in one hand while propping it against his chest. "Breathe," he advised playfully.

Belle's hand was pressed to her chest as if to keep her heart from bursting out of her body. "I didn't know you were stopping by."

"You forgot this at home." Leo lifted his hand a little and swung the lunchbox to get her attention.

Startled, she snatched it up and clutched it against her stomach. "Don't say that so loud," she hissed as nervous eyes roamed to see if anyone was paying attention.

"You're welcome," he said, even though she hadn't thanked him. "Busy day?"

Belle appeared to relax and nodded. Now, he noticed the tendrils of hair that had come loose from her ponytail and how one edge of her blouse had come untucked. With only her, Ivy, and their boss to man the store during this rush, they must have been running themselves ragged.

"Every time we have a new release, it's like the whole town remembers that they have a bookstore and come flooding in. I haven't had a chance to sit all morning. We had a few people waiting at the door before we even opened."

A voice boomed from the front of the store, calling her name. Belle straightened and slipped between him and the bookcase. He followed, only because he wasn't sure where to put the box. Belle was faster, despite her short legs, and was behind the counter with a taller bald man by the time he came up to the line.

They talked too low for him to understand, but he stood and waited.

"Are all of those for you, sweetheart?"

The middle-aged woman beside him with the beginnings of gray in her hair, regarded him with eyes sparkling with humor. It wasn't until he finally glanced in the box that he realized why. He might have been totally disconnected from pop culture, but he recognized the series from the snide jokes some of his coworkers had made. The newest installment in the erotic romance craze had just come out today. And he was holding a box full of them.

Leo made a face and set the box on the counter as the woman and a few other ladies behind her began to giggle. Belle must have noticed, because she came forward and slid the box to the floor, but something was different. Her face, once flushed from the exercise she had mentioned before, was now ashen and her expression was dulled by some somber emotion.

She hurried away from the counter after talking with her boss and though Leo could feel his slightly hateful stare, he ignored it and followed.

"What's wrong?" he asked, leaning in so their conversation would be private, despite the bustling bookstore.

Belle smoothed back the hairs on her head and let out a long breath. "Ray's just in one of his moods today. Nothing new."

Leo looked over his shoulder to the bald man and immediately detested him.

"Don't you dare talk to him," she warned, as if she could read his mind.

He smirked as they made their way toward the back of the store and the breakroom where she'd stash her lunchbox. "Who said I was going to talk to him?"

"You had that look. I know that look."

"I had no look," he teased. "Besides I wasn't going to talk to him. My fist will do the talking for me."

That earned him a smile, which was enough. She opened the breakroom door and he was ready to step through, but she put up her hand to stop him.

"What? Afraid someone's looking?" he asked, unafraid to hover dangerously close to her face as he spoke.

Belle leaned away and tapped on the sign nailed to the door. Employees only. "Don't want customers getting the idea they can ignore this."

Leo made a face. "Well, if you're going to lock me out..."

That didn't amuse her half as much as he intended. "I'd never lock you out, Leo. And I am thankful for you bringing my lunch, it's just..." She nodded toward the rest of the bookstore that he had been able to tune out since he walked in. If only she had the same skill, maybe she wouldn't have been as stressed.

"It's been a busy day. I understand. Promise me you'll take a break when you can?"

She gave him a sweet smile and nodded. "I promise. You might want to leave before Ray chews you out too."

Without ceremony, she closed the door behind her and Leo was left staring at the advisory plaque. He sighed in the face of that defeat and turned to leave. Somehow, he had hoped they could eat lunch together if she wasn't otherwise busy, but it was just the wrong day. They'd get to spend a little time together tonight and maybe take that stallion out for a test ride. That is, if she didn't feel like crashing on the couch with a cup of chamomile tea. And even if she did, he'd be there for her, just like he promised.

The moment Belle had been both dreading and praying for all day had finally come. It seemed as if everyone living in Levi had passed through those front doors at some point that morning, and now that it was a few hours into the afternoon, the traffic started to dwindle. This gave them all a minute to finally breathe, and to possibly talk.

That seemed to be the last thing Ivy wanted to do. Her professional coldness was somewhat expected, but its inevitability didn't save Belle the hurt. They hadn't had a chance to talk about what happened at the party. From the moment she tried to wish Ivy a good morning, Belle knew that her coworker wasn't on her side. She and Drake had been dating, after all. And Belle just sent her friend plummeting into singlehood again. She wouldn't stay there long, but had Ivy been happy with the scumbag?

Belle sat on one of the reading benches near the magazine section and she could hear Ivy sorting books in the aisle close by. Some kid had pulled out almost every Dr. Seuss book they had in the store and made a fort from the stacks. Though she was impressed with the little girl's ingenuity, Ray didn't see it that way.

She could only see the top of Ivy's blonde head as it turned to look from the shelf to the stack of thin hardbacks in her hand. Belle tried to find the right words, sorting through the tightness in her stomach and struggling to push the elephant off her chest.

To be silent, to let this passive aggressive animosity between them fester, would have been worse in the long run, compared to ripping the bandage off and working it all out now. Even if it meant taking the argument into the backroom, even if it meant one or both of them would break down into tears, it had to be done.

It would probably ruin whatever she had with Ivy. Though they disagreed on so many things and she could never boldly open up the way she wanted, Belle had hoped they could be close one day. She had already been a good ally and sounding board in the past. This apprehension was silly, and she knew it. Ivy could be trusted.

"I'm sorry about Drake."

That was all Belle could give. An apology. She didn't try to defend herself or give her side of the story. If Ivy had already decided to be against her, then there was no use in trying to reverse it.

The blonde head stilled, and she heard a sigh before Ivy disappeared below the top shelf. She reappeared a few seconds later at the end of the aisle and came to sit next to Belle as if they were in for a long talk. So far so good.

"It's not your fault," Ivy replied. "Drake was being... he was being a jerk."

Belle gathered that she wanted to say something a little stronger by the way her lips pursed momentarily. She couldn't sugarcoat or hide her own true reaction though.

"You've been acting like you hate me all day."

Ivy hid her face in her hands and propped her elbows on her knees with a groan. "I don't hate you. I just... I hate myself. I always do this. You know I do this. I pick the wrong guy. I always pick the charming, troubled piles of mess, because he says I look pretty and I think there's a diamond somewhere underneath all the trash." She looked up, frustration creasing her face. "But then I take a big bite of that trash and realize it's not superficial. Why do I do that?"

She knew exactly what Ivy was talking about, but there was no right answer. Belle had her own assumptions, of course, but she wasn't ready to be that honest.

"For that, you may have to go to the self-help section."

They both giggled, the strain between them finally dissipating.

"I mean, seriously," Ivy continued, still piqued beyond reason. "What he did to you, trying to make you go out with him while he was already dating me! It's insane! I've had guys cheat on me before, but trying to ask a girl out and force something like that is just..." Her fingers curled to resemble claws, no doubt imagining Drake's thick neck trapped between them.

"Drake is scum," Belle said flatly, unafraid to insult the man that no one in town liked anymore.

"Drake is scum," Ivy repeated, letting her hands drop into her lap. "But you were awesome. That nose was bleeding for so long."

Belle's face puckered as if that compliment caused her pain. "I honestly wish I had never done that. I know everyone's saying it was great, but it was so unladylike."

The look she received was almost enough to make her take it back. "Girl, that man needed a wakeup call. I'm only sorry I didn't get a swing at him for trying to cheat on me before he left the party. And if that was unladylike, then you need to be unladylike more often. You stood up for yourself and didn't give a... didn't give a crap for once." Ivy reached out and took Belle's arm. "You were brave for standing up to him. I know you must have been scared out of your mind, but you stood your ground. Didn't know you had it in you. Like, I knew you were always pretty anxious and stuff, so punching Drake must have been terrifying, but it really was cool."

Instead of rejoicing in her affirmation that what Belle did was good, her mind snagged on one seemingly unimportant part. *I knew you were always pretty anxious.*

"You... you knew?" Belle could feel all her blood sink south and her body broke out into a cold sweat.

Ivy smiled in that way people always did when they felt sorry for someone else. "Girl, I've known for a while. You've only been coming out of your shell recently. Ever since Leo showed up."

Again, Belle ignored the part about Leo, the part that should have sent her in a tizzy. "You've known and you never..." She couldn't even word it. All the times she had been almost too anxious to function, all the times she almost came undone right there in the bookstore, and Ivy never did anything. She didn't necessarily make it worse, but she could have helped.

But how could she have known how to help? Belle wasn't even completely sure how to cope when the mask was on and she was nowhere near any essential oils or hot tea. She'd just come unraveled the moment she was home and never bothered to learn. It was true that Leo was helping her in some small ways and teaching her self-care, but why didn't Ivy reach out?

"I didn't think you really wanted me to know," she confessed solemnly. "You are good at hiding it. I just see through that sort of thing sometimes with certain people. I may have bad taste in men, but I can read a person pretty well. So, I just left it alone. If it was really important or if you really wanted to open up to me, then you would have."

Now it was Belle's turn to feel ashamed and hide her face. "It's not that I didn't want to open up," Belle whined. This one outpouring felt like strapping on a faulty parachute and getting ready to jump. It couldn't end well, but she was doing it anyway. "I didn't want you or anyone else to think I was crazy or pathetic. I didn't want you to look at me any differently, like I was some mental case waiting for the one episode that would put me in a straitjacket. I didn't want you asking me every day if I was okay, because I'd either lie or tell you the truth and sound like I was complaining. I've already been complaining a lot with Leo and I don't want to be a burden."

In an unexpected move, Ivy hugged her around the shoulders. Belle sat there, confused about how to return it.

"You're not a burden," Ivy said. "You couldn't be, even if you tried. And you haven't been complaining. You need to talk about it. We all need to vent sometimes, or it'll make us go nuts." Ivy pulled away and grinned. "I always wondered if you just didn't like me and that's why you were hiding. But then I saw you in public once and knew you weren't doing it on purpose. Honestly, I'm just glad that whatever Leo's been doing to help you, it's working. You seem so much happier."

Belle let herself smile, sincerely smile. "He's really been pushing me in all the right ways. Remember that time you asked me to the movies and I texted you to cancel? I felt so bad about that, but Leo was the one who encouraged me to bail. Not in a controlling way, but you know how awful that day was. I wasn't in the right mind to go out."

Ivy nodded. "I know, and that's why I wasn't mad at all. I thought inviting you to the movies would be a chance to unwind, but I guess we unwind in different ways."

That was an understatement, but Belle just nodded. "We do. You'd think I could go into business selling tea out of my kitchen drawer. I have a membership to this fragrance company that sells candles and bubble bath stuff. My idea of a good time is sitting on the couch with a book and not talking to anyone."

Ivy listened, but Belle could tell when she was going too far with her confession and stopped before she could talk about the meditative techniques she utilized almost daily.

"I never thought it was that bad."

"It is," Belle said, feeling a bit of the weight finally lift off her chest. "But it's manageable... sort of. It is now, anyway."

"Is there anything I can do to help you here at work?"

Belle never thought she would ask, and for the first time, she initiated contact. Her hand closed around Ivy's. "I'll let you know if there is."

For the first time since she had invented the mask, she felt comfortable letting it drop around someone else besides Leo. Her gut, as unreliable as it was, had been right. Ivy could be trusted. She had known the truth for so long and respected her in spite of it. She wouldn't lord it over her or purposefully embarrass her. She didn't call her crazy or weird or give her useless advice. There was no judgement, only a willingness to understand. She wanted to help. She cared. Belle's inner circle now included one more person, when she never thought it was possible to let someone so close without everything falling to pieces.

Chapter 9

"So, is this your place?"

Leo wasn't one for small talk and the former owner of the stallion was already too chatty for his liking.

"My employer's," he replied as they led the new stud from the trailer. His heavy hooves crashed against the metal track, his head drooped, but dark eyes wide as he took in the new surroundings.

The man, Mr. Rumsey, had his eye on the three mares grazing in the pasture. Snow's white head craned up to look at the new male on the property, while Maggie and Chestnut were more intent on munching the grass. "Are them the mares you were talkin' about?"

Leo nodded and kept his focus on the stallion, whose name – almost predictably – was Buck. "Yep."

"Fine mares," Mr. Rumsey said. "You know they might not be in heat this winter, right? Suspect's it'll get mighty cold and they won't wanna have anythin' to do with ol' Buck."

Belle had spent almost an hour the night before going over every detail of how to get the stallion acclimated to his new farm and she hadn't spared him the particulars about the process of getting her girls pregnant.

"Aye, we're aware. But it might take him that long to get used to all three of them."

Mr. Rumsey huffed. "Buck's pretty docile. He shouldn't give you any problems."

Leo thought of Snow's dominance over the other two mares, despite her youth, and frowned. "It's not Buck I'm worried about."

The stallion snorted and tossed back his dark mane once he was just a few paces out of the trailer. Almost at the same time, a cold wind swept across the farm and chilled Leo's exposed arms. The sun had been warm enough that afternoon that he didn't see the need for a jacket. Clouds formed overhead and blocked out much of that light and it was as if the whole property had fallen under the shadow of a giant.

Mr. Rumsey, however, didn't notice and went on to talk about a few mares he had that were dominant. The words rolled off Leo as he continued to lead Buck toward the stables and tried not to assume the worst about the sudden darkening of the sky. His skin didn't tingle like it usually did during an impending storm and the air didn't smell moist like it did just before a sudden gush of rain. There was something else at work here, and he didn't want to believe it was the darkness.

However, if it was, Mr. Rumsey needed to leave. Soon.

Leo managed to get Buck into the stall nearest to the mares' easily enough and gave him plenty of food and water to hold him over.

"Do you have some of his old feed?" Leo asked, cutting into the middle of the man's sentence.

He paused, but recovered quickly from the rude interruption. "Yeah, it's in the truck."

The fifty pound bag was retrieved and Leo did exactly as Belle instructed, leaving it next to the rest of the feed so they could mix it during his regular mealtime. The temperature continued to drop when he paid out the other half of the sale price for the stallion. Leo didn't leave the stables until he was absolutely sure that Mr. Rumsey and his trailer were completely out of sight. Only then did he make his way toward the house.

With the horses and sheep in their pastures, and Ranger tormenting the hens, Leo had no other chores. Dealing with the darkness was not something he wanted to do. Not today when everything seemed to be going fine. Just one day without a crisis, that's all he wanted.

It should have stayed away after all the pain he inflicted and blood spilled last Friday. That many rounds of fighting should have taken care of his blood payments for at least another week or so. But he should have known this was coming after what had happened with the stove.

He found the darkness on the front porch, reclining in one of the deck chairs and his ankles propped up on the railing. It was a picture of relaxation that Leo hadn't expected, especially after their last encounter on the farm. That night, he had been scared out of his mind and then dissipated in a burst of moonlight, but not before giving out some hefty threats.

Leo stood on the top step and hooked his thumbs in his belt loops. One look should have told the demon enough. He wasn't pleased and not in the mood for the usual banter as they had exchanged at the fight club. But when those dark eyes turned, Leo got the same impression. Neither of them were happy to be here.

"You need to leave," the darkness grumbled, so little conviction behind it that Leo wondered if he realized he sounded like a broken record.

"I could say the same to you."

"I'm actually serious this time," the darkness' mean eyes narrowed into slits. "Matthew's here."

For a moment, he wondered if his heart had stopped beating completely. His limbs went weak and a heaviness settled on him, greater than anything he had ever known before. The world went deathly still for just a few seconds while his frozen mind tried to grasp the full meaning.

Matthew was here. Not coming. Here. In Levi.

He didn't know what to ask, what to do. Once the shock wore away, other emotions, stronger and consuming, took over. Fear and anger went unchecked, but he couldn't move. Couldn't speak. He simply stood there and wondered what he was going to do now that his brother had finally caught up with him.

"Matthew will kill you and banish me for trying to hide you." The darkness shrugged, already reticent to his fate. "Of course, he could toy with you for a while first. Slowly picking off everything you've grown attached to here. The horses, the sheep, the dog..."

"Belle." The name came out breathy, betraying the toxic mix that stormed in his chest.

A rueful smile spread over the darkness' face. "You don't have to worry about your little tart. She'll be fine. You should be more worried for yourself... Unless she..." That sudden thought scared the darkness into silence, but Leo was far more interested in the first part.

"She'll be fine?" he parroted.

The darkness' throat worked before answering. "Yeah, she'll be fine. She's got her own protection."

Leo didn't have to think too hard about what the demon meant. After witnessing all that praying she did at church the day before and knowing that it had some true effect in her life, he understood why she'd be perfectly fine, and he was still in danger. She had God on her side. He didn't.

This new piece of information finally caught up with him. "I was making blood payments for both of us... when she didn't even need them?"

Belle had her own kind of protection. Leo had wasted his blood and his sanity to make sure the darkness didn't come anywhere near her, when in reality, he was paying only for himself and making the darkness even stronger for it. The darkness made him believe his pain was actually worth something.

By his unchanged, pitiless expression, Leo knew he suspected right.

Unable to hide his frustration, he slammed his fist into one of the porch posts. The white paint flecked atop the broken wood beneath. Though hardened by years of fighting and punching soft flesh and bone, his calloused knuckles were cut open. A bit of bright red blood marked the glossy varnish.

It was all completely and utterly pointless. Everything. The cutting, the fighting, the physical pain and mental anguish he suffered, thinking that he was the only line of defense between Belle and the darkness.

He paced back and forth across the porch, minding not to come too close to the darkness or he'd take advantage of this bit of vulnerability. Not even cursing or letting out suppressed screams could ease this new wash of total helplessness.

"It wasn't like that to begin with," the darkness said, as if that was any consolation. "I didn't realize she had her own guard detail."

Leo turned and looked to him questioningly.

The darkness rose from the chair and stood, arms dangling at his sides. "I might as well come out with it since I'll be banished before the end of the week anyway. Matthew's bound to find out how I've been cloaking your trail and that'll be the end of it for me... It was fun while it lasted."

Leo wouldn't have called the last twelve years "fun" under any interpretation of the word. "What guard detail does Belle have?" he asked, beyond frustrated now.

"You don't see them? Interesting. You can see me, but you can't see them."

"See what?" Leo demanded, wishing the darkness was a solid man so he could let out some of his anger in a more violent, satisfying way.

The darkness gave a mirthless smile. "No wonder you were so clueless. It's why I can't stay here when that girl's around. It's why we've needed to leave Levi since the beginning. If they could, they would have destroyed me already, but you've been keeping me just strong enough to merely exist here. I've been restricted to parlor tricks like those electrical shortages, but nothing more. Do you know how embarrassing that is?"

Leo could feel a bit of blood creep down his fingers which coiled into fists. "You need to start making sense."

"The things I've been... I've been scared of. They grow stronger all the time. Matching me. Toying with me. It's infuriating."

"I could name a few other things that are just as infuriating."

The darkness took a slow breath. "Listen, I know your tiny brain can't fully grasp all this, but trust me. The things that are guarding Belle are doing their job very well. I, on the other hand, have been trying to do mine, but they won't let me. But when Matthew shows up, I'll be gone. Poof. Done. And do you know where that will leave you? On the chopping block. I torture you, but Matthew will kill you. If we leave now, we can get away from these..." His eyes wandered to some point beyond Leo. "We can get away from these things and we could both live another day. I can mask you from Matthew again, because I won't have those things weakening me."

Leo took a moment to let it all sink in. If he stayed, he died. If he ran, he would live, but he'd lose Belle. That might as well have been like death. He needed time to think and assess the options.

"Is Belle safe from Matthew?" he asked. "You said she'd be fine, but you started to say something and stopped."

The look in the darkness' eyes wasn't convincing and without having to say a word, Leo commanded honesty.

"Matthew has allies stronger than me, and I've been able to match these things blow for blow. It's... I don't know. I really don't know. She's safe from me, that's all I know. If those things grow stronger, Matthew might not be able to touch her, but..."

"If they grow weaker..." The darkness didn't need to finish the thought for him. If Belle stopped praying, if her own guards grew weaker, then she'd be open to attack from Matthew and the darkness. "I'm not giving any more blood payments," he announced.

The horror in those black eyes might have been satisfying enough. "You can't just stop paying me! We had a bargain!"

"Aye, and the terms have changed," Leo returned with just as much fury. "You haven't been doing anything for Belle and that broke our agreement long ago. I'm not obligated to you at all."

The darkness dematerialized for only a moment, long enough to dart toward him in a mist and reappear too close for comfort. Leo staggered back into the porch railing.

"No, the amendment to our contract is voided, if anything. The deal you made with me after leaving Brooklyn is still valid. You want me to leave you alone, I need payment."

The crazed look about him reminded Leo of a druggy in desperate need of a fix. He could see it in the way his black veins stood out against the pale skin of his face and neck. The darkness was weak, tired, and if he didn't get it, Belle's own protectors would do away with him. Leo could be moved to sympathy by many things, but he had no attachment or feelings of mawkish kinship for the darkness. None whatsoever. Even if he had been his constant companion for over a decade. He could be banished, annihilated, trapped in hell forever for all he cared.

A sinister, devious smile transformed his expression once more, the shift so sudden that Leo almost flinched. "You see, the girl may have protection, but you don't."

He lifted one hand, its fingers spread wide like he would grab at Leo's face. The once blunt, perfectly rounded nails sharpened and extended into blackened talons. He leaned away from its poisonous touch, knowing what would happen if just one tip made contact with any part of him. He could already feel his soul begin to empty and fossilize. Such lifelessness wasn't unfamiliar to him, but he had hoped to never feel it again.

"I still have you, Leo," the darkness whispered, haughty and fully aware that there was nothing his prisoner could do to stop him. "I can zap every bit of happiness right out of you. Do you want to feel that again? Do you want to get sucked into that void? I can send you there and leave you in it."

Leo shut his eyes against the prospect. This was why he made the blood payments in the beginning. Anything to stave off the full impact of the memories, the guilt, the shame, the hopelessness that nearly drove him to end his life just to find some relief.

He couldn't go back. Not when he had Belle. She might have been fine without him, but he couldn't do without her.

"Fine," he barked, quickly moving away to march toward the front door. "But I'm only going to give you what I think is an even exchange. Those... things can do what they want with you."

He left the darkness behind, though he knew it was following him. It always did when he was about to do something he'd regret.

In the kitchen, on the counter, was a block of knives. The serrated steak knives wouldn't leave a clean slice. Though it would be more painful, it would leave a worse scar and he wanted to cut down on the visibility this time. Someone who cared might see it.

He pulled out each of the handles and debated, all while the darkness gave his own opinion over his shoulder. Finally, Leo settled on the boning knife and prepared himself over the sink.

Two cuts? No. Three. That should be enough for a little while. Just enough that the darkness would leave his soul alone, leave it able to feel and enjoy what time he might have left with Belle. He knew for a fact that he wasn't leaving. Matthew might kill him, but he'd die a free and feeling man who knew the love of a woman. Only death could keep him away now.

There had only been a handful of times when Belle felt so mentally and emotionally exhausted that she almost couldn't keep her eyes open. It was ten minutes until closing time. Ray had received an urgent call and left early, and though Ivy had been hesitant, she asked if she could leave, so she could get to her evening shift at the diner in ample time.

So, Belle was left alone in the bookstore, tasked with closing up for the night after one of the busiest days in a long time. She sat at the counter, chin propped in her palm as she watched the front door. No one had come in or out for a while now, and she wondered if she could get away with closing early. Soft jazz music that she hadn't heard for most of the morning, sounded so loud in her ears. The only interruption came from the cars that drove past the store on Main Street.

She let out a sigh and allowed her tired eyelids to close for what seemed like only a minute.

"Excuse me?"

The masculine voice startled her awake and she nearly fell out of the stool she had been perched on. A hand reached over the counter to take her arm to keep her steady, but her brain went scrambling for that mask.

"Sorry," he said. "Didn't mean to scare you."

Belle looked up and was met by a pair of blue eyes that seemed so familiar at first that she had to blink a few times. The eyes belonged to a face that was not as familiar, but there were still trace elements that reminded her of someone. The shoulder-length dark hair didn't help her rationalize that she had never met this man before in her life. Neither did his tallness. There weren't that many tall men in Levi, save for one.

"Oh, it's fine." Belle shook her head to get rid of her grogginess. "I didn't know anyone else was in here."

He smiled, and she instantly found him charming. "I'm a pretty quiet guy. I've been in here for the last half hour."

Belle glanced over her shoulder to the ticking clock on the wall and saw it was already ten minutes past the hour and she was late to close. "I am so sorry." Once more, she tried to find her bearings. "Did you need anything?"

The man held no books, yet he had been in there for quite a while. He must have needed something.

"I was looking all over, and I couldn't find your New Age section."

New Age? Belle's mask, which usually saved her face from scrunching at any customer's strange questions, failed her now. "New Age?... I don't think we have one of those."

The man gave her a blank look, as if he thought she might have still been too sleepy to answer his question. Belle had been working at New Beginnings Bookstore for years and they had never received a book that was labeled "New Age".

What he had to say next made her understand why.

"It's a genre dedicated to metaphysics and spiritualism."

Belle bit her lip. "Like, religious books?"

He shrugged his broad shoulders. "In a way, but it's not a specific religion."

To Belle, religion and spirituality had always been intertwined, but the customer suggested differently. And the customer was always right. "Are you looking for a specific book?"

"Not at all," he replied. "I was just hoping to browse. I travel light, so if I buy any books, they're digital."

The bane of every bookseller. eBooks. But Belle wouldn't be deterred by that, because he would be leaving soon anyway.

"Well, I'm sorry we didn't have more for you to browse," she said as she fully dismounted from the stool – dropping a good way to the ground. "We're just a small-town bookstore. You might have better luck in Little Rock. They've got a lot of big-name bookstores, but you might not find anything in this part of the state."

"I may be staying in Levi for a while, but I'll keep that in mind when I leave."

He followed too close behind her as she made her way to the front door. Belle made an effort to keep her pulse under control. The bakery across the street was still open, their lights were on, and she could see people in the window. If this man intended her harm, she could scream, and someone was bound to hear her.

Jumping to such paranoia wasn't unlike her, but Belle still felt guilty for it. She tried to remind herself that not all men were predators. Then she wondered if women who had been raped or assaulted had tried to keep an open mind too.

"What brings you to our little corner of Arkansas?" she asked, hoping to at least seem polite and cordial.

"Family," he replied a little flatly.

"Just visiting?"

He gave a sardonic smile. "Something like that."

Curiouser and curiouser, as Lewis Carrol had once put it. Belle let out a breath and opened the door for him. For once, she was able to put on that fake smile. "I hope you enjoy your time with your family, then."

He didn't leave right away. He stood in the open doorway, the evening wind gushing between them to fight back the air conditioning. His eyes, the ones that seemed so uncanny, contained a sort of deepness that made the hairs on the back of her neck stand at attention. His stare was piercing, as if he were looking for something in her face and it was a matter of life and death to find it.

Losing her nerve, she dropped her gaze and felt her cheeks tingle with a blush.

"You're Annabelle Clearwater, aren't you?"

The completely enigmatic nature of the question made her look back up. "Sorry?"

"Annabelle Clearwater. That's your name, isn't it?"

Her nametag only read "Belle" and there was absolutely no natural way that he would know her full, given name and her last name too. A bigger question was whether she would confess it to be true or not.

She shivered as the air grew frigid around them. "I'm sorry, should I know you?"

That charming smile returned, but it seemed so out of place with those eyes now that she couldn't find him appealing, even if she wanted to. "No, not really. But I think we'll get to know one another very well before I leave."

With that, he turned up the collar on his jacket and left the store. Belle stood there, trying to make sense of the encounter. She might as well have been trying to dump water on an oil fire. He didn't give his name, but he knew hers all too well. What kind of man parts ways without a formal introduction after something like that? And how cryptic could one person possibly be and still be speaking English?

Belle peeked down the sidewalk, but the man was long gone. She closed the door and immediately locked it tight, leaving only her and the jazz music. It wasn't until she slipped her keys back in her pocket that she realized how badly she was shaking. The man had messed her up for sure.

It's over now and you probably won't see him again. You're fine.

As she made her way toward the back of the store to turn off the lights and do one last trash check down the aisles, her phone buzzed in her pocket. There was only one person who could have been calling her and she struggled to whip the phone out from her jeans to answer.

"Belle, are you all right?"

Leo's lilting Scottish voice had never been more soothing to her raddled nerves.

"Yeah, I'm fine. I just had a late customer. Ray and Ivy bailed on me, so I'm having to close up by myself."

"You're alone?" The panic in his voice might have been contagious if it were coming from anyone else.

"I am now. A customer just left."

"Who was the customer?"

Belle stopped and could feel her brows knitting together as she stared into the darkened storage closet. "Some guy looking for New Age books. He's gone now." The sigh from the other end of the line was so audible that Belle angled the phone away from her face, so it wouldn't ring in her ears. "What's wrong?"

"Nothing," he replied curtly. "You're coming home soon?"

Something sounded so pleasant about that question, as did what Leo had said to her earlier that day. There was a certain appeal to the way he referred to her farm as his own home too, the one they shared. Though, there was nothing totally permanent about the arrangement, she couldn't help wishing that it was.

"Yep. I just have to turn the lights off and hop in the truck."

"Promise me you'll be careful out there?"

Belle laughed as she walked to the breaker panel at the back of the closet. "What is it today with you and promises?"

He didn't answer for a while, even after she flipped the switches and narrowly avoided tripping over a box of paperbacks on the floor. "Nothing. I just want to make sure you know that I need you to be safe."

She shut the door and leaned against it, her eyes roaming over the shadowy bookstore interior. How could she give a comeback for that? Was she supposed to thank him for caring? Make some witty, sarcastic comment to disguise how touched she truly felt? Reply with her own true wish that he, too, was safe and well?

He saved her the trouble.

"Have you... Have you prayed today?"

He hadn't asked that in a while. At least half a week. "No, I don't think I have. I haven't really had the time."

"Please pray before you leave the store."

It wasn't a question, but a gentle, noninvasive order. Belle could certainly oblige. One thing she was never too proud to do was pray. "I will. I promise."

She could hear the smile in his goodbyes before they hung up. Belle continued to hold her phone long after she tapped the red button.

What had come over him? Why was he so concerned? Did this have to do with whatever feelings they shared for one another, or was there something more to that bit of alarm in his voice?

Instead of dwelling on those things that would drive her up the wall with worry, she bowed her head and muttered out a quick prayer for safety, protection, and peace of mind for both her and Leo. The day had been good, despite the absolute rush from earlier that morning and the delicate conversation she'd had with Ivy. She didn't repress a total meltdown and her anxiety only kicked in under extreme circumstances, rather than lingering every hour.

When she was finished thanking God for one good day where she didn't feel like she was totally falling apart, all that remained was her and the empty building.

The long aisles of bookcases loomed like sentinels guarding Levi's only storehouse of knowledge and adventure. There was something peaceful about having the whole store to herself, the door locked, and lights cut. She had toyed with the idea of camping out here some years back, but figured that someone might peek through the windows and find her.

But there was something to go home to for once. A man who cared for her and a puppy who was always up for some cuddling, were waiting for her. How could she ever stay away from that?

Chapter 10

If Belle hadn't reminded Leo about the coffee outing with the men from her church, he would have completely forgotten about it. He would have preferred to stay home, and said so otherwise, but she did her best to kindly suggest that he just bite the bullet and go. What could it hurt?

When he had accepted the invitation, he imagined it would be Mr. Levinson and a few others he met on Sunday morning. He hoped that Mr. Tale would be there, so they could discuss potential work plans for the coming week.

Leo would have to excuse himself from any work he offered until the ewes had begun their lambing, because Belle couldn't take that much time off from work and Mr. Johnson, her usual go-to man about sheep things, was out of town for the next few days. Leo was the only one to be there when the lambs came, and going out for coffee made him feel like he was abandoning his post.

But Belle assured him that she could stay on the farm for another hour or so since she had worked later than usual the previous day. And she showed it. Dragging her feet across the threshold the night before, Leo wondered if she'd collapse on the living room floor. She managed to make it to the sofa. He didn't mind reheating leftovers and serving it to her, so she could rest. But when he went to put on the kettle to make her usual evening tea, she refused. As exhausted as she was, she said she didn't need it to help her get to sleep.

That wasn't a lie. Only halfway through her plate of spaghetti, Belle passed out, her legs curled up on the sofa cushion and face framed by the hair she had let down as she cuddled into one of the throw pillows. Leo had been tempted to leave her like that, but thought better. Instead of draping a blanket over her as he had done once before, he scooped her up and carried her to bed.

Of course, there came the temptation to stay, to slip under the covers behind her and wrap his arms around her torso. He wanted to bury his nose in her hair, feel her warmth, and enjoy the feeling of utter peace and serenity that flowed from her the moment she stepped into the house.

He didn't.

Leo knew it would open the doors for something dangerous. Though it was like leaving a piece of himself in her bedroom, he walked down the hall to the bathroom and reminded himself just why they couldn't get that close.

He kept the scars on his arm hidden. He wore a long-sleeved shirt and fought back the habit to push them up to his elbows so she wouldn't see the bandage. This time, he kept it clean from infection. He even stashed the old bandages in his room, so she wouldn't notice them in the bathroom bin. He even forced himself to stay present, to not let his mind slip back to the day before on the porch when the darkness told him about Matthew and confessed that his pain had been wasted. She couldn't see the worry or the fear that followed him all night and day.

A mask of his own had been forged and he understood a piece of what Belle must have gone through every day. To pretend to be fine when he knew that within a matter of days, he could be dead. Matthew wasn't one to doddle and if he wanted to find Leo, he would. How soon wasn't sure.

He had to think of a way out or a way around the inevitable. Until then, he had to be careful and vigilant. Even here in the coffee shop, far away from Belle and the farm, the darkness could be waiting. He could run into Matthew at any moment.

However, when he stepped through the door and allowed the warm vanilla coffee bean aroma to encircle him, Leo felt something else. That peace that Belle created when she prayed, it was here, too. So stunned by that realization, he stopped on the welcome mat just inside the door and had to gather his wits before taking another step.

The booming laughter in an adjoining room let him know where the other men were meeting. So, he stood in line behind the elderly couple and waited for his turn to order. The two were holding hands and just as affectionate with each other as newlyweds. The old man with white hair planted a kiss on her forehead and she leaned against him.

On any other day, he might have ignored this show of intimacy. Today, he couldn't. What had nearly happened in Belle's bedroom the night before was still fresh in his mind and he couldn't shake the deep, visceral longing to be with her in that moment.

Another thought, one more depressing and heart wrenching than anything else, was that they would never be like that. They would never wear wedding bands or grow old together. They would never be the elderly pair in a coffee shop or a diner, laughing and talking as if they had been friends their whole lives. Belle would live on to find a man who was worthy of her, of course, but not him. His days were numbered.

They moved aside to wait for a bagel and Leo stepped up to order the largest black coffee they had when a hand smacked him on the shoulder. He turned, one hand tightening into a fist and ready to punch whoever it was. His body tensed for the sight of his brother, but was met with Mr. Calloway's smiling face.

Leo told his racing heart to slow, but his defenses wouldn't drop. Not even when the religious man beamed with such vivacious energy.

"Good morning, Leo!" he greeted heartily, and then turned to the cashier who couldn't have been more than one year out of high school. "His coffee's on me."

Hoping that Mr. Calloway wouldn't feel his taut shoulder muscles, he shook his head. "You don't have to do that."

"Of course I do! You took that old stove off my hands. I'm repaying the favor."

It hardly seemed fair, but if the man wanted to treat Leo for such a convenience, he wouldn't argue. While Mr. Calloway paid for their coffees – like he even needed one – Leo peeked into the adjoining room to find the group of men he was to sit with. Mr. Levinson was there, as was Mr. Tale and several others he recognized. The group was far larger than he anticipated, and he wondered how long they could possibly sit around to talk like that. An hour? Maybe two?

He thought of Belle and the farm and the ewes that needed to be watched. He resolved to only stay as long as there was coffee in his cup and then he'd leave.

"Are you here for the men's group?" Mr. Calloway asked as he pocketed his wallet.

Leo nodded and moved away from the counter so the young lady behind them could order. "Are you?"

"Sure am," he replied. "Wouldn't miss it for anything. I've been to every meeting since Chad Clearwater started it, oh... maybe fifteen years back."

At the mention of Belle's father's name, Leo felt his gut harden. "Belle's da?"

"Yep." Mr. Calloway rocked back on his heels proudly, his hands deep in his coat pockets. "It started off with just him and a few other men from church coming to talk, share, and pray. Old Chad may be gone, but he certainly made a legacy for himself."

Pray? They prayed here too? Taking another look at the table, Leo finally noticed the Bibles. Some were open, others closed and sitting beside their cups of coffee and breakfast pastries. Was this why Belle wanted him to go so badly?

"You all right, son?"

Leo started at the word. No one had called him that in... he didn't even know how long. He stared at Mr. Calloway, who was clueless to what he had just done.

The barista called out his order and Leo turned to retrieve it from the counter. "I've got to go," he said. "Thanks for the coffee."

That wouldn't fly and Mr. Calloway only had to say one thing to make him stop dead in his tracks. "You can't run forever... But you're probably figuring that out by now, huh?"

What was it about this man? How did he know everything? Was he some confederate of the darkness or was he on someone else's side, as he had suggested in church? Leo looked to him and kept up his masquerade. Just like with the darkness, he wouldn't show his hand. Not completely.

Mr. Calloway only smiled and jerked his head toward the men in the next room. "Come on. They don't bite."

He walked away, acting on blind faith that Leo would trail after him like some obedient dog. After waiting a few seconds, mentally turning over all of it until he thought he had the right answer, Leo moved.

Room was made for him amongst the grinning faces and with some chagrin, he found he was the only one without a Bible. Mr. Calloway pulled out a small volume from his cargo pocket. Mr. Tale retrieved a chair from another table and positioned it beside himself.

The general consensus was that they were glad to see him, but Leo couldn't shake the feeling that he didn't belong there. These men all believed in something he knew nothing about. Deep down, there existed a faint curiosity about their faith and the power of their prayers, but he had been totally lost during the sermon on Sunday. If he just finished his coffee quickly, he could leave and save himself the trouble of sitting through another boring and confusing teaching.

He did notice, with a little pause, that the pastor who had stood up at the pulpit on Sunday wasn't amongst the group. If this was such an important thing, why wasn't the leader of the congregation here to oversee it?

Taking a sip of his coffee, Leo assessed each of them. They all seemed so happy, chipper, and eager for this meeting to start. Mr. Tale elbowed his ribs.

"We haven't prayed yet," he mumbled.

Looking around, he noticed that no other man was drinking their coffee and the pastries were untouched. There came the vague memory of his grandparents once praying over a meal. All he knew was that he needed to bow his head and close his eyes like the rest of the family at the dinner table and not take a single bite of food until grandpa was finished with some long prayer of thanks. He never paid attention to it. But this was for coffee, bagels, and cinnamon rolls. Why pray over something so small?

Other eyes turned to him, but he only took another long swig of the brew before letting it settle in his lap. Some men chuckled and didn't seem offended at all by his subtle rebellion.

"Care to lead us in prayer, Randy?" Mr. Levinson asked one of the younger men at the table. Besides Leo, the blonde-haired, blue-eyed lad at the other end of the group looked familiar. He thought he had seen him on Sunday, but couldn't be sure.

The instant he smiled, however, Leo could place him. That wide, toothy grin that split his face was probably the most remarkable thing about the man. Randy was important at the church, but not the pastor. He came up to pray over the congregation in between songs and initiated certain proceedings within the service like passing around the collection plate. Afterward, Leo had seen him with a family and their teenage son. The meeting appeared to be an emotional one, but he was too far away to tell what it was about.

In unison, every head was bowed, whether bald, graying, or youthful, as Randy began his little speech to God. Leo thought the prayers pompous and borderline arrogant. It was a time to show off and act like they cared more than they actually did. Granted, his experience was limited. He hoped that Belle didn't pray like Randy or Pastor Kendall.

"Lord, bless this group of men who have gathered here in Your name to fellowship. Bless this coffee and delicious pastries and bless the hands who prepared it. Thank You that we live in a country where we can gather openly like this and talk about You, Your Word, and the love You have for us and all of mankind. Thank you, once again, for sending Your Son to the world, so it may be saved by grace through faith. Let our discussion here this morning be to Your glory. Speak to us through Your Word, so we may know You better. And Lord, thank You that Leo was able to join us. You know he could be in a million other places, but You've called him to be here with us and we are grateful. We pray and ask all of these things in Jesus' name... Amen."

The rest of the men resounded his final close to the prayer, but Leo was left stunned. That was the first time he had ever heard someone openly profess any kind of gratitude for him just showing up. He sunk down lower in his chair, and now that the coffee had been "blessed", he took another sip. It tasted no different.

With his eyes cast down, he resolved to just stay quiet. He had nothing worth adding to this holy discussion and he certainly wasn't going to learn anything of value. God had never helped him before, why should He now? That is, if He was even there.

Mr. Calloway sat up straighter and flipped through his tiny bible. "I know I don't normally propose topics for discussion, but I was reading a passage in Acts the other day and wanted to see what y'all thought about it."

Half of the assembly perked and leaned forward to listen to what he had to say. Others were already turning pages in their Bibles, the thin onion paper crinkling between their fingers as they searched.

"It's chapter nineteen and starts at verse eleven, but I suppose if we want to look at it within context, the story starts at the beginning of the chapter."

Leo let out a long, mostly muted breath and out of respect for the man, tried not to show how much he wanted to leave in that moment.

Mr. Calloway's voice rang loud and clear across the table, the cadence of his voice rising and falling as he read through some part about a guy named Paul going to a place called Ephesus. Leo assumed that was some country overseas. Maybe in Africa. The passage talked about how he baptized people and preached about Jesus for a few months before leaving.

Then, he came to the part he wanted to ask the others about. By now, almost every man was fixated upon their Bibles and Mr. Tale angled his toward Leo, so he could follow along if he wanted to. Again, to show respect for his employer, he read.

It spoke of Jewish men trying to exorcise an evil spirit. Leo's fingertips pressed into the cardboard sleeve around his coffee cup as he read how the men said, "We exorcise you by the Jesus whom Paul preaches." Leo assumed that was the same man from the previous section. It seemed legit, but the logistics didn't make sense. Couldn't they have done it on their own?

"And the evil spirit answered and said, 'Jesus I know, and Paul I know; but who are you?' Then the man in whom the evil spirit was leaped on them, overpowered them, and prevailed against them, so that they fled out of that house naked and wounded."

Though Mr. Calloway spoke the words so blandly, Leo couldn't resist a smile. Who did they think they were dealing with? Puppies? Of course, they'd be assaulted and sent away. What did they expect when dealing with evil spirits?

That was the hook and Leo didn't see any reason to drink his coffee so fast. He wanted to see what these religious men thought about a bunch of Jews losing to spirits, even with Jesus on their side.

"Why do you think the exorcists failed to cast out the demons?" Mr. Calloway asked the group.

"Authority," one farmer answered. "It all goes back to authority."

Mr. Levinson added, "It's authority, but it's also faith. They didn't actually have faith in the name of Jesus. They were just throwing it around, because they saw Paul do it while he was in Ephesus."

Mr. Tale nodded in agreement. "It's like handing a tool to someone who doesn't know how to use it."

"They didn't know the true power of the name they were speaking," Randy said. "All they knew was what Paul had preached and they were just imitating him. They were trying to use it for their own glory as well, rather than doing it to glorify God or Jesus."

Mr. Calloway held up a hand to get their attention again. "But the next part of the chapter talks about how the name of the Lord Jesus was magnified and many came forward to confess their sins and believe. In the end, their failure did glorify God in a way."

One man whom Leo didn't recognize huffed at the assumption. "Only because it made the Jewish exorcists and the sons of Sceva look bad."

Mr. Levinson nodded again. "It showed that there was true power in Jesus' name and even the demons and evil spirits acknowledged him."

"That word!" One man sitting beside Randy pushed up his thick glasses and then pointed to his text. "My Bible commentary goes on about the direct Greek meaning of the word 'know' in this passage. The evil spirits acknowledged and knew Jesus intimately – that is, not carnally, but personally. So they were saying that they would respond to Jesus and Paul, because they were given authority over the spirits, but they had no obligation to the Jews, because they didn't own the authority."

The farmer who had first spoken waved his hand. "Like I said! It's all about authority."

"And we only obtain authority through our faith," Mr. Calloway reasoned. "But we have to walk in it, otherwise it's useless."

Many more nodded and agreed, adding in their own comments and conjectures about the scripture. All the while, Leo could feel himself edging closer and closer to the table, his stare darting to every man who spoke as he tried to follow. One minute, it all made perfect sense and then the next, they were throwing out words like faith and he was lost.

"You're saying," Leo began when there came a brief pause, "that a man can have authority over a demon?"

They all looked to him and seemed just as surprised as he was that he even dared to ask the question. Mr. Calloway closed his pocket Bible and folded his arms over the edge of the table. "It's a little more complex than that, but yes. All men who believe the Lord has empowered them can do it through His name."

Leo blinked and tried not to look as stupid as he felt. "But how do you get that kind of power?"

"In the first chapter of Acts," Mr. Tale explained, "Jesus says that he'd send the Holy Spirit and with Him, they would have power to do all the things that Jesus did during his ministry."

Randy ticked off the abilities on his fingers. "Healing, exorcism, being a witness to the lost, empowering one to proclaim the truth of the gospel, and to recognize sin within yourself."

Leo continued to struggle. "So, the exorcists should have been using this Holy Spirit to cast out the evil. Not Jesus."

"Jesus is the Holy Spirit," Mr. Levinson corrected. "And Jesus is Lord as well."

"You're only confusing him," the hollow-cheeked farmer chided. "He needs milk, not meat."

What Leo needed was stronger coffee. He wanted to understand, no matter how long it took. If anything they said could benefit him, it might have been this. He wanted to know the trick to controlling the darkness, if it really was a trick at all. "Wait, go back to the part about authority. Who is the one with authority here? Jesus or me?"

Mr. Calloway spoke slowly, probably in response to his frantic tone. "Jesus gives the authority to those who call on Him, receive His forgiveness, and invite the Holy Spirit into their lives. Only then would they have the same power that Jesus had when he cast out demons and commanded evil spirits."

"Just like he did in the book of Mark, chapter four," one of the other men joined.

The farmer with the thick glasses chimed in a little loudly. "No, it was chapter five when he cast out the legion of demons from the man in the cave. You're thinking of the book of Luke in chapter five when the demons throw themselves at Jesus' feet."

Another member of the group smirked. "Yeah, and Jesus told them to shut up and get the heck out."

Mr. Calloway grinned as if the next bit of scripture made him ridiculously happy. "And then they spoke among themselves, saying, 'What a word this is! For with authority and power He commands the unclean spirits and they come out.'"

Leo had to know this power, had to wield it for himself. Maybe that was the key to finally being rid of Matthew and the darkness. But how could he get a straight answer out of these guys? They talked about faith and authority and all the things he didn't know. This was the tip of the iceberg and he had a feeling what lay beneath the surface was far more complicated.

He only hoped that Belle could wait a little longer before he came home.

For the first time in what seemed like ages, Belle felt like everything was finally coming together. Maybe it was the spell of calm after the storm of emotion she had weathered the day before. After the reconciliation with Ivy, the difficult day at work, the creepy customer, coming home to Leo's comforting arms was like stepping into the eye of a tornado. Calm and still, with chaos swirling all around, but never touching her. He blew away every trouble and she was able to forget long enough to let exhaustion take over.

Waking up that morning to Leo cooking breakfast downstairs completed the picture of home she had always dreamed of. No anxiety, no worry, just this warm feeling in the pit of her stomach that everything would be all right.

But that word, the one she feared to even think was barred from the picture. No need to ruin it with false expectations. The way he seemed to care was enough. There was no need to complicate this with anything more than that. This deep, meaningful friendship would stay just as it was until she witnessed something stronger in return. The kisses, and near kisses, wouldn't count until she further understood their purpose.

Until then, Belle would let business continue as usual. The eyesore of half-burned cabinets in the kitchen was the only catalyst for the slightest bit of panic, but Leo assured her that he would get them replaced. And she trusted him.

As she looked over her shoulder, one hand on the backdoor knob, Belle tested that feeling. Trust. She was learning to give it a little more freely these days, now that Leo had taught her that not everyone was out to embarrass her, ridicule her, or use her anxiety against her. So many things had changed since he came around and she prayed that they would continue to change for the better.

With Ranger yipping and chasing after a dangling shoelace, Belle made her way out to the sheep pasture to give out their feed.

The stallion, Buck, was still getting used to his new home. He wandered in a smaller, fenced-in portion of the pasturelands adjacent to the enclosure where the mares roamed. After a few days, she decided that she'd introduce Maggie first. She might not have been the mellowest or the most submissive, but that middle-ground temperament would set him off on a better foot than if she tried to pair him with Snow right out of the gate.

Looking to the docile stud, Belle couldn't help but smile. Not because she could see the small ways in which he was warming up to the place, but because of what his presence on the farm meant. This place had a future. The path to growing her business was being slowly cleared and she had Leo to thank for it. She would have never been able to afford Buck so soon, but he and God made a way.

And she wouldn't deny God's hand in all of this. The way the community came together to help her after the barn burned down, the way Leo had saved her countless times, how despite evil trying to stick its grubby hand into her affairs, she came out of it alive and in better shape than before.

All things work for good for those who love Him and are called to His purpose. Belle liked to think that this was God's purpose. To be at peace and to honor her family by growing the farm they began so long ago.

She took up a bucket of supplement feed out to the sheep pasture. Before she even approached the fencing, she could hear their loud bleating and cries for attention. This seemed a little odd, given that they usually didn't demand treats until she was within sight.

Ranger slipped through the fencing and scampered among their spindly legs, but none of them seemed frightened of him. Hopefully that would change when he grew a little bigger over the next six months.

Belle cooed and talked to them as she always did and spread out the supplements in their feeding trough. But as she walked away, some of them didn't stay at the trough. They followed close on her heels, nudging their heads against her knee and calves as she tried to step around them.

It was then she realized two were missing. Sunflower and Heather were not amongst the few who hungrily gobbled up their feed, and neither were they part of the bunch that crowded around Belle. They were off near a section of fencing about a dozen yards away. They rubbed against the fence and though the facial expressions of sheep were rather limited, she understood that look.

One peek at Heather's backside confirmed it. The wool seemed a little extra damp and dingy, as if she had sat in something.

Belle inspected each of the other sheep and though they didn't show the same signs as Heather, she knew what would be coming later that day. Out of the seven Finn ewes, five were ready to lamb.

For a moment, she stood dumbstruck and counted the days from when she knew Butch had worked them over. Was it really that time? She knew it was close, but she had no idea it had been that close. With everything that had happened, the date snuck up on her.

Standing there, with three Finns almost clamoring up her legs and two more that needed to be moved into the barn, Belle realized how alone she was. And with that feeling of isolation came the panic. She tried to breathe and mentally listed out everything that would need to be done. All her supplies were either in the house or the shed, and though she knew it was best to assist with the lambing, her ewes were perfectly capable of doing it on her own. The prep work was what sent her heart into palpitations.

She set the bucket down and grabbed for her phone in her pocket. The absolute first thing she would need to do was call Ray at the bookstore. There was no way she'd be able to go to work now.

Chapter 11

Leo had stayed far too long at the coffee shop. Checking his phone on the way to his bike, he realized just how late he was. Hunger didn't even register to him, but he had skipped lunch entirely. Not everyone stayed in the group after the first couple of hours and he was tempted to feel a little guilty for dominating the discussion. No one called him out for it, but he could sense the slight annoyance in the other men whom he didn't know all that well.

The others, like Mr. Tale, Mr. Levinson, and Mr. Calloway, were far more patient and willing to answer his many questions in the best way they knew how. But after so many hours of deliberation over the topics of demons, angels, and the miraculous ability to command any of them, Leo still felt confused and like he was lacking in something. It was as if his mind and heart wanted to understand, but something kept him from fully grasping the concept.

Mr. Calloway had written down a heavy reading assignment for him to complete before the next time they met. Two whole books in the New Testament. It seemed like a monumental task for a man who hadn't read a book from cover to cover since grade school, but

Mr. Calloway assured him that it wasn't so difficult. He also said that Belle would be more than willing to help.

Leaving the coffee shop, he sent Belle a quick text to apologize and let her know that he was headed back to the farm. He received no reply, and when he pulled up to the house, her truck was still parked near the porch steps. The moment he shut off the engine, he heard her shouts from the barn. That sent him running. The worst scenario passed through his thoughts that Matthew had finally come and decided to go straight for Belle, rather than face him like a man.

But when Leo saw that Ranger sat just outside the stables, tail wagging and completely unfazed, he suspected that his brother hadn't made his grand appearance yet. Ranger had already shown himself to be intuitive when it came to matters of the darkness, and if Matthew had been anywhere close, Leo suspected Ranger would have been the first to know it.

What he found in the sheep barn might have been more distressing than if Matthew, indeed, had arrived to the farm.

A few of the pens that lined the interior wall of the barn were occupied, and the pitch of the bleating sounded strangely high and less robust than he was used to. In the center, Belle knelt in a fresh, shallow pile of straw, one hand deep inside the ewe laying in front of her. Her hair was back, but one long strand hung over her cheek as she tossed her head to look his way.

Despite the cold, sweat glistened on her neck and down her chest and arms that were exposed by the tank top she had stripped down to. The fabric hugged the slender curve of her waist and showed off the strong, lean muscles of her back. This might have been the first time he had seen her in something so form-fitted. Though he might have enjoyed the sight, the dirt and unidentifiable substances along her forearms made him hesitate.

Her emerald eyes spoke enough. She had probably been doing this for hours and he hadn't been there to help. Scattered around her were other tools she had mentioned before when she talked about lambing. An oral syringe, medicines, a spray bottle of disinfectant, and new tags littered the operating area.

"What can I do?" he asked, unsure himself if he was ready for this. But he had let Belle down by staying at the coffee shop too long. She didn't have the luxury of opting out, so he didn't either.

"Just keep her steady," she replied breathlessly. Her face scrunched as she twisted her hand further into the ewe. "Shouldn't be too much longer for this one."

Leo wasn't about to ask how she could possibly know that and hurried to crash down in front of the ewe. As gentle as possible, he braced his hand on the sheep's back and shoulder, mindful to let her tense if she needed to, but he applied just enough pressure, so she didn't thrash too much.

"Before you even think it," Belle said with a note of humor, "I haven't been doing this all day. Daisy's been having issues for a couple of hours now. The rest lambed just fine."

Leo shrugged his brows. "I would hope you haven't had your hand up a sheep's... up a sheep's bum all day, but I wasn't going to ask."

She slid him a smile. It seemed a wonder at all that she could joke and tease in a moment like this.

Silently, he watched Belle work and probe. She was right. Within moments, he witnessed what some would call the miracle of birth. To him, it looked more like a slimy, bloody mess.

Belle held the lamb by the forelegs and gave a firm, constant tug to help it leave the birth canal. Its head emerged after the legs. The rest slipped through quickly and easily. Belle pinched her fingers between the lamb's jaws to break the mucus seal and then blew on its nostrils to help it breathe for the first time. The newborn flailed as she took up a wad of hay and rubbed it against its chest. It gave a short bleat to let them all know it was alive. After administering the dose of vitamins with the oral syringe and spraying its underbelly, Belle swiveled the lamb toward Daisy's head in his direction.

"She'll lick the rest off," she told Leo, referring to the coating of slime that covered the lamb's body.

There was no hiding his look of disgust when the ewe began to do exactly as Belle said. But what startled him more was when she sat back on her heels again and reached inside one more time.

"Another?"

Belle smiled and nodded. "Finns usually crank out twins or triplets." She gave a nod toward the other occupied pens and saw that each one was filled with at least two lambs who were testing out their knobby, unsteady legs.

His head hung for a brief moment before he looked back to Belle, unable to contain an apology any longer. "I'm sorry," he said. "I wasn't here and I have no excuse."

"You were at the coffee shop with the guys, right?" she asked as she continued to search for the forelegs of the twin.

"I was, but I didn't need to stay as long as I did."

Her eyes flitted in his direction, but he sensed no aggravation or resentment in her question. "Did you have a good long talk?"

Leo's lips pressed together. After a few seconds to come up with a hasty answer, he said, "I guess so. I wasn't... I wasn't expecting all of that, though. You could have told me."

Despite how tired she must have been, Belle's face brightened with a look similar to mischievousness. "I knew how it used to be when my dad arranged everything, but I didn't know if they kept it the same. They didn't talk about cars and sports?"

Leo huffed. "No. Nothing like that."

"Well, I'm glad they're keeping some traditions alive. Who all was there?"

If she was trying to make conversation to distract him from the fact that the ewe was still licking her newborn lamb, she was failing. But he talked back anyway. He went into listing off the men who were present, all the while trying not to look at the ewe or the way Belle's hand continued to reach.

She nodded at a few of the names and her brows twitched at some others. "Mr. Calloway's always there. He never missed a meeting, but he never could stay consistent with church attendance."

From what Leo witnessed, he had a hard time believing that. Out of all the men present, he appeared to know the most. He even surpassed Randy on a few topics and corrected him on citing his sources within the Bible. If he knew more than the assistant preacher, then he might as well have been the most reliable teacher in all of Levi.

"He seems like... I don't know. Just really devout." Leo didn't know how to say it without sounding like he condemned the whole religion.

Zealous, arrogant, pompous, and know-it-all didn't seem like the right words. He knew a lot, but he never gave the impression that he was holier than anyone else. Maybe that's why Leo finally decided that he liked the man in the end. He wanted to help without being overbearing. He didn't drag Leo into the conversations and welcomed his questions and input without putting him down for not knowing the simplest of things.

"He's certainly a man of God," Belle said, sounding a little distracted by what was at the end of her fingertips. "He and my dad talked all the time about spiritual things. They didn't always see eye-to-eye, though."

Leo frowned. "Did they argue?"

She shrugged her shoulders, making the collar of her tank top rise and fall in a way that drew his attention too effectively. "Not really. I mean, some of their discussions got a little heated, but my dad never really got mad. They just agreed to disagree."

"From what you told me, it's hard to imagine your da getting upset about anything at all."

Belle made a face. "I only saw him really upset once and he had a very good reason. He was on the phone with my mom and had to break the news that he wouldn't let me see her anymore until she got her act together. It didn't go well. There was a lot of screaming."

It was still hard for Leo to fully wrap his head around how much of a train wreck her childhood had been. Of course, he was in a similar boat, but at least she appeared to have moved on from it all and made the best of it. Yes, she still had her anxiety issues, but she had the strength to persevere through them. Leo only knew how to run from everything. What Mr. Calloway had said in the coffee shop just before Leo was ready to run out the door had stuck with him. Maybe he had been running all his life. He made himself believe that he had no choice, but the choice was there all along. Only now was he making up his own mind to stay, to face it, to fight it.

In Leo's silence, Belle had grabbed the twin lamb's legs and pulled it out just as easily as the first. She carried out the same procedure as before with no issues, just in time for the ewe to trade out lambs. Belle took one of the towels from nearby and wrapped up the first lamb to transfer it into a vacant pen.

"How many more?" he asked, monitoring the ewe as she left to put the lamb away.

"Three have lambed now, but there's still two more that should be ready soon. When their first fluid sack ruptures, you'll know it's time."

"Like their water breaking?" Leo might not have known much, but he remembered a few things from school.

She nodded. "Something like that."

"And the rest?"

Belle came back with the towel and used the clean side to wipe off her hands. "The Suffolks are out in the pasture with Butch and the other two Finns who haven't shown any signs yet. But it's only a matter of time before they start lambing too." She plopped down onto the hay and watched her ewe with a mixed look of exhaustion and fondness. "I totally lost track of the days. I knew this was soon, but I didn't think this soon."

Once more, Leo felt the pangs of regret. "I truly am sorry for not being here."

She waved him off and almost brushed back the loose strand, but thought better of it when she looked to her dirty hand. "Even if you were here, I would have left work to help. Not that you couldn't do a good job, but it would have been a little hard to explain all of this over the phone."

He nodded and allowed himself a tiny smirk. "I won't disagree with you on that."

"Granted, most ewes don't have a problem on their own, but there's all the extra bits that go along with taking care of the lambs."

Leo dropped his stare back to the ewe and its twin, wondering how much longer she needed to keep cleaning off the gunk and slime. "I take it you've done this a lot?"

"Every year since I was a kid," she replied proudly. "Sometimes twice a year. My dad did most of the work back then and I did what you're doing now. Just watching and holding."

It occurred to him that his hands were still on the ewe and he lifted them away to allow her to shift a bit. "Is there anything else I can do?"

Belle looked around to the ewes in their pens and shook her head. "I don't think so. They've all nursed a little and haven't had any issues yet, so this is going pretty smoothly so far. You could go out and check on the other Finns in the pasture and see if they're showing any signs yet."

Leo didn't hesitate. "Just looking for that water break?"

"Yep. And if they are, bring them here so I can see how far along they are."

He left the barn, eager to get away from the slightly sickening sight of the ewe's cleaning ritual. Though, he didn't want to be away from Belle. He had let her down once by not being there and he didn't want to make that mistake again.

The sheep were slightly disappointed that he brought no treats with him into the enclosure, but their crying didn't bother him. He went to the two Finn ewes and checked their backsides.

One was clean, and the other wasn't.

Something didn't seem quite right about the second. Not only was her wool matted and damp, but there were remnants of blood as well and a similar goo as he had seen from the ewe that just gave birth. He called for Belle and she hustled out to meet him. For a moment, he was worried about her standing in the cold this way, especially since she had been sweating.

He pointed out the Finn and her eyes went wide.

She threw open the gate and bolted inside to get a better look. She didn't seem sure what to do. Her hand came up a few times as if she were ready to check the birth canal, but she hesitated. Her gaze began searching around the feeding trough and the immediate space inside the pasture.

"She's already lambed," Belle reported, leaving the ewe to continue looking. "This happened last year, but I was hoping Azzy wouldn't do this again."

"Do what?" Leo only became a little panicked by proxy. If this was serious enough for Belle to become flustered over, then he had a right to be the same.

"Some ewes just aren't good mothers. Everyone told me I should have sent Azzy away after she abandoned a set of twins last year, but I wanted to give her one more try." Belle stomped her foot in the grass and he could see her begin to shiver. "I should have listened."

"So, where's the lamb?" He found himself searching too. A blob of white amongst a field of green shouldn't have been too hard to spot.

"It could be anywhere. It only takes a few hours for the ewe to lamb, so she could have done it any time since I started working with the others."

The fevered rise in her voice spurred Leo to take action. He came forward and took her by the arms, ignoring the way some of the cold slickness on her skin transmitted to his palms. "Hey. Take a breath. We will find it."

As if Belle had completely forgotten how to breathe, her mouth hung open. Nothing came out at first, but one severe look from him helped her lungs to work again. Belle took a big breath and then another before nodding. They both needed to be calm, especially when they found the lamb. He wanted to ask what happened when a mother abandoned her baby, but such a question would only make Belle panic more.

So, they combed the pasture, heads swiveling in all directions. Even though the sun was high in the sky, the autumn breeze kept either of them from fully enjoying its warmth. While Leo looked for the lamb, he also watched Belle. Her lips quivered, but he couldn't tell if it was from the cold or fear of what they may discover.

After a few moments, they both spotted the mass of white and yellow amongst the grass. They ran and found a set of twins. A few yards separated them. Upon close inspection, Belle pronounced one to be dead.

"Probably from the cold," she said sadly. "Azzy never licked her clean and with this wind... It didn't have a chance."

Leo took bounding steps toward the other and saw it moving. Shivering, but moving. "This one's alive."

Though the filmy layer remained on its body, its dark eyes were cracked open and nostrils flared as it continued to breathe laboriously. Without much thought to himself, Leo stripped off his jacket and scooped up the lamb. His shirt would have been a warmer place for it to cuddle against.

"Take him into the barn and get him cleaned off," she ordered. "I'm getting the thermometer. If we get some colostrum in him quick, we could reverse the hypothermia."

They both moved swiftly to take action. Leo had been used to being the one with the level head between them, but Belle had proven that this was her field. Her area of expertise. This was in her blood, ingrained in her from an early age, and coded in her genes. She understood these sheep better than he ever could, and that's how he knew this farm would become everything she wanted it to be. If she could handle a crisis like a dying lamb, she could take on anything.

Belle returned to the barn with her arms full of supplies, including a jug of water, a thin hose, a feeding syringe, and a tub of something tucked between her elbow and her waist. She dropped in front of him and took the lamb.

"Mix some of the powder colostrum in the water and fill the syringe."

Leo did as he was told while she took the lamb's temperature. He heard her utter up a thanks to no one in particular and then took the syringe from him.

"Is he going to make it?" Leo asked, remembering how Belle had called the lamb a boy earlier when they were in the pasture. How exactly she could tell so soon, he wasn't sure.

She nodded and began to slip the tube down the lamb's mouth and throat. "His temperature isn't so bad, so he just needs to be fed and monitored. If Azzy does what I think she'll do, she won't let the lamb nurse either." Belle shook her head in dismay. "Why didn't I listen to everyone?"

Leo reached out and rubbed at the bare skin of her shoulder. "Because you always think the best of everyone, even animals. There's nothing wrong with that. There's nothing wrong with caring too much."

She passed him a weary smile and attached the syringe to the open end of the hose. "There is when I endanger the lives of someone else... I know it's just a lamb, but a life is a life. I was able to save Azzy's lambs last year, but I knew if it happened again, I might not be so lucky."

The colostrum flowed through the tube and into the lamb's stomach at a slow, easy pace. Leo watched the way he continued to shiver and adjusted the towel around his back while he sat upright in Belle's lap.

"You couldn't have known for sure what Azzy would do if she lambed again, but you hoped for the best. That hope is what matters, right?"

He remembered bits and pieces of what Mr. Calloway said at the coffee shop. Things about faith, hope, and a love that Leo couldn't begin to understand. Seeing Belle try to revive this lamb gave him a glimpse into those ideas that eluded him before. She cared for these lambs as if they were her own children, even if they were bound for the slaughter in a few months. She might have had a feeling Azzy would slip back into her neglectful tendencies, but she hoped the ewe wouldn't anyway. She chose to do what she was supposed to, what was best for her and her lambs.

That kind of hope and blind faith in the positive wasn't something Leo practiced. His life had been spent expecting the worst and getting exactly that. Maybe it was time to make a change.

This would have been a lot easier if just one of the ewes had accepted the orphaned lamb. No matter how hard they tried to coax Azzy into taking back her baby, she wouldn't. The sheep wanted nothing to do with any of the lambs. Belle had no choice but to bottle feed the orphan according to the time table her father had written up years ago. His old pencil markings were nearly faded and she knew one day, she'd have to type up every piece of notebook paper in the beaten plastic binder. Crucial information had been recorded for her, as if he knew that one day she would have to raise the flock without him.

Belle nestled her head in the crook of her elbow and stared down at the sleeping lamb. Just one more hour until she'd have to scoop him out of the makeshift bed in the shipping box and feed him again. Night had settled in and the house was still. There was only her and Ranger in the living room, but while she chose to lounge on the sofa, the puppy wanted to be close to the lamb. Already, Ranger had the instincts of a shepherd.

Leo was in the stables, finishing up the evening chores while she looked after the lamb. She wouldn't be inside for much longer. This orphan was just one of several others who needed to be monitored. The other ewes knew what to do with their young and while some farmers were content to leave them alone for the night, Belle hadn't been raised that way. She and her father would take shifts, just as she and Leo would have to do now, and make sure that every lamb was suckling as needed and none of the ewes acted out as Azzy had.

Her eyes were growing heavy when the backdoor opened. Ranger lifted his eyes, ears popped up and alert. The heavy tread of footsteps through the kitchen disturbed the tranquil silence, but Belle didn't move from her comfortable spot.

"How is he?" Leo asked, leaning over the back of the sofa to take a look into the crate.

Belle smiled. "He's doing just fine. It's a good thing we found him when we did."

This orphaned lamb wasn't her first. He wasn't anything extraordinary. Lambs had survived worse in their first twenty-four hours. But to her, this one was special. It was the lamb she and Leo both tended. Their hands had cleaned him and fed him. Together. This lamb would forever hold a special place in her heart, even if Leo never knew it.

Unlike the others, she wouldn't give him up. She needed another ram anyway, if she wanted to build up her flock. Why not keep him after everything they had been through?

"I just came in for some coffee," Leo said. "Do you want any?"

Much unlike herself, Belle hesitated. Coffee, though it would screw with her anxiety after such a long and trying day, might have been just the thing she needed. The lamb would need to be fed every two hours until the following day, and even then he would need to be fed every three hours. Though she had work the following day, they had agreed on a shift schedule. Five hours each, with Belle running the first round, she'd get just enough sleep to function. While she slept, Leo would take care of the lamb.

She pushed herself up from the sofa cushion and let out a deep sigh. Ultimately, she turned him down.

"I can take the first shift if you need to rest," he said. Could he see how tired she was?

Belle shook her head and the motion made her slightly dizzy. "No, I can take the shift."

Leo wasn't convinced and a gentle hand pushed her back onto the sofa. "You look like you're about to fall over. I don't mind taking the shift. You've had a rough day as it is."

That shouldn't have been a factor in anything. Belle always had rough days. Some were just rougher than others, and not all of them involved looking after pregnant ewes. But she was too tired to argue and settled back down onto the cushion, though a hot bath and plush mattress would have been heaven.

The aroma of percolating coffee revitalized her a little, and the muffled, distant noises of Leo's movements in the kitchen kept her from tipping over the edge of total sleep. Her thoughts wandered, as they always did just before she drifted off to sleep. She thought about Leo, all that she had failed to accomplish that day, what the morning and following afternoon would bring, and everything in between.

But unlike before, those worries didn't latch. Maybe she was just too tired to let them take hold. Or maybe it was the fact that, regardless of all the troubling things she could have thought about, the feeling of rightness had encased her spirit and acted as a barrier against it all. How could it have survived after everything they had been through that day? How could she still feel this good without even trying? She didn't want to think that her anxiety had been totally cured, but it was certainly a nice idea.

The backdoor closed and the soft, creeping smile on her lips stopped. She hadn't expected Leo's sudden absence to hit her so hard. Pulling herself up, she looked into the kitchen. The pile of quilts and pillows she had set out on the dining table were gone and half a carafe sat in the warming coffeemaker.

She sat there, weighing her options. She could stay on the sofa and sleep until her next shift, or go upstairs to officially ready herself for bed and rely on Leo to wake her when the time was right. But there was a third option, one that might have been crazy to even consider.

With one deep breath and mustering of bravery, Belle gathered up the lamb with its blankets and bottle. Ranger was up and awake by the time she shuffled toward the door. With the lamb bleating in her arms, she leaned down to don her boots and jacket.

The night air blasted her with cold the moment she stepped out into the yard. Cradling the lamb close to her chest so it wouldn't be as chilled as she was, Belle hurried to the sheep barn. The silver glow of the electric lamp illuminated Leo's confused face when he saw her walk into the barn. Already settled on the quilt that lay overtop a mound of hay, a steaming cup of coffee in his hand, the scene looked every bit a mistake waiting to happen.

Belle didn't care. For once, she didn't care.

"I thought you were going to sleep?"

Ranger preceded her and began to excitedly sniff around the pens, inspecting each one. Occasionally, a lamb would poke its pale snout through the planks to meet his.

"I thought so too," she replied as she made her way over and sat down next to him. The lamb wriggled in her arms and she let him down to prance and explore with Ranger.

"You probably should get some rest," he said.

Belle nodded. "I know and I will. I just... thought you could use the company." It was a lie. A total boldfaced lie, but it had to be spoken, because Belle had no other way to explain why she wanted to be close to Leo. It wasn't about company or peace or the fact that he had become something like a security blanket. She couldn't name it. Didn't want to. Naming it would bring with it all sorts of complications that she couldn't stomach yet.

For now, she just wanted to enjoy what they had and let herself believe it would last forever.

Leo offered her the mug and against her previous inclination to deny the coffee, she took a sip. The brew was every bit as strong and bitter as she remembered. He laughed at the face she made when she handed it back to him.

"That bad?"

She stuck out her tongue and wished she had some water to chase it with. "Needs sugar or creamer or something."

"It can be an acquired taste." Leo took a long draft of the brew without difficulty and she almost envied him for it. She wasn't sure how she'd stay awake without any caffeine at all.

Belle turned to watch Ranger and the lamb sniff one another and play as if they wouldn't grow up to be on opposite sides of the farm dynamics. Hunkering down on her grandmother's old quilt, she let her tired muscles relax. "Can you make sure he gets fed?"

Leo gave an affirmative as she folded her arms over her stomach and closed her eyes. The only sounds in the barn came from the puppy and lamb's occasional roughhousing, and the shifting of hay coming from the pens. It was just as she remembered from when she was a little girl, the night she had snuck away to hide out in the hay loft. The musty smell of earth and straw, the odors of the animals, and beneath it all, the symphony of quiet that leaked through when the crickets weren't chirping in the forest beyond.

But that barn was gone now. Only her memory remained. Now, she made new ones. With Leo.

After some time, she felt a disturbance beside her. All she could tell was that Leo might have put down his mug – presumably empty now – and shifted so he could stretch one arm above her head while reclining against the hay.

Her heart rabbited against her ribs as she did the unthinkable. Belle rolled into him until she drowned in his warmth and the smell of his deodorant that wafted around her. In response, he didn't shy away. His arm angled in such a way to hold her there, one hand resting comfortably on her arm and her head pillowed by his bicep.

Fingers that trembled curled against his chest, though she longed to reach out and hold him around the waist. Was it right? It felt right, but what would he think of her if she did? Belle curbed this one temptation, reasoning that out of all she had just done, she should hold back this one impulse. No need to go completely insane.

So she let the back of her forearms graze the soft fabric of his shirt, but that was all. Just to be this near, to hear his breaths and know that he was completely and totally real, that was enough. For how long, Belle didn't want to guess.

Chapter 12

It would have been so easy for him to stay like this, holding her beneath this fleece blanket while dawn broke across the Arkansas horizon. The rest of the farm slept except for him. But soon, like clockwork, the rooster would scream as it always did just after sunrise. Until then, he wanted to enjoy this. Having Belle so close, their bodies tangled together, Leo couldn't think of anything better in the world. He kept time with the steady rise and fall of her breathing, counting them and synchronizing them with his own.

He had let her sleep the whole night through. Though they didn't start out this way, he was thrilled when she inched closer and closer each time he laid back down beside her after feeding the lamb and checking on the ewes. Maybe it was drowsiness or perhaps it was her subconscious urging her to wrap her arms around him. Whatever it was, he didn't fight her, didn't resist it.

He would have let them stay that way for eternity, but his coffee mug was empty and he had a long day ahead of him. She would need to go to work and life would carry on. But he'd never forget the serene look on her face, as if she were completely at home with him. To be so wanted, so needed, even like this, was a miracle in itself.

The ephemeral thought came to mind that if things could change, if he had his way and the darkness wasn't around, he'd be with her like this every morning of every day for the rest of their lives. He wouldn't mind that at all. Even if Levi was small and he'd be watched by all the men of the town to ensure he didn't hurt Chad Clearwater's daughter, Leo could call this place his home. His final destination. The deep feeling such a concept brought with it made him grin.

Could such a living be his? Could it be within reach, now that he was learning the secret to controlling the darkness? More Tuesday coffee shop meetings, a little reading in the Bible, and a few long discussions with Belle and Mr. Calloway would equip him with the right knowledge. He just needed time.

Being careful not to wake her, Leo slipped out from under the blanket and made his way out of the barn. Not even Ranger or the lamb, who stayed curled up together near the base of the hay pile, had noticed his absence.

With his mug in hand, he entered the darkened kitchen. He flipped the light switch, but nothing happened. This small occurrence, though simple and harmless as it may have seemed, sent a streak of panic through Leo. He froze and peered around the house, looking for the signs. The temperature hadn't dropped. The shadows around the counter and table didn't lengthen. He didn't feel such an ominous dread in the air. Was it the darkness, or for once was this a natural glitch in the wiring? Belle was on the farm and if her own variety of protection could hold out, the darkness shouldn't have had any power here.

He tried the lights again, keeping his senses attuned to any change. The lights finally kicked on. The sudden brightness startled him and he blinked to let his eyes adjust.

When they did, he saw it. The darkness was tucked away near the partition wall on the living room side, safe from the nearly blinding overhead lights and well out of range. Leo stood there, his gaze locked on the darkness as it stared back at him with a burning directness that could only mean one thing.

Leo drew himself up to his full height and expelled a long breath, waiting to say what he had wanted to say for so long, but never had the courage. But as he studied the darkness, he saw something else. A feebleness that was so uncommon to its nature. Its stare might have been the only firm and solid thing about him. The rest wasn't all there. His form was hazy, blurred, the edges of his limbs and shoulders undulating like a flame whose oxygen was slowly being sapped, but refused to go out.

Everything he had learned the day before came to mind. The countless stories about demons being cast out by the apostles and disciples of Jesus. He wasn't at that stage yet and he knew it. Giving orders in the name of a man he didn't know or understand wasn't an option. He didn't want to be like those Jews who were driven out, because they tried to claim authority when it wasn't theirs in the first place.

But Leo could do one thing.

"You won't get anything from me," he declared.

The darkness lifted its chin. "Excuse me?"

"No more payments." Leo then strode toward the coffeemaker, showing that he was done with the conversation.

"You can't go back on our deal," the darkness hissed as if anything about this meeting was supposed to be secret or private.

"Watch me."

Leo had gotten this attitude before and lost his nerve when the darkness began making its usual threats. Not today. He was ready for what would come. He had to fight it.

"You know what will happen if you go back on our deal," the darkness said, its voice growing louder as if he were drawing closer to Leo's ears.

He only continued to prepare this pot of coffee, mechanically focusing on every movement as if that would drown out the steadily overwhelming presence of the demon in the house.

"You're making a mistake," the darkness said, the words now echoing in his head. It was already beginning.

Leo slammed the rinsed carafe under the dripper. "I've made plenty of mistakes, but this isn't one of them. I'm making my stand here. No more payments, no more deals. You can stay or go for all I care. And Matthew can come do his worst. I'll be waiting."

He turned to see the darkness seething on the edge of the kitchen, the light streaming through his core as if he were nothing more than a mirage of smoke. That's really all he was. If mere men could use little more than their words to command the demons, entities like the darkness were nothing. He had lost his intimidation factor and Leo wouldn't be afraid. Not anymore.

The darkness, angry beyond articulation, had nothing to say in reply to Leo's affirmation. He understood that if the demon didn't receive his blood payment, he would grow weaker. Especially while he was trapped and tormented by Belle's spiritual protectors. Leo might have opened himself up for attack, but if the darkness was as weak and useless as he believed it to be, the possession wouldn't be as horrendous as it had been in the past.

Soon, the cloud of evil dissipated. The lights above flickered and it began. Leo could feel it first in his gut and tracked its poisonous progress through his veins and into his chest. It wrapped around his heart and lungs, rendering him unable to breathe or think through the heaviness that pervaded his limbs.

A million thoughts, all black and laced with acid as they burned pathways through his mind and soul, consumed him and it took all of Leo's resolve not to listen.

You killed them.

It's all your fault.

You're a burden, a nuisance.

End it now.

She doesn't want you.

No one does.

Leo gripped the edge of the countertop and glanced at the knife block. But that's all he did. He glanced. He didn't reach for one of the black plastic handles. He didn't roll up his sleeves. He just took one look and then turned back to his coffee pot, waiting for it all to pass over him.

The thoughts came, one by one, raking their claws across his spirit until he felt himself grow raw and numb to the pain of their words. He didn't let them dwell or sink in. That's where the danger lay. He understood that after years of suffering under this debilitating depression.

He had to keep going, let himself feel every bit of this agony and then move. That's what Belle did, and he could do the same.

That didn't stop the tears from falling or quiet the tremors. He couldn't remember a time when he had been whole. His soul was always scarred, always cracked by these demons and memories. And he could feel those cracks widen, his cords unraveling and fraying at the ends. The pillar of strength he had always relied on to get him through the day was being dented and after a while, he knew it would buckle. Unless he did something to relieve the pressure.

But he had to keep going. If he was busy, he could outshout the demons with his own declarations.

I am useful.

It wasn't my fault.
Belle does want me.
I am needed here.
I am loved.
I am strong.

Just when Belle thought she was beginning to understand Leo, he threw her off balance again. Waking up alone in the barn wasn't her idea of how to end a romantic evening, but that hadn't been the worst part. Finding Leo tending to the horses, visibly different in everything from the look on his face to the way he walked was what had set her reeling.

No longer the eye of her storm, the calm she needed to think and breathe, something had happened. But no matter how many times she asked, he assured that he was fine. He'd brighten for a few moments, but then slip back into that state where he looked barely alive. The only sign that he was cognitive at all was in the way he carried on as if nothing had happened.

Belle fled to her first instinctual reaction. She must have done something wrong. All the way to work, she wanted to smack her head against the steering wheel. It might have been when she went to the barn last night. Or maybe she had gotten too comfortable with him in the hay. She never asked if it was okay to intrude upon his quiet time. She just barged in and made herself at home. Even if it was her barn, it wasn't her shift.

God only knew what Leo must have thought of her now. Clingy, needy, attached. He knew that she was emotional, so that wasn't all too surprising. But what if he suddenly realized this had all gone too far? If that was ever a concern, he should have known that after their first kiss, or their second.

Futilely, she tried to convince herself that if Leo had a problem with her, he would have said so. If this had anything to do with her sleeping beside him in the barn, he would have told her upfront. And if it wasn't that, then what was wrong?

Maybe he was just tired. He had stayed up all night after all. But he had done that before and never looked this haggard and dead on his feet. He didn't exhibit the typical signs of tiredness. Whatever this was penetrated deeper and radiated from him. She could feel it when she came close. A coldness, portentous and sapping. It made her want to take a few steps away, to flee, so she wouldn't be infected. Not even the animals wanted to be near him and gave him a wide berth as he put out the hay and feed in the troughs or ewe pens.

Belle had left the farm after giving him all the instruction he would need regarding their orphaned lamb and the recovering mothers. A nagging feeling persisted, however, that things on the farm would be far from all right that day.

The same situation was mirrored at the store. Belle would have wanted Ivy's company, but this was her usual day off and she had no one to talk to. Especially since Ray was in one of his moods again. Ordering her about, blowing up over small and seemingly inoffensive things, even getting snappy with a customer – which he never did.

The mask that kept her calm and her tongue clamped firmly between her teeth wouldn't allow her to call him out for it like she wanted to do so often. After ruining things with Leo, Belle realized that she needed to keep a tighter hold over her impulses. Just stay quiet, do as she was told, and don't make waves. That was all she needed to do.

But when the store was empty, and the only sound came from the soft jazz music over the intercom, Belle grew suspicious. Ray had been slamming books and reports almost all morning, but now there was nothing coming from the front counter.

She leaned out from the bookcase she had been sorting to check on him. Ray's elbows were propped on the counter, his hands covering his face. It was the image of a man distraught. She had never seen him like that. Not even on their busiest days or in the periods of utter deadness when the store wasn't making enough money. He had never looked so vulnerable.

Stepping out of sight from the counter, Belle didn't like the choice she had to make. She could pretend she didn't see and move on with her job. She could hope that whatever was bothering him would work itself out in due time and she wouldn't invade his space. That was the safest route. The one her mask told her to take. She wouldn't embarrass herself or open herself up for target practice. If Ray was really that stressed, he'd respond to her questions in the same, predictive way he always had. Yelling and snide remarks about minding her own business.

And that's what she should have done from the very beginning. Mind her own business.

The second option was to cast aside her mask and ask him what was wrong. That was what her spirit wanted her to do. It's what her heart, which cared about the suffering of others, demanded that she do. But just like the previous night when she had overstepped her bounds with Leo, could she do the same with Ray?

It wasn't her job to fix his problems. Nor was it her job to fix Leo's. But just like he had said the day before when they nursed the orphaned lamb back to health, she cared too much about people. She wanted the best for everyone and when she saw someone who could even remotely benefit from her help, she wanted to give it. Freely and willingly, whether they asked for it or not.

Ray wasn't asking for sympathy. In her heart, though, she knew she couldn't walk away. She'd forever wonder what God might have been trying to show her in this situation. Or what he might have been trying to do through her.

This would be the second crazy, reckless thing she had done in the last twenty-four hours. She never thought she could be this self-destructive.

Belle straightened and made her way to the front counter. Ray didn't seem to notice her until she spoke.

"You all right?" she asked.

He lifted his head from his hands and she could see the whites of his eyes were reddened, and the tip of his long nose matched. He couldn't have been crying.

She watched his expression warily, waiting for that miserable look to morph into pure rage at her question. Instead, he only folded his arms and shifted a little on his stool. "Yeah, I just..." He paused, and Belle tried to think of a time when his voice had ever been so void of irritation or didn't hold that commanding tone.

Belle waited and the struggle for the words was plainly written from the way his brows met between his eyes to the way his back hunched under the discomforting weight of his troubles.

"This stays between you and me," he continued, the authority returning to his words. Belle froze, ready for whatever would come next. "My wife... Home hasn't been the best place lately. The kids are acting out. My teenager may be getting in with the wrong crowd at school... It's just a frustrating situation for me and my wife, and I... I'll admit I haven't been the best husband. But she told me last night that she was pregnant."

A long, expectant silence hung between them. Ray looked to be on the verge of breaking down again, while Belle wondered if this was her chance to say something. Anything.

"I have a feeling a congratulations isn't the right thing to say, is it?"

Ray shook his head. "We haven't been sleeping in the same bed for six months. She wanted to get separate bedrooms, because she complained about my snoring. It wasn't like we were going to miss each other anyway. Things have been going downhill for a while. She worked later hours at the hospital and I just trusted her word on it. I never thought... I never saw..."

He rubbed at his bald head and finally, those tears that had been glistening in his eyes during his speech were released. He began to weep, and Belle stood, half horrified and half stunned. She would have never taken him for a crier, or a man who would fall apart like this. Then again, when a man's entire existence was crumbling in his hands, how else was he supposed to respond?

Belle forced herself back to the present and quickly went to flip the store's sign so they could have some privacy. When she returned to him, Ray had dropped his head to his arms, his shoulder convulsing with his sobs.

Forgetting her mask, forgetting any and all potential opportunities for embarrassment, Belle came beside her boss and put her arm around him. Finding the right words would be difficult. This wound deserved more than a band aide. She couldn't just throw out clichés as if they were something profound and all-healing.

She couldn't say that this must be God's will, or that everything works out for a purpose. She couldn't tell him that he was better off without a partner who didn't treat him right. None of that would comfort him, because she knew those kinds of things wouldn't comfort her either.

Instead, she silently asked God to speak the words Ray needed to hear. She'd just be the vessel, the mouthpiece for whatever message needed to be spoken.

"I know it must be hard for you to see past all of this, and I can't give you any advice. All I know for sure is that... God sees you. He knows what's been going on and though He couldn't keep it from happening, He can help you through it. It was your wife's choice to do what she did, but it's your choice what you do about it. You can try to do this on your own or have faith that God can and will heal this hurt."

Ray lifted his bloodshot gaze and regarded her with confusion. "God? What does God have to do with any of this? If He knew what was going on, why didn't He stop it? Why didn't He keep your barn from burning down? Why doesn't He do something about all the problems in the world?"

Belle had wondered that for a long time, as did her father and luckily, she had the sense one day to ask him the same thing. "God is all powerful and all knowing, but He doesn't inhibit free will. People make the choice to do bad things. They choose to sin. He won't come down from heaven to stop anyone from doing what they want. He only came down so that when they realize what they've been doing, they would have a path to redemption. A path back to Him. He can't force anyone to choose Him. They have to do that for themselves. Your wife chose to have an affair, but you can choose to forgive her and ask God to heal your marriage."

She knew that he was listening. He had to. This was the same doctrine he had heard in his Catholic Mass. At least, that's what she hoped. None of this should have been new. But by the strangely fascinated sparkle in his eyes, she had to wonder.

"Forgive her?" he huffed. "How can I forgive her after what she did?"

Belle smiled. "The same way that God forgave you and everyone else that ever lived or will live on this earth. He did it, because He loves you. And you still love your wife, right? You wouldn't be hurting so badly if you didn't."

He nodded and turned away, his puffy eyes staring at the counter-top. It must have taken him a lot of courage to admit that he still had feelings for a woman who betrayed him, lied to him, and cheated on him. But that was exactly what God did every day. Forgave them and loved them.

"Can I pray for you?" Belle asked, knowing that all of this had gone way far beyond the boundary lines that had been drawn the moment she started working there. Ray was her boss. Her employer. These sorts of conversations shouldn't have been had between them. It might have been unprofessional, but the moment Ray opened up about his personal life, Belle couldn't just ignore that. He trusted her, just as she needed to trust him and Ivy with her own problems too.

After some pondering, Ray agreed. Belle closed her eyes and prayed aloud. It might have been the longest, loudest prayer she had ever uttered. Everything else had been reserved for whispers behind closed doors or in her mind where only God could hear her supplications.

This was the third reckless, brave thing she had done in twenty-four hours. How many more would be numbered with it before the end of the day?

The lambs had been tagged. The ewes had fully recovered from their pregnancies. The stallion was acclimating to the new pasture just fine. And Ranger was already learning how to herd the hens near the chicken coup. Then there was Leo, barely hanging on and forcing his way through the black fog.

When there were chores to be done, he was fine. He could pour himself into the task and let himself drift through the process. It had been ages since he allowed the darkness to take over. The blood payments were easier to handle than this, but he couldn't cave. He couldn't let this win.

But when there was nothing to do, nothing to occupy him, he wanted to buckle to his knees or crawl into his bed and waste away. He hadn't eaten all day and not even coffee or a ride on his bike could entice him. He smoked his last cigarette, but not even the nicotine could give him relief. He would have let the exhaustion take him if it hadn't been for the lamb who still needed to be fed every few hours. The lamb stayed inside with him and demanded his affections, which he half-heartedly gave.

In those hours when there was nothing to do, nothing to think on but the past, Leo sat on the sofa and blankly stared into the fireplace. He occasionally glanced to the bookshelves where he saw a few different copies of the Bible, and he remembered the reading assignment Mr. Calloway had given him.

The thing was that Leo couldn't bring himself to move. Just moving his eyes that little bit seemed to take such monumental effort. It was like wading through mud or trying to walk through a brick wall. Stuck. Trapped in the never-ending cycle of grief and guilt that he had pushed off for so long. He had flat lined in the valley and the mountains around him seemed undefeatable.

Time passed, and Belle was home, but he didn't feel the same abounding joy as he usually did when she appeared. He had hoped that seeing her would break this hold over his heart and mind, but he couldn't even bring himself to smile.

And she could sense it in him. Leo knew that. Her incessant questions earlier that day nearly drove him mad. He couldn't stand to lie to her anymore about any of it. He might have battled against the voices in his head that told him he was nothing, worthless, useless, and weak. But he couldn't find the ones that accused him of being a liar. It was the truth. He had been lying by omission since the beginning. She didn't know about the darkness, about his past and the reasons he did what he did. She wanted to know, but he had pushed her aside each time.

Now, with Belle in the living room, bottle-feeding the lamb in her lap, Leo knew he couldn't be silent anymore. He had thought long ago that telling anyone about his past or his trauma was a bad or frowned upon thing. His father used to call them "pity parties" and no one wanted to be invited. It's what had kept Leo silent for so long. He thought keeping it all bottled up would keep the despair contained, quarantined within himself so it wouldn't contaminate others.

But not this time. He couldn't stand the hurt look in her eyes when she tried to greet him and he simply turned away. He couldn't lie to her anymore. And maybe, just maybe, speaking this sorrow into the open could strip it of its power.

Leo brought in an armful of logs from the stack leaning against the side of the house and prepared them in the fireplace. He wouldn't feel the warmth of the flames, but she could and that mattered more. Ranger, ever curious, sniffed at the kindling and jumped when the first embers began to pop and burst. With his back turned to Belle, he stoked the fire until he found the right words.

"How was work?" he asked suddenly.

The tiny intake of breath told him that she hadn't been expecting him to say anything. "Work was... interesting," she said. "Ray, my boss, was in a pretty foul mood for most of the day before we talked."

Leo sat on the bricks of the stone hearth and watched the way the amber light brightened her features. She was always beautiful, always so perfect. So different than him. Better.

"What did you talk about?"

Belle's eyes stayed focused on the hungry lamb that suckled on the bottle she held above its head. "He... I'm only telling you, because I know you won't gossip or anything, though he told me the conversation would stay between us... He's just going through a lot of family trouble and it all came to a head yesterday. It's not good. It's probably the reason he's always been such a grouch. I can't hold that against him. Ivy probably can, but I can't. People act out when they're upset. I understand that better than most, so I guess I can be more forgiving because of it."

Leo took heart in that. She would understand his pain and why he shut her out. He swallowed hard and tried not to let the voices tell him that he had hurt her. He'd make up for it. All of it. Right now.

He started off slowly, gradually, picking his words as if they would be used against him later. They probably would. "You've been... extraordinarily forgiving of me... And patient. I know I haven't been entirely honest with you and you have to know that it's not because of you."

This earned her attention and Belle looked up, meeting his gaze.

"I mean... I don't want to dump all of this on you. I don't want your pity or any consoling. I've done... Well, I'm still working through a lot of it, but I'm saying that so you know that when I'm finished, you don't need to say anything. You don't need to do anything. It happened so long ago and – "

"Leo," she interrupted firmly. "Just tell me what it is that's keeping us apart. That's all I've wanted."

He wasn't sure how far he could go, how far he could climb out of this hole. It'd take him time to tell her everything, but this much he could tell.

"I told you about my family, that they died. But I never told you how or that... We weren't always damaged. We did have a pretty happy home for most of my life. My little sister was already showing that she could probably have her pick of any college she wanted to go to. She was so smart. My da worked as a mechanic and my mum stayed at home. She was a phenomenal cook and baked all the time. My da didn't used to be the way he was. He used to play catch with my brother and I in our backyard. He drank occasionally and had a temper, but he had been able to keep it under control fairly well. My brother... he was more into sports than anything and I was in the middle, just trying to figure things out for a while.

"But something happened, and I can't really tell you a lot about it, but my brother wasn't... he just wasn't right. We caught him doing things he shouldn't have been doing and we sent him to a psychiatrist. He was diagnosed with schizophrenia and he had to take all these medications just to keep him stable... It messed up our family. My da had been so proud of Matthew before his diagnosis and afterward... he was a wrecked man. His drinking got worse. I assumed he was upset and trying to forget that he had a son who was – according to him – broken."

Leo rubbed at his face and felt the perspiration from sitting too close to the fire, but he didn't care to move away. "Everything fell apart after that. The beatings... the screaming from my sister's room... I felt I couldn't do anything. I was just a kid. I didn't know what to do when my mum stopped cooking. I didn't know what to do when Kaitlyn became sick. It was just me. I could handle his drunken rages better than anyone and Matthew didn't do anything to help. He was... untouched by it all."

His heart pumped harder in his chest as new feelings emerged. Rage. Bitterness. Hatred. Leo wanted to break something when he thought of how Matthew was the only one of the family who hadn't been hurt, who hadn't suffered. It was unfair.

"One night, I came home, and the house was dark. I could hear them shouting upstairs. My parents and Kaitlyn were in her room. I went and watched my mum shoot my da in the head. Then, she turned the gun on herself. We saw our parents die that night. Matthew had disappeared, and I never heard Kaitlyn speak again. The doctors that worked with social services said that it was a result of all the trauma she had gone through. She wouldn't even talk to me. We were both going to go to Brooklyn, but her sickness got worse. She died before we could leave Scotland... They never found Matthew and I assume he wanted it that way... In the end, it's my fault."

Belle's voice came soft, but pleading. "How could any of that be your fault?"

Leo wouldn't look at her. He didn't think he could anymore. "I was the one who told my parents about Matthew acting out. If I had just let him do what he wanted and minded my own business, he wouldn't have been diagnosed and my da wouldn't have had a reason to get drunk so much. That's what I thought anyway. That's when all of it started and my family had to put up with it for years before it was over. But it all went by so quickly. It was like a twister touching down out of nowhere, destroying everything, and then disappearing. The only thing left was me."

His throat became too thick with emotion, reliving it all again. There was no more he could say. He had been wrong. Speaking it all now did nothing, but bring back their ghosts. He could hear them, how they were before. He could almost smell his mother's perfume and feel the bruising of his father's fist on his cheek. It was too heavy of a burden for him to carry anymore. For a moment, he wondered how he'd survive this new wave. He already felt like drowning, like his breaths were numbered.

But then, Belle let the lamb down from its mealtime. She came to him and wrapped her arms around his shoulders. He wanted to push her away, afraid that he'd taint her with the darkness and misery. He didn't want this, and he had told her that from the start. No pity, no sympathy. He just wanted her to listen.

She said nothing. Not a word. She just held him, and he could feel for the first time all day. The warmth of her body transferred to him in a rush that he thought he'd never feel again. He thought, somehow, this confession would finally scare her away and show her that he was too damaged, too broken to ever deserve her attention. There was no picking up the pieces from this wreckage and he didn't want her to try.

His hand came up and held her arm in place, feeling selfish despite what the depression told him. He wanted her to stay right there with him, holding him. Loving him. He might not have been out of the hole, but he could start to see the light at the top. And it was her.

Chapter 13

So that was it? That was what Leo had been afraid to tell her for so long?

Belle sat at the dining table, unable to focus as her mind continued to replay their talk the night before. She couldn't imagine the pain Leo must have endured, the courage it took to tell her everything in the way he did, and the bravery to keep it hidden for so long. To be so young and have his whole world stolen from him so quickly. Her father's death couldn't even compete with something like that. His illness had been gradual, stealing the life out of him over eight months. There was plenty of time to say last goodbyes and get affairs in order. It was enough time for Belle to accept the course of the cancer and though they continued to pray for a miracle, she had come to terms with his death long before the doctors announced it.

But for Leo, it was all in a matter of minutes. The fallout had been building over years, he said, but he could have never seen the end coming like it did. There were no words she could say, nothing to ease the hurt that was still so fresh. The way he looked last night, the way his voice deepened with the sorrow of his story, Belle knew those wounds hadn't healed. Instead, they festered and turned into something even worse than grief.

Guilt.

How could she get through to him that he couldn't blame himself for their deaths? If everyone followed the rabbit trail far enough, they could find blame in anyone they wanted. But to go through his life with that cloud hovering over his head every waking hour was unhealthy. Belle knew that better than anyone.

And she was hardly in the position to give advice. She still struggled to convince herself that not every little difference in someone's attitude and behavior toward her could be linked to something she did. Sometimes, it was just circumstance. Like with Leo. She thought his fresh bit of despondency had to do with her and what they did in the barn the other night. All along, it had been him reliving those old nightmares from his childhood. Why else would he have come out and told her after hiding it for so long? It had nothing to do with her, but she had believed it was.

She laced her fingers together and sent up a quick prayer that God would somehow help Leo through this storm, just like He had helped her through her own years ago when her father passed. But when she breathed her "Amen", she felt no less distracted than she had before. Her notebook was still blank and her laptop screen was still dark.

This was her last day off from work until the Farmer's Market that weekend and there was still so much to do. But she didn't even know where to begin with a list. She had already sent off the designs for the banner to the print shop in the next town over, along with a digital copy of the flyers she hastily made up. It was the only place close by that had a large enough printing facility to help her for a good price.

Within reason, she could advertise horse boarding, training lessons, eggs for sale, and wool. Everything else would follow in the months and years to come. It'd be a slow process, but she had to start somewhere.

It was still early in the day and she had told Leo not to feed the sheep that morning, because she intended to shear them in the afternoon when it was a little warmer. But glancing at the clock, it was still a few hours away from lunchtime and she needed something to do. Something to occupy her idle hands.

With a sigh, she stood from the table and got dressed. *Might as well get it over with now.* Maybe talking to Leo or doing something relatively mindless like shearing would motivate her to get more done. Donning a pair of already stained, but clean, work clothes, she slipped into her jacket and boots, and went out to the pasture.

The ease at which Buck acclimated to his new home convinced her that they ought to start introductions. Leo was in the pasture now with the stallion and Maggie, monitoring their socialization closely.

The only thing that came out of last night's long talk might have been Belle's full awareness of his past. The confession did little for Leo's mood. He still seemed dazed, lethargic, and the only thing keeping him moving was the endless chores that he took to so eagerly it scared her a little. He looked for excuses to work, to stay busy.

Even now, walking up to the pasture fence he leaned against, she could see that look in his eyes. The one that told her he was slipping without something to do. For once, they could relate on that score. If Belle couldn't stay busy, she'd go mad.

She got his attention and slipped her hands into her coat pockets, so she could fidget with the bent and twisted paperclip she kept just for this kind of situation. Belle wasn't entirely sure what his confession meant for this relationship between them. Was it the final break, so they could get things moving, or would he treat them the same?

Leo turned and regarded her with a twinge of that same regret she had seen earlier that morning. It made her wonder if he wanted to go back in time and stop him from telling her his big, dark secret.

"Do you think you could help me with shearing some of the ewes?" she asked. "I usually have Mr. Johnson help me, but he's still out of town."

Leo thrummed his fingers against the wooden fence rail as his gaze darted to the barn. "I've never done that before."

Belle gave him an encouraging smile. "All I need you to do is hold the sheep while I work the clippers. You don't have to do anything except keep them still. I want to shear all the ewes and bring a few of the fleeces to the festival, but I'll wash a couple tonight to give people an idea of what the wool can look like when it's clean."

She had already told him much of this. She knew she had rambled a good while about the process and all she would need to do to make herself a one-stop shop for wool spinners and fiber fanatics. By now, he must have been tired of her explaining it all. He never showed it, though. No matter how long she talked, he never tried to interrupt or change the subject.

Leo took a deep breath, his chest expanding, then he slowly let it out as if he were already regretting it. But he agreed and they made their way to the barn. There, the orphaned lamb was carefully looked after by Ranger. The other ewes and their lambs were still in their pens, but she thought that it might be fine to let them out into the pasture later that day once the sun warmed up the farm. They needed to stretch their legs after being kept in pens for the last few days.

Bringing out Sunflower, her eldest Finn ewe, Belle began to walk Leo through exactly how he should hold her for the shearing.

"The most important part is to not let her dance around or wiggle. If she moves, I could accidentally cut her."

Leo nodded and gripped Sunflower's mouth and nose just as Belle instructed while she went to get the electric shearers.

"I used to help my dad a lot before he passed," she told him while she rummaged through the supply bin. Luckily, she had thought to charge the portable battery so the fact that the barn wasn't installed with electricity yet didn't put a hold on the plans. "I wasn't very good at holding them, so he showed me how to be careful with the shearers and that was my job from then on out. Back then, though, we used manual clippers and it was a lot harder. Took a lot longer too."

When she turned back, she saw Leo roll up his long sleeves. She allowed herself to watch and admire the nicely toned definition of his forearms and how a few veins stood out against his tanned skin. But on his left arm, she noticed something else. The blood in her veins turned to ice.

Belle stopped and stared at the dark, puckered lines above his wrist. They were new. She knew that for a fact. She had studied every one of those faded scars, knew their angles and positions as well as she knew the layout of her home. These were not there last week. Granted, this was probably the first time she had seen his bare arms since that day when she caught him leaving the bathroom in a towel. It had to have happened after that, but there was some scabbing and recovery already in place, so she knew it couldn't have been too recent.

Leo looked to her, his eyes questioning her stunned, frozen expression. It didn't take him long to figure out why. Belle swallowed hard as she felt the rush of panic sweep through her.

Why had he done it? When? Where? Was it because of her? No, she couldn't let herself think that way. Just like everything else, it probably had nothing to do with her at all. She had to keep breathing, keep her head clear and be rational. That was the only way she would get answers.

"When?" she asked, trying to avoid the more pressing and disturbing questions for last.

Leo kept a good grip on the ewe that leaned against his legs and she could see the struggle in him whether to answer or not. "Monday."

Belle closed her eyes, thinking back to the beginning of the week and how he had been with her at the bookstore. He seemed so happy and attentive. And then the phone call that evening. He did talk a little different then, wanting promises and making sure she was okay. Did that have anything to do with the cuts?

It was obvious where he had done it, so now there left only one thing to ask.

The word came out shuddering, breathy, hesitant and fearful, because deep down, Belle didn't want it to be about her. "Why?"

He didn't answer. He simply twisted Sunflower onto her rump the way Belle had explained. The ewe's stomach and chest were exposed, legs stiffened in front of her while Leo's elbow pinned her head around against his hip.

She didn't want to start. She didn't want to move or even look at those scars again, but they would be right in her line of sight. How could she just ignore them?

"Why did you cut, Leo?" Belle noticed the fervent tremor in her voice and hated it. She needed to stay calm, but she felt anything but calm.

"I don't want to get into this right now," he replied coolly, his words like ice chilling across her skin.

"Why not? Was it something I did?" Now she was begging for a reprieve to a crisis that was all in her head.

Once more, she wished there was a zipper conveniently sewn across her lips, so she could close her mouth whenever she got like this. Whenever her emotions bubbled up to ruin a perfectly good thing. Whenever her anxiety spoke for her. Whenever she was about to make a huge mistake. It was like watching a freight train barrel toward her and she wanted to see if it would jump the tracks. How stupid could she get and still breathe?

"No, it... I don't want to talk about it." Leo's subtle shift shot up red flags. He was about to say something, but curbed his tongue just before he would say it. Why? What was he ready to tell her, but decided not to? That only sent her mind into a downward tailspin and Belle couldn't find the parachute cord.

"But I do," she whined, taking a few steps forward, though she wasn't even sure what was keeping her legs from buckling beneath her. "I can take it. Just tell me why you did this."

Why hadn't she been this adamant before when she saw the old scars? Maybe because it wasn't so personal then. He said he had been dealing with something and it was over. But that was ages ago according to him. Had it come back? Did it have to do with the death of his family or did this wound go bone-deep?

"Are you going to shear the sheep or not?" Leo barked, his tone raised in anger against her.

Belle gripped the clippers tighter, resisting the urge to run or drop the subject entirely. She wouldn't be scared into leaving the matter alone. He knew shouting was a trigger and he used it against her. This felt like a betrayal, a reversal that broke every promise he had given.

Instead of giving in, she charged forward and began working, being mindful to keep Sunflower's skin pulled tight, so she could make a nice, clean shave. The comb cover allowed her to leave a quarter of an inch of wool behind so the ewe wouldn't freeze.

When they moved to a different position, Belle looked at the scars again and shook her head. "I just want to understand why. Is it that difficult to talk about?"

She could almost feel his frustration radiating from him as they stood close to one another around Sunflower. "It's just... I can't tell you."

Belle eyed him, her fear and worry turning into annoyance a little too quickly. "You could tell me about your parents dying, but you can't tell me about why you willingly harm yourself?"

Her choice of words could have been better. That condemnation was plain in the glare he shot her. "It's not the same," he growled.

"How is it not? Do you cut because you feel responsible for their deaths after all this time? Do you want to die so you can be with them?"

Belle began shearing again, but Leo's voice roared over the buzzing noise of the clippers.

"This has nothing to do with wanting to die."

Her own voice wasn't strong enough to bellow like his, so she stood up straight and let the clumps of wool fall after her last stroke over Sunflower's hind quarters. "Then why do it? Is it because of the guilt?"

"No. Not... Not entirely."

She could admire the way he tried to ease back his hostilities, but they both had a long way to go.

"Not entirely? What is that supposed to mean? You have multiple reasons?"

Leo pointed an accusing finger at her. "See? This is why I didn't want to talk about it!"

"All you have to do is tell me why you did it. Why is that so hard?"

"It's just not something I can explain to you," he pleaded. Belle could almost see him visibly shake with the mounting rage.

Belle clenched her teeth together and tried to let it go as she stooped down again to finish Sunflower's side. But once she was turned over again so Belle could shear off the wool around her neck, she couldn't hold her tongue.

"Can you not explain it because you just don't want to tell me or is it something else?"

His deep rumble of a reply didn't help matters at all. "Belle, drop it."

"I can't, Leo," she cried, her hands fumbling over Sunflower's fleece for a moment. "And you know why I can't? I care about you. I probably care way too much, because you obviously don't care enough about me to just explain something so simple."

"You don't need to know everything about everyone all the time," Leo rebuked. "There are some things that are just better left unsaid."

"Like what?" Belle asked, propping her hand on her hip. "Like what we are? Like where this whole mess is going? I'm tired of feeling like I'm having to piece together all these little bits of you that I find out about by complete accident just so I can have some idea of who I'm sharing a house with. Like the fact that you've only ever kissed me when I'm rambling and being hysterical, but never any other time. Or how you call me that Scottish word, but never told me what it means. And now, when I ask you a simple question, you can't give me a straight answer."

Leo stood up, Sunflower leaning against his leg, still unable to right herself and run off as she probably wanted to. Right now, Belle would have given anything to run from that fiery, intense stare. "It's not simple. No matter which way I could ever try to explain this to you, it's not simple. It's complex, just like what we share. That's why I can't give it a name. That's why I should have left town and never looked back. It's why I can't kiss you like I'd want to, every second of every day. It's all too much to talk about right now."

Belle could feel her eyes misting with frustrated tears. "When will you tell me? Huh? Weeks from now? Months? Years? Do you think it's easy for me to wait like this? You know so much about me, but I know so little. I don't know your favorites, what makes you excited or happy. I don't know what makes you sad and want to cut open your arm and bleed. I want to know! I want to know everything about you, but you won't let me in."

"You don't need to get in!" he bellowed. "I keep you out for a reason. Just accept that and move on. You have to learn to let things go."

She shut her eyes against his lecture. "Don't turn this into something about me. Any woman on the planet would have given up on you long ago. They would have stopped knocking at this locked door, but I kept trying." Belle could feel the fury melt into despair once more. She needed to stay strong, but what could she do? He was her strength and now they seemed to be disconnecting again. "If I hadn't kept trying, you wouldn't be here right now. I convinced you to stay."

A jaw in Leo's cheek flexed and she could see the tendons in his arms pop as he curled his hands into fists. "You should have let me go. I should have never come back here after I dropped off Ranger. I should have driven out of town and never looked back. It would have been better that way."

"Why?" she huffed. "Because you think you deserve to be alone after what you did to your parents? No one should live like that."

"That's what I deserve. It's the way I've always lived and there's never been a problem with that until you came around and lied to me that I could actually be happy here."

Her lungs refused air as she stared at him, horrified at his accusation. Did he just imply that he wasn't happy here with her? That he still wanted to leave?

Had it really come to this? After all the sharing, the late nights, the kissing, the moments when he had saved her life? Was it all for nothing? Had she just wasted so much of her time dreaming about a future when she knew all along that he wasn't meant to stay? He said that he would be there for her no matter what. He said they were on solid ground. Had he lied? Or was that solid ground finally giving way beneath this immense pressure, waiting for the final stroke of the sledgehammer that would reduce it all to rubble?

Belle took a deep breath, and as hard as she knew it would be, she looked him square in the face and swung. "Then go. If you can't be open with me, if this farm and everything you've done for me means absolutely nothing to you, then leave. No one's stopping you. I'm sorry I made you feel like a prisoner... I thought you were a partner. I must have been wrong."

Oh, so very wrong. And now, she would pay for it. Broken and betrayed. If this was what Leo wanted, she wouldn't stand in his way.

But he didn't go right away. His gaze searched hers for something, and then he motioned for her to take the ewe. She did and hated the way her body quivered when their hands touched. Belle wouldn't look at him as he strode away. Caught under the weight of Sunflower, she couldn't chase after him. This was his decision. If he couldn't open up, if he couldn't respect her need to understand, then they had been fooling themselves from the beginning. She, the one who told herself not to get attached, had latched onto his charms and sensitivity. How could she be so blind?

Belle resumed the shearing, but went slow as she continually blinked away the tears in her eyes.

What have I done?

Sitting with his head in his hands, Leo didn't even care what time it was. Mr. Tale had kept the blinds closed over the windows of his trailer, but he thought there might have been slivers of silvery blue leaking out onto the floor.

Last night, he got no sleep. Between the voices and his own self-inflicted guilt for what he had said and done to Belle the previous day, Leo had never felt more drained and hopeless. How could he go back after indirectly telling her that he neither trusted her, nor cared for her? How could he possibly make up for that? In his rage, he had destroyed everything.

He couldn't tell her the truth. Not about the darkness, his brother, or the curse over his soul. There was no way he could possibly explain it, which was why he had pushed her out so adamantly. If she knew the truth. If he told her, she'd just think he was crazy. Maybe he was.

There was something to be said for the fact that he didn't leave town when she had practically ordered him to. He stayed, crashing at Mr. Tale's place until he could figure everything out. His wife was away visiting family in their old hometown, which left the house to the two men.

Though his refusal to explain the cuts on his arm was genuine, the things he said about leaving Levi had been spoken in a moment of thoughtlessness. He couldn't leave, even if he wanted to. Leo was far too invested in Belle's wellbeing and this twisted, confusing thing they shared to ever leave. But how could he tell her so?

Distancing himself from Belle and the farm only made the darkness more powerful. He needed to go back if he ever wanted to mend the hurt he'd inflicted upon her. But for now, he wanted to take this time to reflect. He had to come up with the right way to tell her exactly what he felt without revealing too much.

Not only that, but he had to come up with a plan to take care of this darkness once and for all. The Bible lay open on the sofa next to him, half covered by the blanket that draped over his lap. He had tried for hours last night to read, but the passages seemed to float around the page, unable to stay fixed in one spot. He blamed it on the exhaustion, but no matter how much he rubbed at his eyes, he couldn't seem to focus on the words in red.

After a while, he gave up and tried to get some sleep. It seemed no matter what he did, he failed miserably.

The single bedroom door opened, and Mr. Tale's lumbering steps sounded down the short hallway. Leo almost hadn't expected the man's unconditional hospitality. He asked no questions and didn't want anything in return. Even when he offered to work without pay in exchange for a place to sleep, Mr. Tale refused. Leo had even come up with an elaborate story about how he came to be without a home, but he didn't get a chance to tell it.

"Did you even sleep?" the contractor asked, slipping his way into the kitchen. His eyes were only half open, hair disheveled, and dressed in his pajamas.

"No," Leo replied, glancing back to the Bible he had failed to read. Mr. Tale didn't even bat an eye when his new roommate asked for it. Leo recognized it as his personal Bible he used at the coffee shop. Notes were scrawled in the margins and bits were highlighted that must have meant something important to him.

"So, what did you do to Belle?"

The question caused the hairs on the back of Leo's neck to stand on end. He looked up, brows arched as he watched Mr. Tale fill up the coffee carafe at the sink.

"What makes you think I did anything to Belle?" he asked. Admitting that he had hurt the daughter of Chad Clearwater to one of the men who was closest to him before his passing would have been like putting a target on his chest. He didn't want to end up like Drake.

"Oh, I know that look," he said over the running water, a smile playing in his voice. "I've had that look before and seen it on plenty of other men who've royally screwed up their relationships."

Once more, Mr. Tale showed that he was more intuitive than most. How did he know that Leo and Belle were even in a relationship to screw up in the first place? Had it been that obvious at church or the barn party?

Leo waited until the grounds were dumped into the filter before responding with some measure of difficulty. "She... I wasn't being honest with her about something."

It might have been too much to hope that Mr. Tale would leave the matter alone after that.

"Ah, yes. Typical problem. You don't want to tell her something, because you think she'll freak out, right?"

He could have shut down right then, just like he had tried to do at the coffee shop with Mr. Calloway. But he didn't have the convenience of getting up and walking out. He had nowhere to go. "Pretty much."

"You know the only way to fix that?" Mr. Tale leaned against the countertop and faced Leo. "You go pull your britches up and tell her the truth. So many young men think they need to put on this big show of being mysterious or macho, but a woman wants honesty and sensitivity. If you sacrifice your pride, you're golden."

Leo hadn't thought himself prideful when he refused to tell Belle about the scars. He thought he was protecting her. That wasn't prideful, was it? But, he could admit that he was being insensitive. The way he talked, his choice of words, his tone, everything might have brought back some terrible memories for her. The arguing, the shouting, and most importantly, the leaving. Leo had left her just like her mother did. And he thought he had been doing her a favor by walking out of that barn.

He closed his eyes and tilted his head back against the cushion. "It's not that easy."

"Nothing is when it matters," Mr. Tale replied. "If Belle matters to you, then making this work with her won't be easy. But, it'll be worth it."

Leo already knew that. If he could keep Belle's trust, he could die a contented man. If he couldn't, his life didn't have much meaning at all. He had to make this work.

"What should I do?" he whispered, the question posed to whoever in the entire universe that might have a clear answer for him. What should he do about Belle? About the darkness? About Matthew?

"First," Mr. Tale started as the coffeemaker began to percolate, "you go to Belle and you apologize. Then, you give her the straight, honest truth that she wants. Nothing more, nothing less."

Leo rolled his head to the side to look at his new mentor. "What if the truth will hurt her?"

"She doesn't care. She still wants to hear it. If you can't give her the truth, no matter how painful it is to hear, she won't trust you."

Up to this point, Belle had trusted him. At least, when it came to matters about her anxiety and what she should do about it. Now, she asked him to trust her enough to break down the walls and let her see his dark and dysfunctional mind.

"And if she runs because of the truth?" Leo asked, almost afraid of the response.

"Belle's not a runner. She may be a little timid sometimes, but she doesn't run."

That may have been the strongest bit of sense Mr. Tale had spoken all morning. He was completely right. Belle didn't run. Not from a barn fire, a social engagement, and not from him. He was the one running from the truth. Just like Mr. Calloway said.

Instantly, his mind began to form exactly what he would say to Belle. He knew how to fix this now.

Chapter 14

Belle wasn't sure how she could still be moving, how she was still breathing or functioning after all she had endured. She thought processing the wool, cleaning it, carding it, and picking it clean of all the dirt and bits of grass would somehow distract her from all the pain in her chest. It didn't. It just sat there. Not even a cleansing of chamomile tea or overdose of lavender oils could ease this ache.

She had thought to call in from work. How could she face people while this lingered over her spirit? Not only that, but the Farmer's Fall Festival was tomorrow, and she still had so much to do. The banner and flyers were ready at the print shop and they would need to be picked up before the end of the day. And she had to pick up the lamb from Mrs. Levinson's place. Without Leo, she had no one to take care of him while she was away. She even had to put Ranger inside all day, puppy pads laid across half of the kitchen to keep him from making a mess.

There was so much to do, so much to think about, but all she could focus on was the fact that Leo wasn't there. He didn't just disappear and come back to apologize. He was gone. The dresser in his room was empty and the only thing left was the copy of *Anne of Green Gables*. It sat atop the quilt on the bed and it was all she could do to keep herself from bursting into tears.

Belle could often accept the course of things. The passing of time was inevitable, and no one could break its consistency. But this might have been the one time in her life that she wished she had a time machine, so she could go back and change what she had done. She would have stopped herself from asking for Leo's help with the shearing. She would have made herself shut her mouth when she saw the scars. Anything to save herself this heartbreak.

Leo had become her everything, and she knew it was blasphemous to think so, but he had saved her in so many ways and now he was gone. All because she couldn't just leave well enough alone. He was right. She didn't need to know everything. She didn't need to fix the world's problems, especially when she should have been fixing her own. That realization might have hurt just as much as his leaving.

One day, she knew she would be able to put this behind her. She could never forget Leo and all the times they shared together, laughing, talking, and working. She'd never forget the way his blue eyes looked upon her with such tenderness, or how his smile brightened up the dark corners of her spirit. But she wished with every piece of her shattered heart that she could have been different for him. Been better.

The mask she had always worn to hide her true feelings couldn't save her now. There was no fake smiling to the customers, no uplifted voice in answer to anyone's questions or calls. Ivy noticed her mood and tried to help. Belle had no problem broadcasting her troubles onto her friend anymore. She laid it all down, leaving out some of the details to save Leo's perfect and rugged image.

The only thing Ivy could say was that if she could make Leo come back for her, she would have. But they both knew that Ivy couldn't sweet talk Leo into doing anything he didn't want to do. The one time Belle convinced him to stay in Levi had to have been a fluke.

So, Ivy gave her as much space and time as she needed. Ray had taken the day off for personal reasons. Even if Belle wallowed in her own tragedy, she could be glad for her boss. Maybe he would confront his wife and try to make things work between them. At least someone in Levi had the guts to face their problems.

The shop had been relatively empty for the last hour or so before the brass bell above the door chimed. Ivy went to greet the customer as she tried to do almost every given chance that day. Belle could hear the conversation turn serious and for a moment, her heart stopped beating. She listened for the deep voice that would tell her Leo had come back.

Instead, she was soon approached by Mrs. Kendall, the pastor's wife. If only her mask was working. She could be open with Ivy and random customers, but if Mrs. Kendall saw even the slightest bit of weakness, it would get plastered on their prayer bulletin board at church and everyone would know something was wrong with her.

Looking at the pastor's wife now, though, all she could think about was the last time they had talked. It was on the porch just after the barn burned down. She warned Belle about Leo's terrible influence and she hadn't listened. Maybe she should have.

"Are you all right, darlin'?" Mrs. Kendall asked before pulling Belle into a friendly hug.

"I'm..." She couldn't tell the truth. She couldn't even put this much pain into words. "I'm here. I'm just here."

Physically, she was. Mentally and emotionally, she was scattered. It was enough that her body could stand and be present while she worked. Anything more than that would have been too much.

"We haven't seen you at the Wednesday service or Thursday's prayer meetings for a while. I just felt led to come and see you. I'm glad I did. What's wrong?"

Mrs. Kendall smiled, and they walked toward a bench near the magazine section. It wasn't exactly private. She didn't need it. If it took Belle years to open up to Ivy, someone she spent nearly every day with, then she wasn't about to spill her soul to Mrs. Kendall. Even if she was the pastor's wife and the matriarch of their church in some ways. Belle didn't know her well enough, and she was notorious for publicizing the troubles of the congregation. It was all in an effort to be helpful, but Belle wondered if those people ever wanted their business to be spread around like that.

However, she did come all this way just to see her. And if the spirit of God really led her to come talk to Belle, maybe it was for a good reason that she couldn't see yet.

"Leo and I just haven't been seeing eye to eye lately. He's... He's going through a lot and he won't even let me try and help. He doesn't trust me and I thought he did."

Belle resisted the bit of moisture that collected at the corners of her eyes. She couldn't cry. Not here.

Mrs. Kendall let out a rueful sigh. "I told you nothing good would come of associating with him. You went in expecting too much, didn't you?"

Belle nodded. "I guess that I did... I just had this picture in my head of how we would be together and we'd somehow... Well, it's not important now. He's gone."

There was no need to go into all the fantasies she had of Leo. Of them growing old, having a family, healing together. She didn't need to tell Mrs. Kendall about all the kisses and the intimate moments they shared that made her believe they could be something special.

She had pushed him too hard and too fast and ruined it. That was her reality.

"It's better this way," Mrs. Kendall said as she took Belle's cold hand. "You two would have been unequally yoked. I could tell he wasn't a believer. Just like Second Corinthians says, what communion does light have with darkness? He would have brought you down and taken you away from the Lord. I know it hurts right now, but it really is better this way."

Never had Belle felt more riled when scripture was thrown in her face, reminding her how wrong she had been from the beginning. But she could fire back, and there was no mask of politeness to keep her from unloading on the kindly woman sitting beside her.

"Jesus called us to love our neighbors as ourselves. He broke bread with sinners. He was our example. You can't possibly sit there and tell me that showing hospitality and charity to a man like Leo was going against my faith. The book of Hebrews tells us not to forget to entertain strangers, for by so doing, some have unwittingly entertained angels... And Leo was an angel. He showed me what it meant to take care of myself. He taught me how to see my own value when I couldn't see it."

Mrs. Kendall's jaw went slack in shock. "You should draw on your value from what God says about you, not what man says."

"Oh really?" Belle said, knowing she was about to skip across a line that should never be crossed. "Then why is it that when someone in the church does something that's frowned upon, you and all the other ladies sit on your high horse and judge them for their faults? You should be lifting them up in prayer instead of gossiping about them during your sewing circles. If a stranger walked into our church like Leo did this past weekend, and received the kind of welcome that he did, it's no wonder that so few unbelievers see the goodness of God in us." She laid a hand on her chest, feeling it begin to swell and tighten with repressed tears. "I wanted to be that example for Leo. That lighthouse in the storm that we're meant to be to all those who are lost. It didn't matter where he came from or what he did before coming to Levi. If he was looking for shelter and help, then I wanted to be there for him just as Jesus is there for all of those who come to Him. Isn't that what we should be? A lighthouse?"

She looked away, closing her eyes against a tidal wave that swept her up in this new passion. "Leo was my lighthouse when I didn't know how to be one. And he taught me how to shine and not be afraid anymore."

A few beats of silence went by before Mrs. Kendall caught her up in a hug. Despite all her harsh reprimands, the woman hadn't become embittered by her speech. She didn't cast a stone at her for speaking out against an elder, nor did she condemn her for being disrespectful. And Belle returned the embrace.

"You really love him, don't you?" she whispered against her hair.

Belle had never known the tenderness of a mother's love, but she recognized this picture. It was on countless postcards and shown in all the movies. This was where she was supposed to release the tears and sob into Mrs. Kendall's knitted sweater as she confessed everything. But she wouldn't go that far.

All she could bring herself to do was nod. Nod to Mrs. Kendall, to herself, and to her heart. It was an acknowledgement that yes, she had loved Leo with every cell in her body. Every part of her yearned for him, needed him.

She wasn't an expert on the idea. Everything she knew about love came from her father and the church. She had never loved a man. But this ever-burning fire in her that continued to rage long after Leo turned his back on her was proof enough. She loved him. And he was gone.

Leo went all out, just as Mr. Tale recommended. Though Belle was far from the typical female, he would spare nothing tonight.

He went to the store and bought the food. At the local florist, he picked out the roses he was also advised to get. Though Mr. Tale had also told him to get chocolates, Leo remembered once that Belle said she wasn't into sweets. Everything else, from the settings on the table, the candles, and the crisp, freshly ironed shirt, were all to the man's specifications.

The voices in his head continued to berate him as he cooked the mince and tatties dish. It was the same old lines, but one stuck a little harder than the rest. His mother would never make this same meal. He'd never get to taste her cooking again. He couldn't make it like she did.

Leo countered with his own. He might not taste his mother's cooking again, he might not be a great chef, but he could try. That's all he could do. Try.

This was way out of his realm of expertise. His father had never done anything like this, and the men he had worked with over the years never talked about any romantic outings with their wives or girlfriends. All he knew about proper dating or courtship came from guesswork. He treated Belle how he believed she deserved to be treated. Like the most important thing in the world. Because she was.

He couldn't get this wrong. There was no room for error. If this didn't work, nothing would.

His business in the kitchen for the majority of the evening fought off the darkness to a certain degree. Without Belle on the farm though, he still felt its vicelike grip all too well. But he continued to fight for her. For them. He might have still been too tired to read the Bible, but this much he could do. He would beat this. He had to.

He timed it perfectly, so the food would be ready and warm about thirty minutes after she normally arrived home from work. With the orphaned lamb gone, he assumed Belle had trusted him to the care of another farmer while she was at work. She'd be a little later in returning home if she had to pick the lamb up.

But when the food was prepared, the table set, and the candles lit, Belle still wasn't home. More time passed and still she didn't walk through the door. At the hour mark, he strained his ears to hear the rumble of her car engine from the road. It didn't come. And each time he heard a vehicle pass, he held his breath and waited. Nothing. No headlights, no car door slamming, no Belle.

Ranger kept him company on the couch, but with each passing minute, his hope began to slip away. It was now an hour and a half past the time when he thought she would have come home. The numbness of his depression gave way to the tickle of anxiety in his chest that made it so hard to breathe.

This was a mistake.

You drove her away for good.

She's probably out with someone else, trying to forget you.

Why did you even bother trying?

This was a waste of time.

Leo crimped his eyes shut and ground his teeth. He couldn't let himself believe any of it. He had to try. This wasn't a waste. Belle would come home. Where else could she go?

Then, he heard it. The rumble came from the road and steadily made its way closer to the house. He would have known that old pickup anywhere. He stood and went over exactly what he would say to her. Looking to the kitchen, the candles were mostly burned down and the food would need to be warmed up, but hopefully she wouldn't mind.

Her footsteps sounded up the porch steps, across the deck, and to the front door. Leo hadn't expected for her to walk through with her arms full. The lamb was cradled against one elbow, while the other held a package and rolled-up banner. Her purse was slung over one shoulder and though her hair had been pulled back, it looked as if the wind had caught up a few strands.

She froze when their eyes met. The flustered expression on her face gave way to pure joy. Her one arm that had been carrying the supplies dropped, letting everything crash to the floor. Afraid she would do the same to the lamb, he ran forward to intercede. But she was perfectly lucid. At least, that's what he thought until she reached up and forced him down into a kiss.

Leo didn't buck or pull away. Only partially mindful of the lamb, he gave himself to that kiss and all the feelings that came with it. Excitement, utter bliss, everything that fought the darkness and numbness. With his mouth on hers, he had the strength of a thousand men. He had the strength to fight demons, depression, and everything the universe could throw at him.

Their kisses in the past had been to quiet her and sooth her tangled nerves. This was for him and only him. Revitalizing, bolstering, and burning. Its energy shot through him, passing through his heart and core like a bolt of electricity. Her fingers slipped into his hair as his arm encircled her waist. It was as if they had never left.

She pulled away and he hated to see the glistening tears on her cheeks.

"I thought you were gone," she whispered, her hot breath grazing the skin of his neck as she dipped her chin in embarrassment. "I thought I'd never see you again."

Leo shook his head, wishing they could have stayed suspended in that kiss. When they kissed, time didn't exist. No past or future. Just them. "I never left Levi. I stayed the night at Tale's."

That earned him a puzzled look. "With Mr. Tale?"

Then, she looked into the kitchen and her breath caught in her throat. Now was his turn to say everything he had planned to say, but most of it fell right out of his head the moment she looked at him with those green eyes that he wanted to drown in.

"You made dinner," she mumbled in disbelief.

"I did," he replied, realizing that he was holding her so tightly against him that he could feel her breathing. "It's mince and tatties. Remember I told you about that?"

Belle smiled and all the waiting, the worry, and the trouble was suddenly vindicated. "Yeah, I remember. You didn't have to."

Leo slowly released her so she could stand on her own, though he never wanted to let go. "Yes, I did. The way I talked to you yesterday wasn't right. I was..." He swallowed, knowing that he had to fess up at some point in the evening. It might as well have been now. "I've been struggling for a long time. Some days, it's manageable. Other days, like yesterday, it's not. I lashed out at you, because I was scared, which wasn't fair."

She shook her head and let the hand that had been knotted in his hair, fall to his chest. If only he could have her fingers on him like this all the time.

"No," she said. "I was out of line. I was pushing you to tell me something you weren't ready to tell me and that was wrong."

"But I should have been ready." Leo looked down to the lamb, whose neck craned up, so his nose could almost touch his shoulder, curious and probably hungry. He hadn't realized they were both holding him, the only real barrier between them.

He took the lamb from her and set him on the floor. Ranger then came, claws scratching against the tile and wood flooring as he yipped with excitement at the sight of his friend. He and the lamb went off to prance while Leo drew himself up for the speech he had prepared. If he could just find his voice and not get distracted by his audience of one.

"But I'm ready now... You asked me why I cut and it's because I'm a coward. It has nothing to do with wanting to die or blaming myself for my family falling apart. It's because when I hurt myself like I did... It helps me to ignore reality." Her hands slid into his and gripped hard, almost derailing him from his train of thought. "It's partly about the pain, but mostly about how it fights off something even darker that I feel I can't control." He returned her gentle squeeze and let himself get lost in her heartfelt gaze. "But when I do hurt myself like that, I can control it. I can feel like I have my life back. It's not about dying. It's about trying to live."

He could see that it didn't make sense to her. How could it? She probably only understood self-harm as a cry for help or an act of inflicting punishment that no one else could administer. But there was one more thing she would understand.

"It won't happen again," he promised. The doubtful glint in her eyes made him more earnest to make her believe him. "I don't have to anymore. I'm going to fight on my own now. That's why I've been this way for the last few days. I'm trying to get my life back without hurting myself, because I know it hurts you. But I need you to trust me when I say that I'm working through something."

Belle took a step closer, her stare dropping to his chest. "Then I need you to trust me in return. It doesn't matter what you tell me. I'm not going anywhere and I... I told you to leave, but I shouldn't have. I was being a child and having a tantrum, because I couldn't get my way. That was wrong. I was wrong to do that to you when you were already clearly having issues."

He wanted to kiss her so hard that all that guilt would be blasted out of her mind forever. She had no reason to berate herself for anything she had done.

"You can ask as many questions as you want," he said, shaking his head. "I'll answer every single one that I can. You've been an open book to me and it's time I returned the favor."

The silence told him that she wasn't convinced. He had to make her believe him. He reached up and gently cupped her face in his hands, forcing her to look into his eyes.

"I love you." He tested how the words felt on his lips. The statement came out breathy, weak, but she had to sense the sincerity behind it.

When she didn't answer him, he repeated it again and again until the utterances no longer sat heavy in his mouth, but tingled and flowed easily. After a while, it wasn't hard to say anymore. And with each repetition, her smile widened, and more tears seeped out from her eyes. He brushed each and every one of them away.

"I know I love you, because spending the night at Tale's made me realize how much I hate not being with you. I missed your smile, your laugh, your voice, the way you move and everything about you that drives me mad, because I want you to be mine and mine alone."

Belle took a shuddering breath before finally replying to his outpouring of affection. "I am yours. I think I have been for a while now and I didn't realize it until today either. I've just been telling myself this could never work, so I've been just as scared as you."

Instead of kissing her, Leo encased his arms around her as if that would protect her from every terrible and traitorous feeling that would drive a wedge between them. "We don't have to be afraid anymore," he whispered against her hair. "We'll make it work."

He heard her muffled, "I love you" against his shirt and he held her tighter.

It was then he noticed that he was crying too. But not in fear or rage. These tears sprung from the immense joy at her assurances. They came from the knowledge that things would truly be better after this night. How could they not? Belle had fought off the darkness with just one kiss and now, there were no more secrets between them. No more doubts or fears. Just them and this love they could finally grow together.

Chapter 15

This smile was genuine. For the first time in ages, Belle could truly smile to the strangers who passed by her table. When they asked questions, she didn't have to even touch the mask. She couldn't remember the last time she felt this happy. But she could remember the last time she felt this loved. First at her father's hospital bedside when he whispered the last words he would ever utter on this earth. The other time was when she had knelt at the altar as a teenager, ready to pledge her heart and life to Jesus.

And though both of these moments in her past were special and memorable in their own way, there was something different about knowing beyond a shadow of a doubt that Leo loved her. The way he said it again and again, building his confidence each time he repeated himself, Belle knew this wasn't just a trick to get her to believe him. It wasn't a lie. It wasn't said impulsively. He truly and deeply loved her.

The pessimistic side of her brain told her not to get used to this. He had almost left her twice already. He could do it again. At any moment, he could hop on his bike and disappear forever and there wouldn't be a thing she could do to stop him. Though he seemed

adamant enough about his new commitment not to cut, that could
happen again too. She had read somewhere that self-harm could be
addictive. And if Leo believed he had to cut to feel alive, she knew he
was definitely hooked on the rush that pain gave him.

The other side, the more trusting side of her naïve brain, wanted to
think that was all behind them now. They could plunge forward into
a bright and happy future. And even if Leo did slip once, or threaten
to leave, Belle would still love him the same and forgive him. God did
that for everyone, so she knew that she could too. Right now, she felt
like she could do anything.

The orphaned lamb curled up in his makeshift crate bed, probably
tired and worn out from the multitudes of children that came to pet
him and feel his wool. Belle had been standing for three hours so
far and she was thankful it would all be over soon. Not because she
was too drained from all the social contact, but because her feet were
beginning to hurt. Walking around the bookstore was one thing, but
standing rooted in one spot for so long with little other movement
was something she wasn't quite used to.

Leo had come with her to set up the display, but had gone back to
the farm to check on the sheep and horses. They allowed the ewes
and lambs out into a secure stretch of pasture, but Belle had warned
him to look out for any stuck heads in the fencing. His absence,
though regretful, was temporary since she would need his help to
disassemble the tent and load everything back up into her truck bed.

By all accounts, the event was proving successful. She had made
plenty of contacts within Levi, as well as through out-of-town visitors who came to the festival with relatives. Some were fellow farmers and ranchers, people she could learn from. Others were already
interested in her wool. Belle collected the phone number of one
elderly lady who was looking to sell her own flock, because she could

no longer take care of them. That would add ten more sheep to her bunch, and create more diversity for her next batch of lambs.

At the top of the fourth hour, with just one more to go before the church committee would decide to commence cleanup, Belle received a guest she hadn't expected.

"Hey, Mr. Calloway!" she greeted with a wide grin. "I didn't know you had a booth this year."

The older man slid his hands into his jean pockets and seemed a bit embarrassed. "No, not this year. My wife usually helped me and now... Well, I just can't bring myself to sign up, no matter how much Miss Georgina twists my arm."

The lady did have a way of niggling someone into doing just what she wanted. Belle was a prime example. Her facial expression at the thought couldn't be hidden and Mr. Calloway laughed at the sassy shrug of her brows and quirk of her lips.

"I wanted to check out your display close up," he admitted, his gaze wandering from one flyer handout to the next. "Looks pretty good."

Belle caught onto one part of what he said and tilted her head. "Close up?"

Mr. Calloway lifted his head and looked a little sheepish again. "Oh... I guess I said too much. Leo told me to keep an eye on you just before he left earlier. I hope you don't mind."

Always so protective. "No, I don't mind at all."

"You've got a good man there," he said, startling her with his honesty. "A good man, but... He's got some things he needs to work through."

Her smile faltered, though this was nothing new. "You're starting to sound like Mrs. Kendall." Realizing her mistake, she quickly followed up with, "Did he tell you something on Tuesday?"

Mr. Calloway picked up a flyer and casually examined it. "He doesn't have to say anything. It's written all over him. That boy's got some baggage like you wouldn't believe."

"I know," she replied with a grave nod. "He actually told me a little about it. It's not pretty."

It hadn't occurred to her that Mr. Calloway somehow knew about Leo's problems just by looking at him. That shouldn't have been nearly as surprising, though. Considering that he often got his little bits of insight straight from God and not from human understanding.

"No, it's not." The drop in his voice made Belle shiver. "And I don't have to tell you to be on your guard, do I?"

Belle paused, trying to comprehend his meaning. "If you're talking about my safety, I know Leo would never hurt me."

He shook his head. "Oh, no. I know the Lord and his angels protect you. There are too many praying people in this town for you to ever be unsafe. I'm talking about his safety." Mr. Calloway's mouth twisted in a slightly pained angle. "There's something holding him, and I fear without God's deliverance, he won't break free of it."

That was the case for any sinner. And when Belle thought back on the cutting, the smoking, and fighting, Leo must have had a lot to atone for. He, just like anyone else who didn't understand God's unconditional love, needed that deliverance. Nothing Mr. Calloway was saying was all together special or unique to Leo's case.

So, she smiled and nodded. "I'll be praying for him."

Mr. Calloway became earnest. "Don't just pray for him. Prayer is good, but he needs to find his own way out of this too."

Now, she was concerned. But there was little time to think about it or ask further, because the subject of their conversation was striding toward them, beaming and eager. The two men shook hands like old friends and Leo moved around to stand beside Belle, who fidgeted with the cuffs of her jacket sleeves. Her eyes were glued to him as new and beguiling thoughts raced through her mind, all having to do with what Mr. Calloway had just told her.

"Well, I'll let you two get to it, then." The old man leaned over like he was about to tell Leo a secret, but there was little privacy about what he said. "I looked after her like you asked. She didn't sneak off once the whole time."

Leo chuckled, a sound that she had sorely missed. "I appreciate it."

When Mr. Calloway left them alone, one of Leo's strong arms was instantly around her waist and pulled her so tight to him that the breath was forced out of her lungs. She only had enough time to react by flattening her hand against his chest.

"Leo, not here," she giggled, reclining her head back to avoid the lips that steadily descended upon hers.

"No one's watching."

One glance to the main thoroughfare of traffic between the rows of booths told her enough. "Some are."

"Then let them watch," he purred before finally claiming her.

She went tense for a moment, hoping that no one from the church committee saw this. But then, it suddenly didn't matter and she melted in his embrace. The kiss was tender, sweet, but so possessive that her heart couldn't help but feel branded by his love.

When he pulled away, she waited for the spell of lightheadedness to go away before she smiled up at him. He asked something, but her head was still in a whirl. Belle had never drunk a drop of alcohol, but she imagined this was what being drunk felt like. Drunk off his love and need for her. For a minute, she couldn't think of any way that life could get better.

Leo let her talk. He'd let her talk until her face turned blue. Just as long as that smile stayed fixed on her lips, widening each time she mentioned something amusing that happened during the Farmer's Fall Festival.

Leo wasn't an idiot. He knew what was likely to happen. The darkness would try to get at him harder. It would try to break through the barrier Belle's love had forged around him, protecting him from the despairing thoughts that wanted to drag him straight to hell. And Matthew would know about everything. Some way or another, he always did. He'd come to steal away all this contented happiness and do what he should have done in Scotland.

He should have been on his guard, and he was. His eyes continually scanned the tree line and every car they passed on the way back to the farm. Though Mr. Calloway would have never known why Leo asked him to look after Belle, it was because of Matthew's nearness to Levi. He hadn't seen a single sign of his brother, but that didn't mean he wasn't there somewhere, lurking and waiting.

But the longer Belle talked, the harder it was to concentrate on the grim certainty of the conflict ahead of them. Her voice, bouncing with excitement and eagerness for that future, disarmed him more than the darkness ever could.

"It sounds like you had a successful day," he said when it sounded as if Belle was slowing down.

With a happy sigh, she nodded her head and stared out the windshield. Her eyes danced with a cheerful glow. "I really did. I did a lot better than I thought I would."

Leo wondered if their definitions of success were a little different in this conversation. Not only did Belle make connections, but she seemed to be stable. Not once did she talk about an instance when her anxiety decided to step forward and ruin the experience for her. It was a business and personally successful event.

"Plans for the evening?" he asked, thrumming his fingers on the steering wheel. "Candles? Tea? Bubble bath?"

He felt her eyes on him, their warmth as tangible as a caress. "I may have some tea, but I was thinking about checking on the ewes. Maybe hang out with Buck and the horses too."

Yes, it had been a good day if she wasn't drained or too emotionally spent to do the things she loved.

"All with you, of course," she quickly added. "Unless you have something you need to do."

Leo smiled and thought of the reading assignment he had been putting off for days. After the blowup with Belle, their heartfelt conversation the day before, and everything in between, he hadn't wanted to even look at the Bible. But Mr. Calloway would be wanting some confirmation that he had at least tried to finish. It then occurred to him that the following day was Sunday. That meant Belle would go to church.

"I do have something, but... I don't know if I'll do it."

"What is it?" Belle asked, a hint of a nervous laugh playing in the words.

The thought to lie had entered his mind, but he paused and pushed it out before it had a chance to form. "Mr. Calloway told me that I needed to read something."

It was pointless to hope that she wouldn't probe further.

"Read what?"

Leo's fingers tightened over the wheel. "The Bible. Books Matthew and John. Have you read those?"

He glanced her way and her mouth twitched with the smile that wanted to widen into a broad and giddy grin. "I have," she replied, feigning calmness.

"Are they long?"

Belle turned away and he could see the flash of white as her lips parted to finally release that grin she had been holding. "If you're thinking about trying to read both books before tomorrow for church, you may have a little bit of trouble."

The temptation to groan was there. If he could just skip on church, then he'd have a few extra days before he had to give an answer to Mr. Calloway. While the motivation was there to unlock this secret of how to control the demons, he didn't want to have to explain why it was taking him so long. He didn't want to have to tell Belle or Mr. Calloway about how the words became so jumbled together that he couldn't even pin them onto the page with his finger. Nor how depression had stolen away his ability to do anything beyond the absolute necessary.

But if he didn't go to church, that meant Belle would be left alone and vulnerable. Not in the middle of the sanctuary with dozens of other believers around her, but he dreaded the trip there and back. There were too many opportunities open for Matthew and the darkness, if Belle's personal guard couldn't protect her somehow. Maybe he could drop her off and leave.

Leo turned onto the drive from the main road. "I don't know if I'll go with you tomorrow," he told her, bracing for the disappointment that was sure to come. By her responses to the conversation so far, he could tell she was too excited about his interest in her faith. Or, at least one aspect of it. He didn't care much for the redemption, the forgiveness of sins, or the other principles of Christianity. He only cared about the one thing that would truly set him free from his brother and the darkness.

He watched her expression and found that he had grossly under-estimated her reaction. All color faded from her complexion, leaving her face almost milky white as her eyes widened. If the truck wasn't rocking over the dirt path, he imagined she'd be trembling all by herself.

"If it means that much, I'll go."

Belle's head snapped in his direction as if she had been too absorbed in some terrifying thought and hadn't heard him at all.

It was then he looked back to the drive and found they weren't alone. A shiny red car sat near the porch and a woman was waiting in one of the deck chairs, her slender legs crossed at the knees. Even from this far away, Leo could see the sour lines etched in a familiar, yet unfamiliar face. He had seen this woman before, but younger. Her photograph hung on Belle's wall in the upstairs collage, marginalized for a good reason. And seeing the woman in person now, he could see why. If he had met her mother on the street in any other circumstance, he would have turned and walked the other way.

When the truck was in park and the engine shut off, Belle's mother stood and marched to the top of the steps, her heels drumming so loudly he could hear them through the closed doors.

The air in the cab immediately shifted and one look to Belle told him enough. The mask that had been neglected all day was now in place, and she was forcing herself to be ready for this unscheduled visit.

"Are you going to be all right?" he asked in a mumble as if the upset woman on the porch could hear them from where she stood.

Belle gave him a nod and gathered up the orphan lamb that had been sitting obediently in her lap the whole way home. "Yeah, I'm fine... Just watch what you say."

Leo would do nothing of the kind.

They climbed out of the truck and made their way to the porch, leaving the supplies from the event in the bed of the truck until either of them was ready to bring it all inside. Which, if Leo could have his way, would be fairly soon.

Before a proper greeting could even be given, her mother broke in. "Since when do you work on Saturdays?"

Belle straightened, but Leo could tell she was trying so hard not to get defensive. "I wasn't at work, mom. There was a fall festival in town and I hosted a booth."

Any mother should have at least pretended to be supportive. This woman's painted red lips twisted into something a little less than revulsion, but more than confusion. Maybe part of that had to do with the wriggling lamb in Belle's arms. "A booth? What would you need a booth for?"

"For the farm," she replied with some cautious level of excitement. Apparently, she wasn't counting on her mother being too interested in the topic. "I'm going to start breeding horses and building up the flock."

Her mother looked every part the type of woman who was more at home in the city and on concrete sidewalks than a farm. It was no surprise she would try to leave this home behind her in favor of a busier place like Little Rock. That, however, was no excuse for abandoning her family, and that's why the glare on Leo's face wouldn't waver.

And then, as if he had magically manifested, the green eyes that Belle had inherited, turned to Leo. "And who's this?" By the appraising sweep of her gaze, he guessed that she was more interested in finding out for her own purposes rather than out of simple curiosity.

Belle stiffened as they climbed the porch steps. "This is Leo. He's been helping me for the last few weeks."

"You never told me you had someone working for you. I didn't think you could afford that." She extended a hand that looked just delicate enough for him to crush. "It's a pleasure to meet you, Leo. I'm Belle's mother, but you can call me Melinda."

Leo accepted the handshake and made sure to let her know that he was strong enough to do damage without actually inflicting any. "Hi, Melinda. You need to leave."

Both women gaped at him.

"Leo!" Belle gasped.

"Excuse me?" Melinda slipped her hand away and propped it on her bony hip covered in a skin-tight dress.

"You need to leave." Leo repeated the order a little more slowly this time, so it could make its way into her thick skull without too much effort.

It wasn't slow enough.

"Leave? What are you talking about?"

Beside him, Belle was too awestruck to say anything, which he was thankful for. If she could just stay that way until he had a chance to save her.

"Leave. Now. Get in your little sports car and drive back to the highway."

Melinda's shock morphed into rage. "I'm not going anywhere. I'm here to see my daughter."

"She doesn't want to see you. You've done enough and now you need to go."

In the corner of his eye, he saw Belle shake out of her daze. "Leo, what are you doing?"

"Doesn't want to see me?" Melinda looked to her daughter, still angry but now injured by this new concept that her own flesh and blood didn't want to have anything to do with her. "Belle always wants to see me. I'm her mother." She leaned to Belle, as if to ask something private, but Leo could hear her every word. "Are you safe here? Is he doing something to you?"

Leo stepped between them. "I'm not doing anything to her. You're the one causing the trouble. You need to leave."

Melinda glared up at him. "I told you that I'm not going anywhere. And if you're holding my daughter hostage – "

"Stop!" Belle shouted, an edge of panic in her voice. "Everyone just stop!" She bent down and let the poor lamb escape across the porch deck before looking from Leo to her mother and then back again. "I think you need to go in the house," she said, regaining some of her calm. The mask was shattered under the immense pressure of this confrontation he had created.

Leo's narrowed eyes shifted between her and Melinda, assessing how far he really needed to go. If Melinda became violent or too abusive, he wanted nothing to block his path to intercept. The desperate, broken look written on Belle's face was convincing enough.

He gave a nod and slowly made his way into the house, but kept his ears open to any distressing sound. This would be the last time Melinda hurt Belle.

Belle stood in front of her mother, a hand covering part of her face in total embarrassment. *Why did Leo say those things? What was he trying to do here?*

Then she remembered the fight with Drake at the diner. As much as she could admire the sentiment, Leo's mind was programmed in a way that she didn't approve of. Being rude or fighting one's way out of a tough situation was not the way to handle things. He couldn't go off and deck Drake, and he couldn't order her mother to leave.

Melinda continued to fume and rant about his behavior, saying that he must be mentally ill or completely inept for saying those things. The truth was, he wasn't. What he had said was the same thing she had longed to say to her mother each and every time she went too far with her negativity and criticism. She just never had the nerve to say it out loud.

Leo did, though. And it might have proved to be the catalyst for a change she wasn't altogether ready for.

"The nerve of him to say that to my face with you standing there!" Melinda raved. "Putting words in your mouth like that. You should fire him. In fact, I demand you fire him. The next thing you know, he'll be telling you how to live your life. You'll lose every friend, I'm telling you."

Belle took a deep breath and waited for a pause in her mother's speech. "Mom... He's right."

She didn't want to meet that stunned stare Melinda had pinned her with, so she looked toward the pastures where she could see Maggie and Buck sharing a patch of grass. She couldn't fully think about what she was about to do. She couldn't imagine herself holding that match and standing at the other end of the bridge from her mother. If she allowed herself to visualize or give a complete thought to what she was doing, she would never be able to go through with it. Then, she'd have to go through this again and again.

Maybe it was time to take a stand.

"All my life, I've never known you to be positive or even happy. You always had something bad to say about everything, even if it was good. You like your new job, but you hate your coworkers. You love your car, but it guzzles gas. You say you love me, but you never seem to care about what I do. You're always putting me down, criticizing every part of my life until I don't know who I am anymore. Am I your daughter or a part-time project? Am I a strong and confident woman or a little girl who doesn't know how to put on makeup? I know you say you want to see me, but you don't see me. You see my flaws. And I can't handle it anymore."

Melinda didn't speak and it drove Belle to finally look into her aghast expression, bracing for the worst. A slap in the face. A scream-fest. A turned back as she stomped away and never glanced over her shoulder. Any of those would have been easier than continuing this conversation.

"I'm not negative. I'm a realist."

Belle shook her head. "A negative person sees the glass is half empty. A realist understands that the glass can always be refilled."

"And that's what I do!" she exclaimed. "I see where you can make improvements."

"But what you think is an improvement isn't necessary. I don't need to change. God loves me for who I am right in this moment and you should too."

Melinda was hurt by her words. "And I do love you."

"No, mom," she asserted. "You don't understand what love is. Love doesn't find fault with everything. People who love are patient and kind. They do everything they can to protect the people they love. They trust and persevere through the hard times, because they know that when everything else is gone, love remains. But you..." Belle gave a mirthless laugh. "You don't do any of that. Love is unconditional, but you put way too many conditions on this relationship. If I tell you I won't sell the farm, you think I'm crazy for keeping it. If my mascara is clumpy, you tell me to get something new. If I tell you I won't fire Leo, you'll think I've lost my mind and that there must be something else going on between us. And if there is, you'll probably convince me to dump him, because you don't think he's good for me... But he's right. You're not good enough for me."

Belle felt as if she were speeding down the highway and her brakes were shot. "All my life, I've tried to make sense of the things you've told me. I wondered why I was never good enough for you and it made me doubt everything about myself. I thought that if I just acted right, if I looked pretty, and didn't step on anyone's toes, then people would like me. That *you* would like me. I've driven myself insane trying to measure up and hide the parts of me that you constantly picked at. But I'm tired, mom. I'm tired of trying to make you understand that I can't be everything for you and I can't be better. I'm perfect just the way I am and if you can't accept that... you need to leave."

Before she could say anything else, Belle literally held her tongue with her teeth and pinched her lips together. Even if Melinda chose to retaliate, she wouldn't take the bait. She would want an argument. She'd want to fight.

The fire of the burning bridge flickered between them and Belle could feel its heat upon her face. There was no way to come back from this. No way to put out the words that she had just blasted out without care or heed to politeness. This was the end and she could only hope that Melinda would take it gracefully.

But the longer they stared at one another, Melinda's face slowly morphing from rage to sadness and then to understanding, Belle wished there was some way to lessen their pain.

Nothing else was said on the porch. Melinda turned, her gaze sliding away from her daughter for the last time as she descended the steps and walked away.

Chapter 16

Leo watched as Melinda's car backed up and pulled toward the main road, disappearing in a cloud of dust as her tires nearly spun out on the dirt drive. He waited, listening for Belle's footsteps on the porch. With his hands slung in his pockets, his eyes were set upon the door. When she came through, he expected to see a bright, grinning face. She was finally free from her mother's abusive hold. He braced for her to run to him and throw her arms about his neck. That kiss would be his reward for breaking the links on the last string of chains that bound her heart in fear and doubt.

But when her footsteps sounded across the deck and the door swung open, Belle looked anything but what he had imagined. Her eyes were wide and downcast, her movements slow and deliberate as if she were trying to focus carefully on each step she took. The soft click of the door latch was the only sound for what seemed like an eternity as Leo tried to understand.

He took one step forward and her hand immediately shot up. It was trembling, outstretched to stop him from coming any closer. That profound and clear gesture might as well have been like a loaded gun pointed at his chest. And her gaze was the bullet. So full of repressed emotions that he couldn't begin to sift through.

"You had no right to do that." Her voice was shaky, each word stitched together by anger that he knew well.

Belle was wounded, vulnerable, and scared. He had seen this side of her before. The raw, real side of her that no one else saw. She had unloaded on her mom, and now it was his turn.

"What was I supposed to do?" he asked, trying so hard not to reciprocate. "You know what would have happened if she'd stayed. All the good things that happened today would have been for nothing. You would have been a mess after she left and I couldn't let that happen. I love you too much."

Her fingers curled into fists and she let her arm drop. "Yeah, that might have happened. Or maybe I could have worked through it. Maybe I could have suffered through another one of her visits and been stronger for it. Did you think about that?"

"You weren't ready." His defense came out clipped and harsh, much harsher than he wanted.

"And you think I was ready for this?" she asked, waving her hand toward the front yard. Her lone pickup truck sat there, still loaded down with her event display.

"You're better off if she was gone."

Belle gave him an incredulous smile, her brow furrowed in disbelief. "You don't know that. I don't even know that. Yeah, my mom drives me up the wall, but neither of us knows what the future holds. She might have changed over the years. I might have found a better way to tell her all those things that I just screamed at her. I might not have had to burn that bridge. But thanks to you, I don't know if she'll ever come back."

Leo shrugged. "Is that such a bad thing? After being absent for part of your childhood and then treating you like crap for the rest of it, do you really want to keep that in your life?"

Belle took a deep breath and he could tell she struggled not to break down into tears. "She's my mother, Leo. She's family."

"No, she's a parasite!" Once more, he didn't mean to come across so abrasive. "She drains you. She sucks the life out of you. That's not family."

"And I suppose you would know what family is and isn't."

A deathly hush fell between them and Belle touched her lips, as if she had to make sure they were her own. Wrath transformed into shock, but Leo never faltered.

"If anyone has a right to say what is and isn't family, it's me."

Belle closed her eyes and seemed to take a moment to regroup. "I didn't mean to say that."

"Yes, you did. It's how you feel and I never want you to regret how you feel or what you say. You meant to say all those things to your mom, too." Leo pointed toward the window that looked over the porch. "What you said out there was years of words bottled up in you that needed to be said. I won't apologize for what I did. You may not see it now, but cutting her off is – "

"Leo," Belle snapped. "I don't care about how this is going to feel three months or three years down the road. Right now, I feel like I've just done the stupidest thing of my adult life. Now I really have nobody."

He took it back. That look she gave when he tried to rush forward to comfort her wasn't the bullet. This was. He didn't want to think she had forgotten everything they shared in just one moment. She couldn't have. But he could believe that he just screwed up a perfect thing, just like the demons said he would.

Forcing her to confront her mother was the final straw, the break-ing point. All he wanted to do was help her and she had finally pushed back.

"You... You have me." He hated how his nervousness shined through in that moment. He could feel his face twitch with the fear that she would try to throw away what they had. Their relationship had barely had a chance to start before it all came crashing down. And it was his fault.

Belle leveled a look at him. "Right now... I'm... Just let me figure this out, please?"

Leo shook his head. "If you think too much about this, it'll just drive you crazy."

Those hands that once were slack, contracted again. "Right now, I need time to think. Too much has happened. I just need to figure it out, okay?"

He never thought she would ask for space. Not after all the times she said that she wanted his company more than anything, how he felt like home to her. Leo wanted to be her place of comfort. He needed to be that for her. But now, he was a source of anxiety, just like everything else.

Once more, he had failed to do something good. He hadn't saved her. Instead, he threw her into more turmoil without even meaning to.

But he couldn't be angry. Not at her. It wasn't her fault. So Leo only nodded and turned to walk into the kitchen. If she wanted space, he'd give it. Plenty of it. Whatever she wanted, he'd give it to her.

Her quickened steps to chase after him wouldn't give him hope.

"Promise you won't leave?"

The urgency in the plea did make him glance to her once he reached the back door. She stood there in the entryway to the kitchen, her hand clutching the casing so tightly he saw the tips of her fingers grow white.

"I promise I won't leave."

That might have been the only thing he could promise now. He couldn't give her happiness, peace, or comfort. Not right now.

He knew how it felt to think that one was entirely and completely alone in the world, without a friend or loved one to rely on. He had felt it the moment his sister stopped breathing when her sickness took its final toll. He wanted to hate the world and everything in it for the unfairness he had been dealt, but the only person he could truly blame was himself.

If Belle felt just a fraction of that kind of heartbreak, that kind of devastation, then she would need much more than he could ever attempt to give her. She needed a miracle of healing. And quite frankly, so did he.

If Belle thought it was worthwhile to sew her mouth shut, she would have. This was a new level of unhinged that she had never experienced before. It was like there were no more limits, no filters. She had dove off the cliff without a harness or safety net, but she kept falling and bracing for the impact that never came. There was only this dread that she couldn't stop, couldn't slow down.

After she'd told her mom how she truly felt and come in to face Leo, there was nothing to hold back the tsunami. No sandbags, no barrier, and at the end when she stood in the middle of the wreckage, there was no relief coming to clean up the mess she had made. Leo stayed outside for the rest of the evening and all Belle could do was relive every agonizing moment. Every word, every biting comment and accusation she had unleashed played on loop like a scratchy broken record in her head.

For the first hour or so, all she could do was sit on the sofa and stare at the ashes in the fireplace, trying in vain to breathe and calm her heart. No matter how hard it pounded in her chest, she refused to go to the kitchen to make tea. Nor did she light a lavender candle, reach for essential oils, or draw a hot bath to soak in. She would ride out the storm and make herself face the damage. She'd make herself feel every ounce of pain instead of numbing it.

When the house began to darken and the worst of the tremors finally passed, Belle could see everything a little more clearly again.

Leo was right and wrong at the same time.

While everything she had said to her mother was like releasing the pressure from a valve that was about to bust, Belle knew it wasn't the right time. Then again, when was? If she had waited until everything collapsed, when she was unstable and too emotional to see straight, would the words have been meaner? Could she have put them any better if she weren't so stressed or if the truth bomb had been dropped in her own time? Likely not. She was in a good mood before seeing her mother. When was that going to happen again in the future? Her heart was in the right place for this change, but that didn't make her feel any less guilty for the whole thing.

But now, it was over. There was no going back, no expunging what had been done. This wasn't a dry erase board that could be cleared, the marks forgotten. Her mother would never forget what she said. Maybe it would be enough to make her understand the significance of her influence on Belle. More likely, it would be all the evidence she needed to forget about Levi and her daughter, and move on with her life like she never had a family. She had done it once before. There was no reason she couldn't do it again.

This left Belle empty, just like the day her father told her the whole story about their little broken family. Knowing that her mother, the one who had given birth to her and should have loved her, didn't want to have anything to do with her, had been devastating enough for a child. And after so many years of trying to cope with that hole and slowly patching up the edges with God's help, she felt like everything had come unraveled. She'd have to heal all over again and part of her wasn't ready.

But she had been wrong about one thing. And it was in the moment she peeked out her bedroom window that she realized just what it was. Belle wasn't alone. She knew that when she saw Leo feeding the orphaned lamb. He was perched on a fence rail, holding the bottle up high so the lamb wouldn't suckle on any air pockets in the milk. Ranger sat patiently at his feet, the little tail wagging and ears perked up at attention.

Leo was a good man with good intentions. Through his own brokenness, he had made time for her again and again. He didn't deserve all the nasty things she had said in her outbursts when reason failed to stop up her mouth. He deserved all the love she knew she could give, and so much more.

Belle instantly felt selfish and ungrateful, but she had never loved him more. If only she could find the words to apologize. It took her all night and part of the following morning, but it still didn't seem right or sincere.

He would see straight through any patchwork lie she tried to give him. He would know if she was genuinely trying to heal the wounds or just throwing out the typical platitudes to try and make amends. He could see through all of it, which made her scared to even try.

As she fixed her breakfast and got ready for church – because she wouldn't skip out on service even if she felt like a failure – she tried

to see if Leo was still on the property. His bike was parked beside the
house, but none of the animals had been let out yet.

Careful not to make too much noise, she ventured to the barn and
stables to look. The horses were in their stalls and the sheep were
penned up, and Leo reclined against a warm pile of straw with both
Ranger and the lamb snuggled up next to him.

Belle smiled and felt a tiny bit of the black hole in her spirit shrink.
He hadn't left, just like he promised, and from what she could see,
there was no evidence of a cutting fiasco either. But from where she
stood, it was hard to discern. The only way would be to wake him
and inspect his arms and legs herself, which she couldn't do.

For now, she would trust him and just try to be thankful that she
hadn't destroyed the one speck of happiness she had left.

The longest night Leo had ever lived through might have been the
one where he came home to watch his parents die. He remembered
the sirens, the social workers, his sister in a silent daze. The seconds
dragged on like hours. The minutes were days to him. But this last
night spent in the barn, battling his own demons while trying to
work out this mess he had made with Belle, trumped that night in
Scotland ten times over.

Every waking moment was wasted in an attempt to convince himself that he hadn't failed, that there was hope, that she still loved him
beneath the hurt and betrayal. He shied away from everything sharp
and even went so far as to lock them away in the tool shed.

He had come to accept the fact that he had gone too far. He crossed
a line with the best of intentions. That territory of healing he had
tried to trespass upon was hers alone and she was right. It was her

call to make, her bridge to burn, and she wasn't ready to be handed the matches just yet.

If he knew anything about Belle's mother, he might have been tempted to drive all through the night to find her and undo what he had done, even if he didn't think it was right or necessary. He wouldn't take back what he said. Belle needed this disconnect. And he found that sometimes she needed a little shove. Whether it was a carefully worded, honest text to a friend, or a gentle reminder that she didn't have to be everything for everyone. But Leo could accept that he had pushed too hard.

What his demons and tormentors had to say was far less consoling. The voices condemned him, told him that he had no business being a lover and a friend when he treated others this way. They made him feel worthless, useless, a failure. And Leo, whether by some miracle breakthrough or maybe Belle was praying for him in secret, had found a happy middle ground in their criticisms. Maybe he did deserve to die, but not today and not for this.

He held onto the promise of life with both hands, because for once, he wanted to see the dawn. With daybreak would come a new day and a fresh start. If Belle still didn't want him after the sun rose, he would deal with it then. But if she wanted him, if she could forgive him, if she could continue to love him, then all the pain and sorrow he endured would be worth it by morning.

When he finally awoke to the rooster crows in the chicken yard, Leo forced himself to move though every muscle in his body ached. He must have only managed to get an hour or so of sleep and not in comfort either. He checked on the sheep and fed the lamb before leaving the barn to find Belle's truck was gone.

His panic was momentary before he realized it was Sunday. Ranger continued to trip over Leo's heels as he followed him up to the house. After feeding the pup and still ignoring the voices that tried to tell him that Belle had left him for good, he found a note that alleviated almost all his fears.

Leo,

I've gone to church. When I come back, I want to talk. I'm sorry for the things I said last night. I was upset and shouldn't have taken it out on you. I want to be better. Please forgive me?

Belle

If only she understood how much Leo needed her forgiveness first. He put the note down and braced himself against the countertop, holding himself together one more time as the relief descended upon him. Dawn fulfilled its promise and it wasn't over. For once, things weren't over.

But there was no way that Leo could wait another hour or two before Belle came home. If he could take a quick shower, jump into a pair of clean clothes, and hurry, he could make it in time to sit beside Belle in the pews for the service. They didn't have to speak, and he honestly didn't want to. Just being close to her again would be enough to quiet the noise of the demons in his head.

Belle turned up the volume of her radio. Her father's old Alan Jackson cassette tape had been nearly played to death over the years and she never knew when she'd hear *Midnight in Montgomery* for the last time.

But she needed to hear it, even if it was for the last time. Because that cassette tape reminded her of simpler times. Times when she rode next to her father in the truck, her little body bouncing along down dirt roads, even when she had her seatbelt on. She needed to listen to the ghost of her father's voice singing along with his favorite artist. She needed to remember his bright, wide smile when she would speak up in her tiny voice and sing along with him.

Every bit of it was vital to helping her forget about that letter she wrote. That honest, pathetic letter. Just for a little while as she drove to the church, she didn't want to think about how Leo would read it and begin to wonder if her damage was worth the time he wasted trying to repair it.

She could have just not left a note. She could have worded it a little differently. But she couldn't crumble it up or erase a single letter. Something in her gut told her not to. It told her to be honest, be truthful, to be herself. That's what Leo had wanted from the beginning.

A smile found its way to her lips and she took a deep, shuddering breath as the next song rolled out of her speakers. *Love's Got A Hold On You*. It sure did.

Belle drove up to the only four-way stop on her way to the church and she hadn't expected to see anyone else stop with her. Even over the car radio, she could hear the rumble of another engine on the road. Its volume alone told her that it wasn't any normal car.

Her heart nearly stopped as she looked all around for the motor-cycle, expecting to see Leo.

But it wasn't.

The man who eased up to the stop sign to her left was familiar, but definitely not Leo. It took her a second to recognize him and she wondered how she could forget a face like his, even for a moment.

It was her turn to go. She had been sitting at the line for almost a full minute, but she found herself staring fixedly at the guy she had met at the bookstore earlier that week. He had asked for some New Age books. Despite the twangy melody battling against the roar of the bike, a shiver ran up and then down her spine. This guy still gave her the creeps.

His blue eyes turned to her and another minute stretched on as they stared. Did he recognize her too? With his hand still gripping the handle of his Harley, he gave her a three-finger wave and nod. He must have known who she was. And that slight gesture broke the spell.

Even though she doubted that he could see through the sun glare on her windshield, she gave him the same greeting and her feet found the motivation to drive ahead. Maybe a little faster than she would have normally. Luckily, no one was behind her and waiting for her to get a move on.

In the rearview mirror, she watched the man drive across the intersection and she felt she could breathe again.

Then, the radio began to skip at the end of the song. She sighed and recognized the way it looped and scratched. It had nothing to do with the cassette, but something in the radio itself. The only way to fix it was to give it a firm, but loving smack on the plate.

Belle did, but it continued to skip. A few more times and she began to wonder if she really was listening to the death of her dad's favorite tape.

Then, she heard something like a thunderous boom and her truck rattled harder. Belle looked through her windshield for the first time since she left the four-way stop. Across both lanes lay the thick trunk of a fallen pine tree.

She slammed on her brakes. The tires squealed. The smell of burning rubber seeped into the cab. Knowing she couldn't stop in time, Belle turned the wheel hard. She closed her eyes, bracing for impact.

Belle felt her world tilt and the squealing stopped. The shattering of glass and scraping of metal replaced it. Her seatbelt held firm and cut into her chest and shoulder. Something hit her face and her hands were thrown back from the wheel as the airbag deployed. Her head snapped back and banged against something hard.

Her hands reached for anything to hold onto just before the skipping on the radio finally stopped and the truck went still. She could smell gas and she heard a hissing noise through the ringing in her ears.

Nauseous and her head pounding, she tried to gasp for air, but consciousness was slipping. Her hands continued to grab, to search for something to hold onto, because somehow through the chaos, she understood that she was upside down. By the time she was ready to open her eyes, she didn't have the strength to.

There weren't enough curse words in English or in Gaelic that Leo could scream to make him feel any better. He had dialed 9-1-1 before the engine died on his bike. He ran to the mangled truck on the side of the road. The grass was saturated with petrol that leaked from the fuel tank.

Once he reported the accident, he dropped to his knees and pried out the heavy shards of broken glass from the bent window frame of the driver side door. The razor edges cut into his hands, but he didn't feel any of it. Nothing but the anger and fear that perpetuated after he saw the hex carved into the tree in the road.

This was Matthew. All Matthew.

Hot tears clamped around his throat as soon as he saw Belle's face. The airbag was deflated. Its rough seams had ripped through her sleeves like serrated knives. Her cut arms hung to her sides, the back of her hands resting against the dented roof of the cab. A leaking cut on her forehead just below her hairline was in the beginning stages of swelling. But her face showed no signs of distress. It was as if she were sleeping.

Leo tried to yank the door open, but it wouldn't budge. The frame was too damaged. He pushed back the airbag and cleared the path, so when he reached out to unbuckle her seatbelt, Belle could fall safely into his arms.

Doing his best not to jostle her, he slipped her out of the car and onto the road. He glanced back at the totaled truck before he checked her over for any other injuries. Leo wasn't a doctor. He didn't even know how to do CPR, but he understood injuries. He had seen enough, inflicted enough.

While the cut in her forehead continued to bleed, producing a single line of blood that curved around her temple and cheek, he couldn't find anything else to worry about. She was breathing, that much he knew. Her chest rose and fell, the vein in her neck pulsed, and she wasn't cold. Not dead.

Leo heard the sirens coming, but he didn't care. He held her to his chest, afraid to let go or something else would happen. As long as that hex was there, as long as Matthew might have been close by, they weren't safe. Not anymore.

He cursed himself for being so stupid as to let his guard down. He let this happen to her. He let his pride and love for her get in the way of protecting her. How could he have given her space when being apart for more than a moment might have killed her?

For a time, he wanted to hope that maybe Matthew wouldn't come after them. Not while she prayed and the darkness was weakened by whatever agents protected Belle. But he had been wrong. So wrong.

The squad cars, ambulance and firetruck came to the scene. Car doors slammed and the voices of men assessing the carnage should have been his cue to let the professionals do their job. But the moment one of the medics reached for Belle, he lashed out like a desperate animal and held her tighter.

"Sir, we need to check her over."

"She's fine!" he bellowed.

One woman from an ambulance in a blue uniform managed to find Belle's wrist and checked for a pulse. "It's sporadic," she reported.

"Sir, let us take care of her."

Leo looked to them and once he realized none of them were Matthew or the darkness, he began to loosen his grip. Belle was snatched from him and the medics hoisted her onto a gurney. Questions came at him from every direction as he tried to make sense of their medical talk. He stood and followed, pushing aside the cops looking for answers.

"I want to go with her," Leo demanded.

The man who had convinced him to finally let them take her turned and blocked his path to the ambulance. "We're taking her to Mercy Hospital. You can meet her there.

"Please, let me go with her."

"Are you family?"

Leo knew how to answer correctly. If he said he wasn't family or kin, the man would turn him away. If he was, he might let him into the ambulance. He couldn't go so far to say they were relatives. It'd be too much of a lie. But he could say something else.

"We're engaged. I just proposed this morning. I hadn't bought her a ring yet. It was a spur of the moment thing."

Maybe something in his lying ramble struck a chord with the man, because he finally nodded. "Okay. You can ride in the front. There's a window in between. We can keep you updated on the way."

Chapter 17

Leo paced up and down the stretch of the waiting room, his fists jammed into his jean pockets. Those seated in the musty cushioned chairs watched him, but he didn't care. He had to move. He couldn't just sit and twiddle his thumbs until a doctor or nurse came to tell him something. He had to keep moving or he'd scream. He had already called Mr. Johnson – who was back in town - and told him to keep an eye on the farm until they returned, but he wouldn't tell any of their friends about the accident until he had all the information.

Over and over he thought of everything he could have done differently. He should have never left her last night. He should have gone with her to church. Maybe then he could have prevented the accident. Better yet, he might have been able to convince her to stay home entirely. Then again, if Belle wanted to go, there was no stopping her. Church and God were too important in her life. He only wished he could take comfort in any of that right now.

He remembered a man he worked with years ago. His wife had died of cancer and said that it was God's will that she let the illness take her. The man said that she wasn't in pain any longer and that was what was best for her. Leo had thought it a bunch of rubbish then, and he thought it was rubbish now. God didn't want Belle to get in that accident. But he might have wanted to punish her for trying to love a man like Leo. And the darkness would surely want to torture him by toying with Belle's life like this.

After the hundredth pass about the room, Leo came to the conclusion that this wasn't a plot to kill Belle. It must have been a warning, whether from God or the darkness or Matthew. It was a warning to leave, to abandon her and anyone else who could be targeted. He knew the signs. If he didn't leave, something worse would happen and Belle might not survive it.

If it were anyone else, if it were Mr. Tale or Mr. Calloway, or Ivy, then he would leave. He would put Levi behind him and drive in any direction on the map just so the darkness and Matthew would follow him. But it was Belle. She was the only woman he had ever loved and he couldn't leave. Not anymore. He was too involved. He had become too involved the night he comforted her after Melinda's visit. That same night, he kissed her to quiet that troubled mind. He did it, because he knew she wouldn't slow down otherwise, but that simple act had catapulted them into this mess. That was the night of the first warning, when the barn burned. And this was the second warning. He should have never started this. Then she wouldn't have been admitted into the hospital.

His head swiveled to the door the moment he heard the latch click. A nurse stepped through in bright blue scrubs, her eyes on the clipboard. "Leo Thompson?"

He rushed forward before she had a chance to ask him to follow. They wound their way past offices and other waiting rooms.

"Is Belle awake?" he asked.

The nurse skimmed over the charts, but wouldn't look at him. "I'll let the doctor explain everything."

"But is she going to be okay?"

"Please, save your questions for Dr. Stevens." Leo took the hint from her frustrated tone not to probe further, though he wasn't sure how much longer he could wait.

They came to one door that looked no different than any of the others, but somehow Leo could sense that Belle was inside. He didn't wait for the nurse before plunging in.

She lay on the bed, a gauzy wrapping of bandages around her head and both her arms. A monitor beeped rhythmically with her heartbeat, relieving the fears that the nurse couldn't. Belle was still alive and that was all that mattered.

He went to her bedside and saw the tube coming out of her arm that trailed up to a bag of fluid suspended above her head.

"We have her on an IV for hydration," the nurse explained, probably seeing the hint of fresh worry in his eyes.

Leo tried to make sense of the blinking lights and numbers, but he barely had time before the doctor arrived. He was a little older than Leo, with dark blonde hair cut short and pale eyes full of the warmth and comfort that a patient and their loved ones always needed. They shook hands and exchanged greetings, though Leo couldn't give a crap about his name. He only cared about Belle.

"She's going to be okay?" he clarified, needing the reassurance that no one and nothing else seemed to be able to give him.

"Yes," Dr. Stevens replied as he took the chart from the nurse. "She suffered a mild concussion in the accident. We disinfected the cuts on her arms and gave her some stitches to help with the healing process. The swelling on her forehead has gone down significantly since she arrived, so I believe after she gets some rest, the worst is behind her."

"Why hasn't she woken up?"

Dr. Stevens looked to Belle and then the monitors. "We believe she passed out from the trauma of the accident. Patients who come in with concussions aren't often unconscious."

Leo willed his muscles to relax. "She will wake up though, right?"

The doctor didn't seem bothered at all and nodded. "Oh, yeah. I suspect she'll wake up within the next few hours. These periods of unconsciousness are important for the body to rest and recover. Because of the concussion, she'll need to take it easy for a while. No physical activity. No exertion. Do you know if she's allergic to any medications?"

For a second, Leo had to retrace every conversation and scrounge for the answer. He couldn't remember a time when they had ever talked about it. Nothing like that seemed important enough.

"I know she doesn't want to be dependent on anything."

Dr. Stevens smiled and nodded. "Well, this isn't addictive, but she might have a hefty headache when she wakes up. I'm going to prescribe a pain reliever that will help. She only has to take it as long as she needs to."

Leo looked back to Belle and slowly lowered himself into a chair near the bed. "And the cuts?" His stare latched onto the white bandage and he felt his throat tighten.

"She can come back in a few weeks to remove the stitches once the wounds have healed. Just make sure the bandages are clean. Really, Mr. Thompson, she's going to be all right. It could have been much worse, but your fiancé was very lucky."

All Leo could do was nod and slip his hand into hers, even though she couldn't return the gentle squeeze he gave. Though, he couldn't ever say that she was lucky. It would have been better if Belle never met him. That would have been the luckiest thing for her. Not this. Anything but this.

"Is there any other family we need to contact?" the nurse questioned.

He quickly turned on them. "No. There's no one."

The thought of Melinda coming to the hospital to visit her was frightening enough. Thankfully, neither the doctor nor the nurse picked up on his urgency.

"We'll monitor her condition until she wakes up. Once she passes a physical, then she'll be ready to be sent home."

Leo nodded and answered as much of their other meaningless questions as he could. They hadn't talked about so many things. He didn't know enough, but neither did she. And as long as they would let him sit here, he'd be there when she woke up to explain it all.

The hours waiting had also allowed him to come to another important decision. Belle had to know. He could only do so much on his own. He could try to convince her to stay home from church, to pray more, to give him another chance when he clearly didn't deserve it. But she had to understand why. If she knew the real reason he cut, the real reason he roamed around the country without a home or friends, then maybe it would be easier. Then again, she might reject him completely. She might think he was crazy, and maybe he was. But he couldn't go another day without her knowing the whole truth.

For her own safety, she needed to know.

At first, Belle could feel nothing. There was just the blackness of deep sleep. Then, some things came into clear focus. The beeping of some machine. The itchy blanket on her bare legs and feet. Then a smell she never thought she would have to encounter again. She knew it as a cleaning chemical they used in the hospitals.

She could feel her heartrate pick up as the memory came back to her. The tree, the truck, the airbag. And that man. The one she had seen at the intersection. The image of his face burned behind her eyelids as the rest caught up to her.

But then she felt something else. A hand. Big and rough, holding hers. She knew it as well as she knew her own and she gripped it as tight as she could. But she still couldn't open her eyes. Because as soon as all these other things resurfaced, so did the pain.

Her head pounded and everything ached. But Leo was here. Somehow, he was here with her.

She forced open her eyes, as much as they protested against the harsh light of the lamp lit somewhere in the room. She winced at how it made the space behind her eyes throb and she had to blink a few times before she could adjust.

Just as she suspected, she was in a hospital room. She had never seen one from this angle before. She had always been where Leo sat, in the chair meant for visitors and family. Never had she been the one lying in the bed with an IV in her arm.

She turned her head and felt the bandage above her brow shift. It was then she realized both of her arms were wrapped too. Just the slight rotation of her left arm made the stitches pull underneath. Compared to the rest of her pain, that felt more like a tickle.

To her right, Leo stood and leaned closer, his blue eyes flitting over her features nervously.

Her lips couldn't help but twitch into a tiny smile at the sight of him. The smell, the bad memories, the pain, all of it was worth seeing him look at her again with those eyes she loved so much.

"How do you feel?" he quietly asked, a note of panic in his voice that made her wonder if there was something seriously wrong.

Wiggling her fingers and her toes, she knew she wasn't paralyzed. The fact that she was awake at all seemed like a good thing.

"I hurt," she replied, her voice barely above a hushed whisper.

The desired laugh came out and he didn't seem to expect it either. He pulled her hand to his lips and kissed the back of it. She could sense the relief in that simple, yet meaningful kiss and for a second, it chased away the pain.

"How long have I been out?" she asked, her voice hoarse as her throat worked through the grogginess.

"Just a day," he replied. "Do you remember what happened?"

The hopeful, yet frightened look on his face told her enough that something wasn't right at all.

"A tree fell in the road. I swerved... Did the truck roll?"

Leo nodded. "It did. You were upside down in a ditch. I was going to meet you at the church when I found you. I didn't see it happen, but..." His pause scared her more than the fact that she was literally hanging upside down in the cab of her truck in a ditch. "Did you... did you see anything before you rolled?"

Belle swallowed, even though it hurt. "I didn't see the tree fall, if that's what you mean."

"Did you see anyone?"

The face of the stranger popped back into her head and she wished she could have forced it out again. Her hands reflexively closed around his one more time. "I did," she answered. "It was some guy. I don't know his name, but he was at the bookstore earlier this week."

The air in the room shifted. Leo still seemed scared, but he took on a new level of anger that she hadn't seen in him before. Protective wasn't quite the right word. Outraged, offended, and murderous were much closer. But she knew it wasn't directed at her.

"The guy didn't make the tree fall," she said.

"What did he look like?" Just then, the door to her hospital room opened and a nurse tried to enter. Leo turned on her and nearly shouted. "Get lost!"

Trained to handle irate patients and families, she was unfazed. "We need to check her vitals if she's awake."

"Did you hear me? Get lost!"

The nurse looked to Belle, insensible to Leo's outburst. "Do I need to call security?"

Belle rapidly shook her head. It felt as if her brain was sloshing around inside her skull. "No, it's fine. Can we please have a few minutes?"

As if those were the magic words, the nurse sighed and slipped back out of the room.

"You can't talk to people like that, Leo," Belle scolded softly. "She was just doing her job."

Leo grabbed a hold of her hand with both of his. "This is too important. I need you to tell me what he looked like."

Confused and feeling a little dizzy from all the excitement of the moment, Belle tried her best to recount the man's looks. Blue eyes, black hair down to his shoulders, tall, and slightly creepy.

The more features she named off, the redder Leo's face became. After a while, she couldn't bring herself to say anything else.

"Do you know him?" was all she could finally ask.

Leo was shaking with that contained rage, but she wouldn't let go of his hand. She never would.

It took a long moment for him to finally force away the crimson in his vision long enough to speak. "I need to tell you the truth, but you have to promise me that you won't... Just listen to everything I have to say, okay?"

"You're scaring me. Is this bad?"

Leo blinked hard before taking a deep breath to continue. "I told you that I didn't know what happened to my brother, but I do. Matthew was... he had a lot of problems. He was... Please don't laugh or give me a weird look, but he was... is into magic."

He paused to gauge her reaction, but Belle did exactly as he asked. She didn't laugh, didn't smile, and patiently waited for him to finish, hoping that there was some sense in it all.

"When we were kids, before our family started to fall apart, Matthew started reading these books and messing around with the wrong crowd at school. He'd lock himself in his room a lot and he started acting strange around us. My mum said it was just him being a teenage boy, but it got weirder. His teachers would sometimes become seriously sick or one of our neighbors would up and move without reason. When we... When I found dead cats in our basement, I finally told my parents that he wasn't right in the head."

Belle nodded in understanding. "And that's when he started to go to the psychiatrist."

Leo's speech became more urgent. "The medications were supposed to help. He was better for a while and then he became even more secretive about what he was doing and where he was going. But no one cared after a while. With da's drinking and my mum being so out of it every evening, no one was stopping him. He disappeared that night when my parents died, but I saw him after that. I saw him in Brooklyn just before I graduated. He... He blamed me for our family falling apart and he... cursed me."

Belle tightened her lips together at the mention of a curse. The magic she could overlook. She had heard of people dabbling in what they believed was witchcraft or sorcery. It was often a phase or relatively harmless for those around them. Of course, Belle didn't believe in any of it. Magic was the stuff of fairytales and nightmares.

But curses seemed different. Curses might as well have been like hexes or just plain bad luck. It was a vague thing people joked about, but never really believed in. For Leo's sake, however, she would indulge this idea that he was somehow cursed by his brother who practiced magic.

"Ever since then, I've been followed by something evil. It haunts me night and day, like a leech sucking the life out of me. It won't let me rest or be happy. It's just this... darkness that won't let me go. It feeds on my pain. That's why I cut and got into prize fighting. The more pain I caused to myself or others, the more it would leave me alone. The more pain, the less sad I became. I wouldn't be so depressed, and I could feel real again."

A sense of wonder and fascination gripped Belle tighter than she expected. Was he talking about a real entity now, or something spiritual? It sure sounded spiritual, or at least metaphorical. Was this what he meant when he said that he cut to keep reality away? Maybe there was something to this curse after all, even if it was something that only existed in his head. The tears that glimmered in his eyes were real.

"But when I came here, when I met you, I couldn't live that way anymore. I want to break the curse because I know I can be happy with you and I want to have a life with you... The darkness won't let me. It wants me to be miserable, because my misery feeds it and makes it stronger. Drake harassing you, the accident at the mill, the barn fire, the stove exploding, and now this... It's all been the darkness' doing. It's been trying to hurt you, because it knows that it hurts me too. He's trying to make me leave, because my brother's back. He knows that if Matthew found out that I've been fighting the curse, then he'd be destroyed and so would I."

Belle tried to keep up and she found herself interrupting, just as he requested against. "You think every bad thing that's happened to us is because of this curse?"

"I know it is," Leo affirmed, holding her hand so tightly that it hurt. "And that's why I was cutting. I thought if I could cut, then the darkness would lay off or at least keep Matthew from finding me. I did it to protect you at first too. I thought if I cut more, then the darkness would leave you alone like it left me alone, but... you never needed my help."

The sad smile made her ask, "What do you mean?"

"The darkness told me you have something else protecting you. You never needed me, but I don't know why it didn't protect you from this. Maybe because you were off the farm or maybe Matthew really is that powerful."

It was then that the pieces finally fit together. "The man from the bookstore, the one I saw at the intersection... That was your brother."

Leo nodded. "I think so. I haven't seen him in a long time, but it sounds like him. You have to believe me that I never wanted to drag you into this. I wanted to find a way to break the curse or maybe control the darkness before it had a chance to really hurt you, but so much happened and I can't... I can't read the Bible, so I couldn't learn how to control the demons like the prophets did. I thought that would help."

Now it made sense. It wasn't a curse or some vague evil Leo was talking about. It was a demon, or maybe a team of demons. And her protection was the angels she prayed for. Those angels were supposed to protect her property. That's what she prayed for at least. Those prayers had sometimes been half-heartedly spoken, mostly out of habit, because her father always prayed for the same thing each morning and each night. Never did she think she would see it manifested like this.

If she accepted the existence of angels, then she had to believe there were demons too. And if Leo was really being plagued by demons, assigned to him by Matthew or not, Belle would definitely take that seriously.

"I've never been able to shake this curse or my brother for years," Leo continued. "But I want to. I desperately want to. If not for me, then to keep you safe. That's why I wanted to leave Levi, but you convinced me to face this head-on and stop running. I'm not running anymore, but... I don't know if I have enough in me to stand against Matthew. I'm not sure how to beat him anymore."

Belle smiled, but it wasn't in mockery or pity. Where Leo lacked in knowledge, she abounded. She knew the stories from the Old and the New Testament about demons and the spiritual realm. It wasn't something that she thought about often, but she understood the authority she wielded as a faith-filled believer. That would be enough to help Leo, even a little.

But she couldn't do it all on her own.

"You do have enough strength to stand against him," she said. "You just haven't tapped into it yet."

Leo gave her a skeptical look. "What do you mean?"

"Our strength comes from God."

The grave shake of Leo's head told her enough. "I'm... I'm not ready for that, Belle. I don't think God has much to do with this."

"God has everything to do with it," she encouraged. "He's where we get our strength, our hope, and everything we need to defeat the darkness. You just have to believe in it."

That sorrowful smile returned. "I can believe in you and you can believe enough for the both of us."

Belle didn't want to hear that. She wanted this hospital room to be the moment Leo believed in the faith and grace that could save him from this demon that haunted him. She wanted this moment to be the one where he accepted God's love. Then the angels that protected them would rejoice. But that could come later. And like he said, she would have to believe enough for the both of them.

"It doesn't matter how you got this curse, but it can be broken. I'll help you like you've helped me."

A twinge of regret crossed his face. "Belle, I haven't been helping you at all. I've only been causing more problems for you."

"Don't say that," she insisted, twisting her body, so she could take hold of his hands on hers. "You have been... You've saved me from so much. You helped me to see that I deserve a better life and a happier one. I always thought something was wrong with me, but you showed me that I'm just fine the way I am and to embrace that. I knew that for so long, but I never had the courage to do anything about it. You helped me find that courage and I'll always believe that God sent you to me, whether you believe it or not."

For a moment, she wondered if he would accept what she said. It was all the truth, but she understood how hard it must have been to see through the clouds of despair and grief. He believed there was nothing good in him, but she saw nothing but good. And just like he saved her, she would save him. Belle owed him that much. She owed him her life.

Chapter 18

The only reason Leo was now slumped in an uncomfortable chair in the hospital lobby was because the nurses had kicked him out of the room. They wouldn't even let him sit in the hall just outside Belle's door. He had already pushed the limits of visiting hours, but there was no way he could go home. Not while he still believed Belle was in danger.

Leo shifted his shoulders and laced his fingers over his stomach, willing himself to stay awake. Even the cafeteria shut down that evening. The one cup of coffee he drank before leaving Belle's room was given to him by Dr. Stevens. He had to stay awake all night. None of them understood why. He even doubted that Belle could fully grasp the depth of everything he had told her.

There was no sarcasm in the way she tried to quiet his fears about their future. He had known her long enough to hear the authentic sincerity in her tone when she told him that they would break the curse together. But she might have been a little too hopeful in his eyes. Just before he had to leave her, she requested a Bible and notepad. The nurses granted her that request, though the doctor had urged her to get as much rest as possible. She promised, but again, Leo could see through one of her lies. She was probably as awake as he was in that very moment.

He understood that the Bible held the answers, and now that he had her help in decoding its secrets, maybe they could find a way to shake the darkness once and for all. Leo felt his eyelids go heavy and his head listed just before he jolted awake again.

Pushing himself up onto his tired limbs, he walked about the cluster of chairs. Only the two nurses at the front desk were there to see him pace. His footsteps on the tile echoed throughout the high-ceilinged lobby. Down the halls, he could hear the voices and occasional noise of hospital activity.

He never wanted to be in a place like this again. He didn't belong here and neither did Belle. Hospitals only meant death and pain. That's all he knew of them anyway. And no matter how much they tried to convince him that she would be all right, Leo still felt the talons of the demons digging ever further into his spine. He should have asked for Belle to pray for him too.

"I know what you're up to."

Leo spun to see the darkness sitting with his legs propped up on the table between two rows of chairs. In his hands was an outdated magazine. On his lips played a sinister smile, one he hadn't shared with Leo in a while.

Passing a look to the nurses who were busy gossiping to one another under their breath, he moved toward the empty chair next to the darkness and sat down.

"I know what you're up to and it won't work," he repeated.

"You're just saying that," Leo whispered back, knowing that if either of the nurses noticed that he was talking to himself, he would become their newest patient.

The darkness flipped a page, pretending to be interested in the ads and articles they contained. "She won't find it; the cure-all for this curse. And even if she did, she's just as useless as you."

"She has more faith than I do."

The chuckle from the demon made his skin crawl. "If she had any faith in God, she wouldn't be as mental as she is. She would be perfect. God would heal her and make her happy if she believed enough, but she doesn't. She needed you to finally break free. She's just as addicted to feeling worthless as you are. God can't help either of you."

Leo closed his eyes and tried not to let those words make impact. They couldn't be true. This was just another game and Leo was done playing.

"Nobody's perfect," he said. "Belle doesn't proclaim to be perfect. But... But God is perfect and that's what matters."

Something of the sermon from last Sunday had sunk in. The pastor said it briefly. It wasn't even part of the message he tried to preach, the one that Leo couldn't really follow. But that tiny nugget was something he could understand. He had never strived for perfection and never thought it was obtainable. He knew what it must have looked like, though. Yes, Belle wasn't perfect, but they could both recognize it when they saw it.

"What even makes you think that God would waste His time on you? You killed your parents. You killed your sister. You've done nothing but ruin the lives of everyone you come into contact with and you think God's even paying attention to you?"

Leo swallowed hard and shook his head. "He may not pay attention to me, or listen to me. But he'll listen to Belle."

"Not for long."

He shot a glare to the darkness, who hadn't even looked up from the magazine since they began the conversation. "What are you talking about? Belle's fine."

The darkness didn't reply. Just flipped another page and kept reading. Leo balled his hands into fists and abruptly stood from his chair. He stormed toward the desk and leaned over the counter to get the attention of the nurses.

"Can you page the nurse's station near room 625?" he asked, trying to keep his voice steady and calm though all he wanted to do was force his way to Belle no matter the cost. "Please ask them to check on the patient."

The blonde one indulged his odd request and picked up the phone. In a few minutes, they had their answer.

"They say she's fine, but she's not getting the rest she needs. Apparently, she's reading." The nurse glanced at the clock on her computer monitor. "It's way too late into the night for her to be reading."

Leo tried to relax, but he might as well have been asking for Niagara Falls to flow backwards. He thanked them and turned back to the lobby chairs to find every single one empty. The darkness was gone, but that didn't mean it was done messing with him. If he had to, he'd have the nurses check on Belle every hour until dawn came. It'd be a long night, full of doubt and futile pep-talks to keep him from going insane.

Something of what the darkness said seemed to stick. If Belle really was a woman of faith and believed that God could heal and break curses, then why did she still suffer from anxiety? Couldn't her faith fix that problem? Or maybe it was more complex than that. Maybe it took more than a little faith to undo years of emotional abuse. And if that was the case, then what else would they need to defeat the curse?

Before he took another step toward the lobby, he turned to the nurses and asked, "Can one of you two get me a Bible?"

A small part of Belle was thankful that Leo hadn't called everyone in Levi to tell them about her accident. Only Mr. Johnson because he needed to take care of the farm, and Ray who needed to be aware that Belle was sick and wouldn't be coming in for a few days. Of course, once her white truck was taken to the local mechanic to be deemed totally irreparable, word would spread around.

While she should have been calling the insurance company to get an estimate for a new vehicle, or even resting in her bed upstairs, Belle refused to leave the living room for anything more than a bathroom break and food. The coffee table was littered with books and notes that were more for Leo's sake than her own.

She had to make it look like she was bending over backwards to find a solution to his so-called "curse", when in reality, she learned the truth when she was in the hospital.

There was little she could do. It was all up to Leo.

But he didn't want to hear that, so she continued to look for more answers. She looked for every reference to demons, evil, and curses in every paraphrase of the Bible. If she only knew a little bit of Hebrew, she could go back to the original translation.

It was difficult to ignore the bits about faith and salvation, however. And the Old Testament was riddled with situations where God had been the one to do the cursing, not the devil. Of course, she wouldn't tell Leo that. Not only did they not live under the laws of the Old Testament anymore, but also because he didn't need another reason to mistrust the man upstairs.

No matter how much she tried to focus on the situations where demons and evil were cast out in both the Old and New Testaments, the same theme continued to pop up.

Faith was the active ingredient in each and every situation. Jesus talked about faith being the healer to the sick, the light to the hopeless, and the only thing that anyone on this planet needed to have in order to be saved. That's what Leo needed all along. Those words, however, would fall on deaf ears.

Leo wanted a formula. He wanted a step-by-step guide to breaking the curse and ridding himself of the darkness that plagued his life. He wanted a magic pill, but it wasn't that easy. If she knew anything about expelling demons without the use of faith, she'd be just as bad as the posers in the book of Acts.

He wanted a way out, and God was that way, but Belle could only direct him on the path. She couldn't tell him how to believe or how to have faith. He either had it or he didn't, and he had to make up his mind to have it. After all the talk about getting through the curse together, she was helpless in the end.

The research wasn't without its rewards, though. Her dive into the concept of faith and that God could heal all wounds and make even the most despicable of sinners new in His eyes was enlightening to say the least. She found herself sitting and staring ahead at her bookcases, stewing over the principles that she hadn't had to think about in a long time.

It occurred to her, that after being raised by a deacon and attending countless services at her church, that she still had a lot to learn about faith and trust in God. It was a subject she didn't want to touch, because it was far too sore, too raw even after all these years.

But she couldn't ignore it. If she had enough faith to believe that God could handle all her problems, why did she hold onto them so tightly? Why didn't she just give them to the one who could alleviate her pain? She'd breathe easier if she did. She knew that. But Belle still clung to her anxiety with white knuckles.

Yet, just like Leo's situation, there was no magic pill. It'd be hard for both of them to simply let go and believe that God loved them enough to take away their curses.

"You should be resting."

Belle jumped at the sound of Leo's voice from the kitchen. She didn't even hear the back door open. Turning, she watched him slip off his muddy boots.

"I am resting," she replied, holding up the book while her finger held her place between the onion paper pages. Even with the bandages off and her cuts well on their way to becoming healed, Leo still fussed over her as if she were still suffering from the mild concussion. The stitches didn't bother her so much anymore, either.

Just as she expected, Leo perked up. "Have you found anything?" he asked a little too eagerly.

He rushed over and snatched up the notepad. She couldn't take offense at his excitement. After living with demons for so long, he was ready for the solution right this minute.

He read off the bullet points, but it wasn't what he wanted. "Christ became a curse for us... New creation... Your faith has healed you... Resist the devil and he will flee... Overcome evil with good... What about that stuff with demons?"

Belle hated to see him so disappointed, but she could only shrug. "Demons are just a symptom of the problem."

Leo's eyes narrowed. "No, the demons are the problem."

"Demonic influence only happens when we're susceptible to it. We have to guard our hearts against it. It's not an easy fix."

Leo dropped the notepad on a stack of books on the coffee table. "The demons are the roots. I feel like crud, because the demons make me feel that way. Get rid of the demons and you get rid of the problem. It's that simple."

Patience was not one of Belle's virtues, especially when she felt as if she wasn't being heard in the first place. Closing her eyes, she took a steady breath and silently asked God to speak through her. "Think of yourself as a patch of dirt. Before your brother cursed you, what do you think the dirt was like? Was it rocky and loaded with thorns? Or was it clean and fertile? Could good things, good thoughts, take root there? Think of the curse and demons as... weeds."

By now, Leo was seated beside her, his face hard with concentration. He wanted to understand.

"You can try and pull a weed up by the stalk, but it's only going to break and then it'll grow back over time. That's what you were doing when you cut yourself and fed this demon with your pain. You were just breaking it off temporarily, but it wouldn't stay that way. It wasn't fixing the problem. We need to not only pull up the weeds, but pull up the roots. Yes, we have to get rid of the demons and the curse, but what will that dirt look like when it's over? It'll still be rocky and filled with thorns and bad things. That kind of dirt is what the weeds look for."

Belle took Leo's hands in her own after putting down the Bible. "The rocks represent the guilt you feel for what happened to your family. The thorns are all the thoughts and feelings that make you think you don't deserve love or acceptance. It's the hatred for your brother and what he did to you. The demons didn't put them there. You did. We have to get rid of those too. That's what we need to be prepared for when you do break the curse. Till up the ground and make sure we can plant good things there instead."

For a long, pensive moment, Leo gazed into her eyes and she hoped that he could take that halfway parable as a true lesson.

"Are you still cleaning up your dirt?" he asked.

Belle felt her body go cold at the question. Again, she didn't want to think about this, that she still had so much to learn. It wasn't a good example to Leo. God had called them to be the shining light upon the hilltops, but Belle hadn't shined in ages. She doubted if she ever really did.

With her throat too tight to speak, she only nodded.

She expected him to be mad, to accuse her of being a hypocrite. In all reality, she was. Anyone could easily condemn her for being a fraud. She wasn't perfect. Her anxiety still got the better of her. They could accuse her of not trying. Before she met Leo, she hadn't. But all that was changed now. Leo saw her flaws, the cracks in her porcelain that weren't supposed to be there.

Instead of being mad, instead of pointing out how damaged she really was, Leo only pulled her into a hug. It was then she remembered how this all began. He had seen through her façade and loved her anyway. Loved her flaws, her anxiety, and all the broken bits that made up her soul. And what was better? She wasn't the only one clearing her fields. He was helping her. They were getting their hands dirty together, preparing the land for something great in their future.

Maybe that allegory was as much for herself as it was for him.

"We don't have to do this." Leo stared at the white-washed church ahead of them. His motorcycle would have been the only vehicle in the parking lot, but the preacher's sedan sat lonely in one of the front stalls near the entrance.

Belle slipped off as he let the bike lean to one side. "I'm not an expert, Leo. I know I said we would do this together, but it kind of occurred to me that I can't point out the speck in your eye when I have a plank in my own."

With some degree of hesitance, he pulled off his helmet and looked at her. "Are you talking about the faith thing?"

Ever since she started talking in metaphor and euphemisms, Leo had a slightly harder time keeping up with their conversations. He wasn't sure if it was the work of the darkness making him daft or if she really wasn't making any sense.

Once her helmet was also off, she combed her fingers through her hair to work out the tangles and kinks from the short ride. "Yes, it's about the faith thing. It's the only way you're going to break the curse and I'm not the best person to help, as much as you want me to be."

Leo made a face when he looked back to the church. A crow cawed in the distance and the wind seemed to blow colder. The place looked so lonely and abandoned without children and elderly people roaming around the outside. It was quiet too. Much too quiet. He might not have known as many Holy tunes as Belle did, but he would have taken the hum of the old piano in the sanctuary over this silence. He couldn't even think about how it was on the inside, devoid of a congregation.

"I don't know the man," he said, working to make one more plea to escape this meeting.

"He's friendly," Belle replied, taking his helmet from his hand to hang on the back seat. "Maybe a little overly friendly, but you can get used to it."

"Are you used to it?" Leo wouldn't dismount. There was still time.

Belle gave him a wry smile. "Not really, but he means well and that's the point."

He reached for Belle's hand and held it firm. "Hey, I opened up to you about this curse, because you deserved to know. I never told anyone else for a reason."

By the slight tilt of her brows, Leo knew she understood his need for privacy. Still, she dragged him here in some hopes that the preacher could work a miracle. He had hoped they could solve this quickly and secretly if they only worked together. There was no point in dragging the whole church into his affairs.

"I'm not asking you to tell Pastor Kendall about the curse. You don't even have to mention demons or anything. I just want him to explain more about authority and faith to you. Maybe pray for you too. He'll know how to put it way better than I can."

Leo rubbed his thumb over the back of her hand, but she didn't look any closer to throwing in the towel and saying they could go home. He could name off several people he would have rather talked to than the preacher. Mr. Calloway would be his first choice, followed by Randy or even Mr. Tale. At least he had spent some time with them and they knew his temperament. None of them were invasive either. But he knew just by watching the preacher last Sunday that Leo wouldn't like him at all.

As if hearing his thoughts, Belle stepped closer and flashed him a pair of pitiful eyes that could have melted even the coldest of hearts. "Just give it a try. If you're not comfortable with him after say... ten minutes, then we'll go home. I promise."

Leo smiled and propped out the kickstand. How could he say no to her? He stood and they were just inches apart. One soft, but short-lived kiss was hardly enough, but they were on hallowed ground.

When their lips disconnected, he noticed a tiny blush coloring her cheeks.

"What? Never kissed on church grounds before?"

She giggled and dipped her chin like she had just been kissed for the first time. "No, as a matter of fact, I haven't."

"Well, you might want to get used to that, m'eudail. You might be doing it a lot in the future."

It took her a little longer to comprehend the hidden meaning in his words, but Belle caught on and he had to back pedal before anymore unnecessary damage could be done.

"I mean, like stealing kisses between services or just before service or something... Not... Not that."

And then, he put the other foot in his mouth. Leo cringed at the way her lips pulled in that look of confused disappointment. What he wouldn't give to have her smile again. So, instead of dashing her hopes any further, Leo rushed forward in another kiss. This one more passionate and driven by a need to show her that marriage wasn't off the table, but it wasn't a main concern as of that moment.

In the quiet of the church parking lot, they both heard the front doors open and pulled away before Pastor Kendall had a chance to see them making out.

Wearing a formal polo shirt and pair of khakis, the preacher cut a slightly less offensive image than the man who fastened his necktie too tight on Sunday mornings. With his fat not bulging over his collar, Leo wouldn't have thought him the same man. But the jovial grin that seemed ever-present on his face was a giveaway.

Belle waved and they all met at the base of the stairs. She received a hearty hug that made Leo bristle on the defensive. Couldn't the man tell that she was uncomfortable? The handshake Pastor Kendall gave was far too loose for Leo's liking, but he let it slide.

"So, this is Leo Thompson."

Belle nodded. "Yep. I'll leave you two to talk a while. I'm going to visit my dad for a bit."

Leo's gaze shot from Pastor Kendall to her and he tried not to look as upset as he felt. "Alone?"

The pacifying smile wasn't enough to make him relax. Ever since they'd left the hospital the other day, Leo hadn't let her out of his sight for more than thirty minutes. The animals and lambs were doing fine on their own, but they weren't his prime worry. Now that the darkness was onto them, he imagined attacks would be coming from the left and right. He even thought his depression would spike again. However, things had been relatively calm since the accident. Too calm.

Belle pointed toward the alleyway between the church and extra building. "The cemetery is just behind here. I'm within shouting distance."

That wasn't enough.

"Why don't you stay in the church until we're done?"

Pastor Kendall clapped him on the back and started to guide him up the stairs. "It's all right, Leo. It'll be just us guys in there. I won't bite."

The preacher might not bite, but Belle would be out in the open, away from his protection. "Is there a window that looks out over the cemetery?" he asked them both, resisting each step as much as he could without seeming too rude. Instead, he sounded like a scared child who didn't want to be apart from his mother for more than a minute.

"Oh, no," Pastor Kendall laughed. "As appealing as heaven is, we don't want any of the flock looking out over those whom God's already taken up."

Leo found the comment rather morbid and one more look to Belle told him he wasn't alone in the thought. "Not too long, okay? You know why."

Now, it might have seemed like they had something to hide. They did, but Pastor Kendall didn't need to be suspicious.

Belle nodded. "I won't be long. Ten minutes, remember?"

Watching her disappear between the buildings, Leo wondered what those ten minutes would hold for him. If she had enough confidence in Pastor Kendall's abilities to teach or instruct, could ten minutes be enough to tell him everything he needed to know? In ten minutes, could he be free? Could he have his life back?

Belle didn't care if the ground was a little wet. She found her father's grave and sat with her legs crossed. The headstone was well taken care of. Cleaned, polished, and free of debris. He was numbered with the other officials of the church who were buried in this section of the yard, but the rest of his family were laid to rest on the other side.

She read the words over and over, even though she had already committed them to memory. The engraving of the single dove over his name holding a ribbon and olive branch had always seemed a bit corny to her, but her father had picked out his own headstone weeks before he drew his last breath. Though they were still holding out hope for a miracle, they both knew by that point that it was better to have these things taken care of.

He had even chosen his own final epitaph. *"Loving father and man of God. Missed, but never forgotten."*

Belle let the corners of her mouth twitch into a tiny smile. Why he picked such a phrase, she would never know. How could anyone forget him? It had been years and anyone who barely knew him was liable to get misty when he was brought up in a conversation. He had touched the lives of every family in Levi. No one would ever forget his kindness and faith.

The wind swept back her hair, sending it flying around her shoulders and rustling the branches of the trees around the church property. It had been a while since she took the time to visit the grave. Her father wasn't there anymore, not really. His soul and spirit were in heaven and what lay six feet under was just the shell, the vessel that God had used to make an impact on so many.

All at once, thinking about her father's place in the community and how he certainly was missed, Belle felt inadequate. If her father were here, he'd know exactly what to say to Leo to help him believe. He would know what to do about the demons and how to clear out the land she had referenced before. She had to laugh at herself at how silly it sounded, even if it made sense.

"I don't know how you did it, dad," she mumbled to the grave. "You would always know exactly what to do or say to someone at the right time. You and God were like this." She crossed her fingers for unnecessary emphasis. "And no matter how hard I try, I can never seem to get to that place. If I was there, I'd be able to help Leo. I wouldn't be pawning him off on Pastor Kendall like he was some troubled kid or something. Which, he's not. He's actually pretty amazing. I know he looks rough at first, but he really has a good heart. God knows he does and I see it. He just doesn't see it in himself and that hurts more than anything, I think."

Belle licked her lips and lifted her gaze toward the tree line. "I guess he could say the same for me too... He's been helping me a lot in the last few weeks. He's helped so much and it's almost not even right. I should have been turning to God more or letting others help me, but I know better now. I know how to heal, but I wouldn't have gotten this far without him."

She nodded to the statement she would say next, agreeing with herself and the idea. "I think you would have liked him. He's really... aggressive about me. But in a good way. He cares. He really does. He cares like you did and he's really proactive in making sure I learn how to take care of myself... He's a good man. He's everything you would want for me. You once said that all you wanted was for me to be with someone who makes me happy... Leo makes me very, very happy, dad."

Her father didn't need to hear this. He wouldn't. But saying it out loud, confessing it to the slab of marble with his name on it, somehow made her feel better about what was coming in the future. Once this curse business was over, once the demons were gone and they didn't have to fight so hard every day to feel normal, the doors would be thrown wide open. They could love and have a life together in Levi. There was so much they could do. The possibilities were endless, and they'd be free. Leo may have doubted Pastor Kendall or whatever truth he needed to hear, but she didn't doubt. Not anymore.

She heard footsteps behind her and didn't have to turn to know it was Leo. His gait was unmistakable. Slow, but confident.

"I don't think it's been ten minutes yet," she teased.

She turned and the last thing she saw was a pair of bright blue eyes, colder than the middle of winter and full of something Leo would have never given her. Hate. Pure and unbridled hate.

Chapter 19

Leo was done playing nice with Pastor Kendall. He could take the shallow friendliness, and the insinuating comments, but this was too much. "What exactly are you saying?"

The preacher steepled his fingers over his desk calendar and gave a heavy sigh like he actually cared. "The Bible is very specific about these situations. You and Belle are unequally yoked. She was raised in this church. Her father was a great man of God and you... I'm sure you're a great man too, but Belle needs someone who will help her grow as a Christian. She needs someone who will stand with her during the service and sing the hymns with her. She needs someone to talk to and study the Word with. And from what others have told me, you're not that someone."

He wanted to give this man a chance for Belle's sake. But he could only take so much offense and ridicule. He had been called mean things in the past, names that he wouldn't dare utter in the preacher's office. He had done many things and been accused of worse. Now he was being told that, essentially, he was unworthy of being Belle's friend and lover.

"Who are these other people you're talking about?" he asked, doing his best to keep his voice down. The anger, however, was still prevalent.

"It doesn't matter," the preacher said calmly. "What matters is doing right by Belle. If you love her, as I suspect you do, you need to let her go."

"I didn't come here to talk about Belle and whatever you think is going on between us." Leo balled his fists on the armrests. "I came here, because she asked me to. She wanted me to talk to you about... something that's out of our realm of expertise."

Pastor Kendall nodded. "I know she did. She wanted me to talk to you about the Lord and what it means to believe. But I think you want to know about those things for the wrong reasons. You want to make Belle happy and I can admire that. It's the job of every man to make his woman happy, but you have to want to believe for you, not for Belle."

Leo's jaw clenched tight against the harsh things he wanted to blurt out. Even if this man was arrogant and assuming, right now, the preacher was his only hope of defeating the demons.

"Listen," he began coolly. "I asked Belle some very specific things about her religion. I have a problem and it needs to be taken care of. She can't fix it for me, and she's pointing me in your direction for guidance. You're supposed to be like a shepherd, right? I may be a black sheep, but I need just as much guidance as anyone else in your congregation."

Now he was the one spitting out metaphors. Maybe something was catching.

Pastor Kendall watched Leo for a minute before shaking his head. "I think you're looking for a straight answer, but I can't give you one. Neither can Belle. Faith isn't an easy thing to explain. It can only be felt."

"Then tell me how to feel it, so I can solve the problem myself."

The first hint of a smile appeared since they sat down in his private office. It was tinged with a bit of sadness, but it was still a smile. It infuriated Leo. "You can't solve this on your own either, not even with faith."

Silence fell over the office. The ticking from the clock on the wall was only rivalled by the pumping of his own heartbeat in his ears. Faith wasn't going to fix this? Faith wouldn't fight off the darkness? It had before when Belle prayed. Wasn't that faith?

Leo lowered his gaze and stared at the polished mahogany desk top. Maybe if Pastor Kendall knew the truth. If he knew what Leo really needed, maybe he would try to be more helpful.

"Are you and Belle living together?"

His eyes snapped up. With that one question, he had reached his limit.

"Excuse me?"

"Are you living together? It's a simple question."

Leo looked to the clock. It may not have been ten minutes, but he was finished here. "You know what? Forget it. I wasted my time here. Keep your faith and your rules." He stood to his feet, shoving back the chair a few inches with the force of it. "If this is the way you treat people, then I don't want to be in your little club or cult or whatever it is you think you're doing here. Belle can do whatever she wants. She can come here every day of the week. I don't care. But I swear if you talk to her the way you just talked to me, I will come here and make you regret it. Am I clear?"

Instead of cowering in fear as Leo expected the man to, he simply sat back in his chair, his rotund belly appearing out from behind the desk. "Very clear."

Not one raise of the brow, not one note of panic. He stayed calm to this threat. Obviously, Pastor Kendall didn't know who he was dealing with. Leo wouldn't hesitate to wring that fat throat of his if he made Belle feel any less than she really was.

Leo stormed out and turned to walk around the platform where the podium stood like a pillar in front of the rows upon rows of pews. He paused and looked to the stained glass behind the choir seats and to the heavy wooden cross hanging on the wall. He shook his head, furious at God and everything that had failed him in such a short span of time.

This had been his last hope, his only hope. And now, who was left to explain this to him? Who was left to tell him how to use faith as a weapon against the evil he needed to purge from his life? If the church couldn't help him, then who would?

He strode down the center aisle toward the doors, passing through the empty sanctuary as if he were making his final exit from a place he hadn't been welcome in from the beginning.

Outside, the sun seemed to be shining brighter than before and the cold autumn wind had died down significantly. The warm turn in the weather seemed incongruent with the ordeal he had just been through.

He made his way to the cemetery and thought he would find Belle fairly easily. She would have stuck out like a sore thumb in her blue blouse amongst the gray and darkening headstones. But he didn't see her. Not her shirt or her long, wavy brown hair.

He called her name, but there was no answer. He checked the door to the Sunday School building, but it was locked. Neither was she at the motorcycle waiting for him. Standing in the middle of the cemetery, he turned in circles, his eyes skimming over every plot and along the tree line.

Belle was gone.

His breaths came faster, his heart hammering harder in his chest. A long moment, he stood there, his mind circling around this one thought that Belle was missing.

He ran to the woods and peered beyond the dense foliage and pines. He called her name again, letting it echo through the canopy that shaded him against the noonday sun. Still, nothing.

He trudged deeper, pushing aside ferns and bushes, thinking he would find her laying on the forest floor somewhere, maybe sleeping. As absurd as it was, he had to tell himself she'd be sleeping, because to think that she'd be anything else would destroy him.

No sign of her, no matter how thoroughly he searched. He stood, so far from the churchyard and completely isolated from the rest of the world. Alone. He felt himself begin to crack and buckle, but he couldn't allow it. He had to stay strong.

He pushed back the need to collapse and tried to think. Belle wouldn't have run off on her own. She wouldn't have left him. This had something to do with the darkness.

He opened his mouth and his first impulse was to call out for help. But he stopped before a breath could be wasted. Nor would he pull out his phone to call the police. What would he say? That a demon stole his girlfriend away? They wouldn't believe him, and he knew that a person had to be missing for a full day before the police would even lift a finger.

So instead of calling for help, he did the next best thing.

"I know you're there," he said. "I know you took her. Show yourself."

The minutes ticked by and he muttered a curse before turning his attention back to the forest. He found a bush riddled with thorns. He yanked one loaded branch and raked the sharp spines through his palm. Bright red blood soon peeked out from around his tightly clamped fist and he rushed to the nearest tree trunk.

While he aggravated his cuts to make sure blood still seeped from them, his other hand clawed at the bark to make a clear patch. With his nail, he copied from memory a certain hex he remembered seeing during the dark days of his childhood. His brother had carelessly left his bedroom rug flipped up to reveal the circular seal engrained in the floorboards. Dark burgundy stains were prevalent around the edges and he came to learn of its power once the bottom fell out on their family.

He passed over the perfectly ordered lines one more time and then he slammed his injured hand on the summoning seal to wet it with his blood.

"I know you're out there. You know where she is. Tell me." The trembling in his demand was as much from fear as it was from rage.

A few seconds dragged on before he finally received his answer.

"How did you know to do that?"

He spun, his hand still pressed against the tree. The darkness stood there, looking disgusted and yet oddly pleased at the sight of his longtime ward using the same magic that had poisoned his existence. Leo released his hold of the seal and charged toward him.

"Where's Belle? Where did you take her?"

The darkness gave a mocking surrender, knowing that the mortal couldn't do anything to him anyway. But Leo could certainly try.

"I didn't touch her. That was your brother's doing." A fleeting bit of surprise passed over the demon's face and Leo could guess why. He had confidence in his authority over him. God may have failed him, but tried and proven magic had gotten him what he wanted. That was enough.

"Where is he? Where's Matthew?" Leo hurriedly asked, wondering how long the summoning spell would last.

The demon seemed hesitant at first, afraid to speak. But it was as if something stronger was pulling on him, forcing his mouth open to answer the one who had called upon him.

"There's an abandoned farmhouse to the north outside of town on a dirt road marked by a single wagon wheel on the county highway. The house is at the dead end."

It was Leo's turn to be surprised and for a second, a bit of his anger left him. "Is she hurt? What is he doing with her?"

The demon bit his lips together as if that would work.

"Tell me!" Leo bellowed.

"She's unharmed. Matthew wants you. Just you. He was going to send me after a few days to tell you. He wanted to drag it out. He won't be expecting you to come this soon."

Well, if his big brother wanted him, he'd have him. Leo got close to the darkness and bristled with the seething fury he'd unleash on Matthew. "If you tell him I'm coming, I'll do much worse to you than he will. I remember plenty more than just that summoning spell."

That alone inspired enough terror to make the darkness shake. After the stunt Leo just pulled, he probably had no idea what else he had up his sleeve. The demon didn't need to know that was all Leo remembered.

He didn't wait for the spirit to dematerialize. He turned and marched back toward the church grounds. Though he could trust that the demon would obey this last demand, Leo couldn't stand the thought of Belle being held captive by his brother. She might have been fine for now, but Matthew was unstable, a loose cannon. There was plenty he could do to her and Leo wouldn't let any of it happen. Not again.

Nausea turned her stomach as Belle could slowly feel herself returning to consciousness. Her world spun out of control, making her feel light and lost in the blackness. It didn't feel this way when she passed out after the accident and the thoughts weren't nearly the same as her mind caught up with her. She remembered what the doctor had said about incurring another head trauma shortly after the concussion. It could cause complications in her recovery.

But as she rehearsed in her mind the basic facts of who she was to make sure her memory was still intact, other thoughts crowded for attention. She felt the prickling nettles of something like sticks or dried leaves on her cheek and arms. The cool air blanketed her, making her involuntarily shiver. All felt dark and heavy as she reached through the basics and grabbed onto the present.

There had been a man at the cemetery. He came up behind her and that was the end. She saw the blue eyes and then nothing. It was as if everything had been turned off and now, she was slowly coming back to life.

Thankfully, nothing ached. Not even her head. It was more as if she had just been lightly dropped from the sky after doing several dozen tailspins. She opened her eyes and saw it was still daytime. Light seeped through the cracks and jagged holes in the ceiling above her. The walls seemed to be leaning, giving her the impression that she was still off kilter somehow, but then she saw that it had more to do with the tilted house than her dizziness.

The air was musty, old, and earthy like the inside of a barn. But by the scattered pieces of broken furniture and the cramped space, she knew this must have been a farmhouse. Another moment produced a theory. When she was young and stupid, she had followed a group of kids from school to an abandoned house on the north side of town. The walls leaned in much the same way. They didn't stay long, but all of her class believed the place was haunted.

Now, reclining against a pile of dead leaves on the inside, she understood why. This place, though it seemed harmless from the outside to any passerby, had a certain feel about it that creeped her out. She never believed in ghosts, but in this old house, she could almost feel them pressing down on her, suffocating her and filling her with an inexplicable dread like the world outside would collapse in at any moment. Maybe it would. The structure had never seemed safe to begin with.

"I wondered how long you would be out."

The voice that caught her by surprise seemed familiar, and yet different. She turned to see a man in the doorway. The man from the bookstore. The one she had seen at the intersection before her accident. Leo's brother. Matthew. And it was his voice, but now it held a distinctly foreign quality. It was as if the two brothers had melded somehow into one new sound.

He must have been hiding his accent the whole time to avoid suspicion. She wouldn't have guessed that at all. She watched him, eyes wide and portraying all the fear she didn't want to feel. After everything Leo had told her, she had reason to fear him. One perfectly good reason. If he would do something so purposefully heinous to his brother as to curse him with demons – which Belle questioned anyway – then what more would he do to her?

"I won't hurt you," he said as he came closer. "It's not you I want to hurt."

It didn't take her long to figure out what he meant.

"Please, let me go?"

Belle had always thought the weak, powerless females in the action movies were overrated and romanticized. But right now, she could relate to them as she never could before. Out of all the things she had been through, kidnapped wasn't one she ever expected to add to her list.

Matthew gave her a mirthless smile and shook his head. "No can do, lass. You'll be here a while."

It was then she realized she wasn't tied up. He either had too much faith in his ability to keep her in one place, or he thought she was too scared to run. Though the thought wasn't far from her mind, running wasn't an option and she knew it. This place was so far removed from any road or homestead that even if she tried, he would catch up to her.

The bulge in her back pocket, however, gave her some hope. She reached for her phone and checked the signal before trying to make the call. Matthew didn't move to stop her. He must have known there was no service out this far. She was trapped. Plain and simple.

"Are you hungry? Thirsty?"

Belle swallowed hard and gripped her phone. "No," she replied breathlessly.

"There's no reason for you to starve yourself. It will be a few days before my brother finds you."

Something didn't make sense. Matthew was pretending to be kind, pretending to care. He said he didn't want to hurt her and was offering to feed her. Was this normal for a hostage situation? Clearly, he was more interested in Leo than her.

She couldn't take the risk and hope for a safe way out of this. It was still possible that Matthew would kill her or Leo. Then again, a lot of time had passed since they had last known one another. Maybe Matthew had changed.

"What did you do to me?" she asked, noticing that her nausea had ebbed rather quickly. "Did you drug me or something?"

"Drugs are primitive," he returned. "That was a simple knockout spell. Nothing too complicated or messy. You should notice you feel perfectly fine now. And no, it won't affect your recovery from the concussion."

Belle blinked at the mention of the spell. There was no such thing. There was no magic. It was why she doubted his involvement with the demons in the first place. But, she could believe that he believed enough in magic that it was real to him. "How did you – "

"Know about the concussion? I was there, lass. Or don't you remember?"

She nodded. "I remember... Leo said you made the tree fall in the road."

He smirked. "At least he knows to give credit where it's due."

Leo had also mentioned a hex symbol on the trunk of the tree. No doubt another sign that Matthew really put a lot of faith in this magic stuff.

But there was no magic. Everything Matthew had done was completely of his own power. It had to be. Belle remembered the barn, the stove, and the trees falling. Leo blamed the demons, but it might have been Matthew from the start. Though she couldn't exactly explain how, it was completely possible that he sabotaged everything. Either that, or it was coincidence and Matthew was looking to take the credit just to inspire fear.

A wild idea came to mind and Belle took this chance while Matthew had his back turned to a small table in the corner. She navigated to her phone's tools and went straight to the voice memo recorder. She hit the red button and waited until she saw the seconds begin to tick down.

"What else have you done?" she asked. Belle waited until the screen had gone black with hibernation, the red recording light still blinking, and then set the phone on the ground by her feet.

"Now, why would I tell you any of that?" Matthew questioned, turning to her with a tin cup and water bottle in his hands.

"Isn't that what villains are supposed to do? Gloat and rant about their master plan to take over the world?"

Belle didn't expect him to laugh. A genuine, amused laugh. There was nothing sinister in it, nothing menacing or mocking. He actually thought she said something funny.

"If you think I'm the villain here, my brother's been lying to you."

"But, you just kidnapped me. That's a bad thing, if you didn't know."

Matthew poured water into the cup and strode toward her. She took the time to review his walk and noticed it did resemble Leo's. There were so many commonalities between them that she hadn't thought to look for before. They had the same eyes, but she never thought they would have the same walk or the same laugh.

"I kidnapped you, because my brother is too scared to come out in the open." He handed her the cup. "He knows I'm going to kill him. He knows I'm done playing games and he doesn't want to face me. I'm just giving him the right reason to find me and get it over with."

Belle felt her stomach harden and her heart nearly explode. "You're going to kill him?" she whispered.

"Aye. He's suffered long enough. It's humane, really. Take it."

She took the cup with a shaking hand and a little bit of water sloshed over the rim. She wouldn't drink, though her throat became as dry as an old well.

"Leo was the one who started all of this. His price was greater to pay, so it's taken this long for him to finally deserve death. Just when he's found real love and happiness, I'm going to take it all away from him."

Belle brought her arms closer to her stomach, still clutching the cup of cool water. "I thought you said you wouldn't hurt me?"

"I won't," he replied. "I'm going to make him believe that I did. Mental manipulation isn't hard. Not anymore. And Leo's so easy to trick."

She glanced down to make sure the little red light on her phone was still blinking. "Is that why he thinks he's haunted by demons?"

Matthew twisted the cap on the water bottle to close it. "Oh, that part's true. Everything he's experienced up to this point has been true. The demons, his struggles, our family dying, all of it's true. I didn't have to do much to make him really suffer over the years. He did that to himself. I just gave him a little nudge in the right direction and his weak mind did the rest for me."

Thankfully, Belle's mind wasn't so weak. She could put the pieces together. "So... all that stuff about him feeling guilty for killing his parents... that's because you 'nudged' him?"

"He has a right to feel guilty about them. It's his fault. It's all their own faults."

The rigidity in his voice startled her and Belle drew in her legs as if he would suddenly lash out. But he seemed to notice his slip and collected himself again. Matthew turned and walked back to the table where he kept his supplies.

"What Leo told you about his childhood was true. We were happy once. And then he decided to rat me out. I wasn't hurting anyone. Not anyone who didn't deserve it. I'll admit it was childish at first. Making my teachers sick, changing test results, making girls like me. It was all so easy and satisfying for a while. But if I wanted to go big, I had to learn more. I had to do more."

He set the bottle down and turned back. Something in his eyes called out to her. She knew that look of desperation, of loneliness. It might have been enough to make her pity him, but she couldn't. Matthew was admitting to delving into dark, twisted stuff that she didn't believe in. Stuff that her faith condemned.

"That's when Leo found me out. He told our parents and... and they hated me for it. They thought I was crazy. They all did. But results don't lie." Matthew raised his hand and his fingers twirled.

In less time than it took to blink, a dagger appeared out of thin air. Belle wanted to think he had just pulled it out of his coat sleeve, but the blade was so long and sharp. There was no way he could have simply let that slide down his arm. With just one flick of his wrist, it was there, and it made her stop breathing.

"I wasn't crazy. They were the crazy ones for thinking it was all some bad joke. An imbalance of the hormones, they said. My brain chemicals weren't level. It made me believe I could do things that weren't possible. They gave me those meds, but I never took them. I flushed them away, but I learned my lesson. Stay low. Bide my time. Make them pay."

He took a few steps closer, his brows angling together in a scowl as if she were the one who had doubted him all his life. "They chose to medicate me instead of believing me. They wanted to change me, sedate me, humiliate me. So, I did what I knew how to do. A few deals were made, a few bargains struck, and their world fell apart. Da started drinking. Mum stopped feeling. Kaitlyn got sick. And Leo was untouched, because I wanted him to watch them all die. I wanted him to be alone just like I was. I wanted him to feel what it was like to be abandoned and unloved. It took me a while to catch up with him after he left Scotland, but I put the curse on him to finish him off."

A derisive, hateful smile spread over his lips. "One thing I will give my brother. He's relentless. He found a way around the demon's games and he'd been doing just fine until he met you." He spun the dagger until its glinting tip was aimed right at her.

His voice rose to a shout that intensified her quivering. "Then you had to come along and make him think he could have a life, make him think he could be happy again like he was before he ruined my life." And then as suddenly as the storm came, it died away. "But I'm going to fix that. The moment Leo comes here, he'll see a vision of your dead and mangled body on the floor. He'll beg me to take his life and I won't. I'll let him take his own."

Belle's jaw went slack, and she marveled at the whole story of loss and hatred. It was like something out of a crime novel. This was the villain monologue and no matter how long Matthew talked, he was still the villain, unworthy of sympathy.

"Do you get a kick out of torturing other people, or just family?" Belle's fear had done nothing to her mental filter. One wrong word could push Matthew over the edge. He could easily decide that Leo would truly find her corpse in the derelict house rather than an illusion.

Matthew laughed again. His attitude was spinning on the wheel of emotions and every passing minute produced something new and unpredictable. "I don't torture as much as I dispense justice. I'm not psychotic. Those people deserved to die. Not just my family, but everyone else."

Like a man listing off something as casual as the weather, Matthew began to tell her of his crimes against humanity in both Scotland and in America. It was as if that one burst of honesty had broken the dam wide open. She knew the feeling. Once the stream began to flow, it was hard to stop, hard to slow down. He confessed to it all and her phone was picking up every word.

It was all enough to make her blood run cold and hardened stomach turn. It was too much, too gory, too descriptive. She didn't even like reading about serial killers or watching horror movies, and Matthew's detailed accounts of murder and carnage pushed her too far.

"Stop! Please, stop!" Belle cried, tossing aside her cup and wrapping her hands and arms around her head to block it all out. But it was too late. Even when she closed her eyes, she saw their faces. The faces of his victims crying for mercy that neither he, nor his team of demons, would ever give.

The house went quiet except for one distinct sound.

The rumbling of a motorcycle.

Chapter 20

L eo threw his bike to the ground and ran to the crooked front door of the farmhouse. Not a sound was louder than his own footfalls and panting breaths as he prepared himself for what was on the other side. He expected to find his brother at least, and all the way he had wondered what Matthew would look like after all these years apart. He wondered what he would say or do to rescue Belle. He had no weapon except himself, but Matthew had a whole arsenal of magic. There was no way he could win, but he had to try.

What he saw when he skidded through the doorway wasn't anything like he envisioned.

The demon had lied. Blood was everywhere. In scattered pools across the floor, in speckled streams across the walls. Furniture was turned over and broken. What met him was nothing short of a crime scene. The victim lay faceup in the middle of the floor. Her limbs twisted and angled unnaturally, her clothes torn. Long brown hair was caked and matted from the battle, her face slack and white.

Leo's heart stopped beating. He couldn't hear it raging against his ears as he had on the way here. He couldn't breathe, couldn't think. He just stared, unable to tear his eyes away from the carnage.

Matthew was nowhere in sight, gone before the coward could be caught in the act. How long had it really taken him to get here? Ten? Fifteen minutes? Could all of this have happened that quickly? How could he have come so late?

One foot staggered in front of the other, scraping against the roughened wood flooring that creaked under his weight. The farmhouse began to spin and he couldn't keep his balance. He fell to his knees, sullying his pants in her blood. Belle's blood.

He was bent forward, leaning against his hands before he could realize how unsteady he had become. Still warm. Her blood was still warm to the touch. Finally, a breath came. Gasping and shuddering, but he was still alive. Still breathing when she wasn't.

On impulse, he thought to check for a pulse. Maybe she could have survived through the damage, but he couldn't bring himself any closer. He gulped for more air, though he knew he didn't deserve one single bit of oxygen. Not after how he had failed her.

The darkness was right all along. He did kill her. It was done with Matthew's hand, but none of it would have happened if Leo had left Levi and turned his back on Belle. He should have never brought her into this. There was no chance from the beginning. Nothing but a hallucination. Blinded by a need for change, a need for hope.

This would be his greatest sin. His last sin. Nothing else could compare to letting Belle die like this. Painful and alone.

Sobs ripped through his chest. His throat, achy and sore, could only emit that raspy kind of pathetic wail. He hadn't cried this hard since he was a child. And just as a kid who couldn't save his family, he couldn't save Belle.

Maybe something in Leo's brain finally snapped. Maybe it was the stress of the moment or just his imagination. Because even when he paused in his crying, he thought he could hear her voice. Belle's voice. Calling, screaming out his name.

Leo swallowed back his tears and looked up to her corpse. The lips, so soft and pale, weren't moving. But he could hear her. As soft as a whisper at first, and then growing louder and louder. He was losing it. Even the walls, so plastered with blood, began to shimmer and flicker out of focus. He blinked, but his surroundings continued to deconstruct in front of him.

"Leo! It's not real! I'm still here!"

He blinked hard a few times, clearing the moisture from his eyes enough to see that Belle's body was changing. Transparent and blurred, she began to disappear. The warm blood on his hands and knees evaporated. The pools turned to piles of dark autumn leaves. Backed against the wall was Belle. Not dead and very much alive.

Her hands were out, waving wildly like she was trying to get his attention. Once his wide-eyed gaze could focus and follow her movements, she smiled and started to crawl forward. But her eyes flitted upward, and she screamed.

Leo turned just in time to see the flash of metal. Forgetting all thought of what was happening, he turned and grabbed the wrist that held the dagger. His right hook connected with a bold jaw. Nothing was pulled. The full force of his blow sent Matthew backward and out onto the porch of the farmhouse.

It was the first good look he'd had of his brother in over a decade. His features had matured, becoming sharper and bolder with age. Like Leo, he had built up over the years. He no longer had just the magic on his side, but they could probably match one another in a fight.

Leo wasn't going to wait for formal introductions or meaningless banter. He dove forward and threw aside the knife, wrenching it out of his brother's fist. He could have used it. It would have made killing him that much easier. But he wanted to feel it, feel Matthew's pulse come to a dead stop beneath his fingertips. It was rightful retribution for everything his big brother had put him through.

He leapt upon Matthew and began throwing punch after punch, even while Belle yelled at him from inside the house. They wrestled, rolling off the porch and dropping into the dusty earth. Hands groped for one another, knuckles became bruised and bloodied as they duked it out. And just like the first punch Leo had thrown, Matthew held nothing back. He was in this for the kill, too.

The two brothers rose to their feet, grappling one another about the shoulders to push the other off balance. Leo had one thing on Matthew. Experience. He shoved him into a tangle of bushes. The branches and vines ensnared him just long enough for Leo to find a rock.

He picked it up and would have dove in for a second round when he heard Belle from the open doorway.

"Stop! Please, just stop!"

Turning, he saw the tears streaming down her face. Frightened, desperate tears. He held the rock, raised in mid-execution for the blow his brother deserved. But she stayed his hand with just one look.

You've gone soft.

Even now, the voices in his head persisted. The darkness was so near, but it didn't sound like him. It was rougher, deeper, its tones more gnarled and wicked.

Kill him.

But Leo didn't. He dropped the rock and backed away. That was all the time Matthew needed to stand and recover. They stared at one another, heavy breaths bursting from their chests and blood trickling from the cuts they inflicted.

He wanted to kill Matthew. He wanted to pay back all the pain and hurt he had wrought. Yet, in that moment, he realized that he couldn't. The darkness was right. He had gone soft.

Matthew hadn't.

With slight-of-hand, the dagger that had been cast aside before was back in his hand and a grin split his face. Blue eyes, the eyes they had inherited from their father, full of hate and bloodlust glared at Leo. He knew the look so well, even if he hadn't seen it since he was a teenager.

This was one beating he couldn't receive.

"Why now?" he asked his older brother. "After all these years, why now?"

Matthew straightened and wiped the back of his hand against the corner of his mouth. Blood smeared across his skin. "Because of her. It's all because of her."

He meant Belle, and Leo understood why.

"Because I was happy."

It was the one thing the darkness had tried to prevent every day and night since the day his brother implemented the curse. The one thing that was always out of reach was standing on the porch of a dilapidated farmhouse in the middle of nowhere. Happiness. Freedom. Love. Everything Matthew didn't want Leo to have.

"I can't let you have what you stole from me," Matthew said. "You ruined my life. You took my family from me. You left me alone. I wanted you to know what that felt like. I can't let you have what I've always wanted. It's not fair."

Leo shook his head. "None of it is. I know I tore our family apart, but I couldn't have known that da would start drinking more. I... I did it because I wanted to help you."

"I was fine!" Matthew roared, charging forward with the knife mirroring the tremor in his hand. "I had what I wanted. Power. Control. You took that from me! You were jealous of me!"

"No," Leo pleaded, keeping just out of swiping range of the dagger's blade. "I loved you. I cared. I was worried that something was wrong and that's why I told them. You had changed so much and I just wanted my brother back. Back to the way you were before all of this."

For a minute, it looked as if Matthew was distracted, confused. "No. You wanted to be better than me. You always did. You were mum's favorite and you wanted to stay that way. You couldn't just let me do what I wanted. You wanted to make me look mental, so they would hate me."

All the time Leo had spent hating himself for his decision to rat out his brother had been validated. "I know I shouldn't have told anyone. I see that now and I'm sorry. I'm sorry for telling on you. I'm sorry it sent everything spiraling out of control. I can't go back and undo what happened with da, mum, or Kaitlyn."

"I wouldn't undo a single thing," Matthew said, a wild and demented look dawning in his face. "I'm glad they're dead."

Leo narrowed his eyes, but kept good watch on the dagger. "They wouldn't be dead if I hadn't – "

He was cut off by Matthew's sadistic laughter. "You think... You think you killed them?"

Too stunned, he couldn't even reply with his own assumptions, the same ones he had confided to Belle. For years, he had thought it was his fault their father turned into a drunk. If Matthew hadn't been deemed psychologically unfit, he wouldn't have been put on the meds, and he wouldn't have disappointed anyone.

"They all hated me," Matthew continued. "They all hated me because of you. None of you cared. None of you loved me. You all had to pay. Demons are easy to control when you know their motivation. Pain. Sin. Death. Promise them these things and you can make them bend over backwards for you. One demon wanted pain, so I gave him our da. One wanted sadness, so I gave him mum. One wanted sickness so – "

"You son of a..." Leo couldn't even bring himself to say it. So brimming with a fresh anger that words failed him.

"But I saved the last for you. A lifetime of suffering. The demon could have anything he wanted from you. All you had to do was stay alive and stay as miserable and alone as I was when you took them all from me."

It all made sense now, and suddenly, Leo no longer felt guilty. It wasn't his fault. His father's drinking, the beatings, the murders, none of it really had to do with him. It was all Matthew. He made the choice to curse them, just like he made the choice to curse Leo. He no longer felt sorry for the brother he thought he had wronged all those years ago.

Now, he had a new reason to kill him. But Belle held him back again. As much as he wanted to witness the life fade from Matthew's eyes, she was watching. Waiting. Hoping that Leo would make the right decision. She wanted him to take the moral high ground, but that had never been his preferred path.

But something happened. Between the time it took Matthew to finally confess his crimes and the single step that Leo took toward his brother, a shockwave blasted through the air around them. It hummed, alive with some energy that he couldn't explain. The heaviness that hung over the farmhouse dissipated within just seconds.

Leo felt himself pulled back as a roaring gust blasted between him and Matthew. The ground beneath their feet began to shake and he couldn't stand anymore. He fell, but never took his eyes off his brother, who bore the most from this drastic change.

He remained standing, but only barely. All around, he looked with a horror-stricken expression as if something were diving upon him. But there was nothing there. Nothing but the wind. Matthew began to shout and slash madly at the air, fending off some invisible attacker.

Leo watched as this one-sided battle raged, and then he thought to look to Belle. She was still on the porch, on her knees, fingers laced in her lap. Praying.

She had to be praying. Every time she prayed, miraculous things happened. Things that he couldn't begin to explain. The darkness fled, the depression left him, and Matthew lost his mind.

Then, like a blaring horn right in his ear, he realized the truth. They were angels. If God was truly more powerful than any evil, then his angels must have been his prime defenders against demons. All this time, it had been angels. The quiet voices that countered the darkness, the unexplainable healing of his wrist that night he cut himself too much, the guidance when the barn was burning, and all the times when Belle could have died but didn't. It was the angels protecting her.

He looked back to Matthew and his cries for mercy began to make sense.

There was one thing he knew, though. The angels wouldn't kill Matthew. Only Leo could.

The dagger had been dropped in the dirt, discarded by its owner when he realized it was useless against this formidable spiritual hoard that had descended upon him. It was within reach. He could grab it and while his brother blubbered like a lunatic, he could end it all.

He gritted his teeth and sat up, his hand extended to take hold of the handle. But he stopped. If he killed his brother, that would make him a murderer. The one sin he had never committed. A sin that could very well be unforgivable. Belle would never look at him the same and he'd be sent to prison.

Was it worth it? Was taking his brother's life and avenging his family worth all the consequences to follow?

His fingers curled and closed around nothing as he withdrew. Cursing himself, he looked away from his brother, away from the psychopath that had ruined his life, and away from the temptation.

Matthew was right. There was a time when Leo idolized his older brother and wanted to be like him. He had been a boy then, thoughtless, and immature. But he was a man now and he saw the truth. He didn't want to be anything like his brother. Matthew had never grown out of his anger, but Leo had a choice. And he chose life.

Three weeks. That was all it took. Three weeks, a few trips to Little Rock for the court hearings, and more patience than Belle ever thought she could possess. Patience with the cops, the judge, the jury, and especially Leo. He had been so quiet since the incident. It was as if he had simply shut down. Stoic, even when facing the courtroom to give his testimony against Matthew.

With Belle's phone recording and quick detective work on the part of the investigators to validate the murders, her kidnapper was facing charges of murder in multiple states. However, just like when Matthew's parents had sent him to a psychiatrist for a full evaluation, the man was found to be clinically insane and unstable. He was temporarily taken off the medications that left him in a mildly sedated condition long enough to spill the beans about everything. The magic, the murders, the demons, and his vendetta against his brother since they were teenagers. DNA traces kept on file at the crime scenes were still being compared to Matthew's, which would take some time, but he was already behind bars at Arkansas Department of Correction in Pine Bluff. His confession to the crime was enough for the judge. His transfer to death row would be finalized when the evidence was substantiated.

That was all it took and it was over. Both Belle and Leo should have been rejoicing, but neither seemed to draw themselves out of their stupor. For different reasons, they both had withdrawn into themselves until the last few days.

Without Leo to comfort her and assure her that turning in Matthew had been the right thing to do, Belle turned to her friends. To Ivy, Mrs. Levinson, and even Lena. The women at church had flocked to her side, their prime concern being her mental state after being held hostage. Surprisingly, Belle wasn't so shaken by it. She had endured much, but none of it seemed as devastating as learning about Matthew's fate. He would be given the death penalty, a sentence he might have rightly deserved for his murders.

Yet, in the back of her mind, she couldn't forget how she had been treated at the abandoned farmhouse. Matthew – on some level – respected her. He offered her food and water, he promised not to hurt her, and he made good on that promise. He might have been a psychopathic killer who gave himself over to the misbelief that he could control demons, but he had a reason for what he did. He might have grown out of his obsession with the dark, spiritual realm if given the right encouragement as a teen. She could halfway understand him and knowing that he would be killed almost didn't seem right. Especially not when Leo was just as upset over the whole thing.

He was hardly there anymore. Sure, he wouldn't leave her alone for more than a few minutes, but emotionally and mentally he wasn't there. He stared into nothingness, lost in thoughts that he wouldn't share with Belle no matter how often she begged for him to speak.

And he never lost his cool. Straight-faced, hardened, with a quality of deadness behind his eyes.

This wasn't the same man she had fallen in love with. Something had changed, and she knew it had to do with what Matthew had said. His whole life, he had condemned himself for being the reason that his parents and sister were dead. Now, he was left blameless. It had all been his brother's fault, and Belle realized within a few days that Leo simply couldn't cope with the truth. The place where all his anger and bitterness had been stored was now empty. His family's murder would be avenged, but he was left alone again.

No, not alone. Leo had Belle. Lately, though, she felt as if she didn't have him anymore.

It hurt sometimes that he wouldn't talk to her. They could never get past the little things and it was as if life had become stagnant in such a short period of time. Work at the bookstore and on the farm had consumed her days, and whenever there was a moment to spare, Leo stayed closed off. He wouldn't even talk about the illusion Matthew had created to break him. It was as if they had taken five steps back in their relationship and she could count the number of times they had kissed one another on a single hand.

Whether out of desperation or some inconceivable purpose, Leo had called for Mr. Calloway to come over. He wouldn't confide in her, but he would in a man he barely knew. As she eavesdropped from the other side of the front door as they sat together on the porch, Belle understood that it had nothing to do with her or some regression in their love for each other.

Once they worked their way through the small talk about Belle's new truck, the horses, the sheep, and how big Ranger was growing, Mr. Calloway said, "I heard about your brother."

Belle felt the grind of the deck chair against the boards as Leo must have shifted in his seat. "I'll bet the whole town knows by now. They'll know all about Matthew, me, and everything else."

"The beauty of living in a small town."

A long pause commenced, which nearly led Belle to wonder if one or both of the men had left the porch. Tiptoeing, she snuck to the window and drew back the curtain to peek out. Both were still there, staring out to the dirt drive that led up to the house. Neither spoke, neither moved. She wondered how men could sit in total and complete silence like that and neither feel uncomfortable.

"I couldn't do it," Leo finally said. She watched his lips move as he poured out his reason for calling Mr. Calloway. "I had my chance to kill him, but I didn't do it."

The older man turned to regard Leo, but she couldn't see his expression from where she spied. "It's good that you didn't."

"But I wanted to," Leo said with a regretful shake of his head. "I had dreamed of doing it for years, even before I found out what he had done to our parents... I wanted to kill him, but I didn't... I'm a coward," Leo replied with a sneer that nearly broke her heart. The bitterness wasn't gone after all. "I didn't do it because I knew Belle would see me."

"I think you didn't kill your brother for more than just Belle's sake."

Another pause stretched between them and Leo took a long, deep breath. "I didn't want to be like him."

Mr. Calloway nodded and turned his eyes back to the landscape before them. "You didn't want to be a killer."

"I've hurt a lot of people in my life," Leo said. "But I've never killed anyone... When I started prize fighting and I found out how easy it was, I wanted to do it more and more. I'd live for the thrill of winning a match and... I didn't want my brother to be like my first knockout. I didn't want him to be the first in a string of easy kills."

"It takes a lot of strength to resist temptation. The fact that you did, and that you thought through it says a lot." Mr. Calloway crossed his legs and settled his hands in his lap. "You might be right. If you killed your brother, you might have realized how easy it is or how rewarding it could be... But you didn't. And you still regret it?"

"I don't know. I know they're going to kill him and part of me wanted to do it myself... but I knew I'd lose my soul if I did. I don't know what to feel anymore or what to do now that it's all over. There's no fight left."

Mr. Calloway pointed in the general direction of Leo's face. "You still have that cloud over your head. You know it's not over."

Leo glanced the old man's way and Belle was at risk of being spotted, so she ducked a little further below the windowsill like a peeping child.

"It is over. My brother isn't... he doesn't have a hold over my life anymore."

Belle had wondered if the darkness had lingered, if the curse had been lifted now that Matthew couldn't keep up his end of whatever bargain he had made with Leo's personal demons. Did this mean that Leo really was free? Or did Mr. Calloway, in all his spiritual wisdom, know better?

"He may not have a hold over your life, but I can still see his chains on you. It's not over, Leo. You have a long road ahead of you and you know the first step."

Leo's brows furrowed in confusion and he spoke again, but his words were drowned out by the loud vibration of Belle's phone. She slipped away from the window and let the curtain fall as she scrambled to silence the buzzing.

Her finger froze over the red reject button when she looked at the caller ID. Her lips parted and she could feel the anxiety rush through her, the first she had felt in a while since the incident. Funny how she could endure being kidnapped and surrounded by well-meaning church people, but her heart skittered when she saw her mother's name on her cellphone screen.

Belle's first thought was to reject the call, but some hidden voice told her not to. It was the first time either of them had spoken since the blowup. She had never thought she'd hear from Melinda again. And here she was, reaching out first.

She tapped the green button and made her way toward the stairs.

"Hey, mom," she said, unable to bring any bit of feigned cheerfulness to her voice.

Melinda's greeting, however, held a note that was amazingly uncommon for Belle to hear. Sadness. "Hey, honey... Don't worry, I'm not coming over. I just wanted to... to see how you were."

A new and dangerous choice laid before her. Belle could be honest and tell her everything about the accident, Leo's brother, and everything else in between. Or she could lie to save time and questions.

"I've been all right. Could be better, but I'm all right."

"Good... I'm glad."

Belle halfway wondered if this was really her mother. The Melinda Clearwater that she knew would have probed or asked some cunning comment about just how "all right" her daughter really was. Instead, she said she was glad? Her mother was never glad. Not genuinely.

"Are you doing okay?" Belle asked, readying herself for the long list of complaints and negativity. Honestly, she would have rather gone back to eavesdropping, even if it was difficult to hear Leo talk about such morbid things as murder and regret.

"I've... I've been better. But I won't bore you... I've been thinking a lot about the things you said, and I want to talk about it. Can we meet somewhere?"

Belle sat down on the bottom step of the stairs and pressed the phone against her ear. What could she possibly say to that? She thought that bridge had been burned. The ashes were everywhere and scattered to the wind. It had been almost a month without a single word from her and now, of all times, she wanted to pop out of the blue and chat.

But Melinda didn't sound like herself. This was a tired, beaten version of her mother that Belle had never heard before. Something must have happened to make her want to start rebuilding that bridge, or to at least shout across the expanse between them.

Should Belle shout back? Was she even strong enough to take up the hammer and nails to rebuild this piece of her life that should have been gone? Leo had a point that what Belle shared with Melinda was toxic and oppressive. Without her mother, she could begin to heal from those wounds that had never been allowed to breathe. She needed that space to make sense of things, but Melinda was crowding back in.

The longer Belle thought about it, the more she began to think differently. She wasn't crowding. She was just asking. Not demanding, not insisting. Asking.

Then, Belle remembered the lesson she had learned with Leo's brother. The murderer, deserving of death, might have had some redeeming quality about him. Maybe Melinda did too.

"Do you want me to meet you in Fayetteville?"

"We can meet wherever you want, honey."

Belle sighed, "Let me think it over. I'll call you later. I promise. I just have to see where I have the time."

Slightly dejected but accepting, Melinda replied, "Okay. I'll wait for your call. Anything that works for you will work for me."

They gave short goodbyes and Belle nearly dropped the phone once the call was disconnected. What had she just agreed to? Why did she open that door that should have been boarded shut? She wondered if she could get out of it. She could call or text and say that she was too busy, that the farm needed her attention now more than ever. It was the truth, especially now that the lambs were growing, and she'd be receiving that addition to her flock within a couple of weeks. There was so much to do, and she didn't have time for a nervous breakdown with her mother.

But once she checked herself, Belle realized that the thought of having coffee or lunch with her mother wasn't so terrifying. If anything, she was curious. Would Melinda really turn over a new leaf or go right back to the same abusive tendencies? And if she did, did Belle have the courage to burn it all down again?

She raked her hand through her hair and propped her elbow on her knee, trying to figure out a way through this new trap.

Chapter 21

S unken eyes refused to meet his from across the table. His ashen complexion made him look sick and malnourished, but Leo knew the prison had to be feeding Matthew. Maybe his older brother wouldn't eat.

One phone call and a four-hour trip brought him to Pine Bluff. His back ached and he was still in no mood to even think of his brother, let alone be in the same room with him. Guards were posted at the door, the single overhead light illuminating the guns strapped to their belts. Only two chairs, now occupied, and a metal desk between them. Matthew's hands were cuffed and bound to the heavy ring on the table. There was no way he could hurt anyone in here.

The prison doctor briefed him before Leo entered the room. He was being treated for schizophrenia and psychosis. Those two labels stung Leo. They were the same ones Matthew had been given so long ago. Only now, he was the only one to know that his brother wasn't crazy. The delusions about demons and magic, it was all real. The all-out fight that would ensue in hell because of his death would be real. All those demons he had made deals with over the years would come to claim his soul. After all he had been through, there was no denying that everything Matthew had done was legit and not some hallucination. But the physicians wouldn't know that, nor would they care. Drug him up and keep him calm until the execution date. That's all they cared about.

Until recently, that was all Leo wanted either. A quick decision and an end to everything. He wanted to believe that it was all over, just like he told Mr. Calloway. But the old man was right. It wasn't over. There was a lack of closure, of definition, of meaning. And he would have none of it until he saw his brother one last time.

For several long moments, the two Thompson brothers sat in silence. Leo could begin to pick out features of their parents in Matthew's face. He had seen them in his own reflection, but to see them mirrored in someone else was new. He could barely remember what Kaitlyn looked like and he had no pictures left from his childhood. He had forsaken them long before he could realize their true value. All he had were fuzzy images, ideas, memories of a time that was dead and gone.

Matthew brought them back to life. He could see a piece of the boy he had once been, before the magic and bondage of evil took him. He imagined, in another life, that they might have been close. Maybe if Matthew had grown out of it, if he had given up on the darkness instead of using it against his own family, things could have been different. But here they were, sitting in a prison and watched by guards who were ready to open fire on a murderer if he so much as breathed the wrong way.

"Stop looking at me," Matthew grumbled.

Leo was slightly surprised that his brother was so lucid, given the way he stared dumbly at the tabletop, but he wouldn't grant this man any favors. "I won't," he said. "I'm going to keep looking at you until I figure this out."

Matthew huffed. "What is there to figure out? I killed our parents. I killed Kaitlyn. I killed all those people."

"I know," Leo replied with a nod. "And I know why you did it."

His shrug made the cuffs rattle against the metal. "Then there's nothing to figure out."

"There's plenty... I need to know what makes us different." The words came out slow, hesitant, as if Leo were in as much of a daze as his brother. "We have the same eyes, same nose... same anger."

"It's easy." Matthew lifted his stare and locked onto his brother, the heat from millions of moments spent in blind hatred searing him like a hot brand. "There is no difference."

Leo shook his head, refusing to give into such a lie. They had to be different. "I'm not a murderer."

"You are," he replied flatly. "You had a hand in every crime I've ever committed. If you hadn't done what you did, I wouldn't have done what I did."

That wasn't what he wanted to hear. He had already heard it in his head countless times, but he couldn't believe it. "No. You made the choice to kill them."

Matthew's cracked and dry lips twitched into a smile. "That's what the shrinks here say too. That it was my choice to be unloved and abandoned."

"Nobody abandoned you," Leo corrected. "We loved you. That's why we tried to help you."

The clanking of the links on the handcuffs echoed as Matthew gestured to the barren walls. "And see where it got me... You've helped enough."

Leo's jaw clenched, holding fast to all the words he wanted to use as weapons against his brother. All the things he wanted to say since he was first afflicted with the curse were bubbling up and simmering in his throat. He felt he would explode with all that fire if he stayed a moment longer.

And then, he remembered what Mr. Calloway said. He told Leo to go see Matthew one more time and try to see through the hurt, through the anger and the harm he had done. He dared him to see them both as they were, as brothers and as humans. They both made mistakes they couldn't take back. They both said and did things that could never be undone. None of Leo's belated words would fix this for either of them.

What was done, was done. They couldn't go back, but they could move forward.

Leo had to leave this prison with a clear conscience and a clean slate. And there was only one way he could do that.

He took a breath and made an effort to untighten every tight muscle in his body. Then, he said what needed to be said for both their sakes. "I forgive you."

At first, Matthew looked stunned. And then he began to laugh. That hysterical, nonsensical laugh that even made the guards tense.

"Forgive me? Why should you forgive me? I don't forgive you! I hate you! You ruined everything!"

"And you ruined everything for me!" Leo returned with just as much venom. "But I forgive you for botching it up for both of us. We could have had a happy life together. We could have been home in Scotland. We could go visit our parents for the holidays and attend our sister's wedding. But we can't and I forgive you. You don't have to understand or forgive me, because your forgiveness doesn't matter to me. I don't need it. Not anymore."

He stood, but then wanted to give him one more parting thought, one he hoped Matthew would carry with him all the way to his execution day. "But, I will thank you. Without you, I would have never met Belle. And now, I'll be happy again. I'll smile, laugh, and raise a family with her and there's nothing you can do about it. You can't do anything to me anymore."

Humor and bitterness evolved into pure, raw terror. Leo turned and walked toward the door just before his brother flew into a tantrum that would have put a toddler to shame. Screaming, banging his fists, he was sure even the table turned over. The guards were on him in an instant, but it wasn't Leo's concern anymore. None of it was.

He had said what he needed to say and as he walked down the hall toward the exit, escorted by a few more prison guards, Leo felt as if a weight had been lifted. Forgiveness was as much for the giver as it was for the receiver. Though Matthew denied him the same courtesy, he would leave the corrections center with much more than he came with.

The toxins in his soul had been sucked out and he left it all in that room. He wouldn't let his brother destroy him anymore. The darkness was gone, along with the demons, and he was ready to receive his redemption. He was ready to move on and be happy again.

Belle recognized an opportunity when she saw one. Leo had told her not to expect him back until the following morning. When she pried further, she didn't think he would answer. But he said he was going to see his brother for the last time, and she couldn't have been more proud of him.

She wasn't about to ruin that meeting with the news that she would spend the evening with her mother. Belle dialed Melinda as soon as the motorcycle was out of sight and made the arrangements. They were to have a cup of coffee together at a café in Fayetteville that her mother was particularly fond of. Belle didn't want to risk meeting in Levi where someone was bound to see her. Reuniting with her mother wouldn't be so embarrassing, but having Leo find out by accident would be a disaster.

Keeping secrets might not have been the smartest thing to do, now that they were getting back on their feet, but Belle knew that if she told Leo the truth, he would have tried to get her to cancel for the sake of her nerves. She couldn't do that. Not after the way her mother sounded on the phone that evening when she called.

They set up the coffee outing for three in the afternoon that Thursday, Belle's day off. All the arrangements were made with Mr. Johnson to keep an eye on the farm, but she still found herself getting distracted at the last minute and left the house a little late. Knowing that her mother was never on time for anything in her life, Belle wasn't bothered.

That was until she saw Melinda sitting at a corner table, her coffee between her hands and looking just as nervous as Belle felt.

There was no time to recover, no time to abort the mission. She steeled herself with a quick breath and walked across the floor. The warm, coffee-infused air of the café soothed her some, but the look on her mother's face nearly negated it.

"How long have you been waiting?" Belle asked as she took the chair across from Melinda. She didn't drop her purse from her shoulder, convinced she wouldn't stay long. Coffee was still not her ideal drink and she had already vowed to herself that if Melinda stepped out of line just once, she was gone. Leo might have been mad at her for setting this meeting, but she wanted to come back with good news.

"Not long," Melinda replied quickly, scooting closer to the table.

It was then she realized that her mother wasn't wearing nearly as much makeup. The lack of lipstick, eye shadow, and false eyelashes almost gave her a sickly look in the ambient light of the café. Then it occurred to Belle that perhaps her mother hadn't called to apologize, but to confess something.

"Are you all right?" she asked, almost compelled to reach out and take Melinda's hand to see if it were cold. The last thing she needed was her mother telling her that she was sick.

She faked a smile and nodded. "Yes, I'm fine. It's just... It's been a long week."

"Did something happen?"

It was then that Melinda must have understood Belle's worries and waved her off. "No, no! Everything's fine. I still have my job, I'm not sick, everything's fine."

Belle could quite literally feel the balloon in her chest begin to deflate. The strap of her purse slipped from her shoulder and down to her elbow. Still, she wouldn't let it drop to the ground yet. "Okay... That's good."

"You don't – " Melinda stopped herself. Belle caught onto the tone. The same one she had heard for years. Her mother was about to go into a lecture and the muscles that had just relaxed began to tighten again. It had been hours since she had eaten, but she felt as if she'd be sick, just knowing what was to come.

But her mother pinched her lips together and shook her head, as if denying what she had been ready to say.

"I don't what?" Belle egged her on, looking for an excuse to leave. If she wasn't here to announce some big disaster, but wouldn't get to the point, she might as well go back to Levi. She had better things to do with her time than be scolded.

The usual fire in Melinda's eyes wasn't there. The same she had whenever she corrected Belle. Instead, she sniffled and looked down to her coffee cup. "You don't always have to think the worst."

The dam that held in her true thoughts and feelings had broken long ago. Belle wouldn't even try to patch up the holes or weaken their impact. "I learned from the best."

Melinda's hands rotated the cup mindlessly. "I know you did, that's why I wasn't going to say it. It's an insult to both of us."

For a minute, Belle pondered that admission. Then, she let her purse drop to the floor beside her chair. Maybe this would take a while. "That's probably the closest thing to 'I was wrong' I've ever heard you say."

She nodded. "It is... And now I'm saying it. I was wrong." Melinda looked up. "But you have to understand why I say the things I say."

Belle sat back in her chair and waited. She had let her mother do so much of the talking in their relationship, and if she wanted some chance to explain herself, she would allow it.

"My mom, your granny, wasn't really there a lot. She raised me and she loved me, but she wasn't there to teach me the things I needed to know like makeup, clothes, or relationships. I grew up without an attentive mom."

"I know the feeling." It came out before Belle had a chance to really understand the weight of her words. They might as well have been like millstones tied around Melinda's neck.

She nodded. "Yes, I know you do. And I did what I told myself I would never do. When I moved out and married your father, I told myself that I would be a good mother and raise my kids the way I should have been raised. That meant I would be involved with everything they did, teach them what I had to learn myself, so they wouldn't have to make the same mistakes."

Belle shrugged. "So, you didn't. You ran off, because you couldn't take the responsibility."

If she didn't know better, she would have thought Melinda was on the verge of crying. "I've long since regretted what I did. Your father forgave me and I came back to make up for the time I had lost. Whenever you were with me, I tried to teach you how to live. I knew Chad wasn't going to show you how to put on makeup or how to dress like a woman. He didn't have any sisters and all the women he associated with were prudes. I didn't want you to grow up plain like that."

Although no one could describe half of the congregation at her church as plain, Belle understood what she meant. Her father wasn't going to take her shopping for clothes or buy her makeup. Even if he did, he didn't know anything on the subject. Melinda did.

"You've always been beautiful and that's something I never made clear to you. My mom never told me that either. Everyone is beautiful in their own way, but I learned about beauty from the wrong places growing up. There's so much I had learned and tried to instill in you, when I should have just let you be yourself. A beautiful, funny, happy little girl... And I wrecked you. I didn't intend to, but I did. You were right, and I was wrong. I couldn't see it until you told me that day at the farm. Whether you believe it or not, I do love you. But love can show in a variety of ways. I'm not saying my way was right, but I had a reason for it. I didn't want you to grow up like I did. That's all."

Belle listened and tried not to let her own hateful bias get in the way of processing all she had said. "I can try to understand your reasons. I don't agree with them, but I can try to understand... You could have spent more time just listening to me instead of trying to correct me. I never asked for more than just you being there. If you showed up for more birthdays, more Christmases, if you came to the mother-daughter days at school or even came to church with us on Sundays... You didn't have to believe, but just being there with me would have meant so much. Instead, you spent a lot of time telling me that I wasn't good enough, that I wasn't fine just the way I am. It hurt. It still hurts."

Melinda reached out, tears pushing at the corners of her eyes. "I know. I know that now. And I'm sorry. I'm so, so sorry. You may not forgive me, but I really hope that you will. I know we can't start over, but we can make a new beginning, can't we?"

A tear slid down her cheek and caught the light from the amber wire bulb overhead. Belle might have come to regret it later, but she had never seen her mother cry. Startled and full of pity for the woman who genuinely wanted to make amends, she nodded.

"You're right, we can't start over. It's going to take a lot for me to forget the things you've said and try to filter through what was useful and what wasn't... But I forgave you a long time ago. I don't know about a new beginning, but... we can work on it. We can get to know each other again and see where it goes."

That was all she could promise. The future, as bright as it seemed, didn't need more shadows cast upon it. An apology could go a long way, but it would take years, if not a whole lifetime to undo the hurt. But, just maybe, this could be the first step.

Belle wondered if she would need a coffee after all. This meeting could take a while.

By the time Belle pulled up to her home, the sun had set and the winter winds were raging. Her old truck would have been rocked by the force alone, but Leo had convinced her to go all-out and put the insurance money to good use. With a bigger truck, she could haul more, and the idea of buying a horse trailer in the future was promising. Sitting with the engine off, she felt so protected inside the cab. Only the whistling of the gusts rolling around her truck could interrupt her thoughts.

She and her mother had talked plenty that afternoon. So much that they had lost track of time. That had never happened before. Belle always kept one eye on the clock during their visits. She'd watched the second-hand tick away and wish with every fiber of her being that Melinda would just shut up and go home. But this evening was a first for both of them. All negativity was left at the door, and for once, Belle almost enjoyed her mother's company.

They found little in common, but what they lacked in similarities, they made up for in small talk. Jobs, coworkers, the farm, and the tedious little things that came with being a woman trying to make her way in the world alone. They even talked about Leo, but in vague and careful terms so that Melinda wouldn't have another reason to hate him.

They closed the reunion with a hug, and each held on for a few extra seconds before walking away. No follow-up meeting had been agreed on, but they knew it was coming. Maybe not next week or next month, but it would happen. And when it did, Belle knew she'd be ready.

Through the high wail of the winds, a loud crash broke through the silence. She looked toward the barn and pasture. The horses were put away, the sheep were all in their own shelters, but the door of the stables was flapping against the stretch of wall beside it.

Belle sighed and didn't bother to grab her purse. It would only get in the way. Mr. Johnson may not have latched the door well enough. He had done it once before already.

She buttoned up her coat and jumped from her cab. The relentless wind whipped her long hair about as if she were standing in the middle of a cyclone and the air felt heavy, despite the cold. A storm was on its way.

She made it to the barn and decided to check on the horses before turning in for the night. She trusted that Mr. Johnson had fed and watered them, but storms always made them antsy.

Belle tugged on the rogue door and bolted it fast as she took shelter in the stable. Combing her fingers through her hair to calm the tossed strands, she let out a long breath. When she turned, she nearly jumped out of her skin.

Leo was there, an electric lantern in his hand and a pleased smile spread over his lips. Belle pressed her hand to her chest as she tried to catch her breath.

"I didn't know you were back," she admitted, laughing to herself that she had been spooked so easily by the man who never managed to scare her.

Leo took slow, ambling steps her way and he lifted the lantern so its light could reach into the darkened corners of the stables. "I got back a few hours ago." Then, he lifted his other hand and she noticed a tiny remote.

He pressed a button and the whole barn exploded with tiny twinkling lights. Around every post, rail, and stall door, were string lights identical to those Belle had installed in her old barn. She smiled and gazed around at all the work he had done while she was away. This new burst of light allowed her to notice what he was wearing. Torn jeans and a black button-down shirt, the one she had given him the night they first met. And just like then, she could only think of how absolutely handsome he was, scruffy and all.

As he lowered the lantern to the floor, Belle relived that moment so vividly. But now, instead of feeling afraid, she could smile. It was a moment that had changed everything for them.

"Don't worry. These are battery powered." Leo wiggled the remote in his hand and then pocketed it.

Belle then understood what he was doing, and she couldn't have smiled wider. Lost for words, she let him do the talking.

"We met in this very spot," he said as he continued to close the distance between them. "And it was right here where you made me feel for the first time in... I don't even know how long. Back then, I didn't know what it was that I was feeling, but now I do. You made me hope. I felt hope the moment I saw you standing there with the crowbar and that cute little scowl on your face."

Belle lifted her hand and hid her smile behind her sleeve. Yes, she remembered that clear as day.

"I knew you were special then, even if I couldn't admit it to myself." Leo's smile faltered a bit as he stopped just a few feet from her. "I know I'm messed up. I know I'm damaged and it's going to take a long time to undo everything I've been through. But I want you by my side every step of the way. Each and every time we're separated, I fail you. I wasn't with you at the party when Drake harassed you. I wasn't there when the stove exploded. I wasn't there when you were trapped in the fire. I wasn't with you at the church when Matthew took you and I wasn't with you when you wrecked your truck."

He took another step and reached for the hand that tried to conceal half of her blush. His thumb stroked over her fingers and she could tell he was shaking.

"But when I am with you, I can protect you. I can pull you out of the way of a falling tree. I can help you deliver lambs. I can shield you from people who want to take your peace. I want to be there for all the moments when you need saving, and I want to be there for all the moments in between."

Now, he was close enough that she could feel his breath on her face.

"I love you," he said, voice husky and full of longing. "And I know it's a lot to ask of you to love me through all the hard times and the days when I can't say what I mean. But you can know beyond a shadow of a doubt that when I do speak, I mean every word. You said you didn't know what it meant when I call you m'eudail. It means you're my treasure, my precious one, my darling. It means that you are my world, my happiness, my joy. I want to spend my life with you, and I want you to be my wife."

Belle could overlook his slightly defaming comments, over the parts about how damaged he thought he was and all the times he'd failed. She didn't hear that. She only heard that he cared, that he knew how to be better and wanted to be better for her. They were each other's reason, each other's courage.

Despite how short she was, Belle leapt up and wrapped her arms around his neck, letting him catch her and hold her close. "And I want you to be my husband," she whispered in his ear, fighting past the happy tears and the pure and utter joy that burst through her core.

All her life, she never thought she'd find the man who could make her truly free. Everyone around her made her so uncomfortable, made her feel the least like herself. With Leo, she didn't have to pretend. She could be real and honest and know that no matter what she did or didn't do, he would always be there.

He was right, that he had a long road ahead of him. But so did she. Together, they would walk it. Hand in hand, knowing that through it all, they had love and they had hope. They had each other.

Afterword

Hello Readers,

It has been a wild and emotional ride. Thank you for coming with me. Through the twists, turns, and feels, I hope you're able to close this book with a sense of satisfaction. It's also my hope that you've come to a greater understanding of not only mental health (anxiety and depression) but of the value of hope, love, and faith. I know I did. It wasn't my intention to get overly spiritual or religious with this story, but it kind of morphed into that without my knowing. I hear a lot of authors say that their characters can sometimes hijack a story and take it in new directions, and that's certainly what Belle and Leo did with this duet.

Writing this story has helped me to face some hard truths about my own life, but has also helped me to be more open to the struggle of others. You never know what someone is going through, whether it's having to wear a mask or battle their own personal demons. I encourage you to always be kind and patient if someone looks to be having a bad day. You'd want the same in return.

I hope you'll check out my other books. They, like the Redemption Duet, strive to teach a moral lesson about the human condition. No, I can't write anything shallow to save my life!

For more information about my books and upcoming releases, please visit

www.moonstruckwriting.wordpress.com.

Happy Reading!

Sheritta Bitikofer

About the author

Sheritta Bitikofer is an author of paranormal and historical fiction. She lives for the deep, engaging stories that enthrall readers from cover to cover. As a wife and mother of eclectic tastes, she can be found roaming Civil War battlefields, haunting her local coffeeshop, or relaxing with a plate of chili cheese fries.

Follow her for upcoming novel releases
www.sherittabitikofer.com

Also by Sheritta Bitikofer

The Outlaw

The Deviants

The Unsinkable

Keeper of Light

Bulletproof

The Nexus

<u>Bewitching Brews Trilogy</u>

Bewitching Fire

Bewitching Darkness

Bewitching Hearts

<u>The Decimus Trilogy</u>

The Beast of Verona

Amber Ashes

Saving the Beast

<u>Redemption Duet</u>

The Rose

The Lion

<u>Standalones</u>

Escape

Clouds

Passions

Silver Screen

By The Book

www.ingramcontent.com/pod-product-compliance
Lightning Source LLC
Chambersburg PA
CBHW071521260626

47170CB00002B/451